A Venturous Fairy

Book Four
of
The Return of the Tribes

By Alice Taylor

First Edition

The Rum Lot Publishing
Lowestoft, Suffolk, UK
2025

ISBN- 978-1-918079-10-4
Paperback Edition

Books of this series are available for download on

Amazon Kindle
or
The Rum Lot Publishing
www.rumlot.com

I have a venturous fairy that shall seek
The squirrel's hoard and fetch thee new nuts.

A Midsummer Night's Dream
By William Shakespeare

Prologue

1959

When Ricky Aeldor was thirty, he had served twelve years as an NCO in the US Air Force. The twelve-year mark is a dangerous year in the life of a military career because that's the year an airman either stays in for the long haul or puts the military behind him while he is still young enough to start a new career. The decision was whether to stay in for two more four-year hitches and put in the full twenty to earn a minimum retirement. There was no point in leaving at year sixteen, and giving up a gold-plated pension for the rest of your life was there? If he'd stayed until twenty, it meant Ricky would be thirty-eight at retirement.

Thirty-eight seems ridiculously young to someone in their sixties and seventies, but to a thirty-year-old, it felt ancient. For Ricky, the issue wasn't age; it was change. He liked the Air Force; he didn't want to leave, and the idea of change made him anxious. So with no discussion with his wife Caddy, he signed up for another four years and bounced home one night waving a brown envelope with typed-up orders inside and said, "Time to pack up, Babe; we're headin' to Texas!"

They were living in Berlin at the time, where Ricky worked for the US Air Force military intelligence doing whatever it was they did. Caddy had no idea because it was all top secret. All she knew was that Ricky did things with maps, and he spoke Russian.

Her husband had orders to Lackland Air Force Base in Texas, just outside of San Antonio. It never occurred to Caddy until years later that re-enlisting and moving across the world to the US was something that really should've been discussed

between them. But in 1959, a good Air Force wife just packed up their few goods and chattels, rounded up the kids, and hoped for the best. Orders were issued. Orders were followed.
There was no appeal.

Texas was hard. Ricky was an E-6 by then, a tech sergeant, and his job was war. The problem was that the Korean War was over, the Vietnam War was still in its infancy, and the Cold War was, well, cold. The US military war machine was still huge, but at the individual airman level the pay was crap. There were plenty of low-level sergeants, and the excess of men on the rolls made promotion opportunities almost nil even for certified Russian-speaking geniuses like Ricky. Caddy didn't know until years later that he turned down a slot in officer school because he liked what he was doing, and that meant going to university and getting a degree, which Ricky thought would be boring. Why should he endure classes in English Lit and biology just to earn rank?

An American sergeant's pay in postwar Germany was great, but in Texas, it was starvation wages. They had three very young kids at home, and base housing was full, so the Aeldor family was placed on a very long waiting list. In the meantime, they rented a cheap trailer situated in a shaved-off cow pasture in the middle of Texas Hill Country, and that meant a good forty-five-minute drive away from the base.

Caddy felt they were living on the moon. There were no shops to walk to, no neighbours to talk to, and no way to get to either. When she looked out of the narrow metal door of the trailer, the sun-blasted, scrubby, dry hills looked like it. Some parts of the Hill Country were beautiful. Hers was not. They bought a used car so Ricky could get to work, and he left early in the morning and came home late at night, leaving his little family to bake in a tin box in the Texas sun.

Caddy had to get a job.

She had no degree, no skills anyone in Texas wanted, no car, and three kids, so she did the only thing she could – she found a job in the grade school kitchen and became a school lunch lady. With the minimum wage and a part-time job she made just enough money to pay for Ricky's car, and she only had to find a sitter for Conary. She rode the school bus to and from work, just like the kids.

It was in the steaming and un-air-conditioned kitchen that she found out about the Texas Normal Schools and the Texas education system. Teachers and office staff, even in elementary schools, didn't hang out with the lunch ladies, so she didn't find out from them. Her information came from a flyer tacked on the employee bulletin board. The Blanco Independent School District was looking for a part-time travelling elementary school music teacher, no degree required, if the lucky candidate was willing to work towards a two-year degree and Texas certification. At reduced pay, of course.

Back then, you didn't need a four-year Bachelor's degree to be a teacher, especially a grade school music teacher in the middle of nowhere Texas. At the two-year Normal College in San Marcos, she could get her teacher's certification. The little, rural school district didn't have a lot of people knocking on the door to teach and hired Caddy as an uncertified (and much lower-paid) assistant instructor to teach the babies to bang on drums and play the flute (it wasn't as if she was teaching anything important, like high school band). To keep the job she took college classes in the evenings and during the summer. It took her four years of night and summer classes to earn her teaching certification. Then the Texas Department of Education moved the goal posts, and she had to get a Bachelor's to teach. That took another four years.

Ricky thought the whole degree thing was silly, but he certainly liked the extra money that came with Caddy working. It didn't take long for "something she did for pocket money" to turn into "necessary". About two months.

It ended up that Caddy graduated from university the same year Ricky graduated from the Army. The day after he retired, he went into a job as an intel analyst for a defense contractor doing something he loved with people who admired and respected him. She continued with her job teaching four-to-eight-year-olds the basics of music, something she could take or leave. Since her occupation had the word "music" in the job title, Ricky didn't see any problem. Teaching music was a job; it had a very good pension, and it wasn't digging ditches. By then, the money issues weren't so dire, and from his point of view, Caddy was an excellent wife and mother. That was enough personal and professional fulfilment for anyone. Life was good.

In 1969, when her diploma finally showed up in the mail, Caddy was forty-four with a son a year away from going to university himself, and two other kids coming along behind him. By the time they all graduated from college, she'd be fifty-seven. Now her teaching job was full-time, and she had three active teenagers at home, so between being the best teacher she could be, doing all of the housework and taking care of Ricky and the kids, finding time to play music, *her* music, seemed a long way off. She stopped playing the guitar and only occasionally picked up her violin. Anyway, her hands were deforming from the arthritis.

Of course, at the time, she didn't know she was destined to be Queen of the Fairies. All she knew was that dreams were for other people, and the best she could do was make sure her kids had a chance to follow their own dreams.

Book Four

Ratna

When Gaia went insane and pulled the sun down on herself, at the ceremonial gathering of the lords for the summer solstice, Ratna was not there. She was fifteen, so she could have gone, and at any other time her parents wouldn't have hesitated to take her, if only to enjoy the festival atmosphere that bookended a frankly boring ceremony.

But Ratna's mother hesitated, and after thinking about it, both of her parents thought that next year might be better. Gaia was going slowly insane from losing her bond-man to a human, and his disappearance over two years earlier didn't bode well. He was either dead or he had never bonded to Gaia in the first place, and both were equal disasters for the primary lord. As Ratna's mother said, it was a tragedy when one person bonded and the other didn't bond back. It meant a total lack of balance in the relationship, and discord and chaos were the only possible results.

It would be sad for their daughter to watch Gaia embarrass herself again, like last year, and Ratna's mother had a visceral distaste for the voyeurism that enticed some lords to go to the ceremony just to see their Primary publicly fall apart.

There was talk that the Elementals would force Gaia to step aside, and they'd install a new Primary to lead. Gaia could then search for her man unimpeded by responsibilities, or she could go quietly catatonic. That was her choice. In the meantime, the world needed someone to do the everyday work of keeping balance, and in the last two years, that chore had been sorely neglected. Humans were getting aggressive, egged on by orcs, lapping up the chaos that came with no balancing justice and with no rules. There were incidents where some elf clans had outright battles with their local humans. There were, some whispered, deaths. It felt like the tribes could go to war.

If truth be told, Ratna was not that disappointed to be left behind. She was always a shy and private girl who kept to herself, so the prospect of going to a bacchanal was not appealing. She certainly wasn't eager to go hunting for a lord to bed and bond with; that was years away. She would have a lot more fun hiking in the mountains and looking for gemstones to use in her artwork, so that's what she told her parents she would do. And they were fine with that.

It was a long, long way to Tall el-Hammam in Middle Ghor, and porting there took hours, especially when such a huge number of lords all wanted to go to the same place at the same time. The tailbacks and queues were horrendous. Ratna's parents kissed her and promised to be back in a few days, but told her not to wait up if they were late. Her last sight of them was her father and mother turning and blowing her a kiss as they stepped into the first of many ports that would take them to the festival.

She never saw them again.

When Gaia pulled the sun down on the festival and incinerated all of the Elementals and probably ninety-five per cent of all of the lords on earth, Ratna was deep inside a cave working on a promising vein of emerald crystals.

She felt the vibration of the explosion even from the other side of the world, and for a minute, she thought there was an earthquake. She wasn't worried about being trapped deep underground; she had an elf with her, and he would port her out to the surface if need be. The elf felt it, too. Startled, he looked up from a scroll he was reading as he waited for the lord to finish whatever it was she was doing and asked if she had felt that. She had. When it didn't happen again, they both shrugged and went back to their tasks.

It took three long days for the news to get back to Ratna about the disaster at Tall el-Hammam, and by that time, things were rapidly falling apart. With no lords around, the elves began to panic. With no Warrior Lords to counter disorder, the orc and humans, who were always jealous of both lords and elves, began to harass the tribes, stealing what they could from the elves' market stalls and spitefully setting fire to the elves' crops. The orcs gloried in the chaos and began to eat elves when they could catch them, causing more panic in the elf clans and causing pitched battles whenever the opposing tribes met. Orcs had never dared to do such depraved things when lords were around to punish them, but with the shackles of civilisation suddenly cut off, the orcs went deep into their darkest impulses, and there was no stopping them. Elves were eaten, weak lords were raped, mutilated and killed, and everyone's houses were looted and burned.

Ratna was in a panic, waiting for parents who didn't come back. The elves who kept their house in order and kept her family healthy and safe stopped showing up for work. They knew that the strong lords were dead, and lords barely above childhood like Ratna were useless in defending them against aggressive humans and orcs. The Ratnas of the world were now a liability, not an asset to the elves, and they abandoned her as they scrambled to save themselves.

The terrified girl wandered the empty, echoing house, crying and lost, not knowing what to do, not knowing whether to stay and wait for her parents or flee for her life. She didn't know how to feed herself. She didn't know how to do anything. From the hills, Ratna could see fires in the distance as other houses were raided and burnt, and she knew that the only reason she was spared was because there were richer pickings to be had. Sooner or later, someone would remember the lord's modest house in the far valley at the edge of the woods.

Afraid that her home would be the next to fall to the humans and orcs, at night she slept huddled in a cupboard; the close, dark space felt like a cave to her, and that gave her some comfort.

On the third day, an old elf who usually worked in the stables showed up with a backpack of supplies and gave it to Ratna. "Child, I'm going to port you to the mountains. I want you to find the deepest cave you can find and stay there until this mess is fixed."

Ratna nodded.

"We're going away for a while, so you're going to have to be brave and manage until we come back. You can do it; I know you can." He didn't want to look at her. The little lord's frightened face broke his heart.

"I don't know how to cook –"

"You'll learn. Hunger will teach you. Watch what the animals eat, especially the bears. If they eat something, you probably can, too."

"When will you be back? Can I go with you?"

He sighed and looked at his feet. In all his long life, he had never told a lord "no" before.

"No. We are going where only elves can go. I don't know when we'll be back. When we hear the call that it's safe again, I guess. In the meantime, you make sure you eat and stay away from humans! Sooner or later, they'll wake up and get sane again, but in the meantime, you have to hide. When you find your ability, you make sure you practise it every day."

The old elf looked at her, anxious. "Every single day, as hard as you can."

Ratna nodded, and she hugged him. Then she stepped into the porthole, and that was the last time she saw her parents' house.

It didn't occur to her until years – decades – later that the elf knew they'd be gone for a long time. She was fifteen and wouldn't have her abilities for at least thirty or forty years.

Ratna found a lovely cave with water and a hidden entrance, well away from any humans or orcs.

She learned to find food by watching the animals, and like the elf said, she learned what to eat. The first winter was very hard, but she survived. The second winter was easier, and by the third winter, she was thriving.

Occasionally, a human would venture into the mountains, and she would watch what they did, especially if they were hunters. When they weren't looking, she'd steal from them, and the mountains she lived on soon earned a reputation for being unlucky. Even fewer came by once that happened.

When she was about twenty-five, a white-haired lord walked through her valley. She met up with him, and they had a cautious and then joyous meeting with both so happy to be with one of their own kind. He crept into her bed that night, and she didn't turn him away. That was the one and only time she coupled with a lord and feasted on his man-scent. The next day, he went out alone to see if he could find a rabbit for their pot. He didn't tell her that the reason he was on her mountain was that he was fleeing a party of humans and orcs who were hunting him – like a rabbit.

He didn't come back, and when Ratna went to look for him, she found his mutilated body hanging from a tree, pierced by dozens of arrows. His head was on the ground, yards away. Ratna threw up everything she had in her and ran all the way home.

She didn't go down that trail again for years and years.

So Ratna lived with the rhythm of the seasons, avoiding humans, trying to be content with her own thoughts for companionship. Every now and then, she would adopt a wolf cub or a raven or eagle to have something living to talk to.

When she was about fifty-five, she found her ability. When Ratna realised she could call crystals to her and shape them to her will, she cried. If she were still living with her parents, they would have thrown a big party to celebrate her passage into full lord adulthood. There would have been lots of food, and all of their relatives and friends would have come by to watch her demonstrate her nascent skills. A giddy crowd of family and friends would laugh and joke and give her tons of unsolicited advice. Knowing her mother, there would have been an Elemental in the room to nod and smile with approval and give her a little gift to commemorate the day.

So this bittersweet rite of passage was her only gift for growing up, and after a good cry over what she had lost, she worked hard at what she had found. Like she had promised the old elf, she practised every day and made sure she ate well.

Ratna passed her one hundredth birthday. Looking neither old nor young, her straight brown hair was now completely white and contrasted sharply with her brown skin and dark green eyes.

To the people in the valley, lords and elves were fading into myth. A few artefacts remained, and the most ridiculous elf-made things like spoons and a bridle became totemic. But after a few centuries, even those items were stolen, lost, or destroyed. The little people became fairy tales to be told to children at night to keep them quiet.

The only remnant of the Before Times left to the humans in the valleys and the few orcs who still lived with them were rumours of a witch who lived in the mountains.

When Ratna was in her fifth century, she had a visitor.

By then, her abilities were very well-developed, and one of the things she could do was sense the tiny changes that came to her crystals when a living being passed by them. This was very handy when it came to hunting a deer or rabbit. All she had to do was place some crystals on a trail, and when the animal came by, Ratna would know it. She could wait upwind and feel the animal walk past a series of crystals and know exactly when the creature would pass right by her. She would be ready with her bow and arrow, and just like that, dinner.

Over the years, she seeded the mountain with rock crystals. Nothing too rare to attract the humans, but enough to let her know when people were passing through her area. Often, she would go and watch them as they marched by, doing her best to stay well hidden. She wasn't afraid of them any more, not if she stayed out of bow-and-arrow range. Her range for shooting a nasty shard of crystal at them far exceeded what they could reach with even the best of their bows. Ratna didn't want them to get any ideas about hunting her down like they did to that one lord she had met so long ago.

Her visitor came one night in the middle of a sudden October snowstorm. He sheltered in the crevice that hid the doorway to her home, and, of course, he had no idea that hidden deep in the crack in the mountain, there was a door. He was practically leaning on it. Ratna knew he was there the minute he stepped in because her crystals told her.

Every time he moved, they told her. When he tried to light a fire and failed, they told her that, too. When he started to freeze to death, she heard. Finally, she couldn't stand listening to him die any more and opened the door and dragged him in. She dragged him down the flights of stairs and deep into the warmth of her house, which was heated by the earth itself. She pushed him by the oven, took away all of his weapons, and then threw a buffalo hide on him. Then she crawled to the other corner and waited to see what would happen. If he died, she'd have to drag him back up all of those steps, so she hoped he would live long enough to get himself up to the surface. That would be nice.

His name was Tatanga, and he was lost. And that's how Ratna found her first man.

She enjoyed her men, but she didn't take one on very often. It was simply too painful to lose them, and they lived such fleeting, ephemeral lives. She never kept one against his will. If they wanted to leave and go back to humans, they could do that. If they came back to her later, she was happy to see them again.

By now, Ratna was confident in her ability to defend herself, and she had bolt holes to escape to throughout the mountain. When you can bend and melt rock to your will, you can make many things to make your home more comfortable and safe, like corridors, steps, rooms and pits to trap invaders. When you can throw crystals so hard they can pass through a buffalo, you don't get worried about being attacked by bows and arrows.

So the days turned into months and the months into years and the years into centuries. Now and then, a man would come by who appealed to her and gave her something to think about and new ideas to learn. Even when he was gone, the fruits of the encounter would last her a long time – five hundred years or more – until the loneliness became so crushing she looked for a new companion.

When the Rangers came to disturb her crystals, Ratna was still mourning her last companion; he had only been dead about twenty years, so there was no new man in her life, and she wasn't looking for one.

But life gives you surprises.

Ratna

Ratna looked up from the micro mosaic she was working on and listened, her long pointed ears twitching. Her last man had given her a book on Italian micro-mosaics, and they were very interesting. She was trying to copy one to learn the technique, but she couldn't concentrate when her crystals were saying someone was walking on her mountain.

There were also deeper vibrations – something big was on her mountain. She put on her coat and went to see what was going on.

She followed the vibrations, and in a valley on the east side she saw what was causing them. A helicopter had landed and disgorged about a dozen men and women who were busy setting up a camp. Ratna could see piles of boxes, tents, a grill – all the usual stuff humans hauled with them when they made a modern camp.

Sighing to herself, Ratna hoped they weren't hunters. Hunters were a pain, and they had to be watched. Their guns were as bad as the crystals she could throw, and the strongest ones could outrange her. Just a couple of hundred years ago, they hadn't been a problem. But in the last fifty years, human activity around her mountain had gotten too frequent to be comfortable and they all seemed to carry guns. For thousands of years, humans had passed by her because they were lost or had some sensible purpose, like gathering berries, hunting, or trapping, but now they walked into the deep forest simply for recreation. Her last man just liked climbing up mountains and looking at the view. Ratna understood the attraction, but now the human world was encroaching on her home, and she wasn't happy about it. They should find their own mountain.

This camp was bordering on the ridiculous. A tent as big as a house was being set up, complete with an outhouse. They brought a shitter with them! With helicopters! That was a new one for campers.

Ratna was quite familiar with helicopters. She knew that humans could fly now with their machines, and she knew all about quad bikes, motorcycles, trucks – all of them. She had never been on one, but she had kept up with the rapid changes of the last century. It's not like she could avoid seeing the things as humans buzzed around her looking for lost hikers, putting out fires, and cutting down trees.

She sat on a hilltop and watched them set up. Then she got bored and went home. The crystals would tell her if they started roaming.

Ratna

When her man brought her a radio, Ratna wasn't quite sure what to think of the silly thing. But he wanted it and said she would enjoy it, so she gave it a go, and after a while, she found he was right. She liked the voices that told stories, she enjoyed the songs, and she became curious about the wider world. When she got tired of constantly charging the thing up with the round handle, she set up a tourmaline battery system, and that worked quite well. Quartz would hold an electric charge, but tourmaline worked so much better.

BBC was her favourite channel, and she would listen to *The Archers* as she worked on her mosaics, then news and whatever music happened to be on. She avoided the religious programs. Humans certainly had some odd ideas.

Sometimes, if she was in a low mood, she would glance at the radio, and she would be reminded of his love. It would physically hurt that he was gone, like a shard of obsidian in her heart, and she would start to cry.

He had loved her so much and had worried about her being lonely when his body gave out and he passed to the Void. Ratna remembered the day he came home with the heavy black box strapped on his back, hauling it across the many valleys and all the way up the mountain to give to her and how she was very unimpressed. What was she going to do with this ugly box? But then he turned the handle and fiddled with some knobs, and the box sang to her. Then she understood the magnificence of the gift. He had given her the world.

So when the modern world started to creep into Ratna's mountain home, she was quite aware of what was going on. She didn't think flying machines or radios were magic; she understood that they were mechanical inventions because humans could be clever when they put their minds to it. She knew about guns and bombs and Hemingway and pandemics and wars and kings and queens and hip-hop and the internet. For all of her 3,500 years of isolation, in the last fifty, she became quite well-educated (from a human perspective) as she listened to lectures, discussions, and the news.

She knew that elves were waking up.

She knew about Lords Cadence and Kyrylo visiting New York.

She was terrified.

Ratna

The helicopter spent the next two days buzzing the mountains to her east. They were looking for something. Then, when they obviously couldn't find whatever it was they were looking for, they flew around the mountain to her south. Ratna saw a strange rig off the side of the helicopter, and at first she thought it was a machine gun. She had heard of those from the war reports on the radio, but then she saw a glint of a lens and knew they were filming.

That was a relief. They weren't hunters. Maybe they were filming a nature documentary! Ratna had heard about nature films on the radio. One day, she would have to get a television and see what the fuss was about.

The weather turned damp and foggy, and since the gods are kind, the helicopter had to rest next to the huge tent and wait out the low visibility. That didn't mean the men and women stayed in the tent. Oh no, these were determined little beavers; they started to search on foot.

The nature documentary theory gained credence when Ratna started to find camera traps placed on trails. That was quite a nervy invasion of her privacy, and she destroyed every one she found. And she found them all. She didn't know that the cameras couldn't capture her on film, being a lord, but by destroying them so efficiently and purposefully, she betrayed that she was there.

Every time they put one out, she killed it, and they put out more and more. By tracking the destroyed cameras, the team began to triangulate her location. If she had been inside the big tent, she would have seen a screen set up with a dot for every camera, the time of its destruction, and which trails were easiest for her to get to and which took some time.

They stopped using the helicopter and concentrated on the camera traps. When a few dummy traps were put out, Ratna ignored them, which told the team she knew the difference.

It became a game.

Every morning, a couple of the team members – always a Ranger and one of the guides at minimum – would hike up a trail and install camera traps. Sometimes they were on a trail, sometimes deep in the woods. They tried hard to hide them, but that didn't seem to do any good at all.

Once Wendell and two of the Nakota guides walked three hours up a steep trail and installed ten traps. They checked that they all worked with their phones. Later, when they made it back to camp, Luke was sitting in front of the monitor and laughing at them. He showed them that minutes after they left the area, the cameras would die. She was following them and destroying the cameras as fast as they were installing them. If they had turned around, the team would have tripped over her.

Frustrated and tired, Wendell snapped that maybe Luke could do better. And if he could, don't hold back.

So Luke tried another tactic. The next morning, he went out by himself with two cameras. He wasn't supposed to go out solo, but he said he had to if this was going to work, and he promised to stay on a familiar trail no matter what happened. Luke set out, and the team sat back and watched the monitors. The Ranger was wired with geolocators, and he had a body cam on that transmitted his voice back to the tent. The team saw the Luke dot slowly inch up the trail, and then, in a big open field above the treeline, it stopped. They heard his breath rasp as he worked to pull oxygen out of the thin mountain air.

Luke hiked to the middle of a big field of scrubby grass and pounded a stake in the rocky ground, and set up a camera. Then he simply found a big rock to sit on and waited.

Do you know when you're being watched?
Can you feel it?

Luke could feel her eyes on him.

"Hello! I know you're there!"

Silence.

"We mean you no harm! We just want to talk! I –"

A rock shot out as fast as a bullet, shattering the camera trap in a thousand pieces.

"I see you don't feel like talking today! I can take a hint, but when you do, we're here. We have a message from the lords for you."

Luke waved, and as he turned to go, out of the corner of his eye, he saw a flash of white hair. As promised, he didn't chase after her but went back down to the tent.

Back in the tent, the team whooped and hollered. A contact!

Now they went into high gear. Teams went out three or four times a day, setting traps and working out where she was. Without meaning to, in their enthusiasm to complete their mission, they were making Ratna stressed and very, very angry. She was being stalked, and it not only scared her, it infuriated her.

What right did these humans have to come to her home and harass her? How was she to know that they were sent by the lords she had heard about on the radio? They weren't here, now were they? She hadn't seen any indication of lords or elves, so how was she to know they didn't want to trap her for their own reasons? For that matter, were the lords and elves she heard about free? Maybe they were trapped by humans and were prisoners, too.

Every time they set out a trap that she had to go destroy, they called to her, trying to lure her out with conversation. She figured out that the cameras were being used as bait, and she stopped killing them all, which, unbeknownst to her, was messing up and slowing their triangulation efforts.

On the third day of the new, stepped-up harassment, Ratna sat in her home so upset that her hands shook. She decided that this had to stop. She couldn't sleep, and she was not eating well. She had to scare them away.

She took some of her precious paper and drew the most frightening things she could think of. Dancing orcs making rude gestures. Orcs doing orc things. It was entertaining, this bit of creativity, and it calmed her. She drew several pictures, nailed them to stakes, and in the dead of night, she crept into their camp and posted them on the path leading to their latrine.

First, they had to know she could get into their camp; the next thing would be to make them feel she could hurt them. In truth, Ratna didn't want to hurt anyone. In all of her 3,500 years, she had never killed a human, even when she could have and probably should have. But she had scared them away, and she wanted these people to go.

A Nakota guide was first out to the latrine, and when he saw the stakes, he ran hollering back to the tent and woke up the Rangers. In a neat line leading to the latrine was a series of signs. They didn't have words; they didn't need to. They were pictures of orcs. An orc eating an elf. Orcs tearing a lord to pieces. Orcs and humans dancing around a fire with a lord tied to a stake on a spit. Humans, you could tell by the ears, in Nakota dress, shooting arrows into a decapitated body hanging in a tree. The head on the ground was a lord.

You could tell by the ears.

"Shit."

They took photos of the pictures of the stakes in situ and then took them down and took them to the tent, where they were copied and sent to HQ. They were on Caddy's and Kyrylo's desks within half an hour.

Forty minutes later, the lords were on the screen. They were quite upset, and their distress came through the blurry image.

Psychologists were examining the drawings as they were speaking, but the first instinct of the lords was to tell their people to stand down. These drawings were a warning to back off, and that had to be respected. They were the shake of the rattler's tail.

"We know she can defend herself; look at what she did to that camera." Kyrylo spoke slowly, thinking as he spoke, "She could hit you as you're walking up a trail, and you'll never know what happened. You'll just be dead. I don't think these drawings are fantasy. You have to remember these drawings are lived experience. You're human, and you're a threat. She is giving you – us – notice that she is pissed."

Caddy interjected, "And pissed also means scared. We're scaring her." Kyrylo nodded. "And that's not the way to get her on our side."

Vernon popped in on another window, as did a couple of the intel people. "There's a fair amount of PTSD in those drawings. The shrinks think she's on the verge of a breakdown. AI has analysed the drawings, and there's a lot of hand shaking and stress in the strokes."

Wendell mused, "Y'know, all of us here know what it's like to be bullied and harassed. Are we bullying her?"

There was an uncomfortable silence.

Kyrylo sighed. "We want you to take a day off while we think this over. No camera traps, no hiking, no calling to her. She doesn't trust humans who are hunting for her, and we can see she has good reason not to. We'll –"

"I'm not human." Tuân blurted it out, and it was rude and against protocol, but he was irritated. "Sometimes I think people forget I'm here. I'm not human, and I've been stuck in this tent looking at this fucking screen for weeks now. Maybe I should go talk to her."

Kyrylo frowned. "Why hasn't Tuân been out on the trails?"

There was another uncomfortable silence. Yes, the two older, more experienced Rangers had, without meaning to, sidelined their younger brother to a supporting role, sitting in the tent, watching the camera monitors. He had never complained, but once he pointed it out, it did seem wrong. Why hadn't they brought out the one huge asset they had – a lord – earlier? If they were honest, they knew why. Getting out and hiking was active and fun. Sitting in a stuffy tent and literally watching grass grow on computer monitors was not. They had hogged the fun and, in doing so, degraded the mission.

"Stand down; take the day off. Tuân, be ready to go out when we have a plan." Kyrylo's voice was clipped, and it was hard to tell if he was irritated, worried, or just in a hurry. Probably all three. He signed off.

That afternoon, all of the Stoney Nakota guides resigned and were flown back to town. The last thing they wanted to do was anger the Witch of the Mountain, especially now that they knew she really existed. That left the three Rangers, the helicopter pilot, the cook, and one of the non-Native guides.

Ratna watched as the Stoneys packed up and flew away. Four down, six to go.

Ratna and Tuân

Ratna looked at the young lord, and for a moment, she couldn't breathe. For a lord he was. And there he stood, studying the sheer rock face like he was reading a sacred ancient text, which in a way he was. He had a small smile as he looked up, and even from her perch, she could see the blue sparks in his eyes. His ears had good points to them, but they weren't as magnificent as they would be when he grew to his full age. He gave the rock face a fond pat and then turned and walked down the goat trail.

She moved with absolute silence behind him, loath to let him out of her sight. When the wind came from the right direction, she could smell him. Once she got a whiff so strong she had to stop and steady herself. Oh, gods – he smelled so good. He was very young, but he was a young man, not a boy, and he smelled like a man should. And she hadn't smelled man-perfume for over 3,500 years. You don't forget it, though. She wondered if he could smell her, but he didn't seem to notice her at all.

He knew where he was going, and he walked quickly. There came a point when Ratna couldn't follow as closely as she wanted to because the mountain goat trail meandered across a sheer and open cliff, and she would be exposed. He, on the other hand, walked as surely as a bighorn over parts of the trail that were only inches wide, the vertical face of the mountain occasionally forcing him to sidle along if the trail was too narrow for his shoulders.

He had very nice shoulders.

Ratna memorised every part of the lord in the short time she could follow him. He wasn't too tall, and he was slim, but under his dark mountain gear, she could see he was all lean muscle. Even his big hands had muscles. From her cautious distance well behind him, she couldn't see his face well, but what she saw reminded her of the Nakota people in a way, but different. He wasn't as pale as the white ones who lived in the valleys. His cheeks were beardless, but he had a thin moustache and goatee. He had the most gorgeous, tightly-curled red hair, like a mountain goat calf. In a few years, it would turn white like all lords, but for now, it was a glorious flame that frothed out behind him and bounced on his shoulders.

He continued down the trail, but she was too afraid to go further. The human men were looking for her; she knew it. But now this lord was here, and what if he was one of her hunters? Was he looking for her, too? Did that mean they meant her no harm? Or was this young lord a turncoat?

He disappeared into the treeline, and as he left, the wind gifted her one last trace of man-scent, and she drank it in.

She was in love – or at least in lust. She knew the difference. Ratna sighed and turned to go back home. There was too much to think about, and she was scent-addled.

Before the humans turned on the elves and lords, when Ratna was a young woman-lord watching all of her friends and family get killed off one by one, she had a single brief encounter with a lord whose scent affected her like this one did. They didn't have time to bond properly before he was killed, so when he died, she didn't go crazy.

She grieved, but not so much for him because she had only known him for one day. She grieved for the possibilities that had died with him.

The occasional human man she had over the years kept her interested in life and sex, but they weren't able to stir her in the primal way another lord could, and it was unfair to expect them to. Most were, to be honest, fondly remembered as any well-loved and useful tool that eventually wore out. If she thought about it hard, she could remember their names, but not remembering their names was protection for the time they would inevitably die. It was best not to get too attached to them.

This lovely lord surely had a woman already, and just having that thought flash through her mind made Ratna grumpy and jealous, and it was nothing but a thought.

Ratna wondered what the lord's name was.

Tuân

Tuân went out hiking alone every day, sometimes in the morning, sometimes in the evening. He promised, on his honour, not to do any free-climbing, but oh, he found some good places, and it was tempting. He didn't hike in the forests but up where the mountain rose proud and naked over the valley, and he would spend hours scrambling over the boulders, listening to the pika's squeak and watching the bighorn and the mountain goats tend to their spring kids.

On the second day, Ratna followed him back to the base camp, and she watched the others come out to greet him and follow him back into the big tent. So he was one of them, after all. They didn't have him imprisoned.

They had given up on the cameras, so this lord was now coming out instead. He must have been in the tent the whole time. They'd been doing his searching for him, and it wasn't working, so now he was doing it himself.

Ratna realised he was looking for her. She thought about what that meant all night.

On the fourth day of Tuân's solo hikes, he saw her. She didn't hide; it wasn't an accident. She sat cross-legged on a boulder on the other side of a steep erosion gully and just watched him approach.

He didn't run to her when he finally spotted her. Tuân froze. He let her have a good look, and he, in turn, had a good look.

She was small. Not as small as an elf, but very small for an adult human. She had smooth, nut-brown skin and long, white hair pulled back in a single, thick braid down her back. Because her hair was pulled back, he could see her ears, which were long, pointed, and utterly gorgeous. Her eyes glowed green, so he knew she was feeling emotional at that moment, and he hoped the emotion wasn't fear – or worse.

Slowly, he held up his open hands. No weapons. What do you say when you meet a lord? They hadn't rehearsed this bit. He yelled across the gully, "Hello! My name is Tuân!" which sounded a bit lame after all this effort.

She smiled. Tuân was a nice name. She couldn't smell him from here, so she could think clearly. She watched him from across the gully as he awkwardly shifted and bounced on his heels, releasing nervous energy. Then she grinned. He had caught her, this Tuân, and now he didn't know what to do with her.

She got up, nodded, and smiled at Tuân. "My name is Ratna, and this is enough for today. Don't follow me."

So, of course, he didn't.

The encounter was captured on Tuân's body cam, and back in the tent, there were excited whoops and back-slapping. Second contact! And she seemed okay with it!

The intel was sent back to HQ, and it was unanimously decided to continue with Tuân meeting her alone. They would build on this success.

Ratna and Tuân

Every day, rain or shine, Tuân went out for a walk above the treeline. He'd find a big boulder to sit on and then have lunch. Sometimes she came out to where he could see her, and sometimes she didn't, but sooner or later, he always felt her watching.

He left her little gifts like a candy bar or an apple, and even if he didn't see her, he greeted her with her name. Tuân wouldn't have called it that, but he was wooing her.

Ratna was quite aware of what he was doing. Didn't she have 3,500 years of experience luring in deer or wolf cubs with bits of food? Didn't she know all about calling them sweetly and clucking and making them feel safe to be around her? So she wasn't fooled a bit, but hey, she wasn't going to turn down a banana out of false pride. Her man had occasionally brought back bananas for her, and they were rare treats.

The first time she sat near him without some huge obstacle protecting her was a happy day for Tuân. It was full summer and hot on the big boulders, and she sat nearby, almost naked in a little sleeveless shift so thin it was almost transparent and a pair of old denim shorts.

Tuân wondered if she wore anything at all when she was alone and it was hot.

He didn't realise she always chose to sit upwind, and her worries weren't over being *safe* but were solely because if she sat downwind, she couldn't *think*. Maybe that was a safety worry, too.

The day she sat near him, she had walked up the goat-track behind him and leapt up onto the next boulder in a single, impossible bound. Tuân turned and grinned.

"Good day, Ratna! So, how long have you been following me?"

Ratna smiled back, and her eyes twinkled. "Since the camp."

She would not sit next to him. Tuân guessed that she still didn't trust him enough to be within grabbing range, and that was a bit painful, but he had to accept it.

He had tried before. If Tuân edged closer, she scooted away, and if she couldn't wiggle any further, she got up and made a wide loop around him and sat on the other side. Usually, when she did this, she would shoot him a dirty look for making her move. Fifteen feet was the safety zone, and she didn't break it.

They began to have little conversations. Tuân told her about his life growing up in Vietnam and how he didn't know Lord Cadence was his great-grandmother because they didn't know what they were, and so they were hidden from the world. So his great-grandmother and his grandfather, Conary, were lords, too, and they had found some others, and now there were ten in the world. And then there was Lester. He told her all about Lester and his role in the destruction of the lords and elves.

She said nothing, but on Ratna's impassive face her narrowed eyes glowed bright.

A few days later, Tuân made an off-hand suggestion that she come to the tent and talk to some of the lords. He offered to get rid of all the humans, even send them off to the town if that made her feel better. He certainly understood her antipathy towards the human tribe! She had a lot of reasons to hate them.

"I don't hate humans!" Ratna was peeved. What on earth made him think that? "I've had several human lovers over the years. They stayed with me a long time, and it was always [and she emphasised the *always*] willingly. They loved me. I was very fond of them."

Tuân knew she had had one human lover, Martha's dad, but "several" took him by surprise. A fleeting fancy passed through his brain, wondering what it was like to be in Ratna's bed. He had this picture of her riding him on top, naked, her long hair – and he quickly suppressed the thought. Now was not the time.

"We thought that since you didn't want to talk to us, it was because the guys are human. We know you haven't had goo –"

Ratna wouldn't let Tuân finish. "I wasn't avoiding your band simply because of the humans; I was avoiding you because of the danger humans and orcs are to me. I haven't lived up here for 3,500 years by being friendly with the locals and jumping into their tents. But while I don't have anything to do with orcs, I don't *hate* humans as a tribe. I hate what some do. I hate humans with orcs and orcs with humans."

Of course. That made perfect sense.

"So come down and meet the team. I give you my word, they will be respectful. I want you to meet the other lords, and we can do that by TV – it's called teleconferencing ."

"You have a television in that tent?" Ratna perked up. A TV! "I've never seen a TV."

"Do you know," she said, and her voice went husky, sexy, and dreamy, "I've never seen a nature film. The BBC says there are shows of all sorts of things. Birds. Fish."

Tuân grinned. He'd found her hot button. You couldn't lure Ratna with promises of celebrity lords, but a 30-year-old David Attenborough documentary? Bring it on!

He'd even throw in a banana.

Wendell, Tuan, and Luke

High on the mountain, the Rangers were having a good run up and down the goat trails, showing off to each other and yelling insults with all the high animal spirits of healthy young men. Tuân was the fastest and the most sure-footed, and he was well ahead on the narrow trail, slowing down to jog backwards and yelling at his brothers that they ran like old ladies waddling to a charity shop bargain bin.

Wendell bellowed Watch out! and Tuân turned and almost fell over Ratna, who was standing in the middle of the trail, arms akimbo, her face scrunched up in anger, and her firecracker eyes snapping an angry green.

"What fools you are! It's going to rain hard, and it's dangerous up here in the rain. You idiots! You'll get washed off the trails! Go home!"

The Rangers skidded to a stop, panting, and Wendell and Luke looked to Tuân. They weren't going to say a word to the furious little lord.

"We checked the weather app, Ratna; it's not going to rain." As he said the word "rain", fat drops started to fall. Ratna pressed her lips together in a thin line and then ran an arc up the sheer wall and came down behind Wendell. She started to jog backwards.

"Follow me," she growled. "And keep up."

She was fast, and while she had to take two steps to Wendell's one, those little legs *pumped*. If the Rangers didn't have miles and miles of running time against elves, they wouldn't have thought her speed possible. The thundercloud wrapped around the mountain, spitting sheets of rain, and right in front of their eyes, parts of the trail disappeared as torrents of rainwater frothed into fast-rushing streams and waterfalls. Boulders trembled, then rolled, noisily bouncing down the mountain, greased with rainwater from their precarious beds where they had slept for millions of years until today when they went a-roaming. As the boulders fell, they dislodged small rockslides that then merged with their friends lower down to create bigger mudslides. The rain poured, thunder boomed, and the boulders crashed and roared as they flirted with gravity.

Ratna had to weave the group up and down the mountainside to find a path to the tree line, and when they reached the tree line, she didn't stop but herded them through the pines and into the tent like a wolf bitch snapping at the heels of her pups, getting them out of danger.

At the door of the tent, she stopped. The gasping men were struggling for air, bent over. Tuân collapsed, gasping and spreadeagled on the ground, his chest heaving. Ratna walked in and nudged him with her foot. He just waved a hand at her. She grinned and winked at the guides who jumped up from their computer monitors and scrambled to the other side of their table. Then she grabbed an entire bunch of bananas and ran out, disappearing into the driving rain.

A half hour later, the sun was out, and the weather app was once again correct.

Wendell, Tuan, and Luke

The next morning, the Rangers went out again, back to where Ratna had found them jogging, to see what damage the rain had done. Where there once were dry gullies, now there were violent freshets of rainwater, and across the mountain face cascades and waterfalls glinted in the sun. Some of the new rockslides were huge, and the leading edges reached well into the forest, knocking down trees. As they jogged, they came across the carcasses of two mountain goats, already food for the living.

Wendell pointed up the mountain to where he thought they were yesterday. The trail had completely washed away. They scrambled across a steep avalanche field to avoid the piles of uprooted trees and debris at the base, and as they crossed, they suddenly understood the terrible mistake they were making. The unstable rock slide began to shift under their feet, and in the space of a second, there was a roar, and what had seemed like a settled rubble field came to life. It bounced and slid, knocking them off their feet. Swept away in a tidal wave of rocks and mud, the men were washed to the bottom of the slide and buried.

Tuân was entombed in mud and rock. He couldn't move, not even a finger; he was so tightly encased in mud and rocks, and for a deadly, despairing moment, he knew he was going to die, his promise of forever-life squandered on careless, youthful impulse. The mountain settled and sat on him and slowly squeezed. He felt unbearable pain in his shin. There was no air, and he started to black out.

Then the rocks and mud began to move again, only this time they separated and spread like an invisible hand was pushing them away from his body, releasing the terrible pressure. He could breathe, then he could move his arms, and he started to push and fight to get out of his tomb. He looked up and saw Ratna's tight, terrified little face looking into his hole. She was glowing, and her eyes were bright green lasers. She mouthed his name. When she saw him move, she disappeared. He was finally able to pull himself from the hole, and he saw a filthy, battered Wendell standing off to the side, yelling into his body cam, calling for the helicopter and the medics. Ratna's entire body was now enveloped in a brilliant green glow, and she was gently moving the earth away from Luke, rescuing him.

Dazed, Tuân looked up the debris field, and there he saw huge, protective crystals forming a rampart and holding back and redirecting the slowly oozing avalanche. The mountain still wanted them, but Ratna was having none of it.

The medivac helicopter screamed in, and Luke was rescued, put on a backboard, and all three Rangers were airlifted to Calgary. As Tuân was lifted into the helicopter, he screamed to Ratna, but he didn't know if she heard him over the thumping roar of the blades.

"I'll come back for you! RATNA!! Don't go anywhere! I'll come back!"

But when the medics turned to look at what he was yelling at, no one was there.

Vrt

The vibrations were getting closer; Vrt could feel it. For the last six months, once a week, she could feel the song rumble through the earth and up her legs. If the song was to be believed, someone was waking the elves up. She first felt the faintest echoes of a tune from someplace in Estonia, but now the rumbles were working their way up the Finnish-Russian border. Not that she paid any attention at all to the markers humans and orcs put on land. It's not as if the Earth belonged to them.

But these noises were getting close to her patch, and since the song was calling elves, she wanted to see what was going on. So she decided to go a-roaming. If she was lucky, she'd kill an orc or two on the way. One could always hope!

It was quite the circus and appeared to be some sort of military exercise. Vrt had watched hundreds, maybe a thousand, of these military encampments over the years and was always pleased to find one. There were usually a lot of orcs to be found, especially on the Russian side. The Rus did like a good invasion, and they worked on the Suomi pretty regularly.

This exercise was on the present-day Finnish side and didn't involve any Russians. There didn't seem to be any orcs in the units, which was a bit disappointing. But it wasn't quite normal either, and that piqued Vrt's interest. The Finnish military didn't matter anyway because even though there weren't any orcs, this wasn't about them. The song spoke of elves.

She settled into a good hiding place high on a hill and watched. With the telescope she had liberated from a dead orc general three hundred years earlier, she could see everything that was going on.

In her heart, Vrt didn't expect to see any elves; they were long gone. But the idea that humans were looking for them was interesting. In over three and a half millennia, she had never seen humans trying to call up elves.

There were trucks, buses, and all sorts of weapons bristling with cannon tubes. Off to the side, a Finnish Army unit was jumping out of trucks. There was also another unit of soldiers, but she didn't recognise these men and women. Their uniform was dark green without the gaudy patterns that were supposed to blend in with the forest and really didn't.

Then helicopters flew in, and out jumped a bunch of officers whom Vrt recognised because you can always tell the officers by their walk – just like you could always spot an orc by their walk. And from the third helicopter out jumped three lords.

Three lords.

Vrt was so stunned she almost gave a low moan, but of course, she didn't. She was too well-trained to even twitch a muscle. Lords! A family group; she could tell. A man guiding a pregnant woman, and another man following them. All three were Elementals. The woman had the most beautiful ears, and Vrt was ashamed to find herself touching her helmet where her ears used to be. Envy was a weakness, and weakness was not to be tolerated.

With a swift, practised efficiency that was so well-rehearsed it was almost a dance, the woman walked around the field, stopping now and then to listen. Then she chose her spot. The soldiers made a ring around her, and then, to Vrt's utter astonishment, she played an instrument but only to guide the powerful magic of her waking song. *And elves awoke!*

Hibernating elves in massive rubbery eggs popped out of the ground in a huge bubbling mass, and the humans *helped* them. No one killed an elf; no one ate them. They helped free them from their sleep cases and threw them in the air so they could go free. And they laughed and were happy to do it.

When the song had done its work and faded into memory, the woman smiled at the taller man, and he kissed her hand. That intimate gesture brought so much water to Vrt's eyes that she couldn't see for a minute. Another weakness not to be tolerated. The three lords walked back to the helicopter, and Vrt made a note of the words on the tail. RumLot Security Services. She had nothing to write with, but she wouldn't forget.

After the last soldier was long gone and the field was deserted, she walked down to the muddy patch where the elves had reentered the world. This was their land, so they would be back, and when they came back, Vrt would talk with them. They would tell her what she wanted to know and port her to wherever she wanted to go. But for right now, the field was already returning to its natural state. The egg sacs were dissolving, and if someone walked by, they would just see churned-up mud like a herd of deer or elk had trampled the area.

She walked to the place where the lords had stood, and she could smell them. The pregnant woman smelled of apples, the man who kissed her smelled nice, like a pine tree, and the other man let off a heady, sensual man-scent that took Vrt's breath away. She inhaled deeply because he was gone, and it was nice, but she knew what that meant. She would have to stay away from that one. He was dangerous.

She walked back to the forest, made camp, and waited for the elves to return.

Kyrylo and Caddy

Kyrylo was working in his office when he got the call. He looked up, thought about waking Caddy up, changed his mind, and then changed his mind back.

She was taking a nap as she did every day now in the afternoon. He went in and gave her shoulder a gentle shake. "*Zaychik*, I need you to wake up."

She sighed and hugged her pillow tighter. "Later, K. I'm pretty tired now."

He grinned. "Sex. It's always on your mind, isn't it? But I have news, and you have to wake up."

Her eyes flew open, and he gave her the message.

A lord was sitting in the RumLot Security HQ. Just wandered in and sat down in the visitor's area. Could they please come down and talk to him/her and find out what they wanted? He/she made the receptionist very nervous.

Caddy and Kyrylo walked into the atrium, and there the lord sat in the middle of the waiting area on the anodyne, grey sofa. He/she was flipping through a defence contractor magazine that was lying on the coffee table and looked like Darth Vader in a dentist's waiting room.

The lord stood up and didn't say anything, just took a good look at Caddy and Kyrylo, and then bowed low and said, "My name is Lord Vrt." And then stood there. The lord's voice was low and musical, and they could see green glints in the eyes, at least as much of the eyes as they could see through a leather mask. So this lord was a female.

She was taller than Caddy, about 175 cm, with long legs and a lean, athletic build. She was dressed in a motley collection of plain black motorcycle leathers, and her face and head were completely covered in a black leather helmet. Something about the helmet looked odd to Caddy, but she couldn't put her finger on what it was.

All you could see were two green, glowing eyes, and later, when she turned around, a thick white braid of hair coiled up at the base of her neck. Let loose, the braid probably went down to her knees. She wore knee boots and had a sword buckled around her waist, and, from what Kyrylo could see, at least three good-sized elf knives on display. And he suspected more were hidden on her body. At her feet was an old military backpack.

Both lords could see why the receptionist was nervous. Something about the way Lord Vrt held herself made her look like she could kill a bear and not break a sweat. She reeked of danger.

Caddy and Kyrylo introduced themselves and asked her back to Kyrylo's office to talk and have some tea. And that's how they first met Vrt.

Vrt was not easy to talk to. Her answers tended to be one word, and she was obviously ill at ease around the two lords, although it was evident she was trying to be polite. Caddy said later that the poor woman probably hadn't spoken to anyone for years.

She said she was a lord who escaped to the north 3,500 years ago and lived alone in the taiga forests, and that's all she said about her past. She did not know of any other lords until she saw the awakening two days earlier.

Then she asked what RumLot Security was, and Kyrylo explained that they had two missions: one was to wake the elves and reintegrate them with the modern world, and the other was to regain Balance and to control orcs and the humans who supported them so that everyone could live in peace. RumLot Security was the military arm created to help achieve those goals.

"Do you kill orcs?"

"Sometimes we have to, but –"

"Then I will work with you." Vrt nodded; she had made a decision. "I'm very good at killing orcs. Do you have any that you want to kill today?"

Kyrylo was nonplussed. "Well, not at the moment. But I think we're getting ahead of ourselves."

Caddy interrupted. "To regain balance in this modern world, we lords need to work together, and we have a place where we gather and learn from each other. Could you go there and learn about us? When you learn about us, you will know exactly the best way you can help. And I'm sure you have much to teach us so we can learn from you."

This seemed sensible to Vrt. It was always best to examine the terrain before leaping into any battle, and that's what this offer was.

So Vrt was sent to Aelfeham House.

Luke

When Rumlot Security was notified of the accident in Banff, they moved into emergency mode. All of the lords were notified, and Conary was sent to Calgary to be the lead rep for the lords. As Conary said later, with Tuân involved, it wasn't as if they could keep him away, so he might as well be the one to go.

Wendell was banged up a bit and required a few stitches, but not much more. Tuân had a fractured fibula (which meant a walking boot), a cracked rib, and some cuts that required stitches.

Luke was crushed. His back was broken, his spinal cord severed, and he had suffered multiple internal injuries. With modern medicine, the broken back and spinal injuries probably wouldn't kill him, but he would be left with permanent paralysis. It was the crushing that the surgeons couldn't fix. At best, he would be in a wheelchair for life, but the prognosis wasn't that good. The doctors put him in a coma to stabilise the Ranger until they figured out what to do.

When Caddy and Kyrylo heard the news, they were sitting in the Ukraine RumLot Security conference room with Luke's shell-shocked parents.

No one knew what to say.

Kyrylo made the decision.

"Bring him home. Stabilise him, and bring him home. We'll get the best doctors in Europe, and what human doctors can't do, maybe the elves can. There are no elves in Calgary."

He looked to Luke's parents, and they nodded. What else could they do?

Luke was put on a chartered medevac 777, and fifteen hours later, he would land in Kyiv.

_____

Dr Mandy

Dr Mandy shook her head. If this were an elf or a lord, there would be no doubt as to what she would do. She'd pop him in the cauldron and let him be reborn. This was exactly the sort of catastrophic accident the cauldron was best at.

"Why can't he go in the cauldron?"

Dr Mandy looked up at the lord and frowned. Ms Caddy was showing a lot of strain, and for a pregnant woman, that wasn't good. She needed to eat more.

"The cauldron was created for elves and lords. I don't think in all of history there's been a time it's been used on humans."

"What is a cauldron?" This was from Luke's mother, Julia. She was a nurse. A human one.

The doctor answered, "It's called the cauldron because it looks like a big pot. But think of it as a totally immersive incubator. A womb. It allows a broken body to heal by dissolving it and reforming it back to the way it's supposed to be. Like any operation, it works most of the time, but sometimes there are accidents. Nothing is perfect, so using the cauldron is always a risk."

Julia nodded and glanced at her husband before continuing. "You've never used this on a human? Why not?"

Surprised, for once, Dr Mandy didn't have a good answer. "Because it's an elf thing. We don't do medicine on humans because, well, humans don't like us," she finished rather lamely.

"Luke likes you. He loves elves."

She looked at Luke's mother. Anyone could see the woman was going through hell. Grasping at straws now. Dr Mandy sighed. It was her habit to be completely honest. It solved a lot of problems further down the road.

"Okay. Let's say I do this. There's a big risk he won't survive because we've never tested it on humans. This process will change his DNA. He might just dissolve and not come back. Then there is the risk he won't come back as you expect. Maybe brain-damaged, maybe missing a limb, whatever. I don't think he'll come back as anything chimaera, like a half-man, half-animal. I doubt it, but hell's bells – I don't know."

"What are the odds of success?"

"Fifty-fifty"

Luke's father nodded. "And today odds now one hundred per cent he die when he leave life support."

Dr Mandy sighed again. She could see where this was going. She looked at Caddy and Kyrylo. "I'm putting this in your hands."

"I'm hardly an objective person, Mandy. My son John died in a car crash. I would have given anything – anything – to put him back together." Caddy nodded to Julia and Marko. "My vote is to give Luke every chance. If he dies, we'll have tried everything possible. If he lives –" Caddy looked at Mandy. "You'll be able to write your own case study for the medical journals."

Kyrylo nodded. His vote was with Caddy. They had to try.

Lords commanded, and elves obeyed, so Luke's plane was redirected to Heathrow because Aelfeham House still had the cauldron set up that they had used for Jack.

Vrt

Vrt stood in the pretty Breakfast Room of Aelfeham House and was introduced to Sam, Jack, and Alizah. Jack and

Alizah were a bonded couple of floaters and seemed to be very nice, even if Alizah was a little noisy. She talked a lot. Sam was a bit quieter and started off friendly, but soon it was evident he didn't have much to say to Vrt. After a few awkward minutes, she was escorted to her room, and there she stayed until the elf came to take her to dinner.

At dinner, she learned that two more lords who lived there were gone. Conary and his grandson Tuân were in Canada (Alizah looked it up on a map and showed Vrt where Canada was). There was some sort of accident, and they were flying back to the UK (another map lesson here). The elves were setting up a cauldron for one of the party who had been crushed in a rockslide. They were there to meet a new lord, but she wasn't coming back with them.

Vrt listened to all of this intently, but it was hard for the others at the dinner table to get any feel for how she felt with the mask on. She didn't eat with them, just drank a bit, and when Alizah asked if she was going to be hungry, Vrt just shook her head. She would eat in her room later and was very good, thank you. No one had the nerve to ask why, which didn't surprise Vrt at all. New people never did.

The next day Conary, Tuân, and two humans called Rangers arrived. One of the humans was put in the cauldron, and the other human went back to his home in Lowestoft. Conary and Tuân stayed on to meet the new lord, which, as Conary said later, could have been done by text; she spoke so little. As it was, since Tuân had hurt his foot and wore a boot, he couldn't go back to work, so he hung around where there were people to talk to.

Conary was the man the the delicious aroma who had been with Lord Cadence and Lord Kyrylo that day. Once he was identified, Vrt could easily handle his man-scent with a tiny, almost imperceptible breeze that always blew away from her. As long as she didn't get trapped with him in an unventilated space, she was fine, and he was none the wiser. She was fanatical about keeping her body and her clothes clean and odourless, and now that she had elves to help, it was easy to have fresh clothes every day. They tailored her a whole new wardrobe, helmets and all, which was very nice. Everything fit beautifully, and even if Vrt couldn't wear pretty clothes any more, it was wonderful to have well-fitting, comfortable clothes to wear.

And while the "old time" lords didn't know what to make of the black-clad, silent woman who sat in the corners and watched, Vrt was quite happy to be around her own people and listen to normal, everyday conversations and banter. She hadn't had anything close to that for years.

Centuries.

Millenia.

Ratna

The valley was very quiet now that the Rangers were gone. All Ratna could see were the ghosts of footpaths around large squares where the tent and other mysterious boxes had stood. Not a piece of paper or old Coke can hidden in the leaves was left behind. Truly, they followed the woodsman's creed and left nothing but their footprints behind.

Deep in the mountain, her home was even quieter. She didn't have the heart to turn on the radio, and so she sat down at the workbench with the micromosaic and tried to pick up where she had stopped so many weeks ago.

Tuân had said he would be back. But Ratna was very, very old, and she knew that there was never any going back. Time only marched forward; it never returned to where it was. Tuân and his companions might return, but it would be different. An older, wiser Tuân would come back one day to visit the fossil in the mountain, probably with a bonded wife and maybe even kids.

He would come back, and he would have grown, and she would be the same – defying time, never moving forward. What do you call something that never grows and never moves forward? There is no name for such a thing because it doesn't exist. It is dead. Even rocks change over time.

For the first time in 3,500 years, Ratna didn't want to be in her mountain.

She looked down at the micromosaic with its fussy, tiny bits of coloured stone recreating the kitschy Greek temple she was copying, and she broke, screaming at herself and the world. She hurled the frame at the wall, where the mosaic exploded into a thousand microscopic pieces.

The sky was black, and every star was a diamond. Like diamonds, at first glance they were white, but if you looked closer, every one had its own subtle shade, its own unique soul.

Ratna lay on a huge, flat boulder that thrust out of the side of the mountain. Every afternoon, it caught the sun and would heat up, and when she came to look at the stars, the sun's heat stored inside would be released, and the mountain felt like a mother, holding her and comforting Ratna with her warmth.

She had a good, old-fashioned shattering that afternoon, and now she was exhausted from the tears and the emotion, and she only wanted things to be the way they were before stupid human Rangers and their lords came and disturbed her 3,500-year peace.

So many years ago, she had come to the mountain, a fifteen-year-old so terrified and alone she was almost catatonic. The old elf told her to come, and he had been right. She did what he said, she fed well, and when her abilities came in, she practised hard every day, and from that good advice, she stayed healthy and alive. He said he'd come back one day, but, of course, he never did. She remembered his words, "I don't know when we'll be back. When we hear the call that it's safe again –

" – When we hear the call that it's safe again."

" – I don't know when we'll be back. When we hear the call that it's safe again."

Ratna bolted upright, a charge of electricity shooting through her. How could she have missed it? It was right in front of her face the entire time.

Elves were back. They had heard the call. It was safe again.

It was time for her to go.

Ratna

She didn't have a phone and wouldn't know how to use it if she had owned one. In their haste to pack up and go, no one thought to leave Ratna a way to contact anyone on the outside. She didn't even know where they were going. She knew Tuân lived in a place called England, and that's where the elves were. She also knew that to get there, the Rangers flew on a plane and that planes lived in airports.

So she would go to an airport and get on a plane and go to England. From listening to the BBC for so many years, Ratna knew the biggest city in England was London and that there were elves in London. That's where she would start. Once she found an elf, they would help her find Tuân. She would command them, and they would obey. Politely command, of course. Her mother always told her to treat the elves politely, or they'd port her to someplace nasty and cold, and she'd have to walk home.

Packing was a problem. To get off the mountain, she'd have to do some old-fashioned hiking. An elf had ported her here, but that was then, and this was now, and she'd have to carry everything she needed in her backpack. She'd also need money to pay for food and planes and whatever. The people on the *Archers* were always worried about having enough money to pay for things. Ratna would give her man gold and gems to trade for the things he brought back, so while she had plenty of both, she didn't know how much to carry with her. What was a gold nugget the size of her thumb worth? Would it buy her a meal?

She looked through her chests and found a fistful of old loonies her man left behind and a water glass full of her best diamonds. They weighed less than gold, so they were easier to carry. She threw them in a pouch, and for good measure, she threw in a handful of gold nuggets. Ratna hoped it was enough, but if it wasn't, she'd just have to go find some more. It wasn't like it was hard.

Into the backpack she added two shirts, some underclothes, and a pair of leather trousers. Add a comb, some hair ties, and a couple of elf knives, and she was ready to go. Oh, and she added a packed lunch and a canteen of water. Ratna debated on whether to carry her bow and arrows, but in the end decided not to. She could always defend herself by flicking a rock at something.

Settled, ready, and now getting excited about moving forward to something fresh and new, she went to bed, slept well, and when the sun came up, she was already halfway down the mountain.

Lord Ratna went a-roaming.

She found a logging trail, which led to a narrow dirt road, which led to an asphalt two-lane road. When she stood on the verge of the asphalt road, she had to decide whether to go left or right, and since England was to the east, that's the direction she took. After a logging truck barreled by, screaming at her, she decided not to walk in the middle of the road but instead walked on the side, even though it was not as nice.

By late afternoon, when the shadows were getting long, she was in a city. It was huge with at least five buildings, a place that looked like what the *Archers* called a petrol forecourt, and attached to that a glass-fronted building labelled "Mini Mart". There were a couple of humans walking around, but no orcs that she could smell. No one paid any attention to her at all. When she walked by the petrol station, she saw it. Behind, parked in a field, was an aeroplane. She had found an airport!

The airfield was surrounded by a wooden fence, and Ratna had heard all about the horrors of airport security on BBC news, so she wasn't surprised. Hopefully, there wouldn't be long queues; they were always complaining about them, too. Nailed on the fence was a battered sign with an arrow that said "Office," and that seemed the logical place to start.

The office was one room. At the desk was an old man with a cowboy hat on, a Taylor Swift t-shirt, and probably the filthiest jeans possible. He was leaning back in his chair, his boots on the desk, snoring.

Ratna looked over the desk, which was piled with bits of paper and half-empty coffee cups. Hidden in the drift of papers, she spotted a bell, and she rang it.

"Hello! I would like to fly to England. Can you sell me a ticket?"

He didn't look up. He didn't take his feet off the desk. But he did stop snoring.

"Kid, I don't fly to England. Too far for my old Cessna."

Ratna considered this and modified her request. *The Archers* spoke of changing planes, and even with porting one had to transfer from one port hole to another.

"Could you please fly me to an airport that will take me to England?"

"Listen, kid, I'm not flying anywhere today. I don't even have money to gas up the plane. Buzz off."

"I'll pay. How much would it cost?"

Now the man was irritated, and he shoved up his hat fully intending to shoo the pesky rug rat away. He didn't have time to play at airports with random –

It was a fucking fairy.

The chair fell back, and he hit his head hard on the wall.

"SHIT!"

"No, thank you. I went earlier." Ratna frowned. "But are you okay? That sounded painful."

"What the hell are you? Are you an elf?"

She pulled herself to her full height, offended. "No, sir, I am most certainly not an elf. I am Lord Ratna. But I'm not here to discuss my tribe. I'm here to get a flight to the best place to get me to England. You have an aeroplane out there. I have money. Can we come to an agreement?"

His mouth dropped. Then he closed it with a snap.

"I can get you to Calgary, which is an international airport, and you can connect from there to England."

Ratna was thrilled. That sounded exactly like what she wanted.

"Wonderful! How much will it cost?"

"Thirty-three thousand, five hundred Canadian. Plus tax." Ratna considered this. Her man had told her that with humans, you never take the first price offered.

"And is that the cheapest you can do?"

He looked at her, at those ears, and her eyes started to glow. Shit. She knew. If he tried to cheat her, she'd hex him.

"No, for you I'll charge four hundred Canadian. Cash if you have it because I need to buy some gas for the Cessna."

"Deal. Okay, here's my problem. I have some cash for you to buy gas with, but I doubt if it's enough for the full fare. Will you take a gold nugget for the balance?" And she pulled out a honking great chunk of gold and put it on the desk. "You should be able to sell this for some loonies and make up the difference."

He cleared his throat and nodded.

"We can leave as soon as I file a flight plan. I'll get you to Calgary International, and you'll have to manage from there."

And that was how Ratna got on the first leg of her trip to England. Easy peasy.

The flight to Calgary was very short, less than forty minutes. Ratna enjoyed every second of it. To fly so high and around and through the mountains in the little Cessna was a thrill, and her delight was so infectious that even the old man was smiling. It felt longer to get from the touchdown on the runway to the tiny independent terminal than it did to fly there. He escorted her in, and she was so happy she gave the pilot one of her smaller two-carat diamonds as a tip.

Calgary International was massive. She wasn't expecting that, not even from the descriptions on BBC. She had to go from an obscure corner of the airport to the international terminal, and that took some figuring out. But after a few polite questions to a trio of very surprised workers standing at the door, a nice man arranged for a wagon called a golf cart to drive her down the long halls to the right place.

Everyone seemed very excited to see her. People chased the little car to take pictures of her with their phones, and a young girl asked for her autograph on a paper cup with *Coke* written on it. So she wrote her name on it in Elvish and hoped that the cup was not hers now. She didn't need it.

She only smelled a couple of orcs, but they didn't bother her, and she didn't bother them.

At the international departures hall, Ratna walked up to the British Airways desk because she was going to England, and that seemed the most logical airline, and that's when she had her first problem of the day.

After some initial disbelief that she was truly a lord and not an elf or – goodness! – a fairy, the woman behind the counter asked to see her passport.

"I don't have a passport. I'm a lord. Lord Ratna."

"Yes, ma'am, but maybe in the computer you do have one on file. If you can give me your birthdate and country of citizenship, that would help."

Ratna thought for a minute. "I was born here, but before Canada existed. Somewhere around 1,520 BCE, on June 29th." She smiled, happy to be able to help.

A crowd was forming behind Ratna, taking pictures and talking so loudly she almost couldn't hear the lady. When Ratna turned to see what the fuss was about, they all backed away in one graceful swoosh, like a school of fish in a pond when you toss a rock in there. Someone screamed.

Everyone was holding up a little square box in front of them and pointing the boxes at Ratna, and all Ratna could think of was that it must be some sort of religious thing. She really should have paid more attention to the BBC religious shows on Sunday, but they were so flippin' boring!

A manager silently showed up and whispered something to the lady selling the tickets, who nodded. The manager came around and curtseyed, which startled Ratna, so she bowed back.

"Lord Ratna, we're having a bit of a problem with your paperwork. Would you mind waiting in the VIP lounge while we sort things out on our end?"

"Will I still be able to get to England today? I'm pretty tired and hungry."

"We'll do our best, and there's food to eat in the lounge. You just help yourself. And there's a comfortable chair you can nap in."

And that's what they did. Everyone was very, very nice. She was settled in the comfortable chair and was shown the buffet, where she proceeded to eat a huge amount of food. They even had a toilet! Inside! In the meantime, her paperwork was going to get sorted.

Norma

Norma picked up the phone, listened for a minute, raised an eyebrow, and told the person on the other end to "do what you have to do. No expense spared."

Kyrylo and Caddy

Kyrylo was having breakfast with Caddy when Norma called. After a second, he put her on speaker so Caddy could hear.

"So, Lord Ratna – *our* Lord Ratna – is now sitting in the BA VIP lounge at Calgary International insisting that she be put on a flight to England, which means Heathrow. She doesn't have a passport. She doesn't have a birth certificate. They don't know what to do."

"DAMN! She got there by herself?"

"It appears so. No one is with her."

Caddy looked at Kyrylo, who looked back and said, "You're the one who's gone a-roaming. What do you think?"

"Hmmph." She looked out the window. "Fax them a letter with lots of seals and glitter and holograms and crap. Tell them it's her Elf Nation passport and that she has diplomatic immunity. Go that route. We'll pay for everything at our end."

Norma laughed. "Extra glitter for the lords! It'll probably work. I'll be back." And the screen went blank.

Kyrylo hooted. "Glitter!"

"Everything's better with glitter."

Ratna

The lovely people at the airport fixed everything, just as they had said they would. Ratna was put in first class on the next BA flight to Heathrow. There was a human assigned to her to take her through passport control and security, and the man stayed with her all the way to her seat on the plane. She tipped him a diamond, and he seemed happy. Ratna noticed that humans did like the shiny things.

He gave her the faxed passport, which was a very impressive document, and told her to keep it as she would need to show it at the other end. When she had time, she looked at it, and it showed that she was a citizen and diplomat of the Elf Nation, which seemed odd as she was a lord. But if it worked, it worked. Lord Cadence had signed the bottom of it.

The aeroplane was a marvel, and there was plenty of food. There were a couple of orcs sitting in the rear of the plane who gave the crew some bother, and Ratna heard the crew talking about duct-taping one to his chair, but they didn't worry her. But best of all, there was a TV attached to her seat. Just for her! The lovely lady in red who tended to her spent a long time showing Ratna how to change the channels, and when she realised that lord's ears and BA earbuds don't work together, she found a set of headphones that did the trick. Ratna spent most of the flight flipping through the channels.

She tipped the entire crew a diamond each, and the flight attendant who was so kind to her got an extra gold nugget. At Heathrow, she was taken to the VIP lounge where her passport was checked, and there, waiting for her, was a wonderful human woman named Ellen and three warrior elves who ported her straight to the house where the lords lived. She was assigned a private bedroom, and she went to sleep and slept for two days.

Aelfeham House was an interesting place. There were lots of humans, lots of elves, and they were all there to tend to the lords who lived there.

LORDS! Plural!

Tuân was there recovering from the avalanche and thumping around in a comical-looking boot as his leg healed. He still smelled absolutely wonderful. He still smiled and talked with her and seemed very pleased she was there. And that was it. No spark at all. At least he didn't have another woman around, and while there was still a chance that his fire was just a slow burn and not a dead ember, Ratna was willing to stay.

Lords Cadence and Kyrylo, the bonded Elementals, didn't live there, but Ratna was told they visited quite often. They were in Ukraine now working on Elf Nation stuff and getting ready for their new baby. Lords Alizah and Jack were a bonded couple who still spent almost every day there working and practising, but they lived in a penthouse in London. They were floaters and liked being up high.

Then there was Conary, who was just learning his ability and was Tuân's grandfather, the one Tuân called the Old Man. He was a funny one, and Ratna didn't mind sitting and talking with him even though there was absolutely nothing attractive about him. He might as well have been her own grandfather for all he smelled, thank goodness. If he had smelled half as good as Tuân, *that* would have been awkward.

Vrt was new like Ratna. She had arrived only a week earlier, and she was a mystery to everyone. She was from the Before Times and, just like Ratna, had lived alone in the wilderness until she learnt about the elves waking up. She wore a mask, and while no one spoke of it, Ratna had a good idea what the mask hid. She knew what the rogue orcs did to lord women when they caught one. The lithe, black-clad lord was very, very quiet and very, very polite and, without meaning to, gave an aura of being very, very dangerous. Vrt reminded Ratna of the cougars who lived alone in the mountains, watching the mountain goats play and dreaming of dinner.

And lastly, there was Sam. Ah, yes, Sam.

Sam worked with rocks and he was pretty good at it. Not as good as Ratna was, but still – pretty good. When it came to rocks, they had a lot in common. When it came to absolutely everything else, they were poles apart. Ratna was open to finding a man other than Tuân because it was becoming obvious to her that while the man liked her – maybe even loved her – he didn't love her *that* way. Tuân acted like he couldn't smell her scent at all. He was not in lust with her, which caused a few tears, but there was nothing she could do about it.

Sam, on the other hand, seemed interested. He was just so darn lumpy. And sexless. Ratna could imagine him rolling on top of her, pumping exactly three times, and then rolling off and going to sleep. For his part, Sam thought Ratna was decent-looking in an exotic way, but her boobs were too small, and she was a bit too clever. She looked at him sometimes as if she was amazed he could tie his shoes.

He was very sure she liked him a lot, though, and if she wandered into his bedroom one night, he wasn't going to push her away. A man had needs.

The young Ranger Luke, who was almost crushed by the avalanche, was in the cauldron when Ratna landed in Aelfeham House, so there were loads of humans and elves passing through to read and talk to him while he stewed.

Ratna was amazed at how well everyone got along. With no orcs around to cause chaos, humans were actually pretty nice people, and for the first time in her life, she mingled and chatted and had good company whenever she wanted. She hadn't talked to an elf since the old stableman had ported her to the mountain, and she was so happy the first time she saw one she cried.

While she missed aspects of her mountain, Ratna doubted she would go back permanently now. Living there had been getting lonely, and after experiencing Aelfeham House, she knew the silence and the loneliness would weigh on her even more.

You can't go back. Time only marches forward.

Vrt

Tuân and Conary were playing chess in the TV room. Vrt was sitting on the couch watching *Dancing with the Stars,* and

Conary wondered what was going on behind that mask. What did a 3,500-year-old recluse think of two humans in sequins and chiffon dancing the rhumba? Would she agree with the scores? If she didn't, would she chop the TV in two with that sword she always wore? He smiled to himself and looked at the board. He wasn't going to let Tuân win this one.

Suddenly, he looked up, and she was there, as silent as the Angel of Death if the Angel of Death wore black leather.

"This game –" Vrt gestured to the board. "What are the rules?"

Tuân explained the rules of chess, and she nodded. She used to play a game very like this – chaturanga. It was a simple matter to make mental adjustments and play this version. It was war, and she understood war.

"When you are done – and it will only take Conary three moves – I would like to play a game with you, Tuân."

Conary and Tuân looked at the board. Three moves? Where did she see that? Then Conary thought he saw the path. He picked up a pawn and set it down, but didn't take his hand off and looked at Vrt. She shrugged; she wasn't going to help him. He released, and Tuân moved, and then it was all clear. Conary won in three moves, just like she said.

Vrt and Tuân had played a game every night until Ratna came, but then he was too distracted by her to concentrate, which made Vrt smile. Ratna was okay. She and Tuân were starting their dance, and it wasn't the rhumba that was for sure. Vrt wished them the best.

Vrt

After Ratna came and Tuân found better things to do than play chess with the Angel of Death, Conary stepped in the breach. He let her have her long silences, although, being Conary, he liked to crack a joke every now and then. While he could never read her expression, her eyes would crinkle up sometimes, and he found that encouraging. Very seldom, but sometimes, she would answer back with something very dry, and it was evident she had a sense of humour and a wry, rather bemused way of looking at the world.

He never asked her about the mask or her past life, and she never offered any explanation of either.

When Tuân's boot came off, he went back to light duty with the Rangers. When Vrt asked if she could come and watch, he didn't think anything of it and invited her for PT the next morning. She was a lord, and she could do what she wanted.

Later that night, he called up the Old Man and told him to never, never do anything to make Vrt mad at him. Ever.

"Why? Did she lose her temper with someone at PT today?"

"No. She walked up and watched the elves do hand-to-hand. I mean, Gramps, these are tough, tough guys, and they beat up Wendell, Luke, and me every single day. So she walks up and watches, and then puts a coin down on the ground. She doesn't say a word, but I guess in old times that was a signal. And you know, I think I saw fear in some of those guys. It was an "oh shit" moment. I don't know how they knew, but they knew."

"What happened?"

"They jumped her. All of them. Every last one jumped her all at once. And I've never seen anything like that in my life. It was like watching a sci-fi movie. In two minutes, they were all on the ground. She didn't use anything but her feet and hands, no weapons. No magic that I could see. Bam, bam, bam. She didn't even break a sweat. They all went off moaning, and they all paid her a coin. Then she took the coins and bought them all pints at the pub."

"So the Angel of Death is a warrior."

"Don't you ever make her mad, Gramps. That's all I'm saying."

Luke

Luke's parents were given a room at Aelfeham House and told the cauldron rules. They met Lord Alizah, who was suddenly an old hand at cauldron-watching, and she took them under her wing and gave them tons of advice which the nurse elves quietly corrected when she wasn't around.

Luke was popular with the soldier elves, and they asked if they could come and talk to him as he lay stewing. His parents didn't see anything wrong with that since that was part of the therapy anyway, so while Luke's parents talked to him for hours every day, the soldiers put in their time for their brother soldier, too. It seemed, too, that hundreds of elves remembered Luke as the first human they had seen at their rebirthing, and each one wanted to come for a half hour or so and talk to the cauldron. Sian came every day and spent hours sitting in the room, talking whenever there was a gap. As Marko told Jack, poor Luke was going to come out of the thing sleep-deprived from all of the elf yakking.

Julia asked Jack over dinner if he remembered any of the talking from when he was in the cauldron, and Jack laughed. "Alizah watched TikTok dance videos while she was waiting and told me all about them. I'm an expert on modern club dance. Can't do it, but I sure can tell you what the dancers are doing in the clubs right now!"

On day four, the egg formed and floated to the top. When Julia saw the outlines of Luke inside, she had to leave the room, and Marko found her in the Breakfast Room, bawling her eyes out. Their boy was reforming. He wasn't going to die.

On the tenth day, he was reborn. The cauldron boiled, everyone was hustled from the room, and they could hear it explode. Everything was normal.

Then there was silence.

The head nurse elf came out, and his face was puzzled. Not grim. Puzzled.

He wouldn't tell Julia and Marko what puzzled him, and he wouldn't let them see Luke. He had to talk to Dr Mandy.

Julia and Marko went into the Breakfast Room alone and talked to Dr Mandy, and when they came out, they were still in a state of shock at what they heard.

Julia looked dazed. Alizah and Jack braced themselves for the worst.

"Luke is an elf. He came back as an elf."

Marko shook his head and said in his heavily accented English, which was worse because he was so upset, "We no expect this. Not in our crazy dreams."

"Is this bad?" Alizah looked anxiously at Julia. She had come to love the woman.

Julia looked at the lord and then smiled. "He is alive, he is normal-looking – for an elf. We love him because he's our Luke. We'll love him as an elf."

Marko shrugged. "He'll make fine elf. He was very short kid; now he'll be a tall elf. He will like that, I hope."

And so Luke's recovery started, and just as his mother and father predicted, he was actually thrilled with his new elf body. No one knew if he would live to be 2,800 years old or a human's four score and ten, but in a hundred years they'd find out. No one knew if he'd be able to port. No one knew if Safe Haven would accept him. Those were all questions for the future. But for now, he was an elf and would go back to his old life, training with the elves but not as a Ranger. He would be one of the Warrior Elves.

All Dr Mandy could say when asked about Luke's curious case was that the cauldron brought you back to your true self. Unless it screwed up. Whether Luke was a screw up or if being an elf was his true nature, no one would ever know.

Ratna

The housekeeper elves tried their best to get Sam and Ratna to hit it off. They put the lords' work studios next to each other. When they set the table, Sam and Ratna were either across or next to each other. Their bedrooms were across the hall from each other. They might as well have been across the planet.

It didn't work. The more they were thrown together, the less Ratna wanted anything to do with Sam. One morning, to avoid Sam who was lingering in the hallway, Ratna crawled out of her bedroom window and hopped down the brickwork. Conary, who was walking on the path outside, saw her.

"So, are you channelling your inner mountain goat, Ratna?"

She jumped and gave the lord a guilty look. "Please, don't tell anyone!"

"So, who are you trying to avoid, Tuân or Sam? I'm assuming it's not me. Usually, women don't climb out windows to avoid me. They just play dead."

Ratna giggled. "I don't try to avoid Tuân. I just can't sit next to him. But Sam –" She shrugged. "I was listening to the Women's Hour on the BBC, and they talked about man-splaining. Sam mansplains to me. I don't want to hurt his feelings, but I don't need anyone to tell me the percentage of crystal and feldspar content in granite. I've been working with granite for 3,500 years."

Conary smiled and nodded. He could see Sam doing that.

"So, without woman-splaining to me, what can you do with granite? It's a rock. Is it your ability to know the feldspar content of granite? That sounds pretty boring. A bore a day doesn't keep the orcs at bay."

Ratnar laughed. "Oh, granite isn't boring. Look at that bollard over there, the one in the parking lot. It's made of granite."

Conary looked, and the bollard began to shimmer as if it were hot. He looked at Ratna, and her eyes were bright green. Then the bollard turned red and began to sag a bit, and up from the base a clear shape rose up, and it was a horse's head. The bollard had turned into a giant chess piece, a knight with a feldspar base and a crystal horse-head top.

Conary wondered at the amount of energy it took to do that, but the lord wasn't even body glowing, much less breaking a sweat. Tuân had told him of the great wall she had built out of crystal that had held back the mountain.

"Very good. Very impressive! Tell me, Ratna, are you an Elemental?"

"Oh dear me, no! An Elemental controls the basic forces of physics. I control a substance, crystalline structures. I can't transfer that control to, say, wood. But I'm pretty strong in my area, and I've been practising every day for millennia."

He smiled and offered her his arm. "Let's go to breakfast. Or is it brunch now?" And they chatted and walked, and Conary wondered why Ratna "couldn't" sit next to Tuân. Tuân, in his self-conscious, awkward, polite, twenty-year-old way, was besotted with her. Conary could tell, and it was a pity. She probably knew and didn't want to lead the poor boy on.

Vrt

Conary, Alizah, Jack, Ratna, and Sam were in the Breakfast Room doing what they should be doing at eight in the morning – eating breakfast.

Sam was complimenting Ratna on how pretty she was this morning and at the same time complaining about the shortage of female lords in a misguided attempt to get Ratna to pay more attention to him.

Jack did not like how the conversation was going, not one bit. For one thing, how any man could think that moaning about not getting any was going to get a woman to volunteer for his bed was a mystery to Jack. Was she supposed to feel sorry for him and offer a pity bonk? It was also a mystery to Ratna, and it was obvious that all she wanted to do was eat her breakfast in peace.

Alizah tried to divert him and pointed out that their ranks were growing all the time and that Vrt had just joined them, too.

"Yeah, but Vrt, she's scary and has no boobs! Not much for a man there to bother with."

And that's when Vrt walked in.

Conary looked up, and for a brief moment, he prayed she hadn't heard Sam, but he didn't know how she could not have. Sam's voice boomed.

The room froze. Alizah looked down at her plate. Mortified, Ratna stood up, and Vrt waved her down.

"Don't get up, Ratna. I'm just going to grab a bite to eat and take it to my room."

And she bustled around the buffet and piled up a plate.

Then she turned and looked at Sam.

"Y'know, Sam, you are absolutely correct. I have no boobs. I have no ears, no nose, or anything that makes me a woman." She tilted her head, and her voice was even and low.

"When I was twenty-five and had no abilities yet, I went looking for my bonded husband and ran right into a pack of orcs who had just killed him. I was the dessert on top of that feast as far as they were concerned. After having their fun, they made sure I wouldn't be useful to any man, ever. They were very handy with their knives, those orcs. They left my eyes, though, so I could admire their handiwork every day. Some elves patched me up, and then they disappeared. I was extremely angry with them for years. They should have let me die with my husband. But I survived and haven't bothered any man ever since. And I won't be bothering you, so don't you worry about that."

She nodded and then left the room.

Then Conary got up, put down his napkin, and punched Sam in the nose so hard he flew across the room.

Kyrylo

Kyrylo put his face in his hands. What a mess.

In front of him was everyone except Vrt, and he had no idea where she was. The elves didn't know, either. She was not in her room.

"How, how, how – could you say something like that to her, Sam? You can see that she's hiding something wrong with her."

Sam looked miserable and rightly so. Everyone in the room was horrified at what had happened, and he knew he had really stepped in it. They were all mad at him. He wasn't even angry at Conary for punching him.

"I didn't mean to hurt her – I just thought she was flat-chested."

Kyrylo shook his head. "Sam, I hate to have to say this to a grown man, but we don't talk about women's parts – full stop. I can't believe I have to say this." He sighed. "Look, we all have to get along. We are a family here. There are so few of us, and some of us have been wandering alone for three thousand fucking years. I can't imagine what that was like. And now we are together, and we can't be punching each other in the nose even when it's probably deserved. "

He looked at the group. "So what are we going to do about Vrt?"

"Well, Sam can apologise." This came from Jack, who was still furious with the stonecutter.

Sam looked down and nodded.

"First, we have to find her." Conary glared at Sam. "I'm going to look for her now, but I think Sam should stay here and think about what he's going to say. I doubt she'll want to see him right now." He left. Alizah and Jack told Kyrylo they were going to go out and fly around and see if they could spot her.

Everyone left to look for Vrt except for Sam, who went to his studio and chipped at rock.

Vrt

Vrt wasn't far; she was only in the back garden. The elves had set up a dummy as a target, and she was practising her knife throwing. She was very good at it, and Conary stopped to watch. That dummy had a neat row of knives going from between his eyes down to his navel. She was about to send the last knife flying to the groin when she stopped and looked around.

"I know you're there."

Conary walked up. It was becoming so natural now that sometimes he forgot he was invisible, and with constant practise, he didn't even have to concentrate any more.

She threw the last knife. Conary winced. No balls on that dummy any more.

"I want to make sure you're okay."

She looked at him, her eyes flashed green, and then she walked over to retrieve the knives.

"Conary, Sam isn't the first to be an asshole to me about my body, and he won't be the last. Anyone who looks at the shape of my head under this mask can see that I don't have a nose or ears. Usually, that's what they ask about first."

"That doesn't make it right."

She walked back and looked at the dummy.

"Probably not, but that's not anything I worry about. I am what I am. It's not like I need any of that stuff anymore anyway. I'm a woman bonded to a corpse, and he's not coming back. There is no changing that."

She threw the first knife, and it landed right between the eyes of the dummy. She tilted her head, judging that throw, and then threw three of the knives in rapid succession.

Thwack, thwack, thwack.

"I'm okay, Conary."

He nodded.

"Why don't you come back for breakfast?"

She turned back to the dummy.

"Not yet. I'll be back for dinner. I need to be alone for a bit. I've had too much interaction with people today. I find them tiresome."

Thwack.

Conary

Conary called up Dr Mandy and asked why Vrt couldn't be put in the cauldron. Isn't that what the soupy thing was for? Dr Mandy refused to tell him why Vrt couldn't be put in.

"It's confidential, Lord Conary. I won't talk about other people's medical issues with you."

"Well, did she ask you? Does she know about what the cauldron can do?"

Mandy looked grim. A lord was asking her a direct question, and she didn't want to talk about it.

"I'm sure she knows about cauldrons. She is from Before Times, and she wasn't a child when the elves left. I won't talk about her case with you."

If Conary could've reached through the phone and grabbed the elf by her white coat and shaken her, he would have. It wouldn't have done any good, though; she'd just port. He tried another tack.

"Okay – if I was messed up, would you put me in the cauldron?"

"Of course, I would."

"What about Kyrylo? He's all scarred to hell and missing an eye – could he go in?"

"Yes, of course, he could – if he asked."

"Then what's the difference? Why can we go in?"

Mandy sighed.

"You and Kyrylo have family. You have someone who loves you to talk you back to this world. All that reading and talking has a purpose. That's the magic part. It keeps the person's soul in the cauldron grounded in this world while the body dissolves. Without that connection to this world, the body just dissolves, and the soul goes into the Void. If you don't have that connection, the cauldron is just suicide by doctor. I won't throw anyone in a cauldron who I know won't come back out. You or Kyrylo – or Vrt – have to *want* to come back out, and there must be a beloved person here for them to come to."

Conary hung up and put his head in his hands. If he went into the cauldron, he knew Tuân would talk him back; hell, he had his mother and an entire clan of relatives in Vietnam. Jack had Aliza. Caddy had Kyrylo. Even human Luke had his parents.

Vrt had nobody, and as she said, no prospect of ever getting anyone. Even if someone fell in love with her, she said she was bonded, and that bond was not broken. She was alive, and her husband was not, and she wouldn't fall in love with someone else while she was married to a corpse. She didn't wander the taiga any more, but she was still utterly alone.

Lester and Lena

Lena was not comfortable. Not at all.

The spiteful baby distorting her body kicked her in the ribs, and when she was hungry, it was hard to eat with the boy jumping around inside her like a chihuahua on crack. And the ultrasounds had made it quite clear she was carrying a boy, much to Lester's delight. He claimed the tiny boy was as well hung as his dad, which made Lena roll her eyes and agree.

She was going into labour.

As the pregnancy came to term, Lester spent every night in Lena's bed, fornicating with whatever other FakeLena happened to be sharing the space, and then rolling over and spooning with the real Lena, his head buried in her hair and snoring in her ear. He said she smelled good, and as long as he wasn't poking anything in her, she could put up with it. It was a small price to pay for being the Empress and Tsarina of All the Rus'. Now that she had given him a proper heir, her place was cemented in, and she didn't have to worry about Lester changing out Lena for a new model. That was the theory, at least.

It never occurred to her that Lester was going to live forever, and "heir" was only something that happened when the previous generation died off. The only person who could tell Lena or anyone in the Russian Court about the biology of lords was Lester, and he either wasn't talking or he didn't know. A bit of both. Because of his virtual social isolation in Before Times and absolute isolation afterwards, there were large gaps in his knowledge of his own tribe.

In Before Times, Lester the Liar had been such an unpleasant character that he didn't have friends to have casual conversations with and hear their stories, and learn from them. He'd been the original incel – a man with a deep ignorance of women mixed equal helpings of distrust and fear.

When the baby, Prince Rurik Lester Vseslev Peter Igor, was born, a few minor issues arose during the birth that Lester wasn't anticipating. For one thing, during her final pushes and as the baby crowned, Lena yelled in pain, and the midwives were flung around the room like cows in a tornado. Then little Rurik came out so hot and fast that the hands of the doctor catching him burned clean off. He backed off from the bed, screaming and holding his stumps out in horror, and then he fainted dead away, which created an unpleasant mess that had to be dealt with.

The unanticipated incident caused panic in the birthing room, and the stupid midwife almost dropped the baby on his head as he squirted out. But quick thinking and a heavy towel saved the day.

Lester was there, partially out of curiosity and partially to make sure the baby that came out was truly a lord like himself and not switched at birth with some other human brat. He hadn't lived for almost four thousand years by ignoring his paranoia. The battering the midwives and doctors took was just further evidence of his powerful genes and superior breeding. Naturally, after the birth, he had them all eliminated so they wouldn't run around shooting their mouths off about demon births. What good was a doctor without hands anyway?

After the birth, Prince Rurik was as calm as any human baby. He had blue eyes, like any newborn, but the sparkle in them and his little pointed ears reassured Lester that this was indeed a lord.

Lester was well pleased. He had the baby brought to him every day so he could look at him, and Lena was given an emerald the size of a goose egg as a birthing present.

Everything was going along swimmingly.

Luke

Luke was back in his flat, his parents returned to Ukraine, and life was slowly getting back to normal. He was still weak and walked with a cane, but he was getting stronger every day. In a few days, he was sure he'd be done with the cane and would start going back to morning PT at Fen Park. Luke was looking forward to it. Being an invalid was boring.

Being an elf was an adjustment, but not as much as you'd think. He'd always been a very short man in a world built for average. Counters were too high, barstools a humiliating nightmare. Just taking a shower meant a step up just so he could reach the taps. And girls – gods help him, the girls. Some were polite. Some were rude. Most just looked right over him as if he were invisible.

But now he was an elf. He had elf ears – big, wonderful elf ears. He was regrowing his beard. For an elf, he was rather tall and pretty decent-looking. The elf girls giggled and blushed when he smiled at them. It was an all-new experience.

Rumlot Security offered to rebuild his flat to fit his new frame, but he didn't know if he wanted it. It felt rather high up, and he thought he would feel better in a ground-floor flat. The Warrior

Elves, who liked him when he was a human, now adopted him
as a brother.

So when Luke took a short exercise walk on the Prom,
he was feeling pretty good about his life, and if he was totally
honest, he would have whispered that the avalanche that almost
crushed him to death was a stroke of luck, not a catastrophe. He
didn't remember any of it. All he knew was waking up in
Aelfeham House and his mother and father gently telling him what
had happened.

"Luke?"

He spun around to see who was calling him. It was Sian,
the pretty elf girl who worked at the counter, and who, when he
had paid a bit too much attention to her, had disappeared. Luke
looked at her, and something teased in the back of his brain. Some
memory he could tease out.

But memories were for later; right now, she was here,
and he needed to pay attention to her. Her eyes were red, and she
looked pretty rough as if she had been crying. He looked at her and
frowned, wondering what was wrong. When she saw him frown at
her, she really did start to cry.

"Sian, what's wrong? Don't cry! Come here. Let's sit
here. I can get off my legs." And then she started to bawl.

He sat down on the bench and pulled her to him, and she
sobbed. If she weren't so upset, he would have enjoyed this. He
was just the right size for her now, and even bawling her eyes out
she was still Sian and still beautiful.

Finally, she got a hold of herself, and it came out in great
gulping sobs. He was an elf, and it was her fault, and now she had
ruined his life forever.

"Sian! You are making no sense! How did you make me an elf?"

"I came to talk to you when you were in the cauldron. A lot of us did. But I'm the one who wished you would come back as an elf, and I told you that. So you did! And now you can't be a Ranger, and that made you so happy." She started crying again. "I didn't think what I said would actually come true! You were in a vulnerable state, and I – I'm so sorry."

The poor thing was wracked with guilt because she thought she had cursed him to elfhood. Luke thought that was so funny he laughed, pulled her to him, and kissed her on the cheek.

"Sian – you did me a huge favour. ALL of the elves who came and talked to me did me a huge favour. No, I can't be a Ranger now – at least I don't think so, but I'm fine. I have a job with Rumlot, and I'm a part of the clan's warriors. I'm very happy with how it all turned out."

She stopped crying. This was not what she expected. Sian pulled away and looked at Luke, not believing her pointy ears. "Really? You're happy?"

"Yeah, I'm happy. I might not be a complete elf. I won't know for a long time if I can port or if I'll live past my human years, but I'll be the best elf I can be while I have the chance."

"Oh – I don't know what to think. I was sure you'd hate me for making you an elf, and then you'd be limited by *terrior* and heights and doing things for lords and all the stuff we have to put up with."

"I'm fine. You don't have to worry." He looked at her. "Why did you disappear? Did I scare you off? Was I rude?"

"I left because everyone was throwing a fit. My parents were beside themselves that I was even talking to a human man. They said if I bonded to you, it would be a tragedy. And they were right that a human and an elf don't have any future together. They said it was unfair to you to lead you on to a dead end. So I left the front desk. I work in the back stockroom now."

"I'm not a human any more." And he grinned at her. "So – how about going to a movie tomorrow? I'm still on medical leave, and I have an open diary."

"I would love that."

LeeAnne

LeeAnne's last year in school was not as much fun as "the best year of your life" was advertised.

She had the stress of A levels to get through, compounded with finding and qualifying for the right uni. LeeAnne wanted to study physiotherapy and really, really wanted to go to the University of East Anglia in Norwich, which was a short train hop to Lowestoft and to Wendell. But her parents were pushing for the University of Southampton near the cruise ship ports. There were lots of fights over the applications, but it was all moot if she didn't pass her A levels with high enough scores. It didn't seem fair that her whole future was hanging on an A-level chemistry score printed on a form.

Then there was the matter of her friends and even some of her teachers. When she was sixteen-going-on-seventeen and had come back from her life-altering cruise with the lords and Wendell, she didn't say too much about it. It would sound like bragging (and it would be), but there was no hiding that she was on *that* cruise that was now legendary in elf groupie circles.

There were twenty-five hundred people on Cunard's Queen Catherine who saw the mermaids dance and heard Lord Cadence's concert. Worldwide, about a hundred times that number claimed to have been there. But LeeAnne really had been there; her dad was the Captain, and so her friends and teachers fell into two camps. Insanely jealous or intimidated. Both groups pulled away and became more distant, which meant "forgotten" invites to parties, finding out that the girls had been to the cinema without her, and teachers who didn't think she needed any help because her parents were loaded and were friends with the fairies.

So to her parents' great confusion, there were no dates, no clubbing – not much of anything social that wasn't part of a blanket school invite. She studied hard, read everything about physiotherapy she could find, obsessively kept up with the elf and lord sites on the internet, and wrote once a week to Wendell.

Wendell wrote back! That was another thing she didn't talk about to her friends – the ones she still had. She was having an epistolary romance with a Ranger. Oh, Wendell never said anything the least bit naughty or romantic because, as he said in his second letter, if someone found out he was writing to LeeAnne, every single thing he wrote was in danger of being stolen out of her postbox and ending up in the Daily Mirror or on some internet site. Nonetheless, he wrote her long letters about what he was doing, his lessons, and what his thoughts were about Rangering. He talked to her about her studies, listened to her moans about jealous friends, and discussed which uni she should go to.

Then, about four months ago, she got a WhatsApp invite to a private chat room from a Mr Bunn. The conversations quickly became much more spontaneous, and while Wendell never once said anything LeeAnne couldn't show her mother and father, they had no idea she was talking with him. She and Wendell joked, they had fun, they teased, and when one was upset over something, they soothed and commiserated and gave advice.

He sent her pictures of places in Ukraine and the mountains of Scotland and the Alps. They were all landscapes and very pretty, but no people, towns, or anything man-made in them at all. Then he sent her some photos of the Banff Mountains in Canada, and a week later she read that a new lord had appeared – in western Canada. Wendell had been working.

So it was only natural that she asked him to go to her prom. It was the last big thing before everyone scattered to university, and while some colleges tried to downplay the American import, her school made a huge fuss over it. She didn't think he'd say yes and expected Wendell to give her an excuse that he was in Timbuktu or some other exotic place, but he didn't hesitate. He'd love to go.

Her hands were trembling when she closed out WhatsApp. She sat on her lacy bed in her bedroom filled with posters of E-Pop bands and fairy lights and just absorbed the minute before she leapt up and ran screaming to the kitchen, hollering for her mum. She was going to the prom with Wendell!

The next day at lunch, she stood in a line at the bursar's office and bought two very expensive tickets to the Prom – one for her and one for her guest. When the bursar asked if the guest was a student at the school, she said no, and he shoved over a form for her to fill out. It was an info form for the guest, probably to make sure she wasn't inviting a pedo or machete-wielding terrorist. She filled it out, putting down his contact details at RumLot Security and that he was employed as a Ranger, and handed it in.

By the end of the day, it was all over the school that she was dating a Ranger who worked for the famous RumLot Security.

So all that LeeAnne needed to do now was finish up the semester, buy the perfect dress and shoes, arrange her hair, makeup and nail appointments, get through a week of hell finishing up her A levels, and then wait three months for Results Day and on to the Prom. Nothing to it.

Results Day came, and much to LeeAnne's tearful relief, she passed everything with As and A*s and one B, so she had her choice of uni. She would go to UEA in Norwich if it killed her. Her dad moaned a bit, but he lost that battle fair and square. LeeAnne had earned her victory.

Leanne and Wendell

Wendell stood at the front door holding the plastic box with the wrist corsage LeeAnne's mother had ordered for him and lifted his hand to knock. He then put it down to fiddle with his jacket lapel. He was nervous.

The uniformed RumLot elf standing behind the Ranger rolled his eyes and then gave him a poke. Get on with it, man. The woman is waiting.

He lifted his hand again, but it was too late. Captain Wilson flung open the door, and Wendell was very glad he didn't rap LeeAnne's father on the forehead.

After that, it was all business, and once Wendell got in the flow of greetings (so nice to see you again) and being stunned by the very gorgeous LeeAnne, he was fine. Poppy insisted on taking loads of pictures and then started to cry, and Captain Wilson ("you can call me Jeremy") had to take her to the kitchen to collect herself. He had a sudden hay fever attack, too, so there was a veritable concert of nose blowing coming through the kitchen doors while Wendell and LeeAnne waited in the living room for them to come back out and say goodbye.

"You look beautiful," he whispered to her as they waited. "So do you!" And she was only being truthful. The last year and a half had honed Wendell to a fine, lean, dangerous edge. Any puppy fat on his face was now gone, and she could see where the laugh lines around his eyes were going to settle in. He had the trim beard that all of the Rumlot security people now wore, but it didn't hide a new scar on his cheekbone. He looked dead sexy in his sleek dinner jacket as LeeAnne told anyone who listened to her talk about this night.

Poppy finally pulled herself together and insisted on taking a photo of her darlings in their limo, and for a second, Wendell looked upset.

"Geez, LeeAnne, I didn't come here in a limo. Was I supposed to? Is that a part of the evening?"

"No worries, Wendell, we can take an Uber." And she pulled out her phone.

Then he grinned, and it became clear he was teasing her. "Don't bother!" And he yelled "Carl!" and an elf in full Rumlot regalia, feather and all, popped in. "Carl is going to port us; it'll be a lot faster."

And so that's what happened, and LeeAnne had the absolute thrill of getting ported and landing with a very satisfying bang in the packed atrium of the hotel ballroom. Carl could have ported them silently and discreetly, but what fun would that have been?

Carl good-humouredly posed for selfies with the friends who were still speaking with LeeAnne and then, with another flourish and a completely unnecessary bang, ported away. Crissy was in tears of joy that Carl was in a selfie with her, and, of course, he was nothing but a misty blob with a feather sticking up out of it. That blob was proof of magic!

They had a brilliant time. The graduates at LeeAnne's table were fascinated with Wendell and pestered him with questions all through dinner. It became a running joke that "I'm sorry, but I can't talk about that" was the answer to almost all of them.

When the band started up and the hip flasks hidden away in handbags and pockets became a bit freer, the party really started to get loud. Wendell didn't drink, so LeeAnne didn't either, but that didn't prevent them from having a giggling, silly time and certainly didn't get in the way of a lingering kiss or two.

It was late in the evening, and they were dancing slowly in a corner when Wendell stiffened and looked over LeeAnne's shoulder. People were starting to leave for afterparties, and the round tables were emptying out. The Ranger spotted something, and he leaned down and whispered in her ear.

"LeeAnne, love, I have to go to work. I'm sorry."

She leaned back, worried. "Orcs? Do we have to go?"

"No. If I have to leave for orcs, I'll call Carl, and he'll port you home." He turned her. "See that girl in the corner? The heavy one?"

LeeAnne looked. He was talking about Grace Vaughn. LeeAnne knew Grace. The V for Vaughn and W for Wilson meant they were often in the same classes and the same queues for school things. Poor Grace was as sweet as can be, but her huge size made her the butt of nasty comments and jokes – when people took notice of her at all. She was sitting at a table, and two guys were standing next to her talking. She didn't look happy.

"Look at her eyes."

Grace's eyes glowed. They were little glows, just subtle sparks of green, and most of the time she looked down at her plate. But they glowed.

"Wendell! Do you think –"

"Would you mind if I ask her to dance?" She could feel his hard arms and hands on her back. He wasn't dancing with her any more – he was on the hunt. Oddly, she found that exciting.

"I'll go to our table, say I have a blister, and wait there. Bring her over if you want." And he grinned at her and kissed her on the cheek. Wonderful, clever, LeeAnne! She knew.

Wendell guided LeeAnne to the edge of the dance floor and, without another word, turned and walked to Grace's table. The two boys with her were drunk. She looked miserable.

"C'mon, Gracie. Let's have a lil' fun – you're big enough for both of us! I'll go in front an' Davin here will go in the back door! A Gracie sandwich!"

"Gentlemen, I think you need to have a little lie down. Sleep it off." Wendell walked over to the table, and Gracie looked up. It was hard to read the expression on her face. Fear? Humiliation? Relief?

"Grace, didn't you promise me a dance earlier? We only have time for a turn around the room, but if you're still –"

Davin lurched at Wendell, and one of the guys at LeeAnne's table, who were all watching what was going on, said he had never seen anyone so fast. One second, Davin was vertical, and the next minute, he was horizontal on the floor, having his little lie down. His unnamed friend flew back, tripped over Davin, and he was napping on the floor, too. To the teachers chaperoning across the room, Wendell didn't look like he had moved at all. The Ranger turned and smiled at Grace, offering her his hand. She laboriously stood up, and they went to the dance floor. He gave her a turn around the room, and they ended up at LeeAnne's table, where Grace collapsed, red-faced and sweating, into a chair.

Grace

Grace and her mother lived in a tiny two-up/two-down council terrace house. She assumed she had a father because, after all, she existed, but her mother never told her who it was. Grace wondered if she knew.

Her mother stayed home with the baby as long as the benefits would let her, and when that ended, she developed anxiety and other mental health problems and was put on permanent disability. Work, as she explained to Grace, which forced her to do something she didn't want to do, made her anxious, depressed, and tired, so she was better off staying at home.

In truth, Wendy G. Vaughn wasn't depressed as much as aggrieved. She begrudged everyone, and she certainly hated anyone richer, cleverer, and especially prettier, and there was no one she hated more than herself. Going every day to a job where she was treated like a slave by people who thought they were better than her just made her loathe the world even more, and she didn't have to put up with it. That's why God made benefits, and she milked the system for all it was worth.

Wendy was short and dumpy, and with years of heavy drinking and constant smoking, she had lost whatever figure she once had. She was shaped exactly like an egg on two toothpick legs, and her gnarled and wrinkled face sagged into a permanent expression of hate and disgust. When Grace was ten, one of the kids at school said her mum looked just like a goblin, and Grace had to admit he was right.

When Grace was a child, Wendy ignored her most of the time. Oh, she fed and clothed the girl and sent her to school, but even though they lived in the same house Wendy was preoccupied with herself, and that didn't leave much room for her daughter. The only thing she did that could be called parenting was to scream at Grace when she didn't clean her plate. "Clean your plate" became a religious obsession for Wendy, a way to exercise total control over her daughter, and with that control over someone else, maybe she could get some control over her own life.

And it was never enough. If Grace finished up a large fish and chips, then Wendy gave her more and told her to finish that up, too. As Wendy fell more and more into alcoholism and mental illness, her obsession with Grace and with food worsened. There was a hole in Wendy, and she was going to fill it with food – by way of her daughter.

School was Grace's saviour, and a series of kind teachers steered the obese girl into books and after-school programs. That was enough to keep her sane and help her understand how distorted her world was. It was when Grace hit puberty that everything really started to go to hell.

Grace began to gain more weight, and the more weight she gained, the more Wendy screamed and fed her. The more Wendy screamed and the fatter Grace got, the more depressed Grace became – and the more she ate. By the time she met Wendell at the prom, she was over twenty-eight stone (she guessed), and she wasn't a tall girl. At eighteen, she could hardly walk, and breathing was difficult.

She knew the prom was going to be the last time she would be out in public, and once school was over, she would end up trapped in her bedroom, dependent on her mother. The only way she would ever escape was to have the fire service knock a hole in the house and lift her out with a crane. She'd seen that on TV.

She just wanted one last memory of something pretty and happy before she walked up those stairs to her bed-tomb and shut the door. Just one happy time.

At twenty, Grace was preparing to die.

Wendy

Ms Wendy G. Vaughn was immediately suspicious of the overtures by RumLot Security. They were offering her fat cow of a daughter a full scholarship to one of their schools. That in itself set off alarm bells. Gracie was book smart, but she was lazy and didn't have the sense God gave her. Besides, she was weird. Sometimes, the way the girl looked at her mother... Anyway, why would they want her? Why would anyone want fat cow Gracie?

And what was in it for Wendy? Giving up a daughter was like giving up her benefits cheque. Gracie was going to bring a good wage once school was over. She already had applications in for till work at ASDA and the CoOp, and Wendy was counting on that money to make up for losing the child benefits Gracie brought in. The girl ate a huge amount of food, but the food banks made that up. Gracie was a net earner.

She talked it over with her friends at Bingo, and while a couple thought going to the RumLot school would be good for Gracie, Wendy dismissed that out of hand. What about her? It wouldn't do *her* any good. Then her friend Phyllis pointed out that the RumLot people were part and parcel with those elves. Satanists, all of them. She would be sending Gracie to hell if she allowed her to go to their school. God knows what they would be teaching her. Ignorant crap, at best.

Elves. Now, Wendy had seen in the Mirror that there were elves back in the world, and they were tremendously rich. Everyone knew that. She had never seen one, but she had heard about them.

Phyllis took a puff of her vape and covered some numbers. "It ain't right, innit. To take away a girl fum 'er mum. Y'da fink the elfs would give'r some compensation. They c'n afford it, rich bastards. Richies are always look'n to screw poor people, aren't they?"

Wendy agreed. At the very least, she should get compensation. Look at what she would be giving up!

Bingo was called, and the winner wasn't at Wendy's table.

Wendy and Tikon

The RumLot reps were not agreeable to giving Wendy compensation for handing over Gracie. For one thing, they pointed out that Grace was twenty, a legal adult and could make her own decisions. And compensation smacked of slavery, of human trafficking, and they wouldn't have anything to do with that. They weren't going to *buy* Grace from her mother.

Wendy was incensed at the refusal. She had already spent the money in her mind. She was sure she could get five or six hundred pounds for her fat cow of a daughter. Maybe a thousand!

She screamed in the phone, shouting at them to stay the fuck away, and her Gracie would leave this bloody house over her dead body. She screamed at Gracie and said that the RumLot people were just jerking her around, and they really didn't want such a fat slob at all; otherwise, they'd do what was right by her mother. Grace sank into a deep depression and refused to leave her room. She didn't cry; she just ate.

The CoOp was full, and Wendy bought herself a bottle of wine on offer and a tub of ice cream for Gracie. There – dinner was sorted. In the crisps aisle, she spotted Phyllis and told her about the rejection by those RumLot bastards. The more she talked, the louder she got, and soon there was a little crowd. Wendy enjoyed the attention.

As she was leaving, a man stopped her. He was a rather nice-looking man with kind eyes that had a pretty, sparkly, purpley glint to them. He sounded Polish or something, and his name was Tikon. There were loads of immigrants in the area – Poles, Albanians, all that lot. He was curious. Why would the RumLot want her daughter to go live with them? She was obviously a loving and supportive mother. A daughter should be with her mother.

Wendy agreed. She did everything for her Gracie. Everything! And now these elf lovers wanted to steal *her* girl away and leave her with nothing. It was enough to bring tears to her eyes. Tikon was a proper bloke and offered to buy her a pint at the pub and even flirted with her a bit, something that hadn't happened for years.

They spent all afternoon in the pub, and when he took her home, she was so plastered she could hardly walk. Like a true gentleman, he helped her into the house. After making sure she was all right, he went up to check on Gracie, and for a boozy minute, Wendy wondered if he was going to touch the girl, but he immediately came back down, holding his hand over his nose and gagging a bit.

He smiled at Wendy and laughed, and he was still laughing when he slit her throat. After a quick phone call, he sat down to wait. Within half an hour, a plumber's van was sitting outside the house, and ten minutes later, a huge bundle was roughly hauled down the stairs by four sweating, grunting men. Wendy was put in some rubbish bags, the room was cleaned up, the door locked, and they were gone.

The house was empty of all life.

Grace

Lord Kyrylo was incandescent, and he made sure everyone knew it.

He would have to explain this fuck-up to Caddy, and in her condition, the last thing she needed was to find out they had lost a new lord.

But lost a lord they had. RumLot Security had flat, no doubt about it, misplaced a lord *and* her mother, and they had no idea where either was.

Ranger Bunn had spotted a lord, a girl (!) and had alerted the Lowestoft branch of RumLot Security. They then referred the case to Ellen's office, as this initial contact was a human/elf interaction, not an immediate security issue. The human on night duty, a Mr McGregor, bungled the case the minute he got it. He didn't call Ellen in the middle of the night because he thought he could handle everything himself, probably because he was angling for a promotion and wanted the kudos. Bringing in a new lord would be quite the coup.

First thing the next morning McGregor initiated contact with the family with a phone call to the girl's mother. He didn't try to talk to the girl first, even though by every measure she was of an age to make up her own mind. That was his next mistake.

McGregor didn't tell the mother that the girl was anything special because all they had was Bunn's report, and no elf had seen the girl yet to confirm her tribe. So, to get someone (himself) into the house, he came up with the idea to offer her a scholarship. What parent wouldn't want a free education for their child? Who wouldn't at least want to talk about it?

Well, it turned out the girl's mother was batshit crazy. A day went by, and then Mum told RumLot she wanted a payoff. Someone (Kyrylo knew it was McGregor because he'd have to get authorisation to spend that kind of money) got all prissy and said no, and the mother told them to get stuffed and hung up.

Because McGregor kept everything to himself, no elves or RumLot Security were sent to watch the house. That was his next, fatal mistake.

That afternoon, when Rashid asked a surprised Ellen how the new lord case was progressing, the shit hit the fan. She confronted McGregor and found out what was going on and learnt his repeated phone calls were being ignored. So Jameson was ported to Southampton with a scholarship offer in one hand and a cheque in the other – "for expenses" – only to find no one at home. The house was empty. Jameson, not being a prissy man himself or overly bothered by the niceties of breaking into a house that held a lord, had an elf port him inside. There were traces of blood on the sitting room floor, and the girl's filthy bedroom was empty. A neighbour told him that a plumber's van had been there about an hour earlier, and that was all they knew.

Jameson had missed them by about an hour. There was no trace of either the mother or the lord. They were gone.

It took Intel over an hour of combing through all the town's CCTV to trace the van. There were an amazing number of plumbers with white vans running around Southampton, but they eventually found their target abandoned on a lay-by, probably on its way to the docks. The kidnappers or whoever they were now had two hours ahead of RumLot, and if they had gone out to sea, there was no way elves could port there once they hit the twenty-mile *terrior* limit. They would have to pursue them the old-fashioned, human way.

Southampton docks are the second-largest docks in the UK, with every possible type of floating vessel passing through them. The container traffic alone is massive. You could hide an army in there, much less two women. Kyrylo was grim. RumLot security had lost Caddy in a dock when she went a-roaming, and then he had lost her at the waterside when she was kidnapped, and now they were going to lose this girl-lord in Southampton docks. He was starting to detest docks.

They had to get to work.

Grace

The little boat rocked, and it would have made Grace violently sick if she had anything to be violently sick with. But whatever was in her guts was long gone.

The man gave her water but no food. When she begged for food, he just laughed.

"Love, you'll just barf it up. Besides, you can live on reserves, probably for months." He looked at her and laughed again. "People pay good money to go on spa cruises. You're gettin' yours for free!"

They didn't bother tying her up. They knew she was too sick and too fat to do anything to anyone, so they just shoved her in the stinking fish hold, threw down bottles of water a couple times a day, and left her to stink and stew in her own juices.

She was a prime catch, she was. The Russians would pay top dollar for this one and not even in worthless rubles. They'd pay in gold.

The man knew he had one of the demon lords that the Russians were asking for. Thank God his mother insisted he go to the Russian Orthodox church with her, which is where he learnt all about the bounty system the Russians had for a live lord.

It'd been like winning the fuckin' lottery when he walked into the CoOp and heard that horrible gnome of a woman telling everyone in the world that RumLot wanted her fat cow of a daughter. As soon as he heard the word RumLot, he knew he was onto something big. When he walked upstairs and saw this one overflowing on her bed like Jabba the Hutt, and saw those devil eyes, he knew. When he smelled her stink, he knew. She was exactly like the Russians said, only fat. God, he wished they paid by the pound!

So he called up Pavel, and Pavel had a couple of mates who knew how to keep their mouths shut. Within a couple of hours, they were on this fishing boat and heading out to sea. In the meantime, he was on the phone negotiating with someone in the

Russian embassy. He sent them pictures. The girl was a little fuzzy, but they could see her terrified eyes for themselves. They glowed bright green.

The trawler would meet the Russians at sea, off Brest, where the Tsar had confiscated a fancy-schmancy yacht from some Russian big shot, and they would make their trade. The Tsar would give him his gold – a cool five million – and they would get their XXL bundle of joy. Everyone would be happy.

Vrt and Conary

Conary could hear her walking. Vrt's bedroom was directly above his, and he had never noticed her moving about on her silent panther feet. But tonight she was pacing, and it was two in the fucking morning. He threw some clothes on and went upstairs to her door and knocked.

"Vrt, I can't sleep, and neither can you. Do you want to play a game of chess?"

The pacing stopped.

"Outside. On the big chess set on the terrace."

Shit, it was cold and damp out there, but if that's what the lady wanted, that's what she got. Conary fetched his coat and went outside to the garden chessboard and made the opening move with one of the massive pieces, a white pawn, and waited.

She walked onto the terrace and, without a word, made her move.

"Sometimes I can't sleep, either." He moved.

She sighed.

"I could sleep, but he keeps waking me up."

Conary looked up, startled. "Who keeps waking you up? Sam?"

"Prana. My husband. He hasn't come to me for years, but since I've come here, he wakes me up almost every night."

She moved her knight. Conary looked at Vrt, studying her, unnerved. Was she going insane?

"What does he want?" He moved, but he wasn't paying attention to the game.

She walked around the chessboard, looking at it from different angles. She was hard to see in the dark, dressed in her matt black leathers, but when she turned her back, Conary could see the flash of white that was her long braid, and when she faced him, he could see her green glowing eyes.

"He wants me to let him go. He says it's time."

"You won't let him go?" Conary didn't ask where Prana was supposed to go. The man was dead. He didn't have many options.

She stopped her pacing and looked at the board.

"Of course, not! He's my husband. He's all I have. I love him. If all I have is his ghost, that is enough for me."

Conary looked at the board, and his heart broke for her.

"I had a wife, and she loved me." He looked up at the black

shadow on the other side of the board. "I wasn't the nicest of humans, believe it or not. I worked with a lot of bad people; probably quite a few of them were orcs, and I probably broke a lot of innocent lives. No, I take that back. I'm *sure* I broke a lot of innocent lives. But she stood by me. She saved me. Helped me free myself from that old life, and she gave up a lot to do that. She gave up everything for me."

He looked at the board. "Gods, I still don't know why, but she did. We had four kids, and I did my best for them. But because of my past – and my past never forgot me – I had to stay hidden, and I think they suffered for that. Everyone who loved me suffered because of me."

He stood and studied the board. He was going to lose. They had barely started the game, and he was already going to lose.

"Sometimes, for someone you love, you have to give up a piece of yourself. You suffer, but they are better for it."

Vrt looked at the board. She was very still. She waved her hand, and a piece moved. Conary thought that was the first time he had seen her use her ability.

"Did you suffer for your wife, Conary?"

"No, not anywhere near enough. The balance on that ledger is still weighted on her side."

He paused and looked at Vrt, a blacker shape in the black night. "She died of sepsis. She was gutting a fish, and the knife slipped, and she cut herself. A tiny nick. But she died three days later. There was nothing I could do but pick up the pieces and raise our kids. That was the highest way I could honour her, by taking care of her children and living my best life. That's all she ever asked from me – to live my best life and be happy. How could I refuse that?"

He moved his knight in a vain attempt to take the black queen. He was still going to lose.

"Isn't your husband asking the same thing? For you to be happy and live your best life?"

The black queen moved by herself.

"Checkmate. Black queen wins. Sleep well, Conary. I'm going to bed now." And she walked off as silent as a ghost.

_____

Grace

Grace stopped crying a long time ago, and when she stopped crying, she started thinking.

The man poked his head over the hatch and threw down bottles of water, trying to hit her with them. He thought it was funny, but he also wanted to make sure she was still alive and hadn't choked on her own puke or something. He liked to tell her how fat she was, as if she didn't know, and he liked to scare her.

Gleefully, he yelled through the hatch that he had killed her mother, and they had dumped the body over the side of the boat on the first night. "The slag is fish food now, love!" He thought that would devastate her, but he didn't know Grace too well.

When Grace heard that her mother was dead, it was like a thousand-tonne weight was lifted from her shoulders. She had fantasised since she was twelve about leaving home, but as she grew fatter and fatter, she realised she could barely walk to the bus for school. Leaving home was an impossibility. She was trapped. The only way out that she could see was for one of them to die. Her mother had thoroughly convinced Grace that *no one* could free her from her mother's grip. The constant lies, the constant disparagement, the constant propaganda – it all wore her down.

Grace was, in fact, twenty when she went to the prom, having lost two years due to her mother holding her back from school. If she had been a stronger person, she could have left her mother four years earlier. But she didn't go ask for help, she never went to a doctor about her weight, she didn't call any hotlines for abuse. She ate.

When Grace heard her mother was dead, it made her think, "If I went home now, I'd be free. I could go to uni like LeeAnne was talking about. I could have a life." That news, that her mother was now fish food, didn't devastate Grace; it gave her hope. It gave her a reason to escape.

She started to study her situation.

She didn't know why she'd been kidnapped. The awful man hadn't said. She didn't have money for ransom; anyone with half a brain could see that.

All she could think of was that they were going to sell her as a sex slave. That's the only possibility. He did ask if she was a virgin, and then he immediately answered his own question. Of course, she was.

The boat rocked, and Grace sat in the dark hold on a wooden pallet and thought about what she would do when she was confronted by some perv with a fetish for fat women.

Vrt

Whether it was the ghost of Prana or demons from her past or simple insomnia, Vrt pushed herself hard to escape them and find oblivion in sleep. But sleep fled from her, and Conary could see that she was slowly falling apart.

Alarmed, he talked to Dr Mandy, who couldn't do anything unless Vrt came to her, and Vrt would not. The other lords were at a loss and could only stand by and try to be kind, but they couldn't exorcise Vrt's ghosts any more than Conary could.

Whenever anyone approached her, she'd get irritable and say she was fine, and she'd walk off.

Conary was terrified she would commit suicide and began to invisibly follow her when she seemed at her worst. He watched her from a far distance if she left the grounds of the house, and only left her when she returned and was around other people. Mostly, she just walked or rode one of the horses from the stables. There seemed to be no purpose to her wandering; she just moved.

One morning, Vrt came to breakfast and instead of sitting at the table and drinking a cup of morning coffee with them, she gathered up a pile of sausage rolls and fruit. Alizah greeted Vrt and asked her what she was going to do today. Vrt was never curt to Alizah – that would be like kicking puppies – so she stopped and said she was going to go to the seashore to practise her abilities.

"It's going to be humid today. Low clouds." Alizah always knew the weather. She was a bit obsessive about it.

Vrt nodded and replied, a good day, especially for her. Conary jumped in and asked if he could go with her.

"Yes, if you stay out of my way. I can't prevent you. It's not like you wouldn't follow me anyway."

Embarrassed, Conary smiled sheepishly. So she knew he was following her.

They were ported to a deserted strand of beach high on the Norfolk coast. Humans tended to think that every bit of England was covered in people, but there were still very wild places miles from the nearest house. This beach was wide and flat, and there was no one around but a few lonely seals.

Vrt stood on the shore facing the sea, and Conary backed off a bit and sat down to watch. She didn't move. Nothing happened. Then he looked out to sea, and far in the distance he saw the thin white line of a waterspout.

The clouds nearby swirled, and another slender finger of a tornado dipped down to the sea, and a new waterspout formed.

He watched as more and more spouts formed. They started to dance and swirl, and the wind picked up on the shore. Vrt's body was glowing now, a pillar of black in a green glittery swirl of light.

There were a dozen spouts off the shore now, and they danced in closer and closer formation until they merged into one enormous whirlwind. Conary saw flashes of lightning sparking from the friction of air masses. Vrt was a bright ball of swirling light now. The wind onshore was fierce, and Conary was sandblasted.

Then it all disappeared. The tornado separated from the sea, the wind died down, the clouds broke up, and all was as it was before. Vrt staggered over to Conary and threw herself on the sand, her chest heaving, and he could see wet splotches on her leather top where she had sweated right through.

She laughed, a lovely musical laugh, and Conary had to laugh with her.

"So that felt good then."

"Always does. I think I'll sleep well tonight!"

"I didn't know you were an Elemental. That was a very impressive display."

She turned her head, her eyes amused.

"Oh, I'm not an Elemental like you. That's all I can do, move the air around. A real Elemental would be able to control all weather because they would control the forces that make weather. I'm just a big blowhard."

He laughed and teased back, "Making wind might be all you can do, but it's quite a lot. I'm impressed."

Her eyes crinkled behind the mask, and she patted his hand. "Time to go back." He held her hand and helped her up, and they called for an elf to port them back. He held her hand all the way back to Aelfeham House. It was the first time they had ever touched.

Vrt

Vrt slept well that night, but then her nights deteriorated. Prana was back.

It was just after midnight, and Conary heard her crying, sobbing, through the walls and ceiling. He trotted upstairs, and this time he didn't bother to knock but walked right into the room. She was curled up in a tight ball in her bed, rocking and sobbing, and her heart was breaking. She wore a heavy nightgown, but she still had the mask on. For a brief second, Conary wondered if she ever took it off.

But only for a brief second. He gathered her up in his arms and did his best to soothe her, never thinking that she would turn and kill a strange man who grabbed her in her bed. She was facing away from him, and he buried his face in the nape of her neck under the heavy braid and rocked her. He made those incoherent "there, there, don't cry" sounds that every living thing gives their love when they hurt.

The sobbing turned into shuddering gulps and then great heaving breaths, and she calmed. All that was left was trembling. Conary slowed his rocking and calmed with her.

Oh, stars, she smelled good. Why hadn't he smelled her scent before?

Vrt felt his breath on her neck. He gently kissed the side of her neck, and the pin that held up the coil of braid fell to the floor. Prana's pin. She shuddered again, but this wasn't the shudder of despair. His hand traced down the side of her body, and he whispered in what used to be her ear.

"Sleep, sleep –"

And she did, a deep and dreamless sleep. When her breathing was slow and even, Conary carefully got up and pulled the blankets over her and left.

Tuân

It was decided to conduct an intervention. Caddy insisted that she would've nothing to do with it as this was entirely a guy thing.

"Get your mates together, call him in for a beer or something, and tell him the facts of life." Caddy was impatient. She had enough on her plate now with a missing lord, a lord going insane, and another doing somersaults in her belly. She was feeling pretty huge lately.

Kyrylo shrugged, called in Jack and Conary, and they decided to talk to Tuân at the Trowel and Hammer. If they did it at Tuân's usual local, they might be overheard. If they did it at The Rum Lot conference room, he'd think he was being yelled at.

Tuân walked into the pub, and immediately his hackles prickled. Something was up.

Seated at the far table were three male lords, all staring down at their beers – Kyrylo, the Old Man, and Jack. With a resigned expression on his face, Tuân slid into the only vacant chair and waited for whatever cards fate was going to deal him.

Kyrylo smiled and shoved a beer at Tuân and asked him how he was doing.

Shit, thought Tuân, this is going to be bad.

"Fine, sir. No problems." The lord smiled again and began.

"Tuân, I don't know how to start, so I'll –"

"Dammit, boy, you stink!" The Old Man cackled so loudly that the bartender looked up. "You need to get some deodorant!"

"Grandpa!" Tuân was deeply offended. "I take showers. Usually twice a day!"

Kyrylo shot an if-looks-could-kill glance at Conary. This was not how he had wanted it to start.

"Is this why you called me here? To tell me I have BO?" Tuân's face turned red. "Is my sweat really worth a three-lord meeting?"

Jack jumped in.

"Tuân, that's not it at all." He paused. "It's a four-lord meeting. This hasn't anything to do with your job or anything official. It's old guys who need to let a young guy in on some facts."

"Tuân, do you smell anything *unusual* with Ratna? Or Alizah or Ms Caddy?"

Tuân looked puzzled. "No, not really. Do they have body odour?"

Jack frowned. How could a healthy young man like Tuân not smell Alizah? That was just weird.

"Okay, this is strange, and I guess we have to spell it out. Here's the facts. Tuân, unlike humans, lord and elf reproduction is regulated by pheromones. It's more the norm than not in the animal world. Think of elephants going into musth or stags going into rut. Lord, women have a special smell, and it drives their men wild. Now, if we're well-matched with a woman, it really drives us crazy. If you're not a good match or if you're related to her, the smell will be faint or just not there at all."

Kyrylo nodded and looked down at his beer, a faint, silly smile on his lips. It was obvious where his mind was roaming.

"So, have you noticed that Ratna won't sit near you? Everyone else has noticed that. It's a topic of conversation." Jack squinted at Tuân, weighing his reaction.

Tuân blushed. Yes, he'd noticed.

"It's because you're driving her crazy. Your smell, your special scent, is sending her up the wall."

"NO!!!"

"Yesssss!" The Old Man laughed and raised his glass to Tuân. "My grand-progeny is a stud!"

Tuân shot Conary with an evil look.

"She's never said a word. She's never come on to me." Tuân frowned; this was so weird. If she liked him so much, why was she avoiding him?

"That's because you don't show any interest in her. You're very polite. You obviously can't smell her scent, so this is a one-way attraction." Jack looked sympathetic. "It would be hugely embarrassing to her to know we are talking about her today, so please keep this confidential. One day, you'll meet a female lord with a special smell that will drive you to do crazy things, but don't feel bad if Ratna isn't the one. She's trying very hard to maintain some dignity, and that's why we're here today. We want you to be kind to her, but please, take extra showers when you come around. Clean clothes from the skin out. De-scent as best you can. And don't go sitting next to her and following her around the room. Maintain some distance. She's trying."

His mouth opened, but Tuân didn't know what to say.

"You're kidding, right? Is this a practical joke?"

They all shook their heads in unison.

"Caddy smelled me the first day she was in Ukraine. She knew I was a lord before I did. She told me later she could hardly think when I was in the room." And Kyrylo smiled that silly smile again, "And I will always remember the first time I got a good whiff of her – I almost embarrassed myself."

Jack and Conary hooted at him. This vision of a goofy, scent-addled Kyrylo was hysterical.

"It's true, Tuân. The scent thing goes with the ears. It's a part of us." Jack grinned.

"But I do like her! But I don't smell anything." He was upset. "I don't smell anything at all!"

"Well, you smell orcs!" Jack couldn't believe it. Surely Tuân could smell an orc.

"Actually, I don't. Not often. Not at all since I left Vietnam." Tuân shook his head.

Conary put his beer down and scowled. "What do you mean you don't smell orcs? Everyone can smell an orc."

"Can you smell flowers? This beer? Conary's truly horrendous bad breath?"

"No, Jack, I don't smell anything. Haven't since I got here to the UK."

"I don't have bad breath, you elongated chicken." Conary turned to Jack, offended.

"Yes, you do. Always after a couple of those vile Vietnamese beers."

With that, the intervention was over. Kyrylo told Tuân to see Dr Mandy first thing in the morning and find out why he couldn't smell orcs. That was concerning and a safety issue.

Tuân went home and thought a lot about what they had said. Ratna had the hots for him.

He couldn't stop grinning.

Dr Mandy listened to Tuân for about three minutes, told him he had a pollen allergy that was clogging up his nose and probably a good sinus infection to add to it. She wrote out a prescription. Usually, she said, lords didn't get ill with such things, but he was half-human and hadn't turned into a full lord yet.

"If this doesn't work, come back to me." And Tuân's doctor appointment was done within ten minutes. Fifteen minutes later, an elf ported into his flat with the meds, which he was to brew in a cup of tea every morning. By mid-afternoon, he could breathe through his nose again and was starting to smell things he didn't realise he couldn't smell before, like the sea and the starch in his uniform shirt.

Tuân wasn't quite sure how to approach Ratna. After all, a gentleman doesn't go up to a lady and say, "I think my nose is working now. Can I smell your pits and see if my nose works now?" She had trained herself to avoid him, so that would have to

be overcome, too. Maybe if they met outside like they had
on the mountain.

He worried about what to expect. The old guys certainly
looked like they enjoyed a woman's scent. Would he – and gods
help him – would he be able to do anything about it, or would he
just pop off and embarrass himself like a fourteen-year-old with his
first porno? What if Ratna got mad at him for approaching her?
What if she laughed at him?

Then he thought, what if I don't get her scent? What if
this is just not meant to be? He pushed that thought out of
his head.

Tuân called her up. "Ratna, it's a beautiful night, and I feel
like an ice cream. Why don't you port here, and we'll have a walk
on the prom?"

Looking out the window, Ratna didn't think it was
particularly beautiful outside, but then the seaside had its own
weather. Maybe it was nicer in Lowestoft than here at Aelfeham
House, and as for a walk outside, no harm in that; she'd make sure
he was downwind. She liked soft ice cream almost as much as a
banana, so she said Yeah, sure. She'd be there in ten minutes.

She ported directly into the living room of his flat. Tuân
was in the bedroom putting his socks on when he heard her call for
him. He walked into the living room to get his shoes, and it hit him
like a judo spinning whip kick.

Oh, she smelled so good. Perfect.

He didn't even think. He walked up to her and picked her
up, and glued his mouth onto hers, and she kissed back. In the
delicious haze that followed, that's all he could remember.

Conary

Conary walked into the TV room, and there was Prana, sitting on the couch watching a football match. He looked confused by the men running around the field chasing a ball, but when he saw Conary, he grinned and waved.

Prana was impossibly handsome. He was very tall with huge elf ears and what can only be described as a roguish glint to his glowing light blue eyes. For a man with a neck wound so deep his head was about to fall off, he was in a pretty good mood.

"Thank you, Conary, for taking care of my beautiful girl." Then he shut his eyes, and the smile faded. "I was stupid and I failed her. You will make her happy."

Conary didn't quite know what to say to that. Do you talk back to a ghost?

"You kept her alive all these years."

Prana perked up and grinned. "That I did. My only success. Have I atoned for failing her? I don't know, but I go into the Void hopeful. I tried my best."

And then he winked out. All that was left was the smell of yarrow.

Conary sat down at the table, set up the chessboard, and waited. If Vrt was going crazy when she spoke of Prana visiting her, it must be catching.

Vrt didn't come for her chess game.

The wind was picking up, and Conary could hear it whistle through the old house's chimney pots. He looked out of the window and saw Vrt at the far end of the vast lawn, glowing.

She was making a whirlwind, and from the funnel out shot bits of wood. Great logs, bits of construction off-cuts, sticks – everything fed down that funnel into a pile on the lawn.

A chill ran through Conary. Vrt was making a pyre.

As he burst out the door to run to Vrt, he was tackled from behind. Furious, he twisted, and the judo lessons he had moaned about so often kicked in, and he threw off the man. But it was Jack, and Jack was not much affected by gravity.

"Stop! Stop!" Jack latched onto Conary's back, and suddenly Conary's feet flew out, and there was Sam, holding his feet like a wheelbarrow.

"Shit, I can't see'm." "Stop!! Conary, listen to me!" "Let me GO! I'll kill you, Jack, I swear!"

"LISTEN TO ME!" Jack was panting. He wasn't much of a fighter. "I'll let you go, but listen to me. Vrt is okay!"

Conary gave a mighty twist and kicked Sam in the gut, and threw Jack off. He spun and regained his feet. "Jack, she's building a pyre! She's going to kill herself!"

Sam was rolling on the ground, the air knocked out of him. Conary hadn't hit him in the gut but a bit lower down.

"NO! Yes, she's building a pyre. It's for her man. She's releasing him." Jack didn't know who he was talking to. Conary was invisible, and Jack was facing away from him, talking to air.

"Look, Conary – we have to get out of here. We're not allowed here. It'll mess her up."

Conary looked at Vrt. She was a mass of energy now, and the pyre was huge. The wood started to move and shake, and he could see the shape of a man forming from it. And a woman. They looked like a bride and groom on top of a wedding cake, only the man was Prana, and next to him was the most beautiful woman he had ever seen.

"Conary, come on, man. Please." Jack was waving his arms, searching the air for the invisible Conary. Conary looked at the pyre with the wooden effigy of Prana. Then he grabbed Sam by the armpit and dragged him over to Jack, who smiled weakly and grabbed Sam's other armpit, and they helped him back to the house. As they struggled back up (Sam was short but broad-shouldered and as heavy as a boulder), Conary saw Alizah and Ratna running down to the pyre. On the terrace, Tuân, Kyrylo, and a bunch of male elves gathered and waited.

"What's going on? Jack! For the love of –"

"She's releasing him to the Void. She's giving her man the gift of freedom and un-bonding. You lords who weren't around in the Before Times don't know this. I've only seen it once in my life. But tonight it's a woman thing down there. No men allowed. If it were a man un-bonding, the women would all be up here and we'd be down there."

Conary turned to watch. All around the pyre, elves, all female, popped in, and their golden sparks as they ported flashed like fireflies. The female lords arranged themselves around the pyre in a circle, and they started to glow green. Conary saw his mother down there, tuning up her violin.

"The women got the call about a half hour ago, and they all ported out. I was with Alizah, and it was like someone had shot her with a bolt of electricity. She just jumped up and looked at me, and said she had to go. She just ran down to the ground floor. Vrt was unbonding, and I don't think she even knew what that meant. An elf popped in to get her, and she was gone." Jack spoke, but he couldn't keep his eyes from the spectacle down below.

The pyre was complete. Conary could hardly make out which green glowing orb was Vrt in the mass of elves. There were thousands of them. Every elf woman in porting distance was there, young and old. At the far edges were the men, watching, protecting, keeping them safe so that their women could concentrate on the grim task ahead.

Conary didn't see where it came from, but a torch appeared in Vrt's hand, and the crowd went dead silent. Then, with a cry of pure and utter anguish, she threw it in the pyre, and the entire pile erupted into a volcano of flame.

Caddy played a song of regret and longing and futures that would never happen, and all of the women danced clockwise around the pyre. Only Vrt walked like a zombie in the other direction, counter-clockwise. It took an hour, and the pyre blazed hot and hard the entire time. The women never paused their dance, but in the end, they slowed. As the fire died, their dance faded away, and then, when the last flame had died away, Vrt stopped. They all stopped to face the pyre, and Vrt threw something in it. There was a blue bolt of lightning that cracked across the valley. She collapsed, and her cry of anguish ripped through the hearts of them all. Her sisters rushed to her, and in the mass, Conary couldn't see her at all.

Jack put his hand on Conary's shoulder. "It's done now. The women will take care of her. Time to go home. We'll see Vrt in the morning."

The men on the hills began to leave, their ports winking in and out as they left. The male lords gathered around Conary for a few awkward moments, then said their subdued goodnights.

"Jack, what did she throw on the pyre? What made the lightning bolt?"

"That was her pin. When lords have a bonding ceremony, the man gives the woman a pin to hold up her hair. That is to show he is joined or pinned to her forever. She's not pinned to him; he's pinned to her. That's why Vrt had to release her husband; he couldn't release her. She gives him a knife to protect the family with. When he died, he lost his knife, so she was released from him already.

"The pin and knife thing – it's tradition. Humans have weddings; we have bonding ceremonies. Humans have wedding rings; we have pins and knives. Same purpose, just different."

"So that was the moment she unbonded."

"Yes, that was the moment. He is no longer pinned to her. She set him free. If he went to the Void as her bonded man, she would die, too, and go with him. That's why he stayed here as a ghost. She had to set him free so he could die and she could live."

Conary nodded, and they all turned back to the house. He was exhausted, but not so exhausted he couldn't apologise to Sam for kicking him in the balls and Jack for fighting him. They were both gracious about it. Sam said he hadn't planned on using that testicle any time soon anyway.

Vrt and Conary

Conary almost tripped over her when he walked out of his bedroom on his way to breakfast. Vrt was sitting cross-legged on the hall floor, waiting for him.

"What are you doing here? Are you okay?" He reached down to help her up, but she rose in one smooth motion and ignored his hand. She also ignored his questions.

"I want to ask you –" And she stopped and looked down the hall. No one was there. She cleared her throat, and Conary realised she was nervous. The Angel of Death had been many things around Conary, but nervous was not one of them.

"Ask away."

"I want to ask if you'll –" Vrt had a white-knuckle grip on her sword handle. "If you would anchor me if I go into the cauldron." And she released a great, shuddering sigh and looked at her feet.

Conary was taken aback. Why was she so nervous? "Of course, I will. Why would you doubt that?"

She shook her head. "You don't understand. I'm asking you to *anchor* me." She looked down the hall again. "Only my bonded man can anchor me. I'm not asking you to sit and read me the daily weather report. I'm asking you to –" And she sighed again.

Conary put his hand to the side of her head. He could feel her cheek under the leather. She was trembling.

"If you're asking me to bond with you, you're too late, Vrt." He pulled her to him. "I bonded with you ages ago."

She fell into him and sobbed. "It's not fair. I know it's not fair. I can't be a proper woman for you, and you don't know what you're getting yourself into," she sobbed again. "I'm a mess – and I might not come out any better than I am now. You're bonded to a freak and will hate me."

He hugged her. "I know. I'm a mess, too. We're very messy people. We'll just have to deal with whatever life throws at us." He kissed her where her ear should have been.
"I love you, Vrt."

"I love you, too, Conary." She wiped her eyes with the back of her hand. "I'm always crying now. I don't think I cried a single time for the last five hundred years, and now I'm constantly leaking."

He took her back to his bedroom and found some tissues. He didn't take her to his bed but to the big chair by the window where she sat on his lap. They talked all morning. She smelled wonderful, and he breathed in her hypnotic scent until he couldn't think.

Dr Mandy was perfectly fine with setting up a cauldron for Vrt now that she had a bonded man to anchor her to this world. On the day she was to enter the cauldron, Vrt told Conary to come down at nine, right after breakfast, which he did, only to find that Vrt was already in the cauldron. The herbs that turned the water to custard had long since been applied.

He was furious with the elves for not coming to get him so he could say goodbye to Vrt, but they just shrugged. Lord Vrt had told them not to fetch him. When he threw a fit the head nurse came up and shook her finger at the lord.

"Do *not* get stroppy with my staff. Lord Vrt had to go in naked, and she didn't want you to remember her that way. Now your job is to sit in that chair and talk to her." She pointed to the chair and stood her ground until he sat down in it.

"Better. Now we'll bring you something to eat. Mind your manners, do your job, and don't hassle my staff." And she flounced off.

A few minutes later, she came back and handed Conary a heavy pouch. In it was Vrt's long braid. She had cut it off before she went into the cauldron and told them to give it to Conary because if she didn't come back or something went wrong, he would have this last gift from her. It smelled of her, and holding the silky hair was almost more than he could bear.

He sat in the chair, and like everyone else, chatted to the cauldron about everything and nothing. He came in every morning at six and stayed there until the nurses chased him to bed, usually at ten. All of the other lords came in and talked, too, even Kyrylo and Caddy, who was so heavily pregnant she could barely walk. Sam didn't see any point in talking to a big, steaming pot of goo, but he would bring in a couple of beers and chat with Conary, which helped pass the time.

Four days later, the egg sac popped up, and Conary could see the faint outline of her form curled up in there. Every part he could see was a hint of how lovely she was going to be. She had ears.

On day ten, the pot boiled over, and he was chased from the room. About an hour later, she was in bed. Unlike with Luke, there were no puzzled elves with worried faces. Everyone running in and out of the rooms looked positively giddy. One male nurse ran by and gave Conary a big grin and a thumbs up, which didn't make him feel better; it drove him crazy. What was going on?

Then he was allowed into her room. Just like the others who emerged from the cauldron, she lay flat on her back, asleep. She was completely bald; all of her gorgeous braid was gone, but in its place was an angel. She had a nose. She had ears. The scars on her face and body were all gone. Under the sheet, she had breasts. She was as she was supposed to be.

Tears flowed down Conary's cheeks, and he wiped them with the back of his hand. He was constantly leaking now.

Vrt opened her eyes the next morning, and when Conary walked into the room with her breakfast, she looked up and beamed with delight at him. It was the first time he had ever seen her smile, and he had to grin back.

"I double you." She whispered and then looked puzzled. That hadn't come out right. Her words weren't working. He laughed. "I love you, too. Triple." And she chuckled.

"My ears!"

He nodded, his eyes getting wet again. "Beautiful ears." And he sat down, fed her breakfast, and talked to her, but she fell asleep in the middle of the conversation, so he just sat and stared at her.

Three days later, Vrt was sitting up, and the puffiness was gone, and Conary could see a white peach fuzz on her scalp as her hair grew back. As her mind cleared and the brain fog melted away, they played chess, and she jabbered happily, almost as much as Alizah and certainly not like the subdued pre-cauldron Vrt. This Vrt was positively giddy.

The head nurse checked in every morning and pointedly reminded Conary not to touch Vrt. Not a kiss, not a stroke, nothing. It became extremely irritating. Did they think he had no control at all?

It turned out that Vrt was the one with precious little control. The day – the hour – the nurses stopped sitting in the room 24/7, she was flirting with Conary. That was a new phenomenon, too, Vrt flirting. And she knew how to do it, too. As they walked around so she could exercise her legs, she leaned on Conary a bit more than was necessary and was constantly touching him. Her shirts all developed issues with their buttons. She turned to kiss him whenever they were in a sheltered place where the elves couldn't see them. It was driving him crazy.

But Dr Mandy wouldn't sign her off, and he had to deal with it.

Vrt, it turned out, was very inventive when it came to playing in bed and yet following Dr Mandy's restrictions.

Ivana, Caddy, and Kyrylo

Ivana was born laughing.

That was Kyrylo's story, and he never deviated from it. While other babies entered the world, as Dr Mandy always said, with messy violence, Ivana fell into her father's hands with a loud, wet, steaming plop, a laugh, and her eyes wide open.

When he looked into her eyes, they weren't blue like a human baby; they were green. And her tiny baby ears had points.

She was a lord.

They had argued about the name up until the minute Caddy went into labour, with Kyrylo offering dozens of elaborate double- and triple-barreled names, each more glorious than the last. But when he came in to breakfast one morning with Fedyanka-Yoddah for a boy and Eudora-Ayudhina for a girl, Caddy informed the lord he was fired from the baby-naming business.

They were going to name the baby Ivana to honour his mother and the male version Ivan if it was a boy. No argument.

She couldn't imagine yelling "Time for dinner, Fedyanka-Yoddah!"

Unlike her first three pregnancies, this one didn't leave her exhausted, mostly because she wasn't expected to keep house, hold a full-time job, and watch the previous children all while waddling around with a twenty-pound growth strapped to her stomach that occasionally kicked her in the ribs. She had birthed her first three children with no family help whatsoever, which shocked the elves when they heard that. She had no sisters or a mother to help and no girlfriends to pick up the slack, and back in the '60s, institutions that were common in Texas fifty years later that would help a mother simply didn't exist. She was as alone in her little house in mesquite country as if she had been on the moon.

But Caddy was a worker, and in the days before the internet she taught herself everything from how to diaper a baby to the other 1,001 things a mother needed to learn like how to get a bug out of a two year old's ear or how to throw together a pilgrim costume for the school play in half an hour flat.

As much as Ricky doted on all of his children, he was absolutely rubbish at the boring bits of fatherhood like making breakfast, dressing a wriggling six-year-old, or throwing some towels in the washing machine. His mother had been a full-time, stay-at-home mom with one very quiet child. Caddy would point out that she had a full-time job and three active kids, but it never connected with Ricky that she would need help and didn't actually *like* scrubbing toilets and ironing his work clothes.

And his wife's music? That wasn't like a real job; it was a hobby. And it got in the way more often than not. By the time Conary was born, Caddy hadn't played much more than *Jingle Bells* with the third graders for years, which to Ricky just proved his point.

She often felt like she had four kids, not three. Ricky's unconcern with the burdens Caddy was under put a real long-term strain on her marriage. After Conary was born, she just didn't have the same respect for him that she did before. She still loved her husband, but it wasn't the same passionate, romantic love between equals. Her love was the love for a dear friend or a favourite relative. It didn't help at all that after John was born, Ricky started calling her Mother instead of Caddy, even when they were alone.

Kyrylo was much better at pulling his share of the household weight, even though he didn't have to. They had elves! Things just got done, and he didn't have to think about it. When he had lived alone, he had a housekeeper who came in and "did" once a week, and with his exacting nature honed in military academies, he was naturally a tidy man. Major Melnyk's flat would always pass inspection.

After they became a couple, and even though they didn't have any kids, Kyrylo was always worried about the stresses Caddy was under as Queen of the Fairies. And for many good reasons, he was paranoid over her safety. He didn't take anything about his fiancée for granted.

Lena was born after his divorce, and other than making sure the support cheques came in, Katya avoided her ex-husband until the little girl was a very bratty six-year-old. It was then that

Katya thought, "This man isn't ever marrying again. I'd better let him see his daughter so he keeps her in his will." She didn't want Major Melnyk to leave his money to a military dog charity or something equally stupid. Intermittent visits during holidays continued until Lena was eleven, and then she announced that she wasn't going to the Major's flat any more. It was boring, and after that, Kyrylo only saw her now and then until she joined the Border Guard. She was his biological daughter, and he owed her his support. But she wasn't any more than that.

This time, it was different for both of the lords.

Caddy worked during her entire pregnancy. She managed the political arm of the Elf Nation, and every week, she went somewhere to wake up more elves. During this pregnancy, she did nothing else. She didn't cook, didn't do piles of laundry, didn't scrub a floor, and didn't chase a toddler.

This time, she could barely blow her own nose without an elf popping up with a fresh box of tissues and wanting to know if she needed some tea to help her recover from the exertion. Kyrylo watched her work schedule obsessively, even to the point of pencilling in naps and mandatory tea breaks. At four o'clock, Caddy's day was done, and no one was allowed to talk to his woman about business, or they would see him in his office the next day.

Kyrylo hadn't been there for Katya's pregnancy and certainly wasn't invited to the birth. He had never been around a pregnant woman, and Caddy's growing belly was a never-ending object of fascination. One night, they were lying in bed asleep, and the baby started to kick. Caddy stayed asleep, but Kyrylo cupped his hand around her belly. He felt his child swimming and turning, and the enormity of what they were about to go through really hit him. There was a child *inside her*, and it was his.

When Caddy woke up at four in the morning and felt her first contractions, she knew what was going on. She gave Kyrylo a shove and told him it was time. The previous month, the elves had set up a pleasant room with a birthing chair and everything they needed to make Caddy comfortable. Whether in a pretty room or not, giving birth was still a painful, exhausting process, and while Caddy's mind knew all about labour and had the experience of three births, for her lord body this was the first time, and she strained for fifteen exhausting hours.

During the final push, Caddy's entire body glowed green with her special fire, and while Dr Mandy stood by with asbestos oven mitts, it was Kyrylo who caught the baby with his big, heat-proof lord's hands.   By the time Ivana was cooled down, cleaned, and swaddled, Dr Mandy didn't know who was more relieved it was over, Caddy or Kyrylo.

As it was from the beginning of time for all bonded parents, the joy of greeting your baby more than made up for the previous months of discomfort and hours of pain. Caddy and Kyrylo were over the moon with their laughing, green-eyed baby girl.

President Meecham

It took a long time for President Meecham to wrap his head around what the Tsar told him. If he'd been told just two years ago that in the Bronze Age the world had four tribes and not just one, and those four were humans, lords, elves and orcs, he would've replied that was patent nonsense. Fairy tales.

This wild story was certainly against everything he had learnt all of his life in church and in the secular university classes he had taken back when he was eighteen. Okay, he hadn't taken any more than the minimum in biology classes, but he would certainly remember if elves were mentioned. No, the only tribe was human, and that was that.

Where was the physical evidence of elves, orcs, and lords? Where was the archaeology? Was there an Elf Week on the Discovery Channel? No. They didn't exist except in stupid fantasy movies and nerd conventions.

And yet, today, thousands of elves were running around Europe, and he had met three lords and shaken their hands. They existed.

But it was the existence of orcs that really blew his mind. The Tsar said these superior beings always lived among the humans, just unaware of their true heritage because they were no longer forced to defend against the evil elves. They had blended in with humans as their natural and rightful partners against elves, and with the elves gone, everyone had prospered.

Lords, other than the Tsar, who understood the danger of the little imps, aligned themselves with elves, and, of course, the Tsar was aligned with the side that followed the human God's word – humans and orcs. Like everything good and right, poor Tsar Lester was in the minority. Lester downplayed the bit about himself being a three-thousand-year-old lord or the tiny detail of the millions of lords, humans, and orcs who had died under his hand. Or the very, very tiny detail that the humans' God wouldn't approve of Lester's enterprising spirit. There was no point in confusing Meechem.

Orcs were a God-fearing, repressed minority constantly attacked by the pagan, demonic elves. By instinct, the long-suffering orcs aligned with humans and stayed away from the lords who were in bed with elves. Lester told Meecham that orcs were so aligned with humans that they actually had an allergic reaction to anyone who had anything to do with elves, and Meecham saw that for himself when Janet got so sick when she shook that fairy queen's hand. The Cadence woman was a living carrier of elf poison.

His wife, Janet, was an orc! The Tsar was worried that she would be targeted by elves and was kind enough to make sure Meecham knew of her peril.

When she found out, Janet was pleased as punch that she was an orc. Thrilled, even. She really didn't know what it meant, just that she was a magical creature of some sort and was unique. No, she couldn't do any magic, but she was born on the side of the angels, and that was special, too. Her eyes glittered a gorgeous purple, and she had the rhythmic, dancing walk of a true orc. She was also very strong. Lester didn't tell her that as a fifty-two-year-old orc she was ageing out fast because that would have been mean. She would find that out after she died.

Janet was sure she was chosen by God.

With the vast PR power she held as the First Lady of the richest country in the world, she had the means and the ability to free and exalt her orc tribe. Her people weren't the Americans who were, to be honest, mostly secular idiots who believed in silly things like a free press and voting and all that rot. Her calling was to bring orcs to their proper place in the world, wherever they were. Her orc people were above the restrictions of country and politics, but her position would give her a voice to rally them to their true place as the first of the four tribes.

Make America Orc Again didn't make a good slogan and was too Trumpian, who was a fine orc in his own right. She would come up with her own original strapline.

Orc Power! Go, Go Power Orcs! Orc – the Other White Meat.

Whatever.

She would think of something.

Vrt, Conary, Caddie, and Kyrylo

Ivana was hungry, and hungry babies weren't worried about the meetings and affairs of state that their mothers and fathers were committed to attending. Hungry babies commanded, and the world stopped to accommodate them.

Kyrylo, Caddie, Ivana, Vrt, and Conary sat around the scrubbed pine table of House's cosy kitchen and waited while Ivana had a right good feed. She was very noisy.

Vrt had only been signed off by Dr Mandy for half a day, and Caddy was feeling very guilty about what they were about to do. But, as they say, needs must. There was no other way.

Kyrylo, as usual, started by laying out the problem they had.

"Lester has captured a lord, a young girl named Grace. We have intelligence about where she is – or at least where she was when the intel was gathered. She is in Russia and is being held in a bunker in Sochi. We think in Putin's palace."

Vrt and Conary shot a glance at each other. Oh, that's why they had been asked to come see the Primaries. What did this have to do with them?

"And we want you two to head up a team to go rescue her. That's it in a nutshell."

Caddy shifted a bit (Ivana was a chunky monkey and heavy). "We know that you have only been signed off for one day, Vrt, but every day this girl is held captive –"

Vrt nodded. She knew. Another day of whatever indoctrination (at best) or torture (at worst). Conary frowned down at his tea.

"It will take a couple of weeks to get everything in place anyway, so you'll have some time. As mission leaders, when you go is up to you."

Conary looked up at the lord. "Mom, we haven't said yes yet. It seems to me that you are asking a lot of Vrt at this stage. She's not used to her new body yet. She deserves some time to be a normal woman, and you're asking her to go back to her warrior past."

There was an awkward silence.

"We know." Caddy looked down at Ivana, who was looking up at her mum. "We know. But you two are the best of our choices for this. You'll be better than anyone else, other than me and Kyrylo or Tuân and Ratna. I don't think Sam, Jack, or Alizah could handle this job."

"Certainly not! Alizah would get herself captured, and we'd end up going anyway to rescue multiple lords if she lived long enough to be a prisoner." Vrt shook her head. And Sam? Oh dear gods. That would be a disaster.

"Ratna could do it, but Tuân doesn't have the experience yet. Conary, you know you wouldn't let him go. He has no lord ability. And Tuân won't stay back if Ratna goes. Everyone knows that."

Conary looked at Vrt and sighed. She was right, of course, but that didn't make him happy. She was already half accepting the job. And Kyrylo and Caddy couldn't do it, either. They were too important to the entire Elf Nation to do missions like this anymore. Who would awaken elves in new areas if Caddy were killed? If Caddy died, the shell of Kyrylo would soldier on, but he couldn't awaken a single elf or bring balance back to the world by himself. And now there was Ivana.

"Let us think about this for a few days. You're asking us to walk into a fortress and rescue a girl who might not want to be rescued. There's a lot of risk here. Lester will be expecting us – or someone like us." Conary temporised, and Caddy didn't blame her son at all.

"Lester the Liar is an idiot. He's a sneaky shit, and sneaky shits can cause a lot of harm, but there will be holes in his plans. There always are with people like him." Vrt picked up Ivana while Caddy adjusted herself to switch sides.

Ivana burped, hugely releasing some air and a bit of spit up, and providing space for round two. Vrt gently wiped the baby's mouth and was rewarded with a smile. She sniffed the baby's neck. What a wonderful smell! Even the nose-blind humans could smell baby scent.

She smiled at Caddy and continued. "I knew Lester back in Before Times. If he sees me, he'll recognise me."

All three were surprised, but it was Caddy who asked for the details.

Vrt had that twinkle in her eye that Conary had occasionally seen even when she was doing her Angel of Death gig and wearing the mask.

"Oh, I was a pretty little thing back then. I had my pick of men. You have to remember – I guess you can't remember because none of you were there – but the lord community was rather small. Maybe two or three thousand of us, so everyone had a passing acquaintance with everyone. And back then we had babies very rarely, so a very pretty young girl with parents who were both Elementals and sat on the Council – well, I was a hot prospect even before I or anyone else had a clue about my abilities. I had my pick of unbonded men of any age and status, and I picked the best just as I have now.

"Lester had the itch for me, but I certainly didn't have feelings for him. And I was vain and proud enough to reject him out of hand and not very kindly either. I was a bit of a snot.

"Lester had very weak powers, and his parents were very weak. Bad blood in so many ways, that one. And he was, not to put too fine a point on it, a disgusting, creepy little shit. But I was naive, like everyone else, and thought that simply because he was a weak creep, he was also powerless and no threat to anyone. No one ever thought that his ability to lie to a lord was not just a character flaw; it was a very subtle power that could do a huge amount of damage. Who could lie to a lord? Who could put worms in their brains to make them turn against each other? Lester could.

"When I found out from Conary that Lester is still alive and had aligned with orcs, that made perfect sense. Who else would have him? As they say, in the land of the blind, the one-eyed man is king. Lester doesn't have to be a powerful Elemental; he just has to be the most stinky piece of dung in his shitty realm." She shrugged. "I will, of course, kill him if I see him."

Caddy said, "Oh, no, only if –"

"Back then, there were elves who thought he turned Gaia's man against her, causing this entire mess. Just to be a jealous little worm hating other people's happiness. That might not be true, but he did incite the orcs, and the orcs killed my bonded husband and caused me 3,500 years of pain. I will kill him." Virt was quite firm.

"Only if he tries to kill you or Conary. Only in self-defence. You have to promise me, Vrt, you won't go rogue. We're not Lester. We're better than he is, and we don't kill lords, even lords as awful as Lester." Caddy looked past them all, at some future only she could see. "Lester is a chaos agent. He needs to be controlled, but it's important that he and the orcs live in this world, too. We can't have balance otherwise."

"We don't need him."

Sadly, she smiled at Vrt. "Yes, we do. I said that once, too. But if you plant a seed in a perfect greenhouse and give it water and sunlight, it will grow, but it will be weak and spindly. Plant a seed and give it some stress and wind, and pinch off some of the buds, and the plant will grow strong and bushy. Lords, elves, and humans – even orcs – need to have something to push against, to battle with, to be stronger. Lester is our balance to all of the good created by elves and lords. Now the world is out of balance because he and his people dominate. We'll break that domination, but it won't be easy. While there are ten lords now and only one Lester, there're millions of orcs, and they are gathering. We'll have to battle with them one day."

Caddy leaned forward. "Besides, if he's as stupid as you say, wouldn't it be better to have Lester as Tsar of the Orcs than someone who might be more competent?"

A muscle twitched in Vrt's jaw. "Conary and I will talk. If we agree – and we are a team and both must agree – then I will follow your orders *during this mission* only because you are the

Primary. But I won't let him live for Balance. There is enough chaos in the world for Balance, and we don't need Lester."

With that, the two lords left. Kyrylo put the baby over his shoulder and walked around the kitchen, jiggling her to get the air out so she would sleep.

"Do you think they'll do it?"

"Yes. I have no doubt at all." Caddy sighed, and for a second, she looked all of her hundred-plus years. "I am sending my son out to war, and he's just come back to me. He's so happy now – I hope I'm doing the right thing."

Krylylo nodded, and Ivana spat up all over his shoulder where he had forgotten to put a towel.

Vrt and Conary

Vrt and Conary ported back to the UK, and an hour and a half later, they were in Vrt's bedroom. Dr Mandy had given Vrt the all clear, and by every god in the starry sky, they were going to take full advantage of it. All talk about missions could wait. Vrt and Conary had their own mission to accomplish, and it was one they both enthusiastically agreed on.

For the last week, Vrt had been teasing and begging and generally making a pest of herself, and Conary had been a man of steely self-control as he waited for Vrt's bones to firm up enough for real, mind-blowing, trampoline sex. In the meantime, they had experimented and explored with every position and part they could possibly think of, and the housekeeper elves were quite happy with their daily Scent-soaked sheets. Vrt was having a very good time.

It wasn't like they didn't know what to do. Both had been married or bonded before, and both had lovers before they made those commitments. In the last week, Conary had had the great pleasure of learning what his beautiful woman's hot buttons were and how to get her worked up. Her job was a lot easier. All she had to do was give him a heavy-lidded look and that little smile, and he was ready.

So when they finally did it, it was a shock to both when he didn't fit.

Oh, he tried. He was as hard as a rock, and it was a good thing they hadn't cheated when her hips were fragile because Conary pushed hard. Really hard.

But she was too tight.

Vrt lay on her back in bed, sweating and panting, and Conary was next to her, literally dripping with sweat, and both stared at the ceiling.

"Are you okay?"

"I'm fine. Just very irritated. I've waited over 3,500 years and now this."

"I'm sorry –"

"It's not your fault. It's me. This new body has a manufacturer's defect." Conary smiled; at least she still had her sense of humour. She rolled over on him, and between her hands and her mouth, three minutes later, she made sure Conary was a happy camper. He told her she didn't have to, but then he didn't object too much either. While he was regaining his composure, she took a shower and got dressed.

"Put a shirt on. I want to call Dr Mandy." Vrt was all business. She was going to get this fixed.

Dr Mandy was available as she always was for one of their precious lords. She was doing her nails when they called, and she was busy painting on a very classy Rhumba Red.

Vrt was quite calm until Dr Mandy asked what the problem was. Then she just fell apart.

"Dr Mandy! I don't fit!" Vrt wailed. Dismayed, Conary didn't know what to do. So he put his arm around her and told her not to cry, but that didn't work at all.

Mandy looked up from her nails.

"What do you mean you don't fit?"

"He can't get it in! I'm too small!" She gulped air. "I mean, he's really tried, but he's hung like a horse –"

With that, Conary threw up his hands and turned bright red.

Mandy pressed her lips together and considered what she had just heard.

"I very much doubt that he's hung like a horse."

"I'm okay with that description –"

"Be quiet, Lord Conary. I'm sure you are perfectly adequate in that department. Lord Vrt, this is what I think happened. When you came out of the cauldron, you rebirthed with your original, unused body. So you have some parts of the body you had as a young teen, and I'm sure that back then, you did things like riding horses, dancing, gymnastics, and playing with the boys, like all young girls do. That stretched your hymen naturally. You haven't done those things with this body so –"

"I've been playing with the boys. Boy. Conary."

"Who's built like a horse and didn't try to get inside the stable if he was following my orders."

"Religiously. Didn't do anything against orders." Conary crossed his heart.

Dr Mandy gave Vrt some gymnastic stretches, told her to go horseback riding, and prescribed some exercises to do – some intimate and some she could do in public – and told them both to keep trying but with lots of lube. And please – do it gently. If that didn't work, in a week to come back to her, and they would do a little outpatient operation, and everything would fit as it should. Vrt was very relieved, and Conary tried very hard not to be smug. Built like a horse indeed.

They went to the stables that afternoon, and after looking over the rather gentle Friesians on offer, Vrt asked for a proper Shire war horse with a nice broad back. In the meantime, she rode the Friesians without a saddle and did her exercises.

A few days later she was fine.

Vrt and Conary

In between Vrt practising her gymnastics, stretching, and riding, they debated about what to do about the captured lord. Conary was not happy with anything that would put Vrt at risk, but in the end, neither could see an alternative lord to pass the job on to.

Vrt was not at all worried about herself. She knew what she could do, and after 3,500 years living at the edge of Orc-dom, she was a formidable warrior. Conary had seen hints of what she was capable of in battle, but he had no clue about her reality. She was more worried about her man. He had given a few hints in passing about his previous life, but he didn't hide that he wasn't as physical as she was. Conary was lean and limber and might land a good punch on Sam, but that wasn't the same as being able to get out of a knife fight with a pack of orcs. Conary was a fighter when he needed to be, but he wasn't a warrior.

As Conary pointed out, there was always an alternative. They could simply stay home and let the poor girl handle her fate herself. On balance, would losing either Conary or Vrt be worth the life of one unknown, potential lord? If either Conary or Vrt died, it would be like killing two lords because neither could live without the other. If they failed to extract the girl, it would be killing all three, and lords were very thin on the ground in this world. Was the risk worth it? He was inclined to say no.

But the girl weighed on them both. Saying no felt wrong when they could do something.

Vrt sighed. "Once I was at the bank of a flooded river and saw a young wolf stranded in the middle on a log. He was scared and crying, and on the far side was his pack, howling and running up and down the bank. If I went into the river to save him and lost my footing, I could be washed away; it was very fast, cold water, but only about three feet deep. And if I made it to the log, what was to say the terrified wolf wouldn't attack me? I would end up killing it anyway. I watched for a while, weighed the odds, and then I just went and did it. I couldn't let him drown. It was hard, but when I got to the log, he let me pick him up. I carried him to his pack, and they all ran off without a glance back. I sat on the bank, freezing and soaked, and it took me two days to dry off."

"So you want to do this?" Conary was still unsure.

Vrt looked at Conary. "I want to go to Ukraine and learn more. Study the situation, see what they have in mind, weigh the odds. I don't mind getting wet, but I won't let either of us drown for the cub."

One of the nice things about living with elves is that you don't have to pack. All Vrt and Conary had to do for their trip to Ukraine was to port to the helicopter pad, take the helicopter to France, and then port across Europe. No bags, no supplies, nothing but themselves. Everything they needed would be waiting there for them.

When they were ready to leave for Ukraine, Vrt came down to the Breakfast Room wearing normal clothes, and it struck Conary that he had never seen her in a skirt. He had only known her in black leathers or RumLot uniforms or in the elf version of a hospital gown, but today she wore a very short skirt, a ruffled blouse, a heavily embroidered jacket, and, of all things, a beret. Her boho clothes were colourful, but she looked very stylish. She earned whistles from the men and oohs and aahs from the women, and she gave them back blushes and a little curtsy in return.

"Look! I had my nails done, too!" And she showed Ratna and Alizah her new manicure.

Conary could see hints of what she had been in Before Times when the twenty-five-year-old Vrt had been a beautiful, cosseted bit of fluff who loved fashion and colour. She would never go back to that old Vrt, but she was regaining bits and pieces of her.

They stayed with Caddy and Kyrylo in House, and that evening the four of them sat around the kitchen table and had a long talk about the mission. No, they had not made up their minds yet, but…

Caddy was not worried at all that they would refuse to go. She was worried about them going and not coming back.

The next morning, the miniskirts and jeans were replaced by navy-blue RumLot lord's uniforms, and the lords went to work.

Jameson had chosen five human operatives to interview with the lords to see if they could work as a team. The three men and two women were very impressive on paper. All had extensive, high levels of military experience, and all brought different skills to the team. They all spoke unaccented Russian.

The human security operatives had no idea who they would be working with or even what the mission was. They had no idea what to expect from that morning's meeting, but they knew it was going to be big and probably dangerous. They weren't officers. They weren't paid the big money to sit on their asses.

While Caddy and Kyrylo were well-known to the wider world, the other lords had been carefully hidden in Aelfeham House. Yes, they wandered around Lowestoft and even had an occasional foray to London, so there were persistent rumours on the internet of other lords, but the public didn't know much about them other than that they existed. Humans who worked for RumLot Security weren't talking, and the ones who left were too afraid to talk. Intelligence agencies across the world knew a bit more but not much.

Jack and Alizah were spotted when they took the penthouse at the Shard, and Tuân was spotted once or twice in Lowestoft, but there was debate whether he was a lord at all. He didn't have much in the way of ears. Of course, Ratna's parade through Calgary airport and her flight to the UK were in the public record. But Vrt, Conary, Sam, and little Ivana never made the news at all. Even Lester thought there were only seven other known lords in the world when, in fact, there were twelve.

So these two were unknowns to the assembled team. What they saw when the lords entered the room was a lean man of average height and average looks who looked to be about forty-five, neither old nor young, with the modest but pointed ears of a lord and amused, bright blue eyes. His short, curly hair was snow white like all lords, as was his closely trimmed goatee. He wore round spectacles. As one later said, if you put a baseball cap on him to cover his ears and stood behind him in a grocery store queue, you'd never notice him. He was invisible.

She, on the other hand, was anything but average. She was about two inches shorter than the man and achingly beautiful. It was hard to pin her race down, maybe because she had no single ethnic group, but the long, thin neck, uptilted bright green eyes, full red lips, pale, creamy skin, and a delicate bone structure that showed both Slavic and far-eastern influences made unforgettable combination. She had very short white hair and the most magnificent elf ears that soared inches above the top of her head. Lord Vrt, it was agreed by the group later, was every boy's wet dream. She didn't smile but gravely examined them all.

Jameson made the introductions and then invited them to sit at the conference table. Lord Kyrylo would be there in half an hour. In the meantime, they could –

Vrt turned to him and interrupted. "Mr Jameson, could I please ask a question?"

"This is your meeting, Lord Vrt. These are your people. Ask away."

Conary glanced at her and then settled back in his chair, watching.

She turned to five men and women and asked each in turn the same question. "Have you ever talked to anyone outside of the RumLot organisation about your job?" They all said no.

Jameson watched, tense. These were all vetted soldiers and, as far as he knew, the best of the best, but you can't lie to a lord. Something was bothering this one.

Conary knew who it was as soon as she got to him. Number four was lying. Vrt came back to number four, a tall, good-looking man with a shaved head. He looked like he lifted weights and reminded Conary of the old Mr Clean adverts from his childhood in Texas.

"Do you have a girlfriend?" Vrt smiled warmly and, by gods, gave Mr. Clean a knowing wink. Conary thought the guy was going to cream his shorts. He returned the wink with a wide grin to the lord who was finding him so very attractive, and he said no girlfriends; he was married. And Conary knew that he was lying. The man was married and had a piece on the side, and that was all they needed to know. He was a liar, and he was talking to one or both of them.

Vrt smiled at Jameson and asked if there were any breakfast doughnuts still about. Everyone left the table to go fetch coffee from the buffet, and elves ported in with trays of brunch food. Conary went up behind Jameson and simply said, "Number four." When they gathered back at the conference table, there were four operatives seated, not five.

Two men and two women. None of them asked about Mr Clean. Their names were Darnya, Adeele, Maksym, and Vanko.

Kyrylo came in, and they got to work. Kyrylo had his tablet (Conary wondered if he slept with the thing), and secured tablets were handed out to the rest of them, which confused Vrt for a minute, and Conary had to open hers up for her. As soon as he did, an elf popped to her side to do the swiping and tapping for her. Conary leaned over to Kyrylo and in a stage whisper said, "My old lady can't keep up with the new-fangled tech."

Vrt made a face at him. "Baby boy, when you're 3,500 years old, you come to me and we'll see who can keep up."

Conary grinned at her, and they all got down to business.

They learned about the girl whose name was Grace Vaughn, British, and that she was twenty and weighed in at almost four hundred pounds, so they had to consider her disabled. She was going to be hard to move. Intelligence had come in that she was being held at Putin's summer palace in Sochi, which was essentially a nuclear-hardened fortress. Getting into Russia was not going to be a problem; getting into the palace was. Then, once they got in and had her, the problem would become how to get her out if she wasn't ambulatory. At her age, she had no abilities of her own that could help her. There were no elves in the area who could port her.

"How do we know she's even there?"

"Conary, we received a tip-off from Ukrainian intelligence. They intercepted a communication and passed it on to us. You can hear it for yourself." Kyrylo nodded to Jameson.

Jameson played it over the speakers; it was someone speaking in Elvish, and the other person was answering in Russian.

Puzzled, Conary looked at Kyrylo. "How would the Ukrainians know what was said? Do they speak Elvish?"

Kyrylo dryly answered, "We think they do now. Their translation had serious errors, and we're not telling them that, but we think that they have cracked some of it. Enough to know that Lester has someone in Sochi. Ukraine intel think it's elves."

The four operatives looked confused, and Kyrylo had to explain that Elvish was a universal language for lords and elves, and the two tribes, if they concentrated, could understand any human language. Orcs understood Elvish but only rarely spoke it. It took too much brainpower to do the translations, so they answered in their native language. Kyrylo admitted that between English, Ukrainian, Russian, and Elvish, he was always forgetting which language he was speaking. The only time he had to think about a language and concentrate was when he was talking with someone who spoke something he wasn't familiar with, like French or Arabic.

Vrt ignored their conversation on linguistics and instead concentrated on the satellite view of the palace and the schematics that were drawn of what was known of the interior.

"How new are these pictures? Can you see this view all the time? Could I see it now?"

"Those photos are about a week old. We have access to new photos every twelve hours when one of our partners has a bird pass over. Ukrainian intel can ask for shots from their NATO partners. Other people either don't care, are afraid of the Russians, or just don't want to help us for their own reasons."

"I think she must come out. Even at her weight, she can't be inside forever. It's unhealthy, and they don't want her dead – not yet – or they would have already killed her. Orcs don't have any control over themselves. They would have killed her because she is a lord if someone wasn't protecting her. So I'm going to assume Lester is keeping her for a reason."

"So why would he keep her?"

Vrt shrugged. Who knew what went on in that creep's mind? "He either wants to breed her or use her as bait. There must be some profit in it for him."

Kyrylo nodded. "That's what he did with Caddy. He wanted to use her as bait to get me. But he was open about that. My life for hers, he said. This one has been captured in secret."

"Doesn't he have a son now? Didn't I read that?"

"Yes, but he's a baby! She's twenty!"

Vrt laughed. "Kyrylo! You're thinking like a human! What's a twenty-year wait for a lord? And what's to say he can't have two Tsarinas?"

"Lena's baby must be human if it's even Lester's at all. Maybe he's decided to make some lord babies."

"Anyway, she's not dead. She's being held in reserve for something. So they must want her healthy. This terrace is private and can be well-guarded. Look at the maps of the building you have here. It's near this thing labelled elevator. That takes you up and down, right?"

They all examined the maps, and Vrt's ideas were debated and discussed.

"I would like to see pictures every time that bird passes over to see if we can catch sight of her. It's not a literal bird, is it? Is it a helicopter?"

"No, my beautiful anachronism. It's a satellite, a machine, and it is at the edge of space, very high up and spins around the earth like the moon does."

Vrt nodded. Humans and their machines.

"Can we have lunch now? After lunch, I would like us all to go to that big field in the back and do a bit of exercising. Is that possible? And could I have a hog?"

"Why do you want a hog? We have a perfectly nice lunch here on the buffet."

"Not to eat, silly man! You will see. I have an idea." And she left her chair to attack the buffet, and that ended the meeting.

Darnya, Adeele, Maksym, and Vanko

After lunch, they all went outdoors to the PT field, and Darnya, Adeele, Maksym, and Vanko were suited up with helmets and mouthpieces and told that they were going to go one-on-one with a lord to see how they were at fighting. They assumed that it would be Kyrylo, but when he came out in his usual uniform, that put paid to that theory. And then Vrt, Conary, and Jameson walked up. No athletic gear on them either.

Vrt stood in front of them, bowed, and then said, "We'll be doing dangerous work together, and it's important that you have confidence in us as leaders. So what we are going to do today isn't a test for you; Mr Jameson says you have already proven yourselves. Today I will allow you to see what I can do. So we are going to play the coin game."

They all looked blankly at Vrt. No one knew what the coin game was.

She took a gold elf coin and placed it on the ground. Then Conary knew. He remembered what Tuân had said. He grinned and nudged Kyrylo.

"The rules are simple. I have a coin here. We'll start fifteen feet from the coin. You have five minutes to pick it up. If you pick it up, you win, and I owe you another coin. If you don't pick it up in five minutes or I'll kill you. I win the coin, and you or your heirs owe me another coin. Mr Jameson is going to be the time keeper and will call out a one-minute warning towards the end. If I put you in a position where I can kill you –" And she looked over to Conary. "I'm not allowed to really kill them, am I?"

"No, my lovely Angel of Death. That would be wasteful."

"Quite right. If I put you in a position where I can kill you (I really won't kill you. Probably.), Then I win. If you put me in a position where you can kill me, you will win, and I will be very embarrassed. Lord Kyrylo will be the judge. I promise not to use any special lord abilities. This is pure flesh-on-flesh, no-magic fighting."

She smiled brightly. "Who wants to be first?"

Maksym volunteered. He walked to the fifteen-foot mark away from the coin, and Vrt walked to her mark. Jameson called start, and they circled for a few seconds, getting the measure of each other. He made a feint to the left, and Vrt exploded towards him. She wasn't fooled at all and flipped and knocked the legs right out from under him. He found himself eating dirt with the lord sitting on his back and her hands around his throat. If she had had a knife in her hands, he would have been dead.

Kyrylo called it, and Maksym left the ring, choking. That took less than a minute.

Adeele lasted a few more seconds, having learned from watching Maksym, but in her first contact with the lord Vrt literally threw her away from the coin, and she landed so hard that it knocked the wind out of her. While she was considered very fast, she was too slow getting up, and Vrt leapt up and symbolically cut her throat.

Vrt made short work of the other two.

When it was all over, Conary walked over and gave them a pat on the back, but not too hard because they were a bit wobbly.

"You all did very well. That took about 15 minutes. Longer than I expected. Here's a coin for each of you because I bet none of you have any money on you. You can pay me back later."

"Are you okay Vrt?"

"Yes, I'm fine. I think I broke a nail on Adeele, though." She frowned at her hand. It was a nice manicure, too.

"So what's next? You asked for a hog, and there it is."

Vrt perked up, the manicure forgotten. "I was thinking – if Grace was out in the open, I wonder if I could pick her up and set her back down someplace else. I've never tried that before. Never needed to. So, to see if that's possible with something living, I'm going to try with this hog because there's no point in me doing that if I kill her. So I thought a hog is heavy and would have the mass –"

"Oh – you mean like when you gathered that wood?"

"Yeah, but that wasn't really controlled. I'll have to be a lot more delicate. Pick her up and put her down without hurting her."

Kyrylo and Jameson looked at each other, and Kyrylo shrugged. He had no idea what was going on.

So the hog was hauled out by two elves and staked in the middle of the athletics field. Vrt told them all to move back. Far back.

She stood in the field, a still pillar in navy blue, and she started to glow. The operatives looked on, all aches and pains forgotten, entranced at the opportunity to watch a lord at work. Vrt glowed brighter, and the wind picked up. Conary nudged Jameson and pointed to the sky. Above them, a cloud started to swirl. It turned dark, then a thick oily green with a bottom that looked like scales on a fish. Off in the distance was a flash of lightning, then a boom. Without warning, a thread came down from the cloud, and that thread got thicker until it was a whirlwind. Now the wind on the ground was intense, and the humans had to lean into it.

The hog looked nervous. The thin tornado shot down and sucked up the hog. The huge sow flew into the sky, spinning around the vortex, and then, about a quarter mile away, the tornado set the hog down in the middle of a road. Two elves went chasing after it and ported it back to Vrt, who was now bent over, shaking and gasping under a clearing sky, her green glow fading away.

The hog was upset but seemed otherwise fine, which was good because Vrt was fully prepared to butcher it if she had broken its leg or something.

Conary ran up to her, gave her a huge hug and a kiss, and they walked back hand in hand. He was beaming at Kyrylo, delighted with his clever woman.

"Proof of concept, Kyrylo! If we can get Grace onto the terrace, then Vrt can suck her up in one of her tornadoes and fly her to a drop zone. Vrt doesn't even have to get into the palace; she can do that from afar if she can see everything!"

Vrt turned to the four team members. "We'll see you guys tomorrow. Jameson will tell you when. I'm going to have a nap now."

And she stumbled to the nearest elf, who ported her back to House.

Lester

They were coming for him.

Lester knew they were, and he alternated between the depths of sheer panic and towering rage. His mole inside the RumLot Security was exposed, and once exposed was quickly kicked out. But not before he found out that they were planning some sort of "mission," and that two unknown lords were leading it.

Their general, a dour man named Jameson, had hand-picked five human Russian speakers, and that was significant. They were coming into Russia, and the next question was why?

Well, the only reason Lester could think of was to take revenge on him for his failed attempt at getting Kyrylo.

They wouldn't be coming for Lena because she could go back any time, and they knew it. Kyrylo didn't want his daughter back. Now, thinking about it, Kyrylo might want to steal his grandson, and with that thought, Lester ordered extra guards around the baby.

But, in the end, Lester's ego and paranoia only allowed for one target who was worthy of two lords coming into enemy territory, and that was to come to Moscow and eliminate Lester himself.

That the unknown lords existed at all was another reason for panic. Lester had no idea who they were or what their abilities were. From their description, they were different from the lords who were known to the world, and that news was scary in itself. Where the hell were they all coming from? For centuries, Lester had been alone, and in the last two years, lords had begun popping up like nasty little toadstools, waking elves and threatening everything he had worked so hard for.

One of the lords in the meeting was called Connally, and the other was Virginia. As hard as he tried, Lester couldn't remember anyone by those names from back in the bad old days, so these must be newly born. The mole said the man Connally (was that Irish?) was a lump who just sat there. The woman, Virginia, was very pretty and a bit of an airhead. Neither of those descriptions gave Lester comfort. All they had to be was stronger than him, and that wasn't hard. And there were two of them.

He hunkered down in Moscow, alerted his spies in the west, and clamped down on the border next to The Wall, limiting any immigrants to three border crossings and only allowing orcs to enter Russia. No human or lord was going to come in, not if he could help it. Then all he could do was wait.

_____

Vrt

For 3,500 years, Vrt had lived in the deep forests of the taiga. Occasionally, she would see humans as they followed the reindeer and the bison – usually the Sami people, and if she was inclined, she traded with them. To them, she was a spirit of the forest – a dark, terrifying, and mysterious cloaked-and-hooded monster who might save a child or rescue a hunter, then the next day kill another for no reason at all. They didn't understand that she was hunting orcs, and that she left the humans alone because they didn't see the difference.

So she wandered the area with no concern over artificial human borders or the diktats of human kings and queens. In the past three hundred years, humans from Russia and the Nordic countries had entered her world more often to fight for territory, and she watched and learned about their new technologies like cannons and guns. She never took them up, preferring her sword and knives because they were silent and didn't need bullets. But she studied the human weapons, and she knew how they worked. When cars, tanks, and helicopters came to her world, she watched and studied them, too.

No one ever saw her face, and very few ever saw her form; she was a wraith who stood at the edge of humanity and watched.

Now, along with the elves, she was reborn and was part of an army herself. Her primary had given her a mission to rescue a lord girl, and Vrt was fine with that. She had by some wondrous miracle found an Elemental lord who first loved her for who she was, not what she looked like, and every time she thought of

Conary loving her when she was still a monster, she had to stop and steady herself.

But now she was too pretty to be useful. The irony was not lost on her.

Darnya was the bravest, and she mentioned it first.

"Lord Vrt, please don't take this wrong, but it's going to be very difficult to get you into Russia with those ears and that face. We're going to have to find a way to make you a bit uglier. You'll attract attention the minute anyone sees you."

Conary looked at Darnya and then at Vrt, and of course, the woman was correct. Even if they managed to figure out a way to hide her ears, they still had her face to consider, and the minute any man or woman started to study her, they'd notice her eyes. Conary, on the other hand, was forgettable, and if anyone did bother to look at him, they'd see that his ears, while elfish, weren't so big they couldn't be hidden by a ski cap.

The elves were given the task of de-beautifying Vrt. By binding her ears under a clever wig, a few subtle prosthetics, make-up, and lumpy Russian clothes, the lord was transformed. When she walked in for lunch at the RumLot conference room, Jameson didn't recognise her and thought she was a new cleaner. He told her to come back later; they were in a meeting, which caused no end of consternation on his part and hilarity on Conary's.

Vrt twirled for the team. "So can I pass for human now? What do you think?"

Maksym said she needed to walk a bit more like a tired babushka; maybe put a pebble in her shoe. The rest thought she looked properly dowdy, and Conary laughed and laughed.

"You think this is so funny! It took me half an hour to get the face bits on! I don't want to take them off now. I'll keep them on when we go to bed tonight. You can enjoy a new woman."

"No." Conary's quick, flat answer made the others laugh and Vrt grin. "Oh, I don't know, maybe you should get used to this. I'm happy having hair again. I'll keep this wig on." But she sat at the conference table and carefully took off the wig. Up popped her red, pressure-marked ears, and it was clear to all she was relieved to get it off. It hurt. An elf popped in and handed her a little tray, and she carefully removed the prosthetics. And there she was, Vrt again.

They turned back to the task at hand before they had been interrupted by Vrt's fashion show. The satellites had taken a series of pictures of the terrace, and one showed humans on it. They were very good, clear photos, and Jameson was quite pleased. While the Americans had been able to take satellite pics since the turn of the century that were so clear you could read the headlines of a newspaper lying on the ground, they hadn't shared that extraordinary technology with anyone else. Photos from their satellites they sent to Ukrainian intelligence, were always degraded so that they didn't reveal exactly what the Americans could see, which was frustrating. The Brits, however, weren't so reluctant to share, and their newest technology was even better in some ways.

The picture with the humans showed a person on a treadmill and three others sitting around a picnic table eating. Two of the seated people had white coats on. The other, a big person, was in a hoodie. There were five guards on the perimeter.

"Is that Grace on the treadmill? Or do you think she's one of the people eating?" asked Adeele.

"They're both big, but look – there isn't any wheelchair out there. Both walked to the terrace."

"Why wouldn't they walk to the terrace?" Vrt was puzzled and then admitted, "I don't even know what a 400-lb person looks like. And what is a treadmill?"

Darya explained the purpose of a treadmill ("humans and their machines, again!" thought Vrt) and then showed the lord some photos from a Google search, and Vrt understood the mobility problems great weight caused. "I know these are overhead photos from very far away, but these two people don't seem as fat as those internet pictures. Is there a way of figuring out their weight?"

"Does it matter for your tornado?"

"Not really, but it does matter if she has lost so much weight that we don't recognise her. She's a lord, and lords need to eat well or we lose weight very quickly. It matters to her mobility, too. Maybe moving her is not such a worry for us. But if she is the one sitting at the picnic table, maybe getting around is still an issue. Either way, it looks like she walked to the terrace unless there is a wheelchair hidden inside. But I don't see the point of that. They could have wheeled her out and left the chair nearby where it would be kept handy."

"Maybe one of them is a decoy," said Maksym, and that made everyone reconsider the photos. Decoys and body doubles – that could be a problem.

The Russians had made extensive use of body doubles and had for decades. Stalin had had a couple; Putin was rumoured to have up to four. Lester had at least three, and that was proven because photos of him were all over the media. Lords and elves blurred out in photos; Lester's body doubles did not. Even Lena had at least six, although only Lester and Lena knew why she needed so many.

A body double for Grace would be concerning but not surprising. The team didn't have any current photos of her; for a modern woman, she was as under the radar as it was possible to be. She hated photos of herself, and aside from a few mandatory school photos taken as a child, there was no visual record of her. They had no idea what she looked like as an adult.

They discussed logistics and wargamed scenarios, and a plan began to come together.

___

Grace

Grace knew in her heart that Wendell would come for her. She wasn't surprised that it would take a while because she knew it would be a very risky thing to rescue her, but she had no doubt he would. He would pick his time, and he would succeed; she was sure he always did.

Unknown to Wendell, or anyone else for that matter, Grace had convinced herself that after the twirl around the dance floor and a half hour conversation with the handsome Ranger that he was her white knight and that she was in love with him. He had literally swept her off her feet at the Prom, and she knew that he was the one behind the RumLot people calling up her mum. If her mum weren't such a shit, she would be there now, going to the RumLot school and seeing Wendell every day.

Wendell didn't love her; Grace wasn't that crazy. But he was kind and brave, and if they had some time together, that might be enough. LeeAnne was pretty, and Grace liked LeeAnne because she wasn't rude to her, but LeeAnne could find someone else.

When the trawler met up with the Russian yacht, Grace was transferred onto it, a horrible, painful operation in itself. They had to winch her up out of the hold, and she was sure she was going to die. The vicious, purple-eyed men who handled her seemed to take a gleeful delight in making the move as painful as possible.

She was filthy, terrified, and almost insane with hunger, but once aboard the yacht, everything changed. To her great surprise, her new captors were very kind to her. They cleaned her up, spoke softly, comforted her, and told her she was being rescued from the demons. They seemed to feel sorry for her. None of them stank or had purple eyes.

She was put in the main cabin of the massive private yacht and fed by a top chef who plied her with healthy meals full of vegetables and protein; she wasn't starving any more. A dietician measured and recorded everything that went in her mouth, and with the first week of starvation and then the introduction of healthy food, she lost at least a stone. She could feel it almost immediately.

When the yacht finally reached its berth in Sochi, she was able to walk off, and she was driven in the back of a van to a palace. Her handlers told her this palace was Revered President Putin's personal home, and she was an honoured member of his household now.

She had people around her who were cheerful and kind, and they said she could go anywhere she wanted when she was fit enough to walk. They were lying about that, but their kindness was true. They gave her a TV set hooked up to an international satellite, and she could watch *EastEnders* and new movies on it. She was not allowed the internet or a phone "for security reasons," and she didn't question it since she knew what the security reasons were. They didn't want her to contact Wendell or anyone else and tell them where she was. She was too precious, they said, and the demons would try to steal her back. But they never told her why.

They never mentioned her mother, and Grace never asked. She was gone, gone for good, and not a part of this new, disorienting life. And Wendy certainly wasn't missed.

To keep her busy, she was assigned private tutors and took Russian language lessons, Russian history, and Russian Orthodox religious lessons. For exercise, Russian folk dancing. They said when she was a bit more limber, they had Russian ballet instructors waiting.

One day, everyone was upset and running around. Tsar Lester was coming to meet Grace and to inspect her arrangements. When he came, he was outwardly very sympathetic – but you can't lie to a lord, and after an initial flush of good feeling, Grace knew the truth. Grace was good at hearing lies – she always had been. When you've been made fun of and teased all your life, not to mention living with a sociopathic, manipulative mother, you can hear a lie before it's even spoken.

Tsar Lester was disgusted with her. She could see the revulsion in his eyes, and she paid close attention to what he said. He was going to take care of her (true), and she could have anything she wanted (false), and one day, when she was ready, she would move to Moscow (false). He told her she was precious to him (true), but that the evil elves and demon lords (false) would kill her (false), and so she had to stay in Russia to live (very false).

After weighing the truth and the lies, she knew what she had to do. She didn't know why they all kept saying she was precious to them, but there had to be something she didn't know. Whatever it was, she had value, and Lester and the Russians didn't want her to go to the elves. And Wendell was with the elves. Therefore, if it meant escaping back to the West to be with Wendell, then that's what she would do. Wendell was going to come for her. The elves and lords would send him, and he was her own *Mission Impossible* hero, her personal Ethan Hunt.

So she would lose weight not only to be able to escape back to the west but to be attractive to her Wendell. She had to outshine LeeAnne, which was going to be hard, but now she had a chance. These Russians were happy to help her get fit, and they would make her as beautiful as they could. She would take their shots of appetite suppressant and walk for hours on the hated treadmill to get fit for her escape. Wendell would come, she knew it in her heart. And she would be ready.

Vrt

Vrt sat at the bottom of the bed and watched Conary sleep. He was her own bonded man, and she loved him more every day, but that wasn't what she was thinking about now. What she was doing was watching him fade in and out of existence as he slept. He had only recently discovered that his ability was to go invisible, and in that, he was like a toddler learning to walk – staggering around gleefully with his newfound talent, trying to stretch and falling, and failing more often than not, but not giving up.

He was an Elemental. She had known that the first day she saw him step off that helicopter, but he was young, only in his mid-seventies, and he hadn't come into his full powers yet. He wasn't anywhere near what he would become.

When Vrt was a child, she knew both of her parents were Elementals, and because they were of high rank and on the council directly under Gaia, she was well acquainted with the Elemental breed. Different lords of all abilities visited her parents' home almost every day, so she met a wide variety of lords and was familiar with their unique talents.. As she grew up and the men started sniffing around her, they would show off their prowess, strutting around like peacocks spreading their tails to impress the peahens.

Elementals were incredibly rare – only Realm Lords were rarer – and even Vrt seldom met one. Elementals were just as described – lords of huge power who could control the basic elemental forces of nature and physics. They could shape change, and their power was not limited to their person but could be cast.

Vrt was not an Elemental. She had never tried to shape change and didn't think she had it in her. She was sure that if she did, she couldn't make it back by herself, and then she'd be stuck in that form like House and Jack. She could manipulate and shape the wind, but only to a certain extent. For instance, she could make a single F5 tornado, but she couldn't make a hurricane. She could move objects and bring them to her, but not reshape them like Ratna or Sam could.

Her parents, of course, knew very early on that she wasn't going to be an Elemental, but that meant nothing to them. They loved her for who she was. They were disappointed that their gorgeous daughter bonded at such an embarrassingly young age to handsome, cheeky, pale-eyed Prana, who had below-average abilities and certainly wasn't an Elemental.

Her father said that he was a good lad but a lightweight pretty boy who couldn't protect his family if need be. To Vrt, that was just ridiculous. Why on earth would Prana ever need to protect Vrt from anything? What bad thing would ever happen to them?

Conary could absorb, emit, and bend light itself. It was an incredibly powerful and subtle talent. He had learnt he could make himself invisible by bending light away from his body. It was so much a part of him now that he did it in his sleep and occasionally forgot that people couldn't see him. Once he started kissing Vrt in the middle of the day, it made her laugh so hard to have this invisible man mounting her. She told him that while invisibility was good for a giggle, she much preferred to see her lover during the act because otherwise she had no idea where his parts were.

An Elemental was usually very slow to develop, and they could take centuries to completely come into their own. Conary didn't have centuries. This was still a very, very dangerous world for lords and elves, and if Lord Cadence was correct about the future, as the orcs coalesced into a fighting force, it would even get more dangerous.

By all the stars in the sky, Vrt was not going to lose this man to the orcs. Not like she lost her first one.

House rang his breakfast bell, and Vrt shook her man awake. They had things to do today. They needed to practise and plan, and she wasn't going to let him laze the day away.

Conary

What she was asking him to do was not possible, but Vrt was absolutely sure he could do it. The only reason he tried was because she insisted. To be fair, just some months ago, he didn't think he could become invisible at will, and now it was easy. Maybe she knew something he didn't.

She wanted him to "cast". What she was asking was that he turn something else invisible, not himself. Instead of thinking of himself as being invisible, he was to think of another object as being invisible, and she had placed a simple teacup on the table to practise with. Make it invisible, she said.

He tried. He tried concentrating on that damn teacup until beads of sweat popped up on his forehead. It was as bad as the feather exercise. Nothing happened.

Move it, she said. She demonstrated, and the teacup moved about a foot. Well, he couldn't do that either. If he couldn't make a feather move, how was he going to move something as heavy as a teacup?

It was starting to make him irritable. He didn't like failing in front of Vrt, and here she had moved the damned cup like it was nothing. It was embarrassing.

She leaned over and whispered in his ear, her lips barely touching and sending a shiver down his back. "If you move the cup, I'll do something extra special for you –"

And he had to laugh. "Vrt, everything you do is extra special. You'll have to do better than that."

"Well, that didn't work. All right. Then try this. Don't think "cup," a solid thing made of clay. Think about the surface, how the light shines on the cup, how it bounces off –" And her voice became low and even. " – Look at how the light defines and makes the cup; look at how it surrounds and wraps the cup like –"

He stared at the cup, and he stopped seeing the cup, but instead saw the light on the cup.

And then, suddenly, he could feel it. He could feel the light on the cup, like pins and needles when his arm fell asleep, but movable, alterable, a substance he could push and pull. Something he could wipe away like condensation on a mirror. Light particles that felt as solid as sand.

Vrt watched the cup slowly disappear. It faded, it flickered, and then it was gone. Conary's incandescent eyes were bright points of blue, and sweat was dripping down his glowing forehead and off his nose. He was breathing hard, and a vein was pounding on his forehead.

"Conary, bring the cup back."

Nothing happened. The cup was still gone.

"Conary, let the cup go."

And then there was a snap, and it re-emerged on the table. Conary fell back in the chair, gasping for air. He turned and looked at her, dazed.

Vrt grabbed a kitchen towel and wiped the sweat from her ever-so-talented man. He grinned at her.

"So that extra special –"

"*Now?*"

"No, maybe not. Later. I think I need to have a little rest now."

Kyrylo

Estonian intelligence sent an interesting observation to select partners, one of which was the Elf Nation. An agent in Moscow was reporting increased military presence around the Tsar's Novo-Ogaryovo Palace. Guards around the Tsar's baby and family were substantially increased. While the Russians had always boasted about an "iron dome" of air defence, it looked like they were truly setting one up.

Kyrylo read the message and called a quick meeting with his own intel guys.

"It looks to me that Lester thinks *someone* is going to go after him in Moscow. Do we see the equivalent change in preparedness in Sochi?"

Everyone on the intel team shook their heads. No.

"So, someone is making Lester nervous. Could it be us? Could he have heard that we are doing something, but he doesn't know what and thinks we are aiming for him? Has anyone gotten a hint of internal issues? Some other operation aimed at Moscow?"

Nothing.

Kyrylo smiled. "Let's keep looking to see what's making him nervous. In the meantime, a little disinformation that the Elf Nation is talking a lot about Moscow might be good. Don't overdo it. It would be good to pin his attention up there for the next couple of weeks."

And the meeting adjourned.

The Team

The plan was agreed on, and now it was just a matter of execution.

The plan was simple in theory but devilishly complicated in execution, and the more complicated a plan, the more likely it was to fail. There were a lot of failure points in this plan.

In Russia, north of the old Kursk bridge, was an area of the Azov Sea, the Priazovsky State Nature Reserve, that RumLot Security had determined was light on defences and radar. The team would land there. A van would be waiting for them, and Maksym and Darnya would be posing as two vegetable vendors with their friends returning from a lovely weekend fishing holiday. Everyone would be returning to their home in Sochi, two hundred miles away. Once in Sochi, they would drive to a safe house that was once the home of two real vegetable vendors who had developed a little business delivering strawberries and melons to the kitchens of various oligarchs – and Putin's Palace. On one of their regular runs, they would try to insert an invisible Conary into the palace. He would look for any weak spots, try to contact Grace, and determine the best way to get her to the terrace. Vrt could pick her up, drop her back at the van, and then the invisible Conary and the entire party would leave back the way they came – if they could. There were various pickup points planned.

Anyway, that was the plan. None of them thought it would really work out that way.

Even before they started, they lost a team member. They started with five and lost Mr. Clean in the first hour of the first day. Then, three days before they were set to go, Vanko ran down the stairs of his house, stepped on a Lego left there by his boy, and tumbled down the last step, twisting his knee so badly that even with elf therapy, he was ordered by Dr Mandy to stay off it for a month.

That left Darnya, Adeele, and Maksym. All a frustrated Vanko could do was help with planning and sit in the Ukrainian control room when the operation started.

Hùng

Nguyen Hùng was born in 1985 and was married with four children. As the oldest boy in his family, he had had an uneventful, poor childhood, and after a lot of effort and probably a few bribes on his father's part, he was given a job working in the medical records department of their local hospital. Thirty years later, he was still in the same job at the same desk. So when he started spitting up blood and getting breathless, it was a quick visit two floors up to the doctor's offices, and they told him what he suspected. Those unfiltered Vietnamese cigarettes he had smoked since he was thirteen had come back to claim a lung. It was cancer.

The doctors said that they didn't have a guaranteed cure, but they could remove the lung, pump him with chemo, and pray. Also, he should really think about quitting smoking.

The other alternative was better, but it would be mind-bogglingly expensive. The French did have a cure, and if he went to the big hospital in Danang, he could buy the French gene therapies and be treated with the most modern drugs. He should still quit smoking.

So to Hùng and his doctors, his choice was stark. Bankrupt his family or die a slow and painful death in about five years.

Hùng had another choice that the doctors didn't know about.

His family name was Nguyen, just like a couple of million or so other Vietnamese. Like his brother and sister, he had long suspected that his father, a white American, was not a Nguyen at all. But hey, having a Vietnamese name avoided a lot of problems, and his dad was a family secret they just didn't talk about in public. No one knew the Old Man's real surname, and frankly, they didn't want to know. Anyway, Nguyen was his mother's family name, so there was a connection.

After he grew up and married, he didn't see the Old Man very often – only at New Year's and about once or twice the rest of the year and only at family gatherings when someone got married or had a baby. Hùng lived in another town, and it was an inconvenient distance from his sister Sen's house, and Hùng was busy with his own life. From all appearances, the Old Man was happy and healthy and living a quiet life with Sen.

If the kids had an emergency, the Old Man would disappear for a week or so and then come and pay whatever needed to be paid to get them through tough times. They never asked where the money came from, and all of the kids felt a deep guilt for accepting any help. It felt like blood money, and they were all getting older. It certainly felt wrong to send out a man in his sixties and seventies to do God knows what to rescue his grown kids.

Then something changed. The Old Man and Sen's oldest son, Tuân, disappeared and reappeared in London, of all places. They both called up and said that Tuân had a benefactor sending him through school and that they would call Sen once a month; otherwise, not to worry.

Now, who in the hell the Old Man knew in the UK who would pay the expensive school fees for an unknown boy from the Vietnamese hinterlands was a mystery, but given their experiences growing up with their father, they didn't talk about it except to each other. Conary's kids clamped down and said nothing to anyone, including their own children and spouses. The Old Man must be back in the Mafia again.

Then Mr. Won appeared and said that Conary was busy and if anything came up, to call him. Mr Won was a very wealthy Chinese lawyer with offices in several major cities, including Danang. Mr Won was so high up the chain that you had to make an appointment with his secretary just to get an appointment to see him. Yet the Old Man's children all had a card with a private phone number and direct access to him. If they needed anything, they were to let him know right away.

But they didn't need him. Nice things happened. Long, the second boy, had a tiny import/export business and suddenly was awarded some very good contracts, and no one asked for bribes. Sen's husband found a very good job. Mysterious bursaries paid for the grandkid's school expenses. They were lucky with the lottery. None of this was life-changing, but suddenly they were comfortable.

Then Long got a bit greedy one day and did the unforgivable. He called Mr Won and asked for something he didn't need. His wife begged for an expensive new car even though his old one was perfectly serviceable, so he called up Mr Won, who politely said that was not possible. The next day, Sen got a call from a very irritated Tuân, who told her in no uncertain terms that they would get everything they needed but no more. And then he said something that put a chill down her back. "Mom, we can't protect you from here. We can't protect the little kids. If you suddenly stand out as having money and people start looking and asking questions, the kids will be at risk of kidnapping. You'll put me and the Old Man in danger, too. We'll make it up to you one day, but until then, remember – the nail that pops up proud is the first to get hit. You've told me that many times." She promised to rein in Long and not "stand proud".

Hùng and Sen came down very hard on Long, and Long told his wife no, they couldn't afford a new car now, and that ended that. But lessons were learned.

When Hùng got his diagnosis, he consulted for a long time with Sen and Long, and both agreed that Hùng should talk to Mr Won. If a diagnosis of lung cancer wasn't an emergency, they didn't know what was. If the Old Man couldn't come up with all that money by himself, then they would see what they could do together as a family.

Mr Won didn't hesitate. He told Hùng they would take care of everything, and the next day he was called by a very exclusive cancer specialist in Danang and set up with appointments, transportation, and everything the Nguyens could want. The only thing they had to do was not to gossip about the treatment, which was to be expected.

The Old Man had come through once again.

Hùng was profoundly grateful for the cancer treatment. It was a new gene therapy treatment where they custom-manufactured a medicine based on his own immune system. That wondrous elixir was drip-fed into him, and his own body then worked to kill the cancer.

The Old Man didn't call him to see how he was doing, but young Tuân did. Tuân refused to be drawn out regarding what the Old Man was doing other than to say he was "busy," and that hurt Hùng a bit. It was not right that one of his nephews knew more about his father than he did, and one day he said so to Tuân. The boy wasn't a kid anymore; he was a man and wouldn't be badgered by his uncle, but he repeated, yet again, that the Old Man was busy and working where he couldn't be contacted easily. As soon as the Old Man could, he would contact Hùng. Tuân apologised for saying so to his uncle, but Hùng would just have to wait.

The therapy was completely painless, and all Hùng had to do was visit the doctor once a week for a couple of months to monitor its effectiveness. He and his wife, Mai, were picked up on doctor day and driven to Danang and dropped off at the clinic. When it was all done, they were treated to a nice lunch and driven back home. The doctor's visits became a bit of a holiday outing for them – a sort of medicalised date night.

One day, as they were killing time waiting for the car to come pick them up, Mai mentioned that it would be nice to take a real holiday when his treatment was done. They had a bit of extra money and, at that moment, happened to be walking by a travel agency. On a whim, feeling healthy and prosperous, they stopped in and looked at the package tours on offer. Of course, they were all very expensive. The salesman was very insistent, very aggressive, and just to gracefully get out of the office, Hùng said they would come back later; his passport wasn't up to date anyway.

Mai looked at him, surprised. "I didn't know you even had a passport!"

"I'm very sure I do. Dad always kept his kids' passports up to date. Just in case –" Then he snapped his mouth shut.

The salesman leapt onto Hùng's words. "Oh, I can look that up for you. No problem. Just give me your name, birthdate, and your government SI number. The computer will find it, and I'll print you a copy so you can get it renewed."

Mai looked at him and raised an eyebrow, and Hùng couldn't see any harm in it, so he gave the salesman his details and let the computer do its magic.

A few minutes later, he walked out with a copy of his old passport printed on a sheet of paper, and as they walked down the street, Mai laughed at the old photo of seventeen-year-old Hùng.

Then she stopped. "Hùng, look at your family name."

Aeldor Hùng.

It was disconcerting. He was plain-vanilla Nugyen Hùng, and now he had this new, foreign family name that he had never heard before. Something else to ask the Old Man and probably get no answer to.

Mai, on the other hand, knew exactly who also had the name Aeldor, and she dragged Hùng to the nearest newsstand. After a few minutes, she came out with a sack of women's celebrity magazines. They walked on to their favourite restaurant and sat down to have lunch while Mai insisted on showing him the fashion sections, the ones where royalty and celebrities from different countries were shown walking in and out of galas and balls. And there were some old photos of Lord Cadence, and since they were very fuzzy, drawings of her dresses. Lord Cadence Aeldor, President of the Elf Nation, but known to the press as the Queen of the Fairies.

Mai thought it was very funny that her husband had the same family name as the Fairy Queen and had a good laugh until she looked up and saw the expression on her husband's face. She stopped laughing.

Hùng was looking at the magazine as if he had seen a ghost, and maybe, in a way, he had.

"My grandmother's name was Cadence," he whispered.

Hùng

Cadence, Kyrylo, Conary, and Tuân all knew this day would come. Even Mr Won knew. That's why he had been hired, and that's why he made the big money.

When Hùng called up the number on his business card and shakily asked Mr Won if his employer was really Lord Cadence Aeldor and not his father Conary, Mr Won went very quiet. As Hùng waited during the agonising pause for his answer, the lawyer was busy sending out a WhatsApp to his employees on the Aeldor emergency team. As Mr Won spoke, people were moving.

"Mr Nugyen, I have been hired by the Elf Nation to take care of Lord Conary Aeldor's family. There are two things I want you to do. One is to not tell anyone – not a soul – until you have had time to absorb what I have to tell you. It is of the utmost importance for the safety of you and your family."

He paused to let that sink in.

"The second thing is that I have a list of family members to talk to, and we need to talk to all of them here in my office. All of you together. It would be helpful if you could call them and let them know that the cars that are being sent for them now are okay to use. They will be upset and scared, and we don't want this to be any more disturbing than it needs to be. Tell them they have a message from their father and grandfather. Will you help me do this?"

Hùng froze into a full-blown panic attack, and Mai grabbed the phone. "Give me the list, Mr Won, and we'll call them. We're still here in Danang. Would it be better if we came to your office now?"

Half an hour later, Hùng and Mai were sitting in a very, very classy conference room drinking strong Vietnamese coffee with the urbane Mr Won and making phone calls. They called everyone in Conary's children, their spouses, and grandchildren who were over the age of fourteen.

It took a while to snatch the fifteen adults and teens from various workplaces, schools, homes, and even from the middle of a busy market and get them packed into chauffeured limos for the two-hour drive to Danang. Children had to be watched, and parents had to trust the very scary bodyguards and nannies who suddenly showed up on doorsteps to do the babysitting. But they all trusted Hùng and Mai, and most of all, they had faith that the Old Man would take care of them.

They hoped.

One by one, they were escorted into the conference room, confused, scared, intimidated, upset, and a couple were really angry at being essentially shanghaied in the middle of their normal day for some crazy shit the Old Man was involved in.

When all fifteen were there, Mr Won asked them to sit and listen to him and to keep an open mind. Their lives were all about to change drastically.

He explained that their grandfather, the Old Man, was Lord Conary of the Elf Nation. He was not a human, but hadn't known about that until he showed up in London with his grandson Tuân. He hadn't known his mother was Lord Cadence Aeldor until he saw her on television. When he discovered who his mother was, he kept it to himself, but when Tuân was being bullied, Conary decided to contact his mother. Maybe she would forgive him for his past and find Tuân a good school. It turned out that she not only welcomed him back with open arms, but she also recognised he was a lord, and so was Tuân. Ever since that day, they had been working and learning with the elves, working for the betterment of everyone, humans and elves, and learning what it was to be a lord.

Here, Mr Won was forced to stop because Sen had fainted. Her father and her eldest son were not humans but magical creatures, and she couldn't process it.

After some water for Sen and a visit by a nurse, Mr Won continued. "Lord Conary, as some of you suspected, had some unsavoury associates in the past. If those associates found out that he is a Lord, there isn't much they can do to him. He now has great power and wealth at his disposal. But they *could* kidnap or harm one of his family members and use that leverage for all sorts of bad things. Mostly to try to force him to do their bidding."

He explained that the Elf Nation didn't have a foothold in Vietnam or anywhere in Asia. So until they did, their choice was either to put Lord Conary's family in a gilded cage and isolate them with full bodyguards and protection, or to let them live normal lives with their friends and families and watch and protect them from afar. Lord Cadence decided to do the latter and to let the humans in her family have as normal a life as long as they could until they could not.

Now, with Hùng's phone call, the secret was out.

And here Mr Won stopped and waited. There was silence, then an explosion of questions, and he tried to answer them all.

In the end, Conary's family had three choices. Go on as normal, but knowing they were now bait for every thug, religious fanatic, or government that wanted to use them for their own purposes to try to influence the lords. Mr Won emphasised that the Elf Nation would not pay ransom or try to rescue them if this was their choice. Doing so would encourage more bad actors and put everyone at more risk.

The next option was to move to a protected, guarded compound in Vietnam that was already set up for them. They would be safe but isolated. The last option was to move the whole family to someplace where elves were living, and that was Europe. Eventually, there would be more places they could choose to live, but no one knew how long that would take. But as long as they stayed in Elf Nation reach, they should be able to live normal, human lives in relative peace. They could change their minds at any time, but if they chose to go off on their own, it would be at their own risk.

They were given twenty-four hours to decide what they wanted to do. Everyone was put in a top hotel, told not to go wandering by themselves without a guard, and given space to think. The next day, they would have a conference call with Lord Tuân, Lord Kyrylo, and Lord Cadence Aeldor, their grandmother and great-grandmother. The Queen of the Fairies.

The next morning, an exhausted, emotionally drained group returned to the conference room. What do you do when your world is upended and you have to make such a decision? No, they were not destitute refugees fleeing a war, but this was still traumatic.

Some wanted to go to England. Tuân's family all opted to go to England and start a new life there. They could see Tuân and the Old Man, whom they loved, and the kids would be safe and have their futures secured. Hùng and Mai were split. She wanted to go to England because it would be better for their children, but he wanted to stay in Vietnam and opted for the compound. When it was explained that they could go to the compound for as long as they liked and visit England later to see if they liked it, and travel back and forth, Mai agreed to try the compound first.

Long, his wife, and family had no doubts. Luxury compound it was. They were looking forward to it.

The grandchild generation all wanted to go to England. No one wanted to go back to their old life.

They had a conference call with the lords, and the world changed for all of them.

Conary, Vrt, Maksym, Adeele, and Darnya

While Conary's children and grandchildren were upending their lives in Vietnam, he, Vrt, and the team were out in the middle of a foggy night riding a RIB to a deserted beach to the nature reserve on the Azov Sea in Russia.

They unloaded backpacks and the old fishing tackle that were props for their cover story, and Vrt and Adeele sat down on the damp sand to wait. Darnya and Maksym walked over the dunes while Conary became invisible and trailed them, looking for ambushes or anything that shouldn't be there.

A few minutes later, they returned with two very frightened Russians carrying a baby and a backpack. The Russians boarded the RIB and left with the insertion crew, and Vrt watched as they silently disappeared into the mist.

Darnya jingled some keys and smiled, her white teeth gleaming in the dark, and she spoke in Russian. "We are now the proud owners of a broken-down vegetable van and a house in Sochi. If the house is twice as good as the van, it will be a hovel." Maksym snorted and picked up a bag of gear. "They said the tank was full. I doubt it."

The van did have a full tank of gas, but not much more. It also had some old military sleeping bags and an ice chest full of fish. They slept on the ground for a few hours like good tourists and got up at dawn to pack up and leave with Adeele driving and Maksym riding shotgun. The rest of them rattled around in the back for the three-hour drive to Sochi.

"Do you know, this is the first time I've ever been in a car! Are they all this uncomfortable?" Vrt sat crossed-legged in the back of the van, her teeth rattling from the vibrations. It was going to be a long trip.

Darnya assured Vrt that she usually sat in seats in proper cars, and sitting on the cargo floor of a van with bad shocks was not how she preferred to travel. Conary sprawled out on the bags and took a nap. It turned out he could sleep anywhere, anytime, a skill he perfected in the bad old days when he spent enough time in the holds of cargo ships and in the back of lorries to last a couple of human lifetimes.

The house was as pitiful as the van. While it was neat and clean, it was tiny and hadn't been updated since it was built as a worker's hut back in the '60s. There was an outhouse in the back and then a row of three PVC greenhouses filled with strawberries and other soft fruits. On the kitchen table was a ledger of deliveries, the amounts each customer ordered, and detailed instructions on how to get through the gates of the guarded estates of the fruit sellers' customers. The Russian couple who escaped to Ukraine on the RIB had tried to make a fair trade as their part of the bargain.

Darnya went out to the greenhouses to check them out and to water any plants that needed it. In the meantime, Adeele swept the house looking for bugs just in case the Russian couple was compromised, and when she declared the place clean, the rest of the team relaxed and studied the ledger. They would make their first delivery tomorrow.

Conary, Vrt, Maksym, Adeele, and Darnya

Very early in the next morning, Darnya and Vrt filled punnets of strawberries and raspberries for the day's orders while Maksym and Adeele worked on the van. Conary cooked up the fish and some potatoes for breakfast. Then they piled in the van and made their deliveries.

They only had four deliveries to make to the oligarchs' summer houses, if you could call such huge palaces by that humble name. To try out their disguises and the instructions they were given, they went to the smallest one first, and to the relief of everyone, it went smoothly. The gate code was correct, the van obviously looked okay to the cameras, and a voice told them to proceed. When they were halfway up the very long driveway to the house, an armed guard stopped them and gave a cursory glance at the van, spoke to someone on his body cam, and waved them through.

The old van rattled and fumed up to the kitchen service entrance, and that was when they met their first hurdle. The reek of orcs was overwhelming. Darnya could see the eyes of the two lords glowing in the gloom of the van, and she hissed, "Eyes down!" Conary disappeared, and Vrt put on her sunglasses and held her breath and made sure the wind didn't take the lord's scent to the kitchen. But other than that, there were no problems. Adeele chatted cheerfully with the kitchen staff, and Maksym brought out the ordered fruit, got a scrawl on the receipt, and off they went. No one asked about the old fruit farmers, and no one cared. Fresh, organic, hand-picked fruit was ordered, fruit was delivered, and the kitchen staff didn't give a flying flip who did it.

The next house was equally uneventful, with exactly the same careless entry procedure. It was as if the guards had all graduated from the same shambolic Institute of Orc (In)Security. They had a key code for the gate, and the guards, human or orc, were too lazy to go all the way up the massive driveways, so they met them far enough away from the house that they were out of sight and then just waved them through. Again, the service entries and yards reeked of orc, and this time Vrt and Conary prepared themselves without being reminded by Darnya.

The last stop was the Palace. As they approached the gate at the service entrance, tension inside the van ramped up considerably. Vrt crouched, and Conary could see her hand down at her side near her hidden elf knife. This was, after all, the full-time retirement home of the great Putin as well as the dormitory of

Tsar Lester's precious guest. The team expected security to be very tight even for humble fruit merchants.

The key code worked, and just like with the others, a voice told them to proceed, and the gate opened. Darnya turned on a video camera system hidden in the patches and grill of the old van. They drove up the drive and were met just out of sight of the house – only this time, there were three human guards. Conary and Vrt tensed. Surely this time, one would check the back of the van, and then they'd have to explain themselves. Darnya already had a well-rehearsed story ready. Hopefully, the guards would buy it.

But no. One of the guards took two seconds to check out the driver and helper, and the other two took the opportunity to have a smoke break. Maksym said later that from the number of cigarette butts on the ground, they smoked every time someone came up. They probably weren't allowed to smoke on duty, but hidden from the house? That was fine. The vendors who drove up the service road wouldn't snitch, not if they wanted to keep their illustrious customer.

The kitchen service door and yard were different, too. There were no Orcs. Nothing. Not even a lingering odour or hint of orc. Adeele chatted even longer this time with the cook as she carefully and slowly wrote down tomorrow's order, and Maksym took his time getting the fruit out and carrying it to the kitchen. He winked at the helper and said it was too heavy for such a pretty woman to haul in, and she giggled and walked ahead of the cute new delivery guy. She opened the door using an old-fashioned swipe card that was part of her ID lanyard. They didn't linger too long, but long enough for Darnya to take some more video and to download micro-body cam footage from Maksym and Adeele. Before they even left the grounds, all of the video and sound were sent by a secure satellite signal back to RumLot HQ for analysis.

They had an order tomorrow for blueberries. Business was good!

It was only ten when they got back to the house, and the team was jubilant with their results. They had penetrated every compound, and no one had so much as blinked. They had good footage of the Palace to look at and discuss.

While they waited for the RumLot intel team to come back with their analysis, Adeele and Darnya went to the area's largest grocery store, a western-style Perekrestok, to shop for food (lords ate a lot!). They bought every fresh blueberry they could get their hands on, while back at the house, the other three watered the strawberries, checked the camera traps for intruders, prepared for the next day's deliveries, and took their turns in the cold water shower.

Later that day, RumLot intel pointed out hidden cameras and a laser trip wire system that was turned off but could still be active at night. There were cameras inside the kitchen, and they were set up the same way, so it appeared that when the Palace was built, the security contractor used the same installation style to hide the cameras. Once you knew what to look for, they were easy to spot. Two of them were broken.

Tomorrow, they'd deliver their blueberries, and Conary would try to slip into the palace and do a recon. Everyone was cheerful and pleased with their progress, except Vrt, who was quiet.

Morning came, and yesterday's routine was repeated. Fruit from the PVC tunnels was gathered, the commercial blueberries repackaged as certified organic, the trucks loaded, and the ragged fruit sellers in their broken-down truck made their rounds.

At the Palace, they were waved in by the same three guards; only two different ones took the smoke break. It appeared that they took turns. At the kitchen service entrance, Maksym jumped out to carry the fruit, but this time he was at the rear door of the truck a few seconds longer while he found a better tray of blueberries for the assistant cook. She almost walked around to the rear of the truck, but at the last minute, Maksym shut the door and turned with his boxes, a wide smile on his face. "Pretty blueberries for the pretty woman!" he boomed, and she blushed and giggled again. He had made a friend.

Adeele chatted with a guard and the head cook, who used the delivery as an excuse to take a break.

The assistant swiped her card, and Maksym propped open the door to the kitchen for her. She went in first, then he took a second to steady the boxes before he stepped in. The door shut silently behind him.

Darnya and Vrt watched all this from the cameras hidden in the front of the van. Darnya looked at Vrt, but she didn't say anything. Vrt glanced back at the woman and nodded. He was in. She had seen a leaf blow in front of the door, but the wrong way. Something had passed by, and the slight wind of its passing had disturbed the leaf.

When Maksym returned, he and Adeele boarded the van, and with a cheery wave, they turned around and left.

Conary

The kitchen was huge – large enough for the preparation of massive banquets – but only one corner was used now. There were only two real inhabitants of the Palace, and neither threw balls or grand dinners. The head chef only had to cook for the staff, and they ate whatever he decided to make. Some days he felt inspired and cooked meals worthy of any gourmand, but most days it was hamburgers and fries.

For Putin, he made Russian slop. The man had been born low class, and, while he had made a show when he was on the way up of having taste and education, in reality, he was a prole, and he liked prole food. Now that he was in his dotage, he liked prole baby food. He loved salo, which was essentially bacon fat on toast, and there was only so much a Michelin-trained chef could do with bacon fat on toast. Some days he cut the toast in circles, other days in diamonds.

The demon girl, now that was a challenge the cook enjoyed. She ate whatever he sent down, and she was always complimentary. When she saw him, to the chef's great surprise, she thanked him for his efforts, which were miles more than anyone else who walked these halls did. She was a prole, too, but a classy one.

She was only allowed twelve hundred calories a day, and the chef tried very hard to make healthy, tasty food for her, and it was satisfying to see the weight melt off her. He had no idea about the high calorie intake of lords, so he assumed that the only reason she was losing weight so quickly was because of his cooking and the treadmill. Diet and exercise that was the key. According to the dietitian, the demon was losing about seven hundred grams a day, which was extreme.

The chef sat in his office thinking of menus for the demon girl, and suddenly he remembered that he had forgotten to see if he was getting low on Putin's salo. He dashed to the walk-in cooler to check.

On his desk, where he left it next to his coffee cup, was his lanyard with his key entry swipe card. When he returned, it wasn't there, but he didn't miss it until the next day when he came into work and couldn't find it.

Conary found the door to the kitchen service hall and silently walked down to the elevator. He would prefer to take the stairs and not use the chef's lanyard, but it depended on how the security system designers had set up access control. Sometimes they'd install swipes on the elevators, and sometimes on the fire doors to each floor's stairwell. It was hard to tell. He also didn't know if the swipe card registered *who* was swiping. It *should*, but this security system seemed to be buckling under extreme maintenance issues. He saw broken locks, a couple of doors propped open so people didn't have to swipe, and there were hanging wires where Conary suspected cameras were moved to replace unusable equipment located in more critical areas.

The palace's service areas were worn and tatty around the edges, and the decor there was frozen in 1990 when the place had been built. But now there weren't many people using the place, and the only sound was the buzz of ancient fluorescent tube lights that echoed in the deserted halls.

There was no one in the hall, but when he stood in front of the elevator, Conary saw it go down three floors to a sub-basement. When he heard voices in the hall, he ducked into the stairwell and started down. The sub-basement was as good a place to start looking as any, and from a security perspective, it was the most defensible and secure area.

The thrifty palace managers were saving on electricity, and only half the lighting units worked. When he got to the floor where the elevator stopped, the door had a swipe box, but someone had put a piece of duct tape over the lock bolt, so he didn't have to swipe at all. The door just swung open. Down the hall, he could hear a voice.

And there she was. The classroom was small, utilitarian, and windowless, but with only one student, they didn't need much space. The only student sat in the only undersized (for her) school desk, and the only teacher stood facing her in front of a pristine and empty mobile whiteboard.

Grace – and Conary was sure it was Grace – listened to a woman lecture in English on Pushkin's poem "Ode to Liberty". Ye gods, the teacher was boring. When her monotone voice read the part "Sing to the world of Liberty, And shame the scum that sit on thrones –" there was no sense of irony at all.

Grace was trying to stay awake, but her head nodded, and on every fourth nod, she would spasm. Her eyes would fly open, and then she'd slowly start nodding again. To Conary, she seemed reasonably healthy, but losing so much weight so fast made her young face sag. Her arms had folds of skin on them, and he could see under her shirt more folds like an overinflated balloon who'd been too long at the party. He wanted Grace to get up so he could see her walk, but she didn't; she fell asleep in her chair, and the lecturer didn't bother to wake her single student up. She droned on like she was being paid by the word.

Conary left and went to the next room, and it was as he expected. All the rooms for Grace were in one area, and across the hall was her bedroom. He left a small card under her pillow, then checked out the next room, which was a small sitting room with a TV. There was no one anywhere, which surprised him. Where were her guards? There were a couple more rooms, but he had found her and her bedroom and now felt like he was pushing his luck. So he left, retracing his route up the stairs and back through the kitchen and out to the service yard.

After almost an hour of constant invisibility, he was exhausted, and he still had to stay invisible until he was out of sight of the house and the guards. The road was hot and dusty, but there was no way to avoid it. Conary started walking.

Vrt

Vrt crouched in the hot, airless van and stared at the tablet. Darnya set up a hidden camera pointed at the service gate, and they pulled off the road to wait for Conary to signal he was ready for his pickup. If he was stuck on the wrong side of the gate, they had a rope to throw over to him, but the team thought he could just open it from the inside. Once they saw him, they'd drive by as if they were heading back home and pick him up, hopefully still invisible.

They waited. Adeele kept an eye on the lord, afraid she'd give up waiting and go looking for Conary, which would make life much more difficult for everyone. But she didn't move and she didn't talk. She didn't do anything but stare at the tablet and watch the gate.

"He's out of the gate." The relief on her face told it all.

Adeele looked at the video and didn't see anything, but the Vrt was sure Lord Conary was there, so she told Maksym to get going. They were only about a mile away and reached the gate quickly. It only took a second for Adeele to open the side door and move to the back cargo area. The minute she moved back, Conary appeared in her seat, looking like he had just run a marathon. Vrt leaned over and kissed him on the side of his head and handed him a bottle of water. Darnya was about to hand him a towel when Vrt swung around.

"Don't touch him!" She took the towel and put it in the lord's lap. "He's very hot. You'll burn yourself."

Darnya sat back. She had heard what had happened to Joan when she touched Lord Cadence after the lord had done a big burst of magic. Third-degree burns.

Vrt balanced behind Conary's chair all the way back to the house and wouldn't let him go.

Grace

It was a card the size of a standard business card. On it, handwritten in black ink, was "Hello". On the back was "привет / privet" as if it were a Russian-language flash card. But it was under her pillow, and she didn't use cards like this for her language classes.

Grace understood immediately. Someone had made it into her bedroom and was telling her they were here. The card was a decoy just in case it was discovered by her keepers.

Or maybe it was put there by the Russians to see what she would do. To test her.

She looked at it, and then she put it on her desk with her other study materials. She didn't hide it or throw it away. If someone was watching her, the card was nothing special to her.

The pillow was cool on Grace's cheek, and she thought about the note. Was it from Wendell? Or some other RumLot person? It really didn't matter to her who rescued her; all that mattered was that someone was coming to get her out of this basement and nearer to Wendell.

She fell asleep and dreamt of Wendell and flying.

The Team

Back at the house, Conary debriefed as quickly as he could, eating and talking at the same time. He didn't understand the lack of guards; the place seemed almost deserted. He hadn't seen any evidence of Putin, but then Conary had been in the service areas and basement the entire time. Grace was being held in a deep sub-basement, probably originally built as a bunker, and Putin could hardly be expected to be down there. The preferred torture method was to bore her to death with nineteenth-century Russian poetry.

He gave the chef's ID and lanyard to Adeele, who scanned it and sent the info on it to the techs at HQ. She didn't have any equipment to make another card, but maybe the techs could learn something from it.

Conary took a three-minute shower just to rinse the sweat off, then flopped on the bed and slept. Vrt stood at the foot of the bed and looked at him for a few minutes, then went back to the kitchen.

Sitting at the kitchen table, eating a late lunch, the four of them discussed the next steps.

"We still have the basic problem of getting her out of the basement and to a place where she can be picked up. I can do nothing in that basement but kill orcs or humans. My abilities are best used outside, but even then, I have a range. I have to be fairly close – maybe no more than half a kilometre away. Conary can make himself invisible, but I don't think he can hold that illusion on himself and Grace at the same time, especially for as long as it would take her to get upstairs and out in the open." Vrt was talking more to herself than to the others, gathering her thoughts as she sipped on a vile instant coffee. The extra milk and sugar she larded it with didn't help.

"We also need to find out where everyone was this afternoon. Surely they don't keep Grace under lock and key with just one Russian Lit instructor." Adeele just didn't get it. "If she were healthier, she could just walk out."

Darnya countered, "That might be the reason she has no guards. They feel she's in a secure bunker, and she couldn't escape if she wanted to. All they need are people to give the alarm if she starts to move. After all, she's not going to move fast, that's for sure."

"We're back to where we were when we first started planning. We can take what we have learned, say we can't do it ourselves because we can't penetrate the bunker, and go back to HQ to say there needs to be a full-scale assault. We go in like Israelis with massive hostage-rescue helicopters, special forces, the whole bit." Maksym was glum.

"Or we do it by stealth, which is why we are here now. A big assault will surely result in deaths, and while our soldiers aren't keen on dying, they will take that risk. But I'm sure it would also kill Grace. Once her guards know they are under assault, I am sure they have orders to kill her on the spot. Better for Lester to have her dead than in our hands." Vrt looked at her companions, and they nodded agreement. Those were the choices, and there was no middle ground. "I'm still convinced that stealth is better. Sneak her out and whisk her away before anyone notices she is gone."

Vrt looked at Maksym. "I think I'll go a-roaming tonight, very late. You'll take me to a spot I saw where I can scale the wall; I'll show you on the map. I'll go around the outside of the Palace grounds and see what the guards and security are like. If it's as awful on the outside as it is on the inside, maybe I can find a hole big enough to get a four-hundred-pound woman through."

"What about dogs? Motion sensors?"

Vrt smiled. "I've run with wolves. Dogs won't bother me. No one will see me, not even the machines of the humans. I'll wear one of your cameras, I think." Then she grinned. "But no wig. That thing gives me a headache."

"And Lord Conary?" Darnya didn't think he'd take it well if Vrt just disappeared.

"Oh, I'll wake him up later and tell him, but it's important he stays behind. If he comes, he'll slow me down, and it's more important that he rest and recover so he can work tomorrow. Our abilities – magic as you call it – take a huge amount of energy, exactly like any human athlete needs energy to move their muscles. He needs to rest and eat, not run around the palace grounds."

They finished their meal and left to do their chores, which were now becoming routine.

Maksym was working on the van and praying some of the frayed belts would hold out a bit longer when a thought popped in his head so violently that he jerked up and hit his head on the bonnet.

Was the girl imprisoned in a sub-basement or a bunker? The team had been using the terms interchangeably, but it made a difference. A sub-basement was probably originally designed for use as storage, mechanical ventilation systems, or utilities. But a bunker – now that was to shelter people and would have an emergency exit of some sort. Even a bunker hardened to withstand a nuclear bomb would have one or two secret exits so those sheltered in there would be able to escape and not be buried inside forever. The team knew there were secret tunnels out of the palace that led down to the beach, but those started at the other side of the huge Palace where the bigwigs lived. They needed to find out if there was one in Grace's area, too.

Rubbing his head, he left the piece-of-shit van to go find Lord Vrt, Adeele, and Darnya.

Kyrylo

The reports from the team showed progress, and while the team was frustrated, Kyrylo was very pleased. They were getting good intel, and that Conary had penetrated the Palace and had seen the girl was excellent news.

When Conary made his recon inside the Palace, he wore a body cam, and even though he was using his abilities the entire time and manipulating light waves away from his body, the camera still worked – badly, but it worked. The images visible in the optical light range of the electromagnetic spectrum were so close to microwaves that at first glance, the video was dark red, but with some brilliant work in the tech department, they refiltered the video and corrected some of the distortions and were able to see a black and white image of what the invisible lord saw.

Then they got a message from Darnya asking if they thought the rooms were a bunker with an escape tunnel or a basement just used for storage and no exit other than stairs and elevators.

And that excellent question led to an emergency meeting.

In the meantime, while the human techs and elf engineers combed over the old construction blueprints they had unearthed and which were now shown to be half wishful thinking and half deliberate disinformation, Kyrylo sent a message back.

"Moscow is worried about a RumLot operation. It's possible they've pulled their human guards to work up there. I think Lester has two tiers of guards – maybe a Praetorian Guard of humans for close-in work and orc guards to work the outer security ring. They can't have orcs working around lords every minute of every day in case they go crazy. A lord girl with no powers can't defend herself against an orc, and I think that's why you don't smell any orcs in the Palace. He can't trust orcs totally, and if he's worried for himself, he might have beefed up Moscow with humans from Sochi. But he can't replace them with orcs, and he can't bring in unknown, untrained humans. Grace was an unplanned addition, and I think that has split his resources. "

Vrt

Vrt read the message along with the others. A worried Lester was a good Lester as far as she was concerned. He would make mistakes, and pulling guards from Sochi to Moscow might just be a weakness that they could exploit. It would only last as long as Lester was worried for his own safety, and end when he increased his guard force to better handle two locations. The team only had a narrow window of time to take advantage of this. Maybe a week, maybe a month, but no more.

Conary was still fast asleep, and as darkness fell over Sochi Vrt decided it was time to go have her walk. She went to the bedroom and shook her snoring man awake. He rolled over and mumbled – "Not now, Sugar – sleep –" But she didn't let him go back to sleep.

"You have to get up. I'm leaving." With that, his eyes flew open, and he sat up so fast she thought he was spring-loaded.

"Leaving!"

"Well, not leaving – going out on a little walk on the Palace grounds. And I don't want to go without you knowing what's going on." She explained everything that had been decided while he was asleep, along with the new intel from HQ.

He wasn't happy, but she promised faithfully not to take any risks and to wear her body cam. She was going to look for the guards, dogs, and most importantly, for any secret tunnel entrances that might be hidden on the beach cliffs.

"I don't know how you're going to see anything like that in the dark." And in answer to that, she smiled and shrugged. You don't live 3,500 years at the edge of orc-world and not learn a thing or two about getting around. The dark didn't bother her once her eyes adjusted, and there wasn't a living thing – and very few dead things – that she feared. Besides, now she had a reason to be careful and someone to come back to. She wouldn't take any risks, and to her wandering around in the seaside scrub of the Palace grounds was no risk at all.

Vrt and Maksym left, and Conary watched the van pull away and then went back to the kitchen in a foul mood. He was tired, he was hungry, and he *did not* like the team making plans while he was asleep, and he said so to Adeele and Darnya in no uncertain terms.

"She told us not to wake you up, that you needed your sleep," Adeele answered. "And truthfully, Lord Conary, she was itching to do something. She has sat on the sidelines watering plants and watching you from the back of the van since we got here. You don't know how much she worried over you when you were in the Palace. It tore her up. We could see it. But she didn't complain, and she didn't say a word to you, now did she?"

Darnya made sandwiches for the lord. Bless them, they ate a lot. They would have to make a trip back to the Perekrestok tomorrow, and she hadn't planned on that. But for now, this "hangry" Lord Conary needed to calm down.

"Lord Vrt doesn't think there's much risk to her at all. She said she lived in the wilderness for many years and can see what average people – humans, I guess – can't see. She promised to put the body cam on, and [Darnya pointed to the tablet] as soon as it's switched on, we'll see what she is seeing. It's got night vision. When I asked her if she needed some night vision goggles, she just laughed and said she was born with night vision goggles."

"No one is making decisions around you, Lord Conary, but even lords need to rest and recover. Y'know – we think of magic as –" Adeele groped for the word. " – fairy dust, not as something that is a physical process that takes effort. Lord Vrt said you need to recharge and recover like an athlete. You're much more valuable to the mission, fully recharged and able to go back to the Palace during the day than on a night recon. Lord Vrt said as much, and she said that you would just slow her down. You know she's right."

Conary scowled and gulped a chunk of the sandwich he was holding as if it were an orc's head. He wasn't going to argue because what Adeele said was all true, but he didn't have to like it. Instead, like Vrt did earlier, he glumly ate his meal and stared at the tablet, waiting for it to switch on.

Vrt

Maksym had never seen the like. Lord Vrt had told him where to go on the perimeter fence, and it was a good spot. There were a lot of scrubby trees in this section, and he could park off the road and hide the van in them. As she left the van, he reminded her to switch on her camera. She waved and, like a ghost, melted into the trees, her RumLot elf-made work uniform blending in perfectly. Since she was wearing a balaclava that hid her ears, pale face, and white hair, all anyone could see were two dimly glowing green eyes like a cat's.

There was enough moonlight that Maksym could see the perimeter fence. The security barrier had two layers at this point – a very tall steel wall that faced the world, probably covered in motion sensors that would light up and alert the guards the minute a person tried to scale it. On the other side, there was a twenty-foot-wide interior dog run and service road, and then another wire fence.

He could see the black shape of the lord as she reached the barrier, and he saw her stop and study it. Then she walked back almost to the road. Suddenly she turned, ran at it at an angle, and leapt right over like a high jumper. She barely skimmed the concertina wire, but she did, and that was the last Maksym saw of her. He left the van and put a special blanket over the bonnet to reduce the vehicle's heat signature, but there was nothing he could do about the underside. Now all he could do was wait and hope no patrols spotted him.

The no-man's-land between the two fences was scrubby and full of dog shit. Vrt could see it was as well-maintained as the rest of the Palace in that the barrier had been built to a high standard when Putin was faux-Tsar. But now, after years of sanctions, economic depression, and Putin's removal as a power centre, it was simply wearing out. When she was outside, Vrt could see that the motion sensors were covered in vines, which would never have been allowed if they were working.

She froze. She could hear them coming.

And there they were, a pack of dogs. They were a motley mix of nasty brutes that had been bred from Putin's old dogs – the labs, akitas, sharrs he had been given as gifts, with a lot of rottweiler thrown in. They growled and snapped at her, circling just out of range. Vrt knew that the pack in front of her was there to distract, and behind her, in the dark, was the Alpha who would make the first move.

She slowly turned, and with her back to the pack, called to the Alpha in Elvish. "I see you. I mean no harm. I belong here."

Slowly, the Alpha crept forward out of the gloom, and she could see him. He was an astoundingly huge, hairy dog made of nothing but snarling teeth, mats, and meanness. She reached into her pocket and pulled out a sausage roll she had brought with her for just this reason.

The Alpha sniffed. Vrt cooed in Elvish. "Look what I have for you. I brought this for you. I'm supposed to be here. I mean no harm to you or your pack. Let's be friends."

The dog growled, his ears back, and inched forward, his head swaying and ropy saliva dripping from his huge canines. Then he sat up and begged like a toy poodle. He wanted the sausage roll, but most of all he wanted Vrt to pet him, which she was happy to do. Alpha got his sausage roll reward for not trying to kill her, and the rest of the pack got a good scratch behind the ears from Vrt.

Vrt trotted with the dogs down the track towards the cliff edge and the beach. She reached the place where the steel barrier followed the cliff down to the water, and the interior fence stopped. The dogs couldn't go further because their shock collars wouldn't let them, and they pooled at the point where shocks started and whimpered. They were having fun running with this new animal who was neither human nor orc but something that smelled wonderful. Something they knew in their bones was good.

The Alpha was upset when he saw Vrt move on down the trail leading to the beach, so upset he made a huge leap towards her and endured the shock until he rolled out of range of the signal. Vrt heard him yelping in pain and waited. If he wanted to come that badly, she was not going to stop him. That would just slow her down.

When he reached Vrt, she scratched him behind the ears as a reward and cut off the collar with her elf knife, throwing it in the bushes. She didn't want him yelping if they came across another signal, and besides, she didn't like it. In Elvish, she told him he was a good boy and to be quiet; she was looking for human holes. She wanted, she said, places where the humans came out of their tunnels, like rabbits.

The dog trotted at her side and thought, as dogs do, that if he did as this person wanted, there might be another sausage roll in it. So he ran off to the nearest human hole he could think of, stopping now and then to make sure Sausage Roll Woman was following.

Vrt knew this one from the maps and the satellite photos. It was used to bring Putin and his guests to the beach and was well-documented. There was the same general air of neglect around it, but it wasn't hidden at all, and she could see that people had been in and out in the last weeks.

"You'll have to do better," she said in Elvish. "I want an old tunnel with almost no scent of humans." The dog was crestfallen. No sausage roll for this one. He showed her two more, which she liked better. But they were lined up with the palace's grander sections rather than the service areas. She mapped them and then gave the dog half a sausage roll and a good scratch.

Holding up the other half of the sausage, Vrt teased the dog. "Find me one more, off in that direction, and you'll get the other half." The dog danced and grinned and then ran off so fast Vrt had to trot to keep up. And there it was, well-hidden in scrub that clung to the sandy cliff and with a good half metre of sand piled at the base of the rusty metal door. She looked around for sensors or cameras and saw one camera barely hanging by a single wire; she didn't see any sensors at all. She tested the door just to see if, by some miracle, it wasn't locked, but was afraid to do more in case it was booby trapped. There was no handle on her side.

She geo-located everything, hoping that she was doing that right, but Vrt knew she could find it again if she needed to. This one felt right.

Vrt gave the dog his sausage roll and a good scratch on his belly along with a "*very* good boy". And then she retraced her steps. About twenty minutes later, Maksym saw her leap to his side of the fence, and they drove back home.

The Team

Conary and the women watched Vrt's recon run with rapt fascination. Conary's lovely Angel of Death talking to the dog pack like a fucking Demon Dr Doolittle was something he would never get over. No wonder she wasn't worried! She had sausage rolls!

When Vrt and Maksym returned to the house, she was greeted with hugs and cheers, which made the lord smile shyly. The intel she had gathered was good, and she hadn't met anyone at all but the dogs. The footage from the bodycam was amazing. While she was in the shower, Conary watched again from the beginning, and the leap over the fence from the body cam point of view gave him vertigo just watching it. He could hear her grunt and gasp for breath and winced at the hard thump when she landed. He could never have followed her, and he readily admitted it.

The video was uploaded to HQ, and the lords sat down to a midnight carb load before they went to bed. Adeele wanted to know how the dogs understood her, and Vrt smiled. "Dog is a language like any other. I spoke in Elvish, and they understood. Any lord can speak to any animal if they put their mind to it, but not every animal wants to or can speak to a lord. It's useless speaking to a wren, for instance. Small birds don't have the brain power to process words, just feelings. And, of course, something like a fish thinks it's going to be eaten, and you can tell a trout it's safe all day, and they will still swim away. Horses are slow, and you have to speak to them in very simple words. Stop, start, left – that sort of thing. But dogs were bred to be around the tribes. Smart *wild* animals are far, far trickier, and just because I can speak to them doesn't mean they will do what I want. Dogs are easy."

Conary looked up from his ramen bowl. "So you think I can talk to a dog?"

"Of course you can. Just speak to them in Elvish, and they will hear it in Dog. Keep the ideas and words very simple and direct. Dogs just want to be loved, and they like lords. We smell good to them. Next time you're around one, give it a go."

Darnya said, "Lord Conary, if you can get inside the Palace again tomorrow, can you look for the tunnel's interior door?

It might be hidden in a closet or behind something. They wouldn't want people to know it's there because to me it looks like a last-ditch escape route for the elite; they wouldn't build an expensive escape tunnel for the cooks and bottle washers."

"If that tunnel still is good, then getting Grace out that way is better than Lord Vrt trying to lift her with a tornado from the terrace and then us trying to catch her outside. We can have an extraction team meet us on the beach."

Conary agreed, and with that, they finished their meal and went to bed. Tomorrow was going to be busy.

Kyrylo

The mission team at RumLot Security HQ was very happy with Lord Vrt's video. After a very close examination of recent satellite footage and with Vrt's geolocation, they were just able to spot a corner of the tunnel door in the cliff.

Kyrylo thought the possibility of using the tunnel was worth exploring. The issues with the tunnel really came down to being able to open the doors at both ends and the hope that there were no ancient collapsed sections in the middle. From the satellite photos, there was no evidence of tunnel collapses visible on the surface.

Just to be on the safe side, he authorised an extraction team disguised as fishermen to wander the Black Sea just off the Sochi coast. And he sent a message to Lord Neptune just to let him know what was going on. You never knew what the old semi-tuna would do. But he liked Caddy, and this was Caddy's son, so maybe he would help.

The Team

The Palace wanted raspberries, so Vrt and Darnya spent a good hour in the greenhouse picking the last of the season's offer from the thorny brambles. Vrt was hot and scratched, and the hated wig was already giving her a splitting headache when they walked out of the greenhouse and saw the orc pulling into the driveway.

Darnya hissed to Vrt, "Stay back; let me handle this." She shoved her boxes on top of Vrt's and walked briskly to the car. Vrt hung back and made sure the wind was blowing her scent in the right direction.

Inside the house, Maksym heard the car pull up, and he strolled out. Adeele stayed inside with Conary, and from the window, she aimed her gun at the back of the orc's head.

The orc was very friendly. He just happened to be doing a construction job up the street and had some extra asphalt, and he wanted to know if they wanted their driveway paved. Cheap. Just the cost of the asphalt, so they didn't have to haul it home. Cash only, of course.

Darnya laughed, and even Maksym had to grin. "Do we look like we can afford to have our driveway paved? We don't have a ruble to pay for a bottle of vodka!" The orc looked at the house and then back at Darnya and her rough work clothes and shrugged. He also had an internet deal if they were interested. Maksym shook his head and dolefully asked the orc if he had any loose change so they could buy some milk for the baby. At that, the man put his car in reverse and backed out of the driveway so fast his tires squealed.

Vrt walked into the house and saw Adeele with the gun. "No, you don't! If anyone's killing an orc, it's me! I haven't killed one for ages."

Adeele pouted. "You can't have all the fun. Anyway, I had first aim at him. I think it's wrong that you pull rank on me about orc killing. I'm going to HR when we get back and submit a complaint."

"You didn't have first aim – I saw him first!" And they argued about who had been better positioned to kill the orc until Maksym called them out to the truck. They had work to do.

Conary

They made their rounds of the oligarchs' homes. Two were leaving for St. Petersburg and cancelled their orders until they came back. Looking at the pitiful amount they made, it was no wonder the previous fruit farmers were so poor!

Maksym pulled up to the Palace, and just like before, insisted on carrying the boxes of raspberries into the kitchen to spare the chef's staff the trouble.

Out in the service yard, Adeele was getting friendly with the guards and asked them if they were going on holiday, as it seemed that so many people were leaving. No, they moaned, they were short-staffed as it was because so many of the guards were on temporary duty in Moscow. But when they got back, maybe next week, they could get some time off. Adeele nodded sympathetically. Poor bastards like us always have to fill in for other people. It's like management doesn't know we have lives, too! The guards glumly agreed. They were all working double shifts, and it was lucky they just had two VIPs to guard.

Maksym came out, the kitchen helper trailing him like an adoring puppy, and with a cheery wave and a "See you tomorrow," they left the yard and drove down the long road to the gate.

Conary didn't linger in the kitchen. The minute he could slip through the hall door without anyone seeing it open and close by itself, he left. The team had discussed whether an entrance door to the tunnel was more likely to be in Grace's sub-basement or on the level above it. Conary decided to start at the bottom, where he could see Grace if she was there, and then work his way up if he couldn't find the door on her level.

Twice, he had to squeeze aside to avoid people walking in the halls. No one noticed him, and of course, no one smelled him because they were all human. Not an orc or any trace of them in this wing of the Palace.

The stairwell was empty because the staff all took the elevator, and his soft-soled athletic shoes made no sound as he trotted down the stairs.

Carefully, he cracked the fire door to the stairwell and listened for anyone in the hall. Hearing nothing but his breathing, he slipped through.

The classroom was empty, as was Grace's bedroom. He slipped a card under her pillow and then went looking for her, which was easy because he heard her before he saw her. She was sprawled out on a big sofa in the horrendously ugly teal and pink TV room watching an old Netflix *Wednesday Addams* DVD. Sitting next to her was another young girl, also extremely obese, with the same general colouring as Grace, but it was certainly not her. She spoke to Grace in very broken English, trying to understand some bit of dialogue in the movie. They had a huge pile of celery and carrots on a tray and bottles of diet Baikal. A girl's movie night, it appeared, only during the morning. Not that night or day mattered in the windowless basement.

For a second, Conary wondered if he had seen the wrong girl at the Pushkin lecture, but that made no sense. They wouldn't have the body double taking lessons in Russian poetry. After a quick look, he moved on to the end of the hall and methodically started searching in every room with a west-facing wall.

The furthest room was a bedroom and was probably where the decoy slept. The western wall was made of concrete block and even after careful inspection hid no door.

The TV room was still occupied and looked to be occupied all morning. He would have to check that later.

The next room was an exercise room. There were some light weights, a treadmill, and an ancient Pilates Reformer. Conary, having never seen or heard of Pilates, worried that it was some sort of torture device. He took several photos of it. The wall in this room was also solid block. No door there.

Grace's room was next. He had been there several times, but this time he paid attention to the west wall. Nothing to see.

The last room before Grace's looked like it was some sort of office space for guards and whoever was there to oversee the girl. It, too, was horribly decorated in what could only be described as 1999 Miami teal and pink bordello. It was empty, but Conary saw a cup of tea on the desk, and it was still warm. Next to it was a clipboard with what appeared to be a menu and a lot of numbers. He took a photo of it.

The west wall was as blank as all the others and a dead end. As Conary turned to leave, he almost ran into a woman in a white coat. She stopped in the doorway and had a few words with someone in the hall, but Conary was too worried about breathing so loudly she could hear him to pay perfect attention. He heard something along the lines of "See you tomorrow." Then the woman turned, and he was able to squeeze around her as she sat down at the desk and took up the clipboard. She was the dietitian.

He took out his camera to take a photo of her and then thought better of it. No risks, not now; and he slipped out the open door.

That was the last room. The next door led to the stairwell and then the end of the hall. He was about to turn into the stairwell when he noticed a recessed door across from the stairwell that led to a women's toilet. On the west side of the hall, hidden by the stairwell and in another recess, was a door to the men's toilet.

He shrugged, and since no men were about, he didn't see the harm in having a pee and went into the men's. There it was – right next to the urinals. A solid blast door, obviously never used, with the dust and spiderwebs on it. It had a swipe box and still had the tiny green light on it that said it was ready. The door even had a sign on it that said it was for authorised emergency use only. Conary stood at the urinal, and during his pee, he studied the door. Who would be "authorised"? He still had the chef's swipe card. Was he high enough up the food chain to be authorised to open an emergency exit? Or could anyone go through if the emergency itself was authorised?

For a minute, he thought about testing the door with his card and then thought better of it. He didn't want to set off an alarm at this point. He would talk with the team and techs at HQ first.

He took a bunch of pics, and like yesterday, he retraced his steps and left the Palace, no one the wiser.

Maybe because it wasn't quite so hot, or maybe because he was not so tense from holding invisibility so long, but the walk back to the van wasn't as bad as before. Like the first time he scaled the gate, since he was invisible, even if he set off the motion sensor, the guards would see nothing and assume it was a glitch. Just out of sight of the gate, the van rolled up, and he jumped inside and relaxed into visibility. Vrt was right there with a kiss on his sweaty head, a water bottle, and a towel. They drove back to the house without talking much.

Grace

There was another card under her pillow. This one was handwritten "Ready" in English, and on the other side was handwritten "Готовый / Gotovyy" in Russian. She put it on her desk along with the mess of papers, school books, and homework each teacher had assigned her and that she was ignoring.

Were they ready to rescue her?

Was she ready to be rescued? Jesus, Mary, and Joseph, she hoped so. She could walk pretty far now, almost a kilometre on the treadmill. While she was still morbidly obese and weighed a lot, the dietitian and exercise coach both agreed that she was trading light fat for heavier muscle. Grace certainly felt stronger and lighter.

They told her that since she was so young, they thought the skin folds would shrink back, maybe disappear altogether. It would take a while, and the coach warned her that she would never look model thin and still be healthy. Not with those boobs, she said. Pay more attention to your waist measurement and not your weight, and don't worry if you have big breasts that add to the number on the scales. Men like'm.

Grace genuinely liked her exercise coach. Her name was Anja, and she was the only one who treated Grace like a normal human being. While the rest were kind to her face, she could tell they were also scared of her. Maybe they thought she would go complaining about them to Lester; she didn't know.

Anja sincerely wanted her to be strong and healthy, and when she said that, she meant it. She was also brutally honest with Grace and told her that her weight wasn't some metabolic thing but psychological. "Suicide by fork" was what she said, and that Grace needed to think of herself as a survivor, not a victim. Anja said that Grace would be very pretty very soon, but first, she needed to think of herself as a person with value. The Tsar thought she was worth saving, so Grace should think that, too. When she lost weight, Anja was certain that the girl would have a body like Anna Semenovich, and she gave Grace an old magazine with pictures of the celebrity. The woman was a figure skater and certainly had big ones.

She wondered if Wendell would like a very curvy woman. LeeAnne was slender. Maybe he would like a change.

Grace was ready.

The Team

They debated whether Conary should try to open the door or not. The big question was what to do if he set off an alarm. Then, if no alarm was set off, should he go in there and test out the tunnel? What if there was no air in there? What if he got locked in?

HQ came back and said they were going to breach the tunnel at the beach door. They said the hinges looked like the door was going to swing in, which made sense if you were worried that it would be blocked by a falling cliff if the Palace complex was bombed. A frogman team was going to go in late at night, pop the door, and then leave. They had some very good explosives that they said could open the door with a minimum of noise.

If that was successful and no one in the palace noticed, then Conary could try the other end.

Since the guards said their comrades were coming back in a week, HQ decided they were going to do this right away before the Palace security was back at full strength. They would try to get Grace out in four days.

There was only one small problem. The Palace cancelled their strawberry order.

The next day, with no Palace strawberries to deliver and with two of their regular customers on holiday, the team only had one small delivery to make, and they finished that up by eight. At loose ends, they rested, watered the plants in the greenhouses, and cleaned equipment. Maksym and Darnya went to the grocery store and gassed up the van, leaving Adeele behind, much to Vrt's disappointment.

Since they had landed in Russia, she and Conary hadn't been able to have so much as a snuggle. Lords were made to do what lords were made to do. With her bonded man sitting just a few feet from her and no way to take advantage of that without offending human sensibilities, Vrt was getting a bit tense.

But the humans weren't going to leave the lords alone without a bodyguard just in case another orc showed up selling raffle tickets or knock-off perfume.

Since they had to work and Vrt was still hopeless with the tablet, Vrt asked Conary to message HQ and tell them to let her know when the frogmen were coming in so she could go there to watch the cliff top and keep the dogs quiet. It wasn't until later that day that he realised that she thought they would be actual frog/men – like mermaids were people/fish – and she'd seen dogs playing with frogs. It wasn't pretty.

He laughed and laughed. "I've seen some bandy-legged men in my life, but never a man with actual frog legs."

Vrt was miffed. "You've seen a mermaid, haven't you?"

"Well, actually, no, I haven't. But I take your point; they do exist." He still chuckled. "But a frogman! That's just weird."

Vrt

While the days were still hot, the nights were getting cold, and Vrt was much more comfortable in the cold than in the heat. It was just after midnight, and she sat in the scrub on the cliff edge enjoying the cold sea breeze, watching the beach, and feeding bits of sausages to the dogs.

The sea was a little rough and dark, but the sound of the waves would cover any unusual noise. It wasn't so rough that it would put off anyone coming ashore.

Suddenly, the Alpha looked up, his nose twitching. Vrt calmed him and told him the strangers she saw walking up the beach were not enemies. The lord was calm and said he and the pack should stay calm, too. The Alpha begged to be able to go have a sniff, but she said no; they had to watch from here. The pack sensed that the lord was interested but not worried, so they lay down to watch, too.

There were three of them. Each one pulled some sort of swimming machine onto the shore. They had tubes of air on their backs that they removed and set next to their machines. They worked quickly and silently, and within minutes they were scaling the cliff. They knew exactly where they wanted to go.

Halfway up, one black shape stopped and scanned the cliff edge, where he saw two glowing, green dots. He gave a little whistle, like a bird call, and got a little whistle in return. Five minutes later, Vrt heard a dull, muffled pop, then another pop.

Nothing happened. There were no alarms, no guards came screaming down to check what was amiss – nothing.

The men scrambled back down the cliff, and one waved in her direction. They put their gear back on, and as swiftly and silently as they had landed on the beach, they slipped back into the sea and were gone.

Vrt waited about half an hour just to make sure no guards would come down to investigate any alarms, and then she and the Alpha went to look at the frogmen's handiwork.

The door was open about a foot. She leaned on it, and it was heavy, but she pushed and it opened a few more feet. The Alpha didn't want to go in. He said it smelled bad. Putrid.

The air inside was stale and old, and the Alpha was right; it smelled bad. Decades of being sealed up had affected the air, and Vrt wasn't worried about the bad smell but about carbon dioxide, which could suffocate a person in minutes. She thought about blowing a wind in there. After a minute of considering just how to do it without getting herself overwhelmed by CO_2, she crouched low, told the Alpha to back off, and blew a great wind into the tunnel along the floor. When it reached the end, wherever that was, it circulated up to the ceiling, and in a few minutes she could see swirls of dust come out of the top of the door. Vrt didn't know how far the tunnel went but hoped the far end was the door to the sub-basement and not a blast door in the middle.

They would have to check the air at the other end, which meant Vrt would need to go with Conary when they went to get the girl. Or maybe she should go back with a gas mask and inspect the tunnel to make sure it was breathable. The team would discuss their options.

She fed the dogs the last of the sausages and returned to the van. Maksym said that while he was waiting, he didn't see anything at all out of the ordinary.

The Team

They simply couldn't know if Vrt's wind had reached the end of the tunnel or stopped at an interior blast door.

HQ was very concerned about the danger of carbon dioxide in the tunnel, and an air monitor was simply not something they had thought to pack in the team's limited gear or give to the frogmen to pass on. They could send one to the extraction boat, but that would take a couple of days, and time was getting short.

Darnya sighed. "It's a pity we can't simply buy one here. It's not like we can just pop out to Perekrestok and pick up one in the housewares department."

"Why not?" Vrt was puzzled. Conary rolled his eyes and waited for another Vrt-ism.

"Because they're pretty sophisticated things, and they aren't sold for normal houses." Darnya was patient. It was bizarre what these lords didn't know.

"But those things in the ceilings that tell you if there is a fire, aren't some of those bad air monitors? Don't they sniff for

carbon dioxide? We had them in every room at Aelfeham House."
Vrt looked at Conary, confused. "Am I wrong? I was told they
were CO2 monitors for bad air."

Darnya looked at the lord, open-mouthed. The Angel of
Death, who had lived in the taiga for thousands of years, was
familiar with smoke detectors and CO2 monitors.

Conary shook his head and chuckled. "You're right; a
smoke detector will also beep if it smells CO2. I can't believe you
noticed those things!"

"Well, when we're in bed, I'm often on my back looking
at the ceiling. You, on the other hand, are busy and looking in the
opposite direction." Vrt sniffed, and Adeele and Darnya had to
laugh at the expression on Lord Conary's face.

The next morning, the women went to Perekrestok and
bought five smoke/CO2 detectors along with nine extra nine-volt
batteries. That night, Vrt would go into the tunnel, and if the
detectors beeped, she would back off right away and blow a big
wind and flush out the CO2.

Vrt

The sand in front of the tunnel door was undisturbed, and
Vrt was sure that no one had been there since her visit the night
before. The Alpha was not happy to go into the dark, enclosed
space, but he admitted it did smell better. He would follow Vrt.

Vrt had the household smoke/CO2 detectors in her
backpack, and the idea was to place them on the floor of the tunnel
every hundred metres or so. If one started to blink red and cry, she
would make a wind circulate through the tunnel and clear the air.
The human sniffing machines had little green lights that blinked

when they were happy, and the team assured Vrt that the batteries would last for a year or so. She didn't have to worry about them getting tired and falling asleep in the next few days.

While lords can see quite well in normal darkness, the pitch black of the tunnel was another level of darkness that even a lord couldn't see through. In their gear, Vrt found a little torch to wear on her forehead that shot out just enough soft light that she could see where she was going and check for booby traps and obstacles.

She stepped inside. The tunnel appeared unused, probably since the day it was sealed in 1990. There was a layer of dust on the floor and occasionally a bit of water that had leaked from a crack or seam, but overall it was pretty dry. It was almost four hundred metres from the sea to the Palace, and so every hundred metres Vrt would stop and set down a sniffer and walk on.

The tunnel was unvarying – a long straight tube about three metres wide and three metres tall with an occasional brittle poster on the walls telling the people who traversed it what to do in the case of nuclear attack. There were also helplines to call for help, which made Vrt smile. She bet the calls would be unanswered.

About two hundred metres in, she passed a blast door, but it was standing halfway open, and when she slipped through, she almost stepped on him.

Sprawled on the floor was a man. A very dead, mummified man. The Alpha sniffed at him and decided the meat wasn't any good, and he went to sit as far away as he could and stay in the light. Vrt crouched down and examined the man, worried that he had suffocated and there could be danger here, but

the mechanical sniffers blinked green, and the Alpha seemed okay
with the air.

Then she saw the bullet holes in his back. He had been
brought here many years ago, either already dead or he had been
executed here. Either way, decades ago, this tunnel became a crypt
used to hide the body. She moved the desiccated corpse to the side
so they wouldn't trip on it later, bits he no longer needed falling off
in messy disarray, and turned his eternally screaming face to
the wall.

She passed two more mummies – a naked man and a
woman in a tracksuit who had suffered the same sad encounter that
left bullet holes in their backs. It looked like they had been there
just as long. How long would it take to make a mummy? Usually,
about a year or so, if the scavengers and moisture didn't take the
body first. Vrt had come across hundreds of them over the
millennia. You walk into a cave, and there would be the dried husk
of a human or orc sitting in a corner (they were always sitting up in
caves, usually watching the entrance and smiling at any visitors),
dead from some long-ago disease or misadventure. The northern
humans would freeze on the tundra, and if the wolves didn't find
the carcasses, they would dry out in the permafrost and curl up to
sit there, usually forever. She had even found mummies on
battlefields, especially in the big war, the humans and orcs had
fought a hundred years ago. They still sat in abandoned tanks and
trucks awaiting orders that never came.

The mummies didn't bother her at all; Vrt was glad to
see they had been shot and not suffocated. But she moved each
one to the side where they wouldn't trip over them and turned their
leathery heads so their grins wouldn't scare the girl.

Then she came to a closed door. She examined it for a
long time, looking for wires or sensors or anything that would send
a signal to the guards that she was there. There were no cameras

that she could see, and that made sense. If people were using the tunnel to flee, who would be watching monitors anyway?

The door had a sign painted on it. "Exit" There was a handle, so she turned it. Vrt heard a rusty click, and she felt the door relax ever so slightly. The old hinges were dry but not rusted, and she pulled them open just a crack, a centimetre, and waited.

Nothing happened.

Vrt pulled and opened it another centimetre, and suddenly there was a sliver of light on the edge. In the gloom of the tunnel, the light burned her eyes, and she had to stop and adjust.

She listened at the crack, her long ears twitching. If there was a human or orc on the other side, she would hear its heartbeat. Nothing was waiting on the other side of the door, but when she stilled her own heart and concentrated, she could hear muffled voices that seemed far away.

The Alpha gave a tiny whine, and she shushed him and told him to wait there and guard her back, which he was happy to do. Then Vrt opened the door just wide enough to peek and then slide in, and she found herself in the men's toilet of the sub-basement just as Conary had said.

This left Vrt with a dilemma. She could go in and rescue Grace right now. Vrt had no doubt she could kill anyone who got in her way and get the girl to the tunnel – if she could walk the distance.

And then what? There was no extraction team at the other end. The Palace would be alerted the minute Grace was found to be missing, and then the place would be infested with furious guards swarming around like a kicked hornet's nest.

Again, then what? She and Grace would be stuck at the other end of the tunnel holding the guards off alone, and the team, with Conary, would come to rescue them and walk right into a shitpile she had created.

So the lord took a wad of rough Russian toilet paper, dabbed it in the toilet water, and wiped away the dust and flakes of rust that had fallen on the floor when the door opened. Slipping back in through the opening, Vrt carefully closed the door, but not all the way. If someone in the men's room fell on it hard, they would nudge it open, but Vrt thought that was a risk worth taking. The Alpha and the lord then turned and trotted back down the long tunnel towards the moonlit sea and blessed fresh air.

Lester

They were hitting Moscow!

Lester was furious, and he watched from the control room as hundreds of drones buzzed the Tsar's family home. The generals standing next to him were grimly ordering everything to bear to repel the assault. There was a ferocious response with ground-to-air anti-aircraft, electronic signal interference, even lasers, but the more they shot down, the more that flew in – then they were confused.

The drones swirled around the palace, but they didn't do anything. No bombs, no explosions. They didn't fight back; they just danced around, easily avoiding the Russian defences.

One of the colonels said it aloud, "I don't understand; what are they doing? These are unarmed. They don't need so many drones as spotters. They would be up high. So why are these drones just buzzing us?"

Then, as if they were waiting for a signal, the drones lined up in formation and slowly passed over the Tsar's Palace. From the bottom of each one dropped a nozzle. They were agricultural drones used to spray pesticides or fertilisers on crops. The entire palace was locked down, and everyone was ordered into full NBC gear, masks and all. The drones were engaging in chemical warfare, and no one knew what poison they would spew out.

Lester had a full-blown panic attack. What if they poisoned Lena and little Rurik? It made him physically sick to think of anything happening to Lena. Gods, she was just a human, but you'd think he was bonded to her.

They all watched the monitors. The drones painted the Palace pink.

When they were done, a drone went to a blank section and began writing. In bright purple glitter, it wrote, "Compliments of RumLot Security". And then the big drones high in the sky exploded a cloud of glitter over the entire wet mess.

Then they all retreated, shooting high and disappearing into the western night sky.

"What was the point of that? All this build-up for two months just to glitter bomb the Palace?" The general turned to Lester, furious and embarrassed. "Were the bastards just pulling us around by the short hairs? Having fun? Creating a distraction?"

Distraction. They all looked at each other, and then the first phone calls from Sochi arrived.

Darnya

As Moscow was gaping open-mouthed at the first wave of incoming drones, the Team was finishing up their work in Sochi.

A few hours earlier, they had been standing in the unmowed grass where the public road ended, getting ready for their last assault on the Sochi Palace wall.

The barrier around the Palace was long, tall, and intimidating, but the section they chose to scale was fairly near the cliff edge. The constant wind and weather from the sea had degraded it. The salt air had rusted the concertina wire props so many were broken, and the rusted razor wire was half hanging off, and that made it a bit easier to scale.

Lord Vrt had gone ahead to quiet the dogs and make sure the extraction team was where they should be. Maksym tossed up the first anchor, and Darnya scrambled up the sheer sides of the barrier and secured a rope ladder for the rest of them. She unrolled another rope ladder on the far side, but she just leapt down.

Everyone was wearing their work uniforms and was fully armed, but they didn't carry anything but the minimum equipment. All gear that wasn't elf-made was abandoned in the house or truck. They wouldn't be going back.

Adeele insisted that they mail nice notes to their customers, including the Palace, thanking them for their business, but regretfully informing them that they were now closing up shop. RumLot Security (Soft Fruits Division) had decided at this time not to expand to Sochi.

Lord Conary awkwardly climbed up the ladder, and at the top of the barrier, he stopped to have a grumble. The man hated heights. Darnya hissed at him not to be a baby and held the bottom of the rope ladder. He was turning to come down when Darnya was jumped.

Out of nowhere, a Palace security guard appeared and grabbed Darnya, but the guard didn't understand what he had when he had it. Maybe his idea was to use her as bait to get the rest of them to surrender, but he just grabbed, and they both fell to the ground. For a few desperate minutes, they struggled in the dark, then Darnya threw him off and in one smooth motion, drew her gun. As she aimed, there was a flash of light, and the guard fell back, the top of his skull cleanly sliced off. She looked up and there, still at the top of the barrier, sat Lord Conary, his eyes glittering bright blue and his body glowing.

She looked back at the guard. The top of his head was smoking, and there was no blood. It was as if the lord had sliced him with a laser. She holstered her gun, happy not to need it and so make noise they didn't need, and returned to business.

"Well, come on down! You're shining like a fucking beacon up there, and you're going to draw fire."

"I hate shaky ladders." But he made it down. Maksym and Adeele followed right behind him.

"Are you okay, Darnya?"

"Yeah, but I think I stepped in some dog shit." She turned to Lord Conary. "I didn't know you could do that!"

"Neither did I." Lord Conary grinned, his white teeth catching the moonlight. "Don't tell Vrt. I want to surprise her."

Grace

Grace was fast asleep when she felt the tap on her hand. Her eyes flew open, two terrified, bright green points of light in the dark. The flamingo night light by her bed was just bright enough to cut through the inky black of the basement, and she saw, kneeling by her, a black shape.

The shape's eyes glowed green.

The elf didn't say anything but put his gloved finger to his lips. No sound, Grace. Then he pointed to her trainers and whispered so faintly she almost didn't hear it, "It's time."

Grace slipped on the battered trainers, and the elf quickly tied them for her. Then he looked out the door and, seeing nothing, signalled Grace to follow him. Her heart was beating so hard and fast she could hear it, but she knew she only had one chance to escape. If they caught her, the elf would die, and Grace would never be left alone again.

They walked as silently down the hall as Grace's bulk and breathing would allow, and to Grace's astonishment, into the men's toilet.

There was a door there! The elf pointed, and it was obvious he wanted her to go through the door, but Grace hesitated. She knew her own size, and the space looked narrow. She pushed at the door, but it was very thick and felt stuck. So Grace sucked in her gut as much as she could and, sidling sideways, tried to squeeze through. On the other side, she felt someone trying to help her, pulling at her arms and pushing down on her boobs to flatten them and get them through the narrow opening. One breast popped through, but her stomach, the other boob, and her folds of excess skin remained stubbornly on the wrong side.

The elf was watching and listening at the toilet's exit door, but seeing that Grace was stuck, he walked over to the blast door and put his shoulder to it and pushed hard. Nothing moved.

"*СТОП!*"

Grace knew that voice; it was the dietitian, Irena. She struggled harder.

The elf spun around and faced the Russian woman. Irena was in a short baby-doll nightgown. Completing the ensemble were a cosmetic face mask and curlers like on a character in a 1960s Jerry Lewis movie. But unlike a comedy character, she was holding a gun, and it was pointed at the elf. Grace could see her out of the corner of her eye, and she groaned and strained. She couldn't budge. The door was ripping skin.

Irena was trained as a killer, but she was not trained well enough. Yelling "STOP!" was her first mistake. A professional killer wouldn't have yelled a warning; a professional would have shot. The warning was only a few seconds, but it was enough.

Irena pulled the trigger, and in the same second, an elf knife inserted itself neatly between her eyes. The shot went wild, ricocheting around the bathroom and scattering vicious, razor-sharp shards of tile. Grace cried and pushed harder.

The elf backed up and ran at the door, attacking it with a huge kick, and by some miracle, it moved. Maybe just a centimetre or two, but it moved. He hopped over to the sink and began pumping soap in his hands and soaping up the soft, doughy mounds of Grace's stomach. Between the soap and the tiny bit of extra space, the elf pushed and the person on the other side pulled, and Grace burst through like a cork exploding from a champagne bottle.

Grace almost passed out from shock and exertion, but a proper English voice said, "Stay with us, Grace. Stay awake." And she stumbled, bleeding and bruised, to a waiting wheelchair that was more like a rickshaw, and she was strapped in. Two huge men dressed in black uniforms, one behind her pushing and one pulling in a harness, wheeled her down the tunnel at a full run. Grace didn't see the elf shut the door and lock it. All she saw was the broad back of the man hauling her and the unending grey walls of the tunnel flashing by.

At the end of the tunnel, others were waiting. They were all dressed in black, and no one spoke. For all of the hive of activity, the beach was eerily quiet. They had a rope system rigged up, and Grace, still in her wheelchair rickshaw, was winched down to the beach.

On top of the cliff, she could see lights flash on, and there were sharp cracks like gunfire in the distance. Two poles were thrust through the base of the wheelchair, and in seconds it was converted to a sedan chair, and four men hauled her to a big rubber boat. As soon as she was safely strapped in, they pushed off, leaving the others behind. Someone held her hand and told her to be brave; it would all be over soon, so she tried her best and squeezed her eyes shut.

Back at the beach, the extraction team and the rescue team managed a controlled retreat. The guards on the palace grounds shot towards the intruders. But everything was black, and they didn't have night vision equipment, and they didn't know what they were firing at. While bullets were flying wildly everywhere, they weren't hitting anything but trees. The RumLot teams only had two wounded members, and they were evacuated first. Within minutes, everyone was off the beach and on the RIBs, speeding as fast as they could to the boat.

Vrt

Vrt watched the wheelchair speed off and disappear into the gloom and let out a sigh of relief. Grace was gone.

When she kicked the door, Vrt felt a sharp pain that wasn't dulled by adrenaline, and she was sure there was a broken bone, but that was a small price to pay for success. The girl wasn't as fat as the photos of equivalent women seemed to be, but even if she had gone down to three hundred pounds, she was still heavy. While the door allowed a slim Vrt and Conary to pass through, it wasn't wide enough for Grace.

The teams had planned and practised for a much heavier person, so in the end the plan worked fine. What they hadn't counted on was the damn door getting stuck partway open.

But she was through it, and now Vrt had to hobble down the tunnel on a broken foot. She gritted her teeth and got on with it. The last thing she wanted was to put the people on the beach in more danger by waiting for her.

The Alpha kept pace with her, knowing that something was wrong, and he whimpered.

Vrt saw Conary's blue eyes glowing far down the tunnel before she saw him. He had run down the tunnel with Grace and the two operatives, still invisible, but when he noticed that Vrt lagged behind and was missing, he doubled back.

He was visible again even if she couldn't see him in the inky tunnel, and he ran up and grabbed her. She could feel his heart racing.

"What's wrong? Are you shot?"

"No, just my foot. I think I broke a bone when I kicked the door."

He put her arm around his shoulder and propped her up, helping her hobble on one foot.

"You're not taking care of this body! If you don't treat it better, I'm taking it away."

"You can take it any way you want." Vrt kissed his cheek, and she could feel him smile. "But not now. I'm not in the mood."

They had made it about a quarter of the way when Maksym ran up, irritated after having misplaced both lords. The men made a sling with their arms, and Vrt had the great indignity of being carried out. If it wasn't quicker this way and if they weren't still under fire, she never would have consented, but the alternative was Conary flinging her over his shoulder like a sack of flour, which would have been even more embarrassing.

As they left the tunnel and made their way to the beach, she saw the big RIB with Grace on board speeding off in the distance. The rest of the teams were all accounted for, and she was unceremoniously tossed into one of the smaller RIBs, and they pushed off. On the cliff, she could see search lights from the Russian guards flickering, but by the time they could fire on the RIBS, they were almost out of range. A few spent bullets splashed behind them, and then they were gone.

The Old Kingfisher

Above the waterline, the fishing boat looked like a total junker, but under the hood was a state-of-the-art jet-fuelled engine, a super slick hull, and a keel made for racing. The captain stood in the wheelhouse waiting for his orders. He had always wanted to stretch The Old Kingfisher under fire, and as soon as all of the passengers were on board, he was going to get his chance. His fingers itched on the joystick.

The big RIB lined up to the net winch, and the passenger was carefully lifted on board. The captain knew this was a person of importance, but so fat she couldn't move. When he had a good look at her, she didn't seem so bad. Not much bigger than his wife.

Then he saw the green glowing eyes. A lord. He worked for RumLot and saw the occasional elf (Who in Ukraine hadn't?), but he had never seen an actual lord. They were rescuing a lord from the Russians! He grinned; now he really had a reason to stretch The Old Kingfisher. He would make her fly.

The woman was hauled on board, and she was in rough shape, all bruised and scraped, but nothing serious. The medics tended to her as soon as she was secured.

On the starboard side, there was some yelling, so he looked. Mermaids! Oh, now he was going to have to tell his daughter about this! Actually, it was a couple of mermen, and they were hauling – and he looked again at the video screen. A huge dog. The mermen wanted the net to winch up this massive dog onto his boat. He looked over to Jameson, who just shrugged and nodded. The Captain gave the okay, and his crew went to work.

When the dog was hauled on board, the mermen gave a wave and a flip and disappeared back into the sea. The dog was not happy but was too exhausted to fight, and after a growl at one of the crew, he found a corner. Aside from standing up to give everyone in a two-mile radius a dog shower, he minded his own business.

Which was good because the two other RIBs were just then pulling up. They called in that they had two casualties, and the medics were ready with the stretcher. But before they could even swing it overboard, one of the casualties was hauling herself over the railings. Another lord! She pulled herself up on the rope, and she limped out of the way. Something was wrong with her foot. The captain turned to Jameson, but he was gone. When the captain looked down, Jameson was excitedly (And when did Jameson ever get excited?) talking to the lord, and then *a third* lord walked up and propped up the second lord. This one had blue eyes.

Holy Mother of God! He had three lords on his boat, and there were mermaids in the water!

The other injured guy (not a lord) was hauled up on the stretcher, and with all of the personnel now on board and the RIBs pushing off to make their own way back to port, the captain told everyone to hang on; they were going to move.

It was like music. The huge engines just hummed, and it almost brought a tear to the captain's eye. He double-checked his coordinates and let her fly the way she was built to fly.

The boat vibrated as it ploughed through the black waves, and the captain sat back to enjoy the ride. The engine room radioed that everything looked fine down below.

An alarm screamed, and the captain looked at his console. The radar was showing something flying towards them.

Expecting something naughty from the Russians, the RumLot people were prepared. On the stern deck, they had two chain guns and a shoulder-fired anti-aircraft MANPADS.

He got on the horn and told the civilians to get helmets on and to get under cover. The captain was a pro, and he let the gunners do their jobs while he concentrated on his vessel. A helicopter was a lot more manoeuvrable than any ship, so he wouldn't even bother to zig-zag until he was under direct fire. He just let her fly.

As expected from the radar signature, it was a helicopter, an old KA-50 Hokum. It was probably the only flying thing the Russians had in Sochi at the moment, and it was making a valiant effort to stop the boat. The captain looked at the radar. It was closing in. The camera facing the rear of the boat showed the chain gunners getting ready. The helicopter's auto-cannon out-ranged the chain gunners, so it was a matter of visibility and who was better and faster.

That damn lord was back there talking to the gunners! The blue-eyed one. He wasn't even wearing a fucking helmet.

The captain grimaced. This wasn't a joyride, Mr Lord; those gunners needed to concentrate, and they didn't need you as an audience.

The lord took off his glasses and tucked them in his shirt pocket, and stared at where the chain gunner was pointing. A blue glow enveloped his entire body. The gunner's head swivelled back and forth between the lord, his gun, and the helicopter, which was a barely visible pinprick in the night sky. Then the lord flashed – and the helicopter exploded into a fireball which made it very visible indeed.

Well. Another story to tell his wife. That was real, heavy-duty magic.

The lord's glow faded away, and he staggered a bit, but then the ship was screaming towards Sevastopol, and it was a bit choppy. He put his glasses back on and gave a thumbs up to the chain gunner and returned to the passenger galley, wobbling and holding on to the rail.

_____

Conary

Conary lay flat on his back and studied the ceiling. Sure enough, just as Vrt said, there was a smoke detector directly above the bed, its tiny green eye winking protectively.

The watery morning light of Suffolk was edging around the curtains, and his stomach was rumbling. Soon he'd get ready to head to the Breakfast Room to load up on carbs and see how everyone was doing, but for a moment, a precious five minutes, he savoured this point in time. Vrt slept next to him, curled on her side with an arm flung over his belly. He could feel her even breath on his ribcage. She was naked except for the boot on her foot, and when she had tried to take it off last night, Conary wouldn't let her. He said he could work around it, and he did.

He played a bit with her hair, which was growing back quickly, but it would be a few years before she regained her magnificent braid. Or maybe she wouldn't. He didn't care; he had the original.

This beautiful creature, his Angel of Death, was mad about him, and he was mad about her. He had a job, if you could call being a lord a job, that was fulfilling, challenging, and a wee bit dangerous, which kept it interesting. Unless he made a stupid mistake, he was going to enjoy both for a long, long time.

For these five minutes in time, life was perfect.

Sam

Sam wandered down for breakfast, and Conary was already there, cutting into a huge stack of American pancakes. Next to that was a plate of sausages, bacon, and eggs. Not one to bother a man when he was eating, and since Conary was looking pretty thin, Sam just grunted, "G'morning," and went to the buffet and made up his own huge plate.

"Good to see you back. Heard everything was good. Where's Vrt?"

"She's still sleeping. Yeah, everything went fine. She busted a bone in her foot, but Dr Mandy says she'll be back to normal in a week or so."

"I guess that's an advantage to being one of the weird ones. Humans take months for those things to heal up."

"Yeah, we can't complain about that! So how was it while we were gone? Anything new happen?"

"Nah, it was quiet. I started carving a life-sized mermaid out of pink granite, which is tricky. Ratna and Tuân are fine, and Tuân is doing some more Ranger training in the Alps, and Ratna is with him. Jack and Alizah will probably be in later." Sam started working on his scrambled eggs. "I heard you brought back a –"

And just as he said that Grace and a human nurse walked in.

"– and this is where you'll have your meals every day. There's always a buffet set up, and you just help yourself. If you want anything, just call for a housekeeper, and they'll fetch it for you."

The lords stood up, and Conary beamed at the girl and walked over.

"Grace! It's so good to see you getting around! How are you feeling? Recovered or still a bit ragged?"

Grace smiled shyly. All cleaned up and wearing flattering clothes and shape-wear that fit her properly, she looked pretty good. While she was still very heavy, she was trimming down to a healthier size, and from what Conary could see she was getting around fine. But the best part was that she seemed to be happy with herself. She was standing up straight, she wasn't scared, and she was looking around, curious about her new world.

Sam cleared his throat, and without turning to look at him, Conary grinned to himself. He and Vrt had a bet.

"Grace, I want to introduce you to my good friend Sam. He's a lord, too!"
Sam stood up, gave a little bow, and then turned bright red and sat back down again without even saying a word.

"Do you want some breakfast? We'd love to have you sit with us even if you just have a cup of tea." Conary winked. "We're just regular guys, but we're not *too* boring, and a pretty girl brings us out of our shells. Otherwise, we just sit and grunt at each other." Grace giggled and sat down next to Conary and across from Sam and nibbled on a plate of fruit.

The three spent breakfast chatting about this and that with Conary filling in most of the airtime, but eventually Sam started talking, too. Vrt came down for breakfast, clumping around in her boot and crutches, and right after she sat down, Alizah and

Jack showed up. So Grace had a nice introduction to many of the lords.

Aliza, Jack, had scheduled a tour of the grounds, and Sam offered to take Grace on a totally unnecessary tour of his studio, but Vrt said she'd rather not do that amount of walking, and Conary stayed with Vrt.

After the four lords left, Vrt turned to Conary. "Okay, I saw the Coke. When did he get it for her?"

"9:35"

Vrt pouted. She had bet that Sam would bring Grace the first Coke after 10:30, so she paid her man a coin.

Hùng

The Old Man called up his children the day he arrived in Suffolk. He was briefed on Hùng's cancer, that it had been arrested and probably cured, and the aftereffects his family went through when they discovered who he and their grandmother were.

The kids (if you can call people in their 50s kids) were packing up and cutting ties with their old lives and within days would be on their way to either the new Rumlot compound in Hanoi or to the UK, where the RumLot people had bought a big house in Oulton Broad with a dock on Lake Lothing. It was all ready for Sen and her family and Hùng's adult kids and grandkids. They would stay together until they found their footing in the UK.

All Conary could say was that he was sorry for the upheaval and how glad he was that Hùng was getting better. When you learn that you will live forever and then find out that one of your children is deathly ill, it's a shock to the system. No one really expects to outlive their children, and Conary was coming to the realisation that he'll watch them, children and grandchildren, pass on before him. All he could do in the meantime was make their lives as comfortable and happy as possible, like any parent.

A person can have unimaginable power and still be powerless. The only real, unimaginable, unstoppable power was owned by Time.

Hùng assured his dad that everything was okay on their end and that they were being well taken care of, and everyone had round-the-clock guards. Mr Won was overseeing every detail, and in a few days, the entire Vietnamese clan would be moved.

The Old Man seemed tired. The picture of him on the video screen was very blurry, but Hùng could hear it in his voice. When Hùng was a little boy and his dad came home from weeks away "working", he would sleep for days, and Hùng could hear the same bone-tired weariness even when he was trying to be cheerful. Whatever he had been doing the last few months had taken its toll.

But whatever work it was, it was providing for the safety and security of his family, and it paid for Hùng's treatment, so no one at their end could complain. Hùng was mature enough to forgive any hurt he felt for having been left out of the loop. The Old Man had his reasons, which were becoming more evident every day.

Conary promised to fly to Vietnam soon and see the family that had stayed behind; he'd go just as soon as Sen's part of the clan was settled in Suffolk. He said he would bring his wife, which took Hùng a few minutes to process. Mai, who was sitting in on the call, jumped in to say that they would love to see her! And with that little bombshell, they hung up, promising to talk again soon.

Hùng turned to Mai. "His wife! And I thought he sounded tired, but I thought it was from going on some adventure! A new wife! The man is pushing eighty!"

Mai laughed. "Well, maybe this new wife *is* the adventure!"

The only thing left to do was throw up his hands and shake his head. The Old Man was full of surprises and secrets. Nothing had changed.

Lester

Humiliated and furious, there was no mollifying the Tsar. Having his palace – his *home* – glitter bombed by fucking elves was a public embarrassment. But privately, the loss of the fat lord was an expensive failure he could not forgive. Heads rolled.

Lena was clever enough to stay out of sight during his rampages and let him have his hissy fit, but at night, he still insisted on sleeping in her bed; only lately he hadn't been fucking the alternative Lenas. He would come in and without a word, just spoon up next to her and bury his nose in her hair and *sniff*. Just sniff and then fall asleep holding her as if she were a giant teddy bear. It was weird. Pathetic and weird.

Then, to make life worse, he started ordering the alternative Lenas out of the bedroom. Now she had to deal with him by herself, and that was no fun. The first time he tried to crawl on top of her, she reminded him that she had just given birth to his heir. To her utter and complete astonishment, he rolled back off, worried that he was hurting her. She was so surprised she let him kiss her neck, and she finished him off with her hands. That seemed to keep him satisfied for a while.

With the other Lenas gone, RealLena knew what was coming, and she wasn't looking forward to it. But it was part of the job. Hopefully, she wouldn't get pregnant again.

For his part, Lester was confused, too. Lords don't get blissed out on the scent of humans, no matter how much they love them, and here Lester was high as a kite on Lena's scent. He thought about her all the time, he worried about the baby, and he was domesticating to a very unhealthy degree. He didn't think he was in love with her. Lester had never loved anyone, and his relationship with Lena had started off as transactional and remained transactional. He was anticipating using her for fifteen or twenty years and then trading her in for a newer model, but now the thought of her leaving made his stomach knot up.

If that Grace had stayed in Sochi, where she was supposed to, when this Lena was washed up, he would have had a real lord to use, waiting in the wings, and trained to his needs. Now he was going to have to find a new one to use if the lord-breeding plan was to materialise. The problem was that whenever he even thought about other women, he just wasn't interested.

One would think he was bonded to Lena, but that just wasn't possible. Lena was human; he had never seen her eyes glow, and besides, her eyes were blue. He was a lord and could not bond to a human. End of story.

Grace

Living in Aelfeham House was like living in an exclusive boarding school, only with adults and no teachers. Grace might have called it a commune, and while no one had to work in the traditional sense, they were expected to learn and help each other.

Grace loved it. For the first time in her life, she was accepted for herself. No one yelled at her for being fat and slow, no one made snide comments about her weight, and no one rolled their eyes when she sat down at the communal table. If anything, the lords ate like every meal was their last and put her portions to shame. Grace would sit with a normal plate of veg and some sort of meat, and they would unapologetically pile on the carbs. There was never a "I really shouldn't" as they dug in.

So she was not impressed after all the weight she had lost and everything she had gone through when Sam brought her a Coke one morning and stood in front of her, hands on his hips, as if he was judging a particularly well-configured heifer. He smiled and said, "When you lose a bit more weight, you're going to be a stunner, Grace."

She didn't take that as a compliment at all, and she gave Sam a dirty look that wasn't missed by Ratna.

Probably the best thing about Aelfeham House was that she had a built-in cadre of sisters. Alizah was her favourite. She was from the UK and wasn't one of the old ones. Everything about being a lord was new to her, too.

When Grace was first told she was a lord and that was why she was so valuable to the Russians and why RumLot had saved her, she didn't believe it. The only thing she could see that made her a member of that tribe was that she could smell orcs. That was it. But the other lords and the elves were convinced and just said she was too young for the white hair, ears, and magic. That would all come in due time, probably when she was about fifty or so, which to twenty-year-old Grace was a lifetime away.

In the meantime, she was to get healthy, learn a bit of self-defence when she was capable, and most of all learn what it meant to be a lord – and there was no pressure. She had all the time in the world. Unlike Tuân, she wouldn't be sent to Ranger school, and for now wouldn't be asked to do anything like going on a mission. Everyone, including Grace, wanted her to get healthy first.

Learning from their mistakes with the other lords who had arrived earlier, the elves and Lords Cadence and Kyrylo changed a few things with Grace's education curriculum. She had all the usual lessons in politics, sociology, etiquette, and so on, but she also had lessons in elf and lord history. She was taught lord biology from the first, so she knew about Scents, about living forever, egg dropping, about bonding – everything.

The "old" lord women, Vrt and Ratna, made sure Grace was not going to get blindsided by a man's scent, and she learned how to control her own pheromones with obsessive cleanliness. The only unbonded lord she had to worry about was Sam, but the women wanted Grace to get into the habit of controlling her own scent. It was only polite.

So when Ratna sat down for a private girl-to-girl in the garden with Grace, a couple of days after Sam's faux pas, Grace didn't see anything unusual about their conversation about scents.

"Ohh – smell the sage, Grace! It reminds me of Banff." Ratna turned to Grace and grinned. "It smells good, but not as sexy as Tuân after a good jog! It's a pity you can't smell him. Or maybe you can?"

"No, he just smells like a sweaty guy to me. Nothing special."

"Good! I don't want to share his scent with anyone! I'll get jealous." Ratna laughed. "Alizah could smell Kyrylo a little bit, but after she bonded with Jack, that went away. I was worried once that if I could smell Tuân, I'd also smell Conary, but that didn't happen. Do you smell any of the guys?"

Grace thought and shook her head. "Sometimes I get a whiff of Sam, but not like how you say." She giggled. "Maybe it's just too much garlic."

"Well, you'll know it when you smell it. I guess Sam's not your type."

Grace fell into gales of laughter. "Sam isn't anyone's type! How can any girl like someone who looks at you like you're a used car and your MOT isn't up to date?" She chuckled. "Sam doesn't love me. He doesn't even like me. He's just a horny old guy, and I'm the nearest thing that can scratch an itch."

Ratna laughed and nodded. She got it. Grace was not interested. Poor Sam.

Sam

When Sam first met Vera, he was twenty-eight and a virgin. He would never, ever, ever admit that to anyone, but it was true.

The reason Sam was a virgin was because he was absolutely, down-to-the-ground terrified of women. He was afraid of their power, their otherness, their magic. A woman could look at a man, and they knew everything about him. They knew if they inhabited a man's dreams, they knew all they had to do was flash a bit of leg or bend over and give a peek (either end, it didn't matter), and just by looking, a man would be, well, unmanned. A woman could smile and a man would forget how to talk, how to walk, and how to think. And the worst part was that they knew it and thought it was funny.

Vera, who was five years older, had been married twice before she met Sam. Her first husband ran off with one of her best friends, and when he returned one evening, confident she would take him back, she had already filed for divorce. He had thought he had the power in that relationship, but he didn't and had found out the first time he screwed up that she was not going to forgive him.

Her second husband was a lot older than her and died falling off a scaffolding. He was a roofer, and that's how Sam met Vera. He knew her from the roofing company where she worked as the bookkeeper, and he would come by occasionally when he had a job that needed work done on a client's eaves. Not long after the accident, Sam stopped by to schedule something, and she was at her desk. As he walked by, he saw a tear fall on a bill. He didn't say anything but went to the nearest corner shop, bought her a Coke and a box of tissues, and silently left them on her desk. He thought Vera fell in love with him because he bought her that Coke. She fell in love with him because he saw her as a person.

Six months later, they were married.

She said to him that he was spending a lot of time at her house, and it seemed to her that having two places was an expense they didn't need. He agreed. But, she said, I'm not going to move in with anyone unless I'm married. He thought that was sensible and said they should do that. Sam always thought he had asked Vera to marry him, but she knew differently.

In all of the years Sam and Vera were married, he never figured it out. He never figured out that when he treated women, including Vera, as a collection of parts who did things for him, they got mad, but when he treated them as people, they liked him. To Sam, women were an indecipherable, unpredictable, unobtainable species, and he knew he was lucky to have found Vera.

All he could do was hope lightning would strike twice in the same place. He just had no idea how to put up a lightning rod and attract it.

———————————————

Vrt and Caddy

Ivana laughed and laughed. She couldn't sit up by herself, but she could grab at things and bat with her hands, making her the patty-cake expert of the world. Vrt lay on the floor, her knees up to prop up the baby who sat on the Vrt-chair and helped her clap her hands. Ivana found this endlessly entertaining.

They were in Caddy's Lowestoft house, the same one she and Ricky had bought so many years ago, in the sitting room. Caddy was on the couch, drinking a cup of tea and scrolling through the playlist on her tablet.

"Well, I have to have that one in, that's for sure." She tapped "Rhumba Queen" into a new playlist.

"What are you doing?"

"I'm making a playlist for our wedding. Kyrylo asked me to marry him a year ago, and now here I am planning the darn thing. We –"

Vrt was shocked. Utterly and profoundly shocked. Ivana pouted because patty-cake stopped, and she waved her little fists and gurgled, telling Vrt to get back to business.

"But you can't do that! That's terrible!"

Caddy looked up, surprised. "Why not? We love each other, we're physically bonded, and we have a kid together. I even have a ring!" And she held up her hand to prove it.

"No, I mean you're planning it. You can't plan your own wedding! It's your bonding party, right? Isn't that what a wedding is? That's terrible luck!" Vrt picked up Ivana and handed the unhappy baby to her elf nanny. This was more important. Patty-cake would have to wait.

"Yeah, I guess a wedding is the same as a bonding party. I wouldn't know either one. I never had a bonding party, and I've never had a wedding."

Vrt looked at the Primary, who should know these things and didn't, and it struck her that she, Vrt, was the only lord in existence now who knew about the old ways. Sure, the elves did, but that wasn't the same. Elves didn't lead; they followed the lord's commands, and if a lord didn't know what to ask for, it didn't happen. Ratna was too young when the carnage happened to understand how to put on a wedding or even a proper banquet, so she wouldn't know. Jack had never bonded and gone through the ceremony. Besides, guys didn't pay much attention to the mechanics of a party; they just attended and attacked the buffet. Vrt doubted if Jack had been to many of them. House might know; she'd have to ask him.

"You can't do anything. You can't choose the music. The next thing you'll be saying you're going to play –" And by Caddy's expression, Vrt knew the worst. "Oh, by the gods in the stars – you expect to entertain your guests at your own bonding. I can see it in your eyes. What's next, cutting the ca –.. Oh, fuck – you plan to serve the food! Are you going to scrub the toilets in your bonding dress, too?"

Caddy laughed. "I guess lords do things a bit differently than humans do."

"Fuck yes, we do. And you're not a human. You are the Primary, and there will be five hundred people at this thing if there is one. It will be the party of the century, and you and Kyrylo each have one thing to do and one thing only. You are going to give him his knife, he's going to pin your hair, and you two will jump over the fire together. Then everyone is going to have a roaring, drunken good time celebrating your bonding." Vrt nodded. "And that's the way it's going to be. If you start managing this, you'll be stressed, he'll be stressed, and you'll have arguments. A very bad luck way to officially start your life together."

"Well, who's going to do it if I don't?"

Vrt sighed. "I will. It's easy. I will go to the elves and tell them the day and what I expect, and they will handle everything. Including the music. You can look at the guest list and throw out anyone you just can't stand to be in the same room with. That's it. Oh – you can choose the day, too."

Vrt shook her finger. "Not a thing other than that. Nothing. The elves will be mortally offended if you take this away from them. It's their fun, too, and we'll never hear the end of it. I bet they're already grumbling and nothing has happened yet."

Caddy threw up her hands.

The lords' tradition was that the bonding party was a celebration and that the bonding couple did absolutely nothing but swap gifts and then have a good time. The very idea that a wedding was work for the couple went against all common sense.

During dinner at Aelfeham House, Vrt was still beside herself; she was so indignant about Caddy and Kyrylo's bonding party. The guys didn't see why she was so upset, but they all agreed that they were lords and should revive lord customs as best they could for this modern world. Tradition did mean something.

"So who gets to come? Will Jack and I be able to come watch?"

Vrt stared at Alizah. What a silly question. "Of course you'll be there. Everyone will be there. I looked up King William's wedding, and they had nineteen hundred guests. I wouldn't be surprised if our final guest list is close to that."

Conary didn't know how to ask this more diplomatically, so he just jumped in, "It's a big deal, Vrt. Do you want to take this on? Can you do it?"

"I don't have to do very much at all. The elves, especially those who have worked bonding parties before, will all have a hand in it. How many elves are out there in Europe now? A hundred thousand?"

"Closer to half a million," said Jack.

"Well, if half a million very talented elves can't keep a dozen lords and a thousand humans entertained for an evening, I'd be very surprised. They'll bring everything in through the Safe Haven. All the local elves will do is set up. The next night they'll have their own party in the Safe Haven and complain and gossip about us." She nodded to herself. "I'll talk with Norma tomorrow. When Caddy and Kyrylo set a date, it'll be absolute chaos at the stampede."

"Don't you mean 'full speed ahead'?"

"No."

Grace, Wendell, and LeeAnne

Grace sent a note to LeeAnne in Norwich and asked her if she and Wendell would like to meet for lunch one day in Lowestoft. She wanted to thank them both for spotting her at the Prom and thought it would be nice to get together when they were available. Nervously, she waited for an answer, and it came back pretty quickly. They'd love to have lunch. Would this Saturday be good? So they picked the Jolly Sailors where they could have a nice fish and chips lunch and a catch-up.

It would be the first time Grace had seen Wendell since the Prom, and now that they had accepted, she didn't know what to do. And once the lunch date was set up, she wished she had never made the overture. She was still heavy, but she looked good; she knew she did, but she would be sitting right next to the gorgeous LeeAnne, and the contrast would be striking.

She didn't know why she had asked them. Maybe she should tell them she was ill? Something came up? She had another date?

But she didn't like lying; too many people had lied to her in her life, and now lying just made her feel bad. The elves had a saying, "You can't lie to a lord". But that wasn't true, and everyone knew it. You *could* lie to a lord; it just was harder to get away with it. And when you knew when people were lying, you started thinking they knew when you were lying, so you just stopped doing it.

But could she lie to herself? She had asked Wendell and LeeAnne to lunch because she knew Wendell wouldn't come alone to something that felt too much like a date. They had seemed to truly like each other at the Prom, and she had no reason to think it was different now. By accepting together, it was clear they were still dating. What did she think was going to happen? Did she truly believe he was going to be so overwhelmed with Grace he'd dump LeeAnne at some point between the fish and chips and pudding?

And she was a lord. The lords who had human wives and husbands all mourned when they died, and so when the opportunity arose, they found other lords to love. Her love for Wendell was based on a thirty-minute meeting. It had kept her focused when she was in Russia. Her love gave her a goal. Maybe she didn't need that goal now. Maybe she didn't need *him* now.

There was only one way to find out, and that was over fish and chips.

Like a condemned woman walking to her executioner, Grace picked out her cutest outfit and prepared to meet her fate.

The Jolly Sailors was nice. Wendell was, as before, heart-stoppingly handsome, exquisitely polite, and very good company. LeeAnne was thrilled to see Grace, amazed at how much weight she had lost and how good she looked, and she was very good company. They both were fascinated that Grace was a lord and peppered her with questions about her training and living at Aelfeham House. Without making a huge point of it, they seemed to be a happy couple with a nice life to look forward to.

Grace learned what Ratna knew. You can't go back. She wasn't the same person who had left the Prom and gone to her bedroom to eat until she keeled over and died. She wasn't the same person that Wendell had twirled around the ballroom floor and who fell in love with the first man who was ever kind to her.

You can't go back; time only marches forward. Grace wouldn't go back for a million pounds.

They had a lovely lunch. Grace thanked them both from the bottom of her heart for helping her that night and starting the chain of events that brought her to The Jolly Sailors that day.

And when it was all done, she picked up the tab, wished them both well, and went back to Aelfeham House to be a lord.

Grace

The dress for the bonding celebration was finally finished, and it was stunning. Grace had worked with the elf tailors closely, and her job was to examine hundreds, maybe a thousand, little cloth swatches looking for the perfect colour, weave, and drape for the dress. The textile samples the elves showed her were fascinating, each with its own personality, and she enjoyed playing with them more than anything else. The colour she chose was a shimmering bronze that played up the dark red of her hair, and the weave had a subtle spider web in it. She couldn't tell you why, but she had always loved watching spiders weave, and this odd damask appealed to her.

Her weight had broken well past the two-hundred-pound barrier, and she was now literally less than half the size she was when she was at the Prom. Her sagging skin was firming up and shrinking back to where it should be, and the little bits that still needed to be worked on could be easily hidden in a formal ball gown. The silhouette the elf designers chose was almost cartoonishly curvy with a full skirt hiding her chubby thighs and knees, and the contrast making her smallish waist seem tiny. A well-structured bodice held everything in and everything up, and the low cut neckline dared anyone to look anywhere else.

Grace was a lord, but she didn't have the white hair and the pointed ears to show off. Maybe it was just her imagination, but she thought her ears were getting a little pointy. So the hairdressers piled up her dark red hair in glossy curls, and with some makeup, she looked really good. Hot even.

On the appointed night, all the lords gathered in the TV room, and Grace stood waiting with her gorgeous, beautifully dressed friends. For once in her life, she didn't feel hideously out of place. Not even when she stood next to Vrt.

The guys were all handsome and so at ease in their dinner jackets; it was like they were born in them. Caddy had insisted that everyone – *everyone* – take dancing and etiquette lessons, and while some rolled their eyes, it was on nights like this that the lessons paid off. The Primary said that every lord was a representative of the Elf Nation and needed to know how to act at the most formal of functions with easy good manners, and that included knowing how to act, dress, dance, and eat at a banquet.

She told Grace that when she was younger, she had read a history book about the different courts in Europe and how some countries were ostracised because their ambassadors didn't know how to act. That wasn't going to happen to the lords of the Elf Nation. She didn't say that she hadn't known how to dance until Kyrylo taught her, which was embarrassing and exciting at the same time.

Some of the lords had never been seen in public before, and part of the preparation for this night was learning how to walk the red carpet, pose for the press, and answer questions for on-the-spot interviews. While this was a private party, Lord Cadence and Lord Kyrylo's Bonding Ceremony was also part of the Elf Nation's public relations and diplomatic strategy. There were going to be representatives from all of the friendly and a few not-so-friendly nations of the world, and most would be heads of state. As well as everyone's families and *some* members of the RumLot Security senior team (because, hey, some people still had to work), guests included celebrities, scientists, writers, artists, and everyone in between.

Ellen paired up each of the lords to walk the red carpet together, and that meant that by default, Grace and Sam were thrown together for that duty. Grace thought Sam looked very presentable in his tuxedo with a barber-trimmed beard and rather impressive pointed ears, and she had no problem putting her hand in his offered elbow and being with him the fifteen minutes it took for them to make their entrance to the ballroom. If he just kept his mouth shut, it would be fine. Besides, once they were inside, she could go off and talk and dance with other people. They weren't on a date.

Sam, for his part, couldn't speak if he wanted to. Grace stunned him to silence. The creamy skin, the low-cut dress, that mouth – and she smelled like sex. All he could do was choke out that her dress was really pretty. She patted him on the arm and said that his tux was very nice, too.

They were second in line for red carpet duty, right after Alizah and Jack. When the PR manager, Trevor, called them up, they were ported to their starting point on the red carpet, where they did their job for the Elf Nation. Then they went on to the ball.

Sam

The bonding party was winding down. It was by all accounts a roaring success.

Most accounts at least.

Sam sat on a bench in a dark edge of a rose garden, nursing a beer and wondering if he should keep looking for Grace or just give up and go home. Around him, partygoers were milling around also looking for lost partners and lost friends. He heard women laugh, and one started to sing. Behind him there were quieter sounds as couples stole kisses in dark corners.

She was gone. The last he had seen of her, she was dancing with Neptune, and he bent down to say something in her ear, and she was laughing. Then they whirled into the huge crowd and disappeared. It never occurred to Sam that the Realm Lord Neptune would show up in his human form, ready for a party, and it certainly never occurred to Sam that the Lord of the Seas would take a shine to the least powerful and newest of the lords, Grace.

He didn't know what to do. He didn't know what to feel. He started insanely jealous of the handsome lord, then insanely furious at Grace for running off with him, then insanely worried for her.

What if she did something she regretted? What if he hurt her? Sam didn't think in a million years Neptune would physically hurt her. He wouldn't rape her. But she was vulnerable, and his Grace could so easily be hurt emotionally. What if she bonded to Neptune during a night of passion? They said Neptune was so old he didn't know how old he was, but he had never bonded, not that Sam had ever heard. He wasn't going to bond to Grace, and after some fun, he'd move on as he always did. Sam had known guys like that back in New York. They had left a lot of broken hearts and damage. They hadn't treated women right.

Sam had escorted Grace into the ball, survived the red carpet, and once in, they did their diplomatic thing and shook a lot of hands. Then Caddy and Kyrylo had a simple and moving bonding ceremony. They jumped the fire, and the party started. Sam had one glorious waltz with Grace, and then Jack cut in, and Sam traded partners to waltz with Alizah, which was fine. Then Neptune cut in to dance with Grace, and within minutes, he had lost her. Sam spent the entire night going from dance venue to buffet to live bands to discos to acrobats and light shows and gods knew what else, looking for her.

Now it was two in the morning.

Conary threw himself down on the bench and took a swig out of his bottle. It was water. He looked a bit worse for wear, too. Somewhere he had lost his jacket, and his tie was dangling around his neck.

Grinning, he turned to Sam. "Some party, huh?"

Sam just grunted. He was in no mood to talk.

Conary gave his friend a sideways glance. He knew what was bothering Sam, but what could he say? Grace had danced with Sam, but then she danced with all the guys. She danced once with Conary, and they both enjoyed it, but it was like dancing with his sister. And to be honest, she *was* his sister now. She was hugely enjoying the party; anyone could see that. It was her debut, her public coming out of the sad shadows of her early life, and she revelled in the attention and soaked up the admiration. Men lusted for her, and it didn't scare her; she welcomed it.

Well, Sam was jealous, and there was nothing Conary could do about that. He would just have to deal with it by himself, and Conary prayed to all the stars above that Sam wouldn't step into shit again and say something to make his situation worse with Grace.

Conary had his own woman to find and get home, and just as that thought flitted through his brain, Vrt staggered out of the crowd. She was certainly weaving, and Conary had to laugh at her. Vrt never got drunk, but here she was, looking for her man, and when she spotted him, her face lit up with a silly, lopsided grin.

"Ohh – I finally found you!" She squeezed herself between Conary and Sam and leaned over to give Conary a sloppy kiss on the cheek. "I think I need to go home now. I'm a little –" And she pinched her fingers together. " –a wee bit tipsy."

"I think you're a wee lot tipsy. Did you have a good time? Where have you been?"

"I've been having a last nightcap with the girls." She slurred and giggled. "I think that last one pushed me over the edge."

Sam sat up. "Was Grace there?"

"No, Grace wasn't there." Vrt shook her head and looked over at Sam, and he couldn't tell if the expression on her face was pity or irritation. "Don't go looking for her."

"Why not?" Sam was incensed. Why not, indeed.

"Because she's having fun and doesn't need a –"

Conary stood up and pulled Vrt to her feet before she said anything more. "Time to go! Bedtime!"

Instead of laughing and making a bedtime joke, she got angry. Her eyes began to glow.

"No – I need to say this. Everyone dances around Sam like he's a delicate little bubble who can't take the truth."

Sam scowled at the lord, and his eyes glowed, too. "Okay, Vrt, tell me the truth. Why shouldn't I go find Grace?" Grace was with someone, and Vrt knew who.

Conary sighed. The shit was about to hit the fan; he just knew it.

"Because she's having fun, and you don't love her. You just want to spoil her fun because you're jealous." Vrt stood up, swaying, and shook her finger at Sam. "She likes you, you fuckin' idiot, but she's just a collection of parts to you. Tits and ass. That's it. And all you want to do is play with her fun parts, and then what?"

"Vrt —"

"No, I have to say this. We lords bond for life. If she gives you her heart, what are you giving her in return? You just think about yourself and what you're going to do to Grace and what she can do for you. You just want her to make you feel bigger and to show off, and that's not being a man; that's being a boy, and she wants a man. I hope she finds a man tonight. Any man. Someone who doesn't walk up and say she has acceptable boobs, but, but, but — Every time you talk to her, you say she's inadequate somehow, that she can be improved, that she's not good enough for you."

"That's not true!"

"Yes, it is! *You're going to be a stunner, Grace, when you lose more weight.* We all heard that. You said that in front of *everybody*! Why didn't you just be honest and say she's too fat to fuck now, but when she meets your standard, you'll think about it?"

Sam felt the air rush out of him, and he thought about all the Cokes he had given her, all the compliments that did no good, and it hit him like a boulder rolling off a mountain. Was Vrt right? Was he always insulting Grace instead? Why couldn't he simply say she was perfect the way she was?

"Y'know, Sam, Conary fell for me when I was a monster. A literal, physical monster who couldn't bed him, but he loved me for who I was. God, I still don't know why, but he did. You just go and leer at Grace's boobs and bring her Cokes and wonder why she's not impressed. What if she doesn't like Coke?

Did you ever bother to ask? No, because it's all about you and your needs. That's what a boy does. Those teenagers over there –" And she shakily pointed to an empty space. "– all they think about are their hard-ons and how to find someone to give them release. They're boys. Men love you for who you are. Men think about their women and children first. Grace is looking for a man, and right now you're a boy. So let her go looking for someone who thinks she's perfect the way she is. Let her bond with someone who doesn't make her feel she's barely adequate."

Conary started to lead her off. "And with that, I think you've said enough, Vrt. Let's go home."

"I love you, Conary –"

"I know you do, Sugar. I love you, too. Let's go." And he pulled her away to go find an elf to port them back to Aelfeham House.

Sam sat on the bench, stunned.

He was still sitting here an hour later when a tired elf came up and asked him if he wanted to be ported back home. Wearily, he nodded and stood up, and seconds later he was back in his own bedroom at Aelfeham House just down the hall from Grace's room. For a brief second, he thought about walking down and listening at her door to hear if she was in there, but immediately quashed the idea. He had no right to do that.

The Angel of Death had judged Sam on her true scales and found him wanting. Once she pointed it out, Sam was honest enough with himself to know that she was right. It wasn't as if he hadn't been given clues; he just refused to acknowledge them.

Even Vera, when they were first together, had told him off a couple of times for being "disrespectful". Once he had had the temerity to lecture her on something about double-entry bookkeeping that was probably wrong, and she wasn't shy about telling him to mind his own business. Why would he do that? He did it because he wanted her to think he was a man and in charge. By disrespecting her, he wanted her to respect him more. By showing off as the alpha man, he was acting like a beta boy.

His dad did that. His dad loved his mom; Sam knew he did. And he knew his mom loved his dad, but the man couldn't sit down to a meal she had lovingly prepared without saying at the end, "That was fantastic. Next time you make meatloaf it would be better if we had mash instead of scalloped potatoes – " or "a bit more pepper" or tell her something else was wrong. He couldn't say anything about stonemasonry to Sam without saying, "Boy, that's very good. It would be better next time if – ". He had to be the final arbitrator, the top dog, the one who determined what was good and what was bad.

So Sam grew up resenting criticism, resenting never being quite good enough for his dad, resenting that Sam could be pretty good if he did this one little thing, and that one little thing was never enough because there was always one little thing more that left him wanting.

Then, with every woman Sam met, he did the exact same thing his dad did. He belittled their achievements; he assumed whatever he wanted was what they wanted because, of course, Sam knew better. He never gave a compliment without a caveat that took the compliment away. He didn't pull that crap with men. Just with women. And then he wondered why women didn't like him.

Even now, his friends were telling him to stop being a jerk, and he just didn't want to hear it. He liked women! It wasn't like he *meant* to be insulting! If they chose to be offended by his well-meant comments and advice, was that his problem?

When he complained to Conary that Ratna wasn't paying enough attention to him when he talked about the art of stone cutting, Conary gently reminded him that Ratna was cutting rocks 3,500 years ago. Maybe he should be listening to her and not lecturing her. Sam shrugged. If she was that egotistical –

He put his head in his hands and moaned. Vrt had held up a mirror and made him look, and he didn't like his reflection. Not at all. Because the image showed true. Ratna never talked to him about the one thing that interested them both because he didn't converse with her like she was a person, like he would have if she were a man. He was more interested in showing that he was better, not in talking about what interested them both, so she stopped coming by.

When Kyrylo told him to stop talking about *and judging* women's parts like he was still on a construction site, he was abashed because he didn't mean to be rude, but he still thought of women as a collection of parts, not as whole people. He hadn't understood the lesson. Now he did.

Vrt had talked to him like a man would. Honestly. Bluntly. In his mid-seventies, Sam had finally listened to what people had been telling him his whole life. The penny finally, belatedly, dropped, and he understood why some men got the girls and guys like him did not. The winners respected women as human beings. It was as simple as that.

Sam stared into the black night, and if he weren't a man, he would have cried. He was crazy about Grace; she was exactly the perfect person for him. He couldn't stop thinking about her, and now she wouldn't have anything to do with him. He had acted towards her like a jerk fourteen-year-old boy who wanted a porno pet, not as a man who loved a human being for who she was.

The other lords might suspect it, but they didn't know that Sam had become as bonded to Grace as it was possible for a lord to be. Unlike Caddy and Kyrlo, who started their dance acting like they were still human, Sam knew what bonding meant. He had seen his lord friends bond to each other. For a lord or elf, bonding was forever, not like the humans Sam grew up with, who fell in and out of love, married and divorced and remarried again. Shit, the Angel of Death was bonded to a corpse for 3,500 years before she could finally release him.

Grace was not going to bond with him. She didn't even like him.

It was too late for Sam. He had blown his one chance.

Kyrylo

The reports were disturbing, and the trends they showed only pointed to one conclusion. Russia was re-arming.

The Elf Nation had its own ways of gathering intelligence, and the European nations bordering Russia had their own methods. Between the two, it appeared to Kyrylo that the sanctions that had prevented Russia from modernising and outfitting its destroyed military during the last decade were weakening.

The further the NATO countries were from the Russian border, the less likely they were to make the same interpretation of the data. The US, for instance, waved away any suggestion that Russia was anything other than a dilapidated mess, and they were more concerned about China. The UK was worried, but in their estimation, Russia was still a decade away from being ready to make mischief. Germany and France thought Ukraine was being alarmist and between themselves, were quite happy for the countries from Finland to Georgia to do their worrying for them.

The Elf Nation was not officially a part of NATO, so their influence was muted; all they could do was share intel with their border state friends and hope that they could convince the rest to keep up the sanctions on militarily useful technology and arms sales. The problem was the pull of commerce, which naturally made many countries classify items like computer chips and lasers as commercial or even humanitarian sales, even though they could also be used to kill on the battlefield.

The RumLot Security analysts were very concerned with the reorganisation of the Russian military that actively created orc units led by human officers called Special Shock Troops or *Специальные ударные войска* (SUV). Entire units were being sent to South America and Africa by invitation of a few particularly nasty dictators who needed propping up, and it was obvious to those watching that they were using those special operations as a live-fire training ground.

Tsar Lester was preparing for something, and it wasn't a glitter bomb. The Elf Nation redoubled their efforts to integrate with their human colleagues in preparation for the day when they would be forced to defend themselves. For the elves limited by *terrior*, there would be no fleeing west if they were overrun any more than they could flee last time. This time, however, they were not going to be surprised by the unthinkable.

Caddy increased her awakening sessions from four times a month to six. Kyrylo wouldn't permit any more, rightly worried that exhausting her would simply set them back to no good purpose. But with a methodical approach developed by the intel people and their human partners, she created a deep web of clans from Georgia to Finland that filled in the holes themselves and gradually spread westward. The immediate practical benefit was a porting web that could take anyone from Finland to a line that went from Athens to Copenhagen. West of that line, there were still holes, but she was filling them in as fast as she could with an emphasis on militarily important locations.

She tried her best to show Kyrylo and Conary how to wake up elves, but they just couldn't do it; their abilities just weren't geared to carry a message the way hers was. The best that could be managed was that Conary could faintly sense the elves sleeping but couldn't communicate that they needed to wake up, trust him, and allow him to guide them to the surface. Conary and Kyrylo couldn't relieve Caddy, and the other lords were too weak to push their voices into the hidden places deep in the earth where the elves slept.

Every day, six days a week, Kyrylo spent his days planning, organising, training, and growing his army. Every evening at five, he spent time with his little family and woke the next morning ready to start it all over again. He was working to keep them safe in a world that became more dangerous by the day.

Sam and Vrt

The Breakfast Room was quiet when Sam walked in. Vrt sat next to Conary, picking at her scrambled eggs and drinking tomato juice. She'd never had the stuff before, but someone had told her it was good for hangovers. They were wrong.

Ratna was there. Tuân was still in bed sleeping off his overindulgences. Grace, Alizah, and Jack were still missing in action.

Sam walked up to Vrt and asked if he could talk with her in the hall. She looked at him with cold, dead eyes. He said,

"Please," and wordlessly she left the table and walked out. Sam followed, avoiding Conary and Ratna's eyes.

He took a deep breath.

"Vrt, thanks for talking to me. I have two things to say, and if you never want to talk to me again, I understand."

Her stony expression didn't change. She was a statue.

"First, it's been almost a year, but it's about that time I insulted you and Conary punched me in the nose. I told everyone I'd apologise, but I never did. I was wrong and stupid, and I can't tell you how bad I felt after hurting you. But when I saw you again, I was – " And he sighed. "No excuses. If you don't accept my apology, I deserve it. I am so very sorry."

The statue nodded but said nothing.

"Second, you were right about what you said last night. I needed to be told off. You were right. Everyone here, all my family here, was afraid to hurt my feelings and tell me I was a jerk, but I wasn't afraid to hurt their feelings. I thought a lot about what you said last night, and the only one who would haul me up by the short hairs and give me a good shake was a true sister. I never had a sister, but you did a good job. So thanks." He looked at his feet because he didn't want her to see him tear up. Of course, he wouldn't, but he was close.

"I'm going to try to be better, Vrt. If I screw up and you remind me, I won't take it wrong."

He didn't know she had moved until he felt her arms around him, giving him a hug.

"Oh, Sam. You're an asshole, but you're our asshole. I never had a brother, either, but if I had one, I'm sure he'd be an idiot just like you."

He gingerly hugged her back for two seconds and then stepped back, his eyes wet. "I don't know how to take that, but I think we're good. Are we good?"

"We're good."

They walked back into the Breakfast Room, and Conary and Ratna pretended they hadn't overheard the whole thing.

Grace

When Grace ran off with Neptune, she didn't leave to have a quick shag in the bushes. She wasn't that stupid. Besides, it would mess up her dress.

Not that he didn't ask! He knew she had never had a man – or half man – before and he promised her a memorable first time. Grace was sure he would deliver, but she just wasn't that interested in him, as hot as he was.

So she laughed and flirted with him, and he flirted back until he got the hint that she wasn't going to go any further than a fumble and a kiss, and he wandered off to find more accommodating ladies. Which he did. Several.

No, what she did was run off to the toilet to reapply her makeup, and then she went to the disco where she ran into Wendell, LeeAnne, and a bunch of young humans. They were thrilled to meet the young lord, and they didn't have any old memories of fat, disgusting Grace. All they knew was hot Grace, who loved to dance. She danced with all the guys and a few girls and partied with them until four, then she went home and collapsed in bed, stone-cold sober, exhausted, and happy.

While Sam was agonising over her, she never thought about him at all. Not once.

When she bounced into the Breakfast Room to see what was on the lunch buffet, well-rested and bright-eyed, she found Alizah and Jack there, and they were fine. Neither were big drinkers, and they didn't suffer from any party aftereffects other than staying up too late and meeting too many new people. Actually, after the bonding ceremony, they were back in their penthouse by eleven.

She and Alizah spent the afternoon looking online at the red-carpet pics of all the dresses and tuxes and reading the reviews and disagreeing with half.

By the evening meal, everyone was recovered and back to their normal routine.

Sam stopped bringing Grace Cokes. He was friendly when she spoke to him, and if they sat next to each other at the table, he didn't ignore her, but he didn't seek her out either. There were no forced compliments about her clothes and especially no comments about her weight, which was getting pretty close to her ideal BMI.

He backed so far off that Grace wondered if he was mooning for someone else now, maybe that human personal trainer who came in to help in the weight room. Whatever it was, he was a lot better than before, and she was grateful for small blessings.

One day her PT teacher came in and said that she was now at her ideal weight, and it was time to start her self-defence training. If she could get to the point where she could defend herself, she could go on trips outside of elf country and start seeing the world and not just their little compound.

Judo wiped her out, and the PT instructor decided she needed more aerobic stamina than her dancing classes could provide. But when she suggested the treadmill, Grace wouldn't even consider it. Instead, she went out for a half-hour morning jog on the horse's exercise loop, thinking she could come back early enough to have a good shower before breakfast and scrape the sweat off.

Then Sam showed up. He ran the same loop at the same time but as far away from her as he could get. On the second day, she asked what that was about "because I know you *hate* jogging."

He shuffled and cleared his throat. "You shouldn't be out here by yourself. It isn't safe, and there are no elves about. I won't bother you, but if you want me to go away, I will." Then he smiled. "It'll probably do me a bit of good, too. Maybe I can keep up with Conary in hand-to-hand. He just stays out of reach because he knows I can take him if I grab'm, but he runs around in circles until I'm tired."

So what could she say to that? "Whatever you want to do, Sam. I'm okay."

Of course, the idea that some orc would dart out of the woods and grab her within earshot of Aelfeham House was silly. But then she had been grabbed out of her bed in Sochi, so maybe it wasn't so silly to be cautious. It was really rather sweet of Sam to think of her.

So every morning, weather permitting, they jogged for half an hour, and true to his word, Sam didn't bother her, and he stayed well out of scent range.

A week later, they were having their normal communal dinner, and Sam turned to Jack and said, "Do you know where the Tate Gallery is?"

"Yeah, we can see it from our balcony. Why?"

"Because I want to go to a show there. They're having an exhibit on George Frampton. He's a sculptor, and I thought I'd go take a look. Maybe we can meet for lunch."

Everyone turned to stare at Sam. Every day, he went and chipped at rock in his studio, but no one looked at what he was doing, and he didn't share. No one thought he was the art museum type, and here he was, able to talk quite knowledgeably about different artists and eras and why he wanted to see the George Frampton exhibit. It turned out he went to the Tate and other museums pretty regularly by asking an elf to port him into a side street. Then he just pulled a ski cap down low to hide his ears, and in his jeans and flannel shirts, he walked in with no fuss and was just another visitor. It turned out that not that many orcs went to art museums, so he never had any problems there.

Ratna thought about her mosaics and piped up, "I'd like to go with you, Sam, if you don't mind." Of course he didn't, and when Ratna said she was going, then Alizah and Grace said they'd like to come. Now they had a party.

Ratna had never been to a museum of any type, and while she had heard them mentioned on BBC radio quite often, she didn't know what to expect. The idea that art of all kinds would be sitting around in a building, and anyone could walk in just to see the pretty (or disturbing) things, was bizarre and charming at the same time – much like most of the art she saw. Grace and Alizah had been to museums as school children and had been to the Tate before, so they knew what to expect, but neither had been as an adult. Jack could take it or leave it, but he had to admit it was a nice place to visit, and he liked the coffee shop.

Grace was particularly taken with the tapestries and weaving and stopped at every single exhibit to look at them.

They had a lovely day out. Sam answered questions when he was asked and didn't lecture or mansplain. He gave them space to enjoy what they wanted because he knew he could always come back tomorrow and see it again if he wanted more time at a particular exhibit.

Grace

The visit to the Tate was eye-opening, and it inspired Grace to ask her teachers if she could learn how to weave. Of course she could! The elves set up a loom in her own workshop, the human training managers hired a tutor to teach her, and weaving became a part of her day.

She couldn't begin to tell anyone how fascinated she was by weaving. Planning a design, choosing the wool, learning the different weaves, setting up a loom – every bit of it was interesting. The actual weaving itself was a dance with thread and required concentration, but the repetition was also hypnotic. Like Caddy with her instruments, the very act of practising and repetition was fulfilling in itself. The day Grace cut the first little table runner off the loom was a thrill, a triumph, and she couldn't wait to start the next project.

Sam could hear the thump of the loom from his studio, and in its regular way, it was as comforting as a heartbeat. He liked hearing it because it meant Grace was nearby, and she was content.

One day she went into her workshop, and there was a box on the worktable. In it were the most exquisitely carved marble gargoyles, each with a hole where its mouth should be. They were loom weights for a warp-weighted loom. Sam had made them for her.

She didn't know what to say; it was the most beautiful, thoughtful present. When she went to thank him, he just smiled and nodded, pleased that she was so happy.

Grace didn't fall in love with Sam because of the loom weights – far from it. But she began to look at him differently, so in the Safe Haven pubs, the elves began to place their bets.

Sam

The pink granite mermaid was a disaster. Sam had started it ages ago before Grace was rescued and came to Aelfeham House. After she arrived and Sam became smitten with her, he started carving the upper torso to Grace's likeness. But she changed so fast as she lost weight, and as Vrt so memorably said, he was looking at her in parts and pieces; the sculpture just never came together. The more he carved, the worse the abomination looked.

There's a point when an artwork just isn't salvageable, and one afternoon Sam reached that point. In a fit of fury and frustration, he destroyed the whole thing. He could move rock, shape rock, break rock, and when he was angry enough, he could turn igneous rock into lava. That night, he threw so much energy into that cursed block of stone that he was lucky he didn't burn down his whole workshop.

The blue flash and the sudden burst of heat set off fire alarms, and when the elves ported in to put out the flames, Sam had to sheepishly apologise and tell them everything was okay; he had just had a meltdown. Grace ran to his place from her workshop next door, and he had to apologise to her, too. She would have been really pissed at him if he had set fire to her workshop, too. Gods help him if he burnt up her loom.

She stood in his workspace and stared at the glowing mass of lava and thought about the amount of power it took to melt a life-sized granite sculpture. Sam stood there grim-faced, a white-knuckle grip on his mallet, and sweat dripping off of him.

And that's when she got a good whiff of him. It came so hard and so fast that Grace involuntarily gasped, and Sam turned to see what was wrong. All she could do was squeak out that she had to go, and she ran out the door because if she stayed in one more minute, she was going to rip off his shirt and lick the sweat off his chest, and that would cause all sorts of issues.

Sam watched her run out, and it just made him feel worse because it was his fault. The heat and fumes from the lava had gotten to her, and now the poor girl's face was bright red, and she was choking. He was so frustrated that he was shaking, and he threw his mallet so hard at the fucking mess that it buried itself deep in the cooling rock. Now he had a big pile of crap rock to clean up, and he wouldn't be able to use his studio until he did. And he'd have to buy a new mallet.

Life sucked.

The next morning at breakfast, Grace asked what he was going to do with the lava pile in his workshop, and Sam sighed into his Cheerios.

"I'll spend the day cleaning it up, of course. It'll be a pain in the ass, but I can't expect the elves to clean that crap up. I made the mess with my ability, and I'll use my ability to clean it up."

He brooded all through breakfast, and she left him alone to deal with it, as did everyone else.

Lena

The mirror didn't lie. Her figure had completely recovered from the ravages of carrying the brat, and Lena was very happy with the reflection she saw in the full-length mirror. She didn't even have stretch marks, and she had been worried about that.

Lena might be well over forty, but with this figure, Lester wouldn't be trading her in any time soon. Lena's time as Tsarina could stretch into the foreseeable future.

She really, really loved being Tsarina. Everyone deferred to her, everyone catered to her every whim, and, best of all, everyone was afraid of her. Living in luxury was wonderful, but living in power was better.

So life was good. Even Lester wasn't so nasty now that the baby had come, and he hadn't hit her since the day he found out she was pregnant. Fatherhood had changed him, and while Lena still didn't like him and wasn't physically attracted to him, he was at least tolerable.

Lester still slept with her every night, spooning up against her back and burying his head in her hair, and the Tsarina knew that she would, pretty soon, have to let him fuck her. But that was a small price to pay for everything else. What was ten minutes a couple of times a week when she was Tsarina the rest of the time? It didn't take much to make him think he was the studliest of studs; it was one of the easiest gigs she had ever done. Lena knew that Lester could convince just about anyone of anything, so it amused her that he was so easily fooled. Lester the Liar could be lied to.

The only tiny fly in the ointment was that Russia's place in the world wasn't as exalted as it should be. Now that Lena was Tsarina, she didn't want to be the queen of a third-rate nation; she yearned for so much more. She wanted to travel to other countries and be exalted by more than the serfs in her own patch; she deserved better.

When she flew to New York with Lester, she had a taste of the international jet set life, and now anything less rankled. The disrespect she saw in the eyes of the other heads of state left a bitter taste. When they were both visiting the United Nations, that horrible Cadence woman had the New Yorkers lining the streets and cheering. Where were Lena's adoring fans? Nowhere. Because Russia and the Tsars were not properly respected by the West.

The western sanctions on imports to Russia were an insult. Sanctions meant she still couldn't travel to anyplace other than to the UN in New York and places like China or Iran. She didn't want to go to fucking Iran and wear a black bag. Lena wanted Paris. She wanted couture and Van Cleef & Arpels and yachts moored off Monaco. Now everything, absolutely every luxury bit, had to be smuggled in at huge expense. She wasn't worried about the expense – that's why God made serfs, to make money for Tsars. What infuriated her the most was that she couldn't choose. She couldn't *shop*. The nasty, petty, grudge-holding West held her back. She couldn't even get the make-up, hair dye, and coloured contacts she needed.

She wanted so much more.

Althea

Through an intermediary, the Elf Nation quietly bought a very fine office building in the embassy district of Ottawa and then secretly requested permission from the Canadian government to set up a full diplomatic presence there. Nothing was said about elves, but a very happy Canadian government was sure that elves would follow. So, of course, they gave provisional permission while the request went through their internal processes. After all, wasn't one of the lords Canadian?

Once the building was made secure to RumLot Security standards, a joint public announcement would be made that the Elf Nation would be opening a new embassy in Ottawa, and President Lord Cadence and Vice-President Lord Kyrylo would make an official visit to open the consulate.

Secrets, though, are only as good as the weakest link, and it wasn't long before the elf-parazzi and the elf-fan sites online were abuzz with the rumours of the Elf Nation making an official foothold outside of Europe.

It was only by accident that Althea heard about it at all. She didn't have a phone; Rev Jimmy said she didn't need one; who was she going to call? And she didn't have access to the internet because Rev Jimmy said it was the devil's instrument, and he wouldn't have it in the house. Althea and the other foster kids in Rev Jimmy's household never listened to the radio or the TV for the same reason. It was nothing but pure evil.

When it was pointed out that he had internet access in his office, he got mad and beat the sin out of the stupid girl. That stopped that. Althea knew better than to point out inconsistencies in Rev Jimmy's rhetoric, but poor Daisy was only fourteen and still thought that women could question what a man said and did.

Althea knew about things like the internet, radio, and TV because she heard other people talking. As much as Rev Jimmy preached against the evils of modern media, others in the congregation thought they could control the evil from leaking out like pus on their living room floors and they could safely watch a bit of football or enjoy a cooking show. Besides, there were church shows and sacred music, and those weren't the words of Satan. Althea listened to the Believers' casual conversations during breaks and at potlucks, remembered what they said about the world, and kept her own counsel.

Rev Jimmy and Sister Lily were very protective of their eighteen foster children. They all attended church school until they were sixteen, and then the boys went on to public high school, and the girls went to work. Althea was given a job in the church basement working on accounts receivable. That meant she chased down slow donations and tithes, counted the money that came in every Wednesday and Sunday and whatever other income that came from money-raising ventures the church did, like the bowling alley, the restaurant, the country store and bookshop, the advertising in church media – you name it. They did a lot, and the untaxed income from all of their charitable enterprises was entered into a very sophisticated computer program by Althea.

The work was incredibly boring.

In theory, Althea made minimum wage, but once the foster money dried up, she had to pay for her keep. After paying tithes to the church, paying for her room, board, clothes, etc, she usually ended up with about ten dollars a week to spend on herself, which was the same pocket money the government said she was due as a personal allowance when she was in foster care.

When she was younger, the social workers would come by and make sure the kids had some books to read, and Rev Jimmy and Sister Lily always made a big deal that they were a book-reading family. But as soon as the social workers left, the books and magazines were immediately gathered up and usually ended up in the used book section of the church thrift shop. Except for Althea's. She learned early on not to look too interested, and since the books were huge spiral-bound volumes in braille and didn't sell Sister Lilly would let her tear out the pages and make origami swans, which did sell well, and the church kept the money. Althea always read and memorised the books before she destroyed them to make the swans, and she learned enough to make her curious and keep her mind active. The few books she loved, she managed to keep at the bottom of the pile of her origami paper, and she read them over and over. Sister Lily never noticed.

Her eighteenth birthday came, and Althea's social workers threw her a big party and left, never to return – not for her at least. The minute she put down her fork from the last bit of birthday cake, her routine was unvarying.

She rose at six, cleaned house for an hour, prayed for a happy and healthy household, got ready for work, prayed for a good day at work serving God and Jesus, was escorted to work by one of her foster brothers or a volunteer, prayed for his safe return, worked ten hours, was escorted back, prayed, helped cook dinner for the men, prayed, ate with the women, prayed, cleaned up, went to bed, and prayed tomorrow would be different. It never was.

But you can't keep out the modern world; it seeps through the most hermetically sealed environment like air leaking out of a mylar birthday balloon. Althea heard about the lords and elves from Rev Jimmy himself, and her congregation was convinced that the End of Days was coming and these magical demons and imps were Satan's heralds. Rev Jimmy preached dire warnings, and every Sunday, the congregation was whipped up into quite a frenzy, and donations spiked. The elves were good for business.

Every day, the other women in the accounting department had lunch at the conference room table, but Althea stayed at her desk pretending to work as she ate. They didn't like her, and years ago, she had figured out that there was no pleasing her boss Patty. That was enough to make all five of them avoid her, so she sat in her cubicle, put her head down, and worked with as little interaction as possible. Working alone when the others were eating also gave Althea the opportunity to pocket the occasional white offering envelope with folded bills in it.

The women would talk and laugh and gossip, and she heard it all. So when they talked about the demons of the Elf Nation opening up an embassy in Ottawa, she thought that was interesting, being a demon herself.

Grace

There was a spider in Grace's bedroom. She didn't notice it until she was in bed and looked up as she was about to turn off the nightstand lamp. The spider had woven a lovely, perfect web that stretched from one corner of the high ceiling to the wall and then demurely sat to the side waiting for flies that would never show up, not in an elf-cleaned bedroom. Grace admired the symmetry and efficiency of the web and the way the bridge threads anchored it to the wall with a minimum of anchor points; the spider had made a beautiful, deadly trap.

The elf housekeepers would come in tomorrow, and as efficiently as the spider hunted and killed a fly, they would hunt and kill the spider. Without a second thought, they would sweep away the web with a feather duster.

Well, that was not going to happen, not if Grace could help it. She put on her dressing gown, and after rescuing a paper cup out of the rubbish, she went to the box room down the hall and found a rickety old ladder and hauled it into her bedroom, only banging it on the floor twice in the process.

She was teetering at the top of the ladder when Sam, who woke up when he heard the bangs, came to her door.

"What the hell are you doing? You're going to break your neck!"

"I'm saving this spider; if I don't catch it, the housekeepers will kill it tomorrow." She stretched out further, but she was just too short.

"Get down from there! That ladder is crap. Here, I'll get it. I can reach it." And he steadied the ladder for her while she climbed down, giving him a good look into her open dressing gown and her skimpy nightgown. When you lose a lot of weight after a lifetime of wearing tents, you get pretty things, and Grace only wore pretty things now. Sam choked a bit and then concentrated on the spider. Much safer.

The spider was easily caught in the cup, and she tossed it out her window as pleased as if she had rescued a drowning child. As he was folding up the ladder, Grace danced up and gave Sam a big hug.

"Thank you! I'll sleep better now!"

I won't, Sam thought, and he stepped away from her. "You're welcome, but please, Grace, no hugs."

She stepped back, blushing. "I'm sorry, Sam. I didn't mean —"

"Yeah, I know." And he put the ladder back in the box room. When he walked back, her door was closed, and the light was off.

Althea

The problem from Althea's perspective was first getting out of the house without being seen, and second, finding transportation out of town. Getting to Ottawa was the least of her worries; she would handle that problem when it arose. Getting out of the house without a male escort – that was an issue.

She was alone but never alone. While no one paid attention to her – thinking she was dimwitted as well as blind – the slow speech and dull demeanour were survival skills honed after years of hearing the screams of those who talked back or were too smart for their own good with Rev Jimmy. He didn't demand obedience from Althea late at night because she was too ugly (she had no idea one way or the other, but that's what others said), and as she got older, her persistent BO turned him off. And she was a girl, so that helped. Rev Jimmy had secret things he'd do with the boys, but he wasn't too picky if need be.

Getting out of the house without being seen was a problem. Althea knew that at twenty-four, she had every right to simply walk away, but she also knew that a loose Althea was a dangerous Althea to Rev Jimmy and Sister Lilly. As stupid as she was, Althea knew too much about the church's money and wouldn't be permitted to leave without a fight. A big fight. Others had tried to escape, and Althea knew what had happened to them because she had heard the men talking. Alabama was a big place with lots of forests, and a kid with no family simply disappeared.

A boy missing from high school might have a truant officer or social worker come by and ask a few questions, and just shrug; they were all disturbed kids. They ran away. A woman of twenty-four who walked away wouldn't have anyone looking for her but the congregation, and if the congregation found her, she would be disciplined, probably to death.

The Rev Jimmy's house was a huge, faux-southern Greek revival mansion that sat squarely in the middle of a vast, bare, treeless, multi-acre lawn surrounded by a ten-foot, wrought-iron fence with a locked gate in the front. The other three sides had wire chain link. It was a guarded compound, not a house and was designed to keep the kids from getting ideas about leaving on their own. There were two ways in, the front gate and a back service gate, both electrified and with cameras to keep the kids safe from the sinners who never tried to break in.

Althea's other options were to escape during work at the church or on the way to and from the church. Publicly, the whole point of the escorts was to keep a poor, simple blind girl and the other girls from being tempted by the sinful, unchurched men who lusted for them or would *gasp* rape them on the way to and from work. But the real reason was to make sure she didn't talk to anyone, and she didn't run off. Althea knew that because the men who escorted her and the other girls weren't chaperones, they were guards.

By the time the news of the demons' embassy in Ottawa trickled down to rural Alabama and the accounting department's lunch table, Althea had been thinking of escaping for a long time.

Years.

She listened, she planned, she slowly gathered supplies. She had over ten thousand dollars gleaned from the collection plate cash, a backpack one of the boys had thrown away, and a pair of old jeans and a t-shirt. And she had her secret weapons – her demonic self and her dog Maggot. If she had an hour head start – Jesus, all she needed was a half hour – she could do it, she was sure.

Grace

Vrt didn't have a phone, so the next day, when Grace was in her workroom and wanted to talk to her she had to call up Conary and ask him if she could talk to Vrt. After a bit of faffing around so they could hear each other (Vrt held the phone upside down) Grace asked Vrt if they were still going to Vietnam in two days and asked if she could go with them.

Vrt was silent for a minute and then said, "Sure, you're always welcome, but why? This trip has been planned for weeks now. This is sudden."

Grace had her own long pause, and then she just came out with it. There was no point in equivocating with Vrt and Conary. "I need a bit of time away. I think it would be good if I got away from Sam a bit."

Vrt's voice was sharp. "Is he bothering you?"

"No, I'm bothering him."

Another long pause from Vrt. "Well, if you need space, you'll get space. Let me talk with Conary, Caddy, and Kyrylo. This isn't just a holiday to visit Conary's children. It has a diplomatic side, and if we bring another lord along, especially one as new as you, the Primaries need to know. They might have something to say about your role, and they may have a job for you."

Grace was happy with that and hung up. She was sure they'd let her go. After all, everyone always made a point of saying she wasn't a prisoner, and they were taking the RumLot Security jet; they'd have plenty of room, and she would be well looked after.

That evening after dinner, Conary told Grace that everything was set up, and the elves would pack for her and get everything she needed on the plane. In the meantime, she had some studying to do. As part of her training she was to tag along on all the diplomatic meetings and watch. To do that she had to learn about each country, learn local etiquette, memorise the names of the bigwigs she was going to meet, and be able to answer a few questions if she was asked. She also had to learn the security arrangements, passwords, alarms, and what to do in an emergency.

Trotting off on a diplomatic road trip wasn't as easy as it sounded.

Conary and Sam

Conary then went out to the fire pit and sat down with a beer and waited. He was sure Sam would show up. And he did.

He had changed a lot since he first came to Aelfeham House with Vera. Conary could see that he had lost weight; at least the dad belly was gone. Exercise and self-defence training had added muscle where none had existed before, and while he was still very broad-shouldered from the constant stone carving, his proportions were more in balance now. His thin grey hair was now thicker and lord-white, and his ears were undeniably elfish now. There was no hiding them. He didn't look like he was in his 70s any more; most people would peg him at 45 or 50. Very soon, he'd arrive at his normal lord adult appearance, neither old nor young. Like Conary, Sam was doing a lot more magic now that he was in an environment where it was an everyday occurrence, and that was contributing to his rapid change as his lord side replaced his human side.

He sat down and popped the top of a Bud and stared into the fire. It took a few minutes for Sam to start.

"So you're going back to Vietnam."

"Yep, need to see the kids who stayed back. Also doing some grip-and-grins for Caddy. We're stopping in Japan, Korea, and Australia. China didn't want us." Conary took a sip of his beer.

"Grace is going, too." It wasn't a question.

"Yeah, she asked to come along. It will be good for her to get out. She can start to learn the family business."

Sam nodded. He opened his mouth and then shut it, thinking better of whatever he was going to say, and instead took a sip of his beer.

Conary knew what was on the lord's mind and answered the unasked question anyway. "It's better if you stay back here, Sam. Give her a bit of time to stretch her wings. She's only twenty-one, and she's not ready to hook up with anyone, human or lord. Cage her up, and that bird will fly away the first time the cage door is opened."

"That's very poetic."

"I have my moments."

Sam stood up. "One's enough for me tonight. Have a good trip."

"We'll try." Conary smiled and raised his can in a salute.

"Conary, watch out for her, won't you?"

"Of course, I will. I can promise you that."

Sam nodded and went back into the house. He didn't walk like an old man, but he certainly walked like a sad one.

Althea

The donations to Rev Jimmy poured in. His sermons against the evil demons of the Elf Nation were well-received by groups of Christian fundamentalists from all over the world, and they donated to the church, mostly online.

It didn't matter that Rev Jimmy had never met a single elf or lord; he didn't have to. He could make up anything he wanted about them, and who was going to prove otherwise? He had an argument for anything and everything. Did they do good? That was Satan luring you in with false promises and lies. Were they peaceful? This was just the calm before the storm. And on and on.

The more he preached, the more famous he became, and the more money they were sent. That success convinced him and Sister Lily to go on a multi-state tour of other mega congregations across the South. She was ecstatic. She would be right up there with him, supporting his message, praising God and Jesus, and living their well-deserved high life as they did it.

Rev Jimmy bought a new bus just for the trip. It was a monster, a million-dollar behemoth with sleeping quarters, a full bathroom, satellite TV – all the bells and whistles. And it was plastered with his photo and message on both sides. The bus he already had was demoted to the crew, guards, and flunkies who always travelled with them. The old bus the guards and groupies used to travel on was traded in for the new one and would be going to the dealer's lot in Tennessee for refurbishment and resale.

A blessing of the new bus was planned for tomorrow night when it arrived from the dealership, and once the keys were ceremoniously handed over, the old bus would be on its way. Long ago, Althea had hidden her escape kit in the church, and today she saw her chance to use it. She would hide on the old bus, and if they kicked her out at the first rest stop, that would be fine. She'd be out of town, where half the people were part of the congregation and the other half were afraid of it. From there, she could manage.

Animals and birds would be her eyes, and God, if he really existed, would be on her side.

That night, she sent Maggot out to look over the parking lot where the buses all were lined up, and he came back and told her where they were parked, who was guarding them, and if they had left any doors or cargo hatches open on the old bus. Being a dog, he couldn't test the doors, but he could see that the luggage bays were all closed up.

Maggot was worried. He knew Althea would have to hide because she was prey, but by not being able to see, she could easily leave a part of herself exposed. A foot or hand sticking out where it could be seen, and all would be lost. She didn't have the teeth or claws to defend herself. He whimpered, but he didn't object. Whatever the wonderful Althea wanted, he would do his best to get for her.

Althea hugged him and told him not to worry; it would be dark, and they would sneak in either the luggage compartment or inside the bus itself. If they couldn't get on the bus, they would use the ceremony to sneak out of the church and simply walk into the thick forest that surrounded the town and leave the hard way, on foot. She pointed out that Maggot had good night eyes, and she didn't need daylight at all. They could manage the forest, and they wouldn't get lost because when the birds woke up in the morning they would tell Althea where to go.

She put on a brave face for Maggot, but she knew this was a long, long shot. But when would a better chance come? The congregation would be admiring and blessing the new bus, and they wouldn't pay any attention to her at all. She was ready, and while they were praying for God to favour and be kind to the new bus, she would be praying for her own miracle.

Lester and Lena

Every day Lester was in Moscow, he made a point to see Prince Rurik if only for a few minutes. Today was clear and sunny, and the baby, five of the Lenas, and the Tsarina were taking a morning dip in the pool.

Lester stopped at the playpen, and little Rurik laughed to see his daddy and held his fat arms up, begging to be picked up, which was exactly what Lester wanted. The baby had bonded to his father, and every day he could, Lester worked to strengthen those ties. He would need those bonds when Rurik was a stroppy teenager, and especially when he grew into his lord abilities. Lester was going to make sure he wasn't overthrown by his son, no matter how strong a lord the boy turned out to be.

The Lenas were all encased in sensible, Russian-made swimsuits, but the Tsarina wore a sexy Western bikini, so she was easy to pick out when she pulled herself out of the pool. RealLena always made sure she was the prettiest Lena, and today she certainly was.

Lester kissed the baby, handed him back to his nanny, and walked over to the Tsarina, leering appreciatively, and stroked her cheek. "You're looking very beautiful today, Lena. Very sexy."

Lena preened and smiled because he was only telling the truth, but as his hand traced down her body to cup her ass, she giggled and backed away. If she wasn't careful, he'd take her right there in front of the waiters, guards, and all of the other Lenas. He thought public sex showed he was a stud; she thought it was undignified. If the other Lenas saw her being used the same way they were, it would bring the Tsarina down to their sex-worker level, and that wasn't good for discipline. Lena wasn't a prostitute.

Instead, she flirted.

"My love, you're looking very good, too. Maybe too good! All the girls here will be hot for you, and that will make me jealous."

He bumped against her, and Lena sighed to herself. Oh, well. She had had a good run, and she might as well get this over with. She purred, "Maybe a few minutes alone? Just you and me?" And that was all Lester needed. He grabbed her by the hand and practically ran inside, yelling at his entourage to wait by the pool.

The nearest empty room wasn't far, and he slammed the door shut and turned to his Tsarina, his eyes glowing dimly in the sun-washed drawing room. Lena laughed and backed away a few steps, letting him watch her wiggle out of the wet bikini. She turned around, giving him a good look at her butt. She fully expected him to start ramming her from behind, but he didn't. Instead, Lester turned her around and started kissing her on the mouth, all juicy tongue and tasting like breakfast sausage. Yuck!

So she pulled away and began kissing him on the neck and chest in the usual, I'm-going-down-fashion. He was breathing hard, and that was a good sign. This wouldn't take long.

Lena moaned, her I'm-so-hot-for-you-I'm-coming signal, and Lester tenderly tilted her head up and took her sunglasses off to look at her ecstatic face when she climaxed. He rarely had the pleasure of seeing her while they fucked. He usually took her in the dark of night or from behind in some dimly lit sitting room. Today, this room was flooded with sunlight, so watching her worship him would be an added pleasure.

He froze.

She stopped. Something was wrong.

"Fuck." He whispered. And he pushed her away, pinning her arms to her side. The expression on Lester's face! His watery blue eyes betrayed a man scared shitless by what he was looking at. A man who had just peered into the abyss and recognised his doom.

"I'm trying to!" Lena wailed, not sure what was happening. She didn't like this at all. She turned her head away from the lord and looked for a way out, but he was holding her arms so tightly she was sure she'd have fingerprint bruises on them later. A happy Lester was predictable and controllable. An unhappy Lester meant a battered Lena.

Lester couldn't take his horrified eyes off of her, his lungs emptied of air, and a shiver ran down his spine. Lena's wet hair was clinging to her head. She badly needed a colour touch-up and had about an inch of new growth showing at the scalp. Her unbleached hair was dark auburn. Her ears – did they have little points to them?

But it was her eyes that made the gut punch that stopped him. Her sparkling eyes glowed a pale green like newly sprouted wheat. Where were the cornflower blue eyes?

Lester's Tsarina Lena, the daughter of an Elemental lord, was also a lord, and she didn't know it. Lester was sure she had no idea.

No wonder she didn't show signs of ageing. She would never age. There would never be a replacement for her in Lester's life because she wouldn't get old and fade away like the many human women he had used.

Then the real horror hit him. He had bonded to Lena. The heady Lena-scent he loved to rub his face into when he slept with her wasn't a commercial perfume. The sick-to-the-stomach feeling he had whenever he thought of pushing her aside or of being in danger – that was bonding.

He had bonded to Lena. And he knew in his heart she wasn't bonded to him.

Lester pushed her away. He couldn't speak to her, he couldn't hurt her, he couldn't do anything but have a full-blown panic attack and run from the room.

Grace

Japan was lovely. Diplomatic visits are heavily controlled by protocols, and since Conary, Vrt, and Grace weren't opening up a formal embassy and weren't heads of state, the pomp and circumstance bit – what Conary called "grip and grin" which is what diplomats did in front of the cameras, shake hands and grin like idiots – was more muted. That didn't mean that the Japanese didn't make a big deal, but they had to hold a bit back in case the

President and the Vice-President of the Elf Nation came to call. Nonetheless, Conary, Vrt, and Grace had a very nice lunch with the Prime Minister and were asked to tea by the Emperor and Empress. Who doesn't want to meet with magic?

When their hosts discovered that Grace had a particular interest in textiles she was provided with a knowledgeable guide, and they went to several of the textile and kimono museums in Tokyo, where Grace met with a Living National Treasure weaver.

The people, though, were another thing altogether. They went, as Caddy would say, bat-shit crazy. Crowds lined the streets looking for the RumLot Security limos, and as the lords drove around, it seemed that half the population was sporting elf ears and white wigs. In particular, they really loved Vrt. There were whole TV shows dedicated to analysing her clothes and how to recreate her ethereal beauty. Grace saw drawings of her everywhere, and once, when Conary saw a Vrt doll on a billboard, he dashed out of the limo to run into a toy shop and buy one, almost sparking a riot. He bought the doll, but not before signing about a million autographs and making the counter girl cry when he signed her arm.

He thought that doll was the funniest thing ever, while the real Vrt didn't see the likeness at all.

"Look at it! It has the same dead-fish eyes you have when you're super-pissed at something. It caught that Angel-of-Death expression perfectly!" Vrt gave him the dead-fish look, and he just laughed harder.

Probably their biggest PR triumph in Japan wasn't in any of the official teas or dinners, but when they went to tour the Sensō-ji Temple. The temple was temporarily cleared of visitors so the lords could freely look around without security concerns. As they left Vrt saw a class of school children waiting for the temple to reopen so they could have a tour. Her weakness for children got the better of her, and she couldn't resist talking to them. The lord asked a little girl what her favourite lesson was, and the girl said gymnastics. Right in front of Vrt, she did a backflip. Vrt winked at Conary. "Hold my beer."

"*You* may hold my hat!" So the girl held Vrt's hat, and then, without any prep, the lord made one of her tremendous leaps and did a triple backflip right there in her business suit and court shoes and landed where she started. The girl returned Vrt's hat, and the lord gave her a kiss and left.

It was all over the news that night.

The trip to Korea was the same – a slightly muted governmental response for protocol reasons and busy trips to shrines, museums, and the DMZ so they could see what the old border was like before reunification. When they went to the Samjeondo Monument, where Grace took photos of the stone tortoises and messaged them to Sam. Every time she saw a statue or a carving, she thought, "I wonder what Sam would think of that?" And it surprised her how often she thought of the stonemason. And she would take a picture and send it to him.

She missed him, and that was confusing in itself. He had been so annoying when they first met, and while he had changed her opinion of him was slow to adapt. She was still irritated by the original Sam, but the Sam that had emerged after the Bonding Ceremony was kinder, more empathetic, and much more interesting. He was even sexier. Was the new Sam there all along inside the jerk, and she had just overlooked him? Or was this new one a temporary, fake Sam who'd disappear as fast as he appeared? It was hard to tell.

Althea

It was dark. Althea could smell it, and she could smell the hot flood lights that lit the parking lot and bathed the gleaming new bus and the small stage that Rev Jimmy would speak from. Everybody was there, even more than on a good Sunday, and the parking lot was jam-packed. Althea lurked in the very back, where no one paid her the least bit of attention. The crowd was chatty and happy; there was a giddy, festive atmosphere when normally church meetings were so serious and dark. No one came up to say hi to the odd blind woman who didn't talk much, especially when there was a party going on, and the men and women were allowed to freely mix. After Rev Jimmy spoke, there was going to be a potluck and singing, so it was going to be a fun night.

She edged back into the shadows of the church and listened. Maggot sat next to her, panting in the humid Alabama air. There was no one around her, not even a courting couple kissing in the shadows. She edged in a little more and stood in the alcove of the side door, which was propped open so people could go in to use the toilets. But she heard nothing. Everyone was gathering around the stage, and Rev Jimmy started to talk.

He said something funny, and the crowd roared. At that minute, Althea opened the door just enough to slide in, and she walked to the toilets. Standing outside of the women's, she stopped to listen – nothing. Althea could hear things other people couldn't. She could hear the breath of a sleeping baby. She could hear the heartbeat of a hiding child. She could hear the intake of breath if someone didn't like her body odour. If someone was standing in the hall or in the restrooms, she would hear them, but now all she heard was Maggot.

She slipped into the utility closet between the two toilets. Behind the boxes of sanitary napkins and toilet paper was her backpack. It was undisturbed because no one went in there except whoever was on rotation to clean the toilets, and, oddly, that was always Althea. She folded up the cane, which she only used for show anyway and put it in the backpack. Listening again, she made sure the hall was clear, and she and Maggot walked quickly down the hall away from the singing and cheering congregation crowded in the parking lot. She silently glided through the unlit classrooms to a door on the other side of the church, and from there she left the building.

Althea followed Maggot around the building and met her first obstacle. In the bushes, two people were fornicating, and she could hear the rustling of the leaves, thrusting, moaning, and wet sounds. Stopping, she bent down and whispered to Maggot, "What direction are they facing?" He nudged her hand. It was all right; they weren't looking her way, so she crept by.

Maggot guided her to the shadows, and then she smelled the diesel of the bus. He stopped, so she stopped. She listened and sniffed. The air was getting wet; it was going to rain. He nudged her forward, and she took a few steps and felt the side of the bus. He stopped, and she knew he was looking and listening.

Althea had no idea if she was hidden in a shadow or outlined against the white bus. She had to trust Maggot that she was not visible to the casual bystander, but from what she could sense, there was no one around. She could still hear the congregation and Rev Jimmy on the other side of the massive church. She walked around the bus, trailing her hand on the side to guide her, and prayed to God that it was the right bus. How would a dog know which was the oldest bus? She had told him to smell for old smells, but what did that mean to Maggot?

Then she felt it; one of the luggage compartments wasn't fully closed yet. The men had left one ajar so they could put their luggage in it, and she lifted it just enough to crawl in. Inside the space, there were two bags and a large ice cooler. Maggot scrambled in, and they both crawled behind the luggage, and with a click that meant either doom or freedom, Althea pulled the door closed. She had no illusions about what would happen to her if anyone in the congregation found her with a backpack of men's clothes and ten grand in stolen offering money. It wouldn't be hard time in a state prison. She wouldn't be so lucky.

They weren't hidden in the luggage compartment for five minutes when the heavens let loose with a massive clap of lightning, and it started to pour, driving the congregation back to the church and the potluck supper waiting in the assembly room. Althea could hear the girls squealing and laughing as they ran out of the rain and the men yelling their hallelujahs and laughing, too. Rev Jimmy could've gone on another hour, but the rain sped things up, and the bus company president quickly handed over the keys to the new bus. Then he and the driver ran to the old one to get out of the rain and start the long drive back home to Tennessee.

Althea could hear one of the men run around the bus, making sure all the luggage hatches were closed, then a few minutes of talking up in the cab and the bus rumbled to life.

And she was gone.

Sam

Sam had never bothered much with phones, not the way younger people did. By the time he bought his first smartphone, he was in his early 40s, and the messaging, social media thing was just not part of his working world. Eventually, he started using the phone to take photos of job sites, which was very handy for his work. Vera went on Facebook to keep up with her girlfriends and her sister, but Sam never bothered.

When Grace decided to send Sam photos from Japan, she set up a WhatsApp between them. He had to go to the tech elves for help because he didn't understand who was messaging him, but after they fixed him up and he started getting photos, it was a breeze.

She'd send a photo, and he'd make some sort of comment. Since he could think about what he said before he blurted out drivel, he was able to cut out a huge amount of condescending lectures and mansplaining. Some messages took three or four edits before he would hit the send button, and by editing, he started to get a real feel for how annoying he could be. He annoyed himself.

Then, a day after her first message, he saw a beautiful spider web in the garden and sent her a photo, and she commented back. They started having conversations. Real conversations. About stuff.

He had a strict time limit of half an hour once a day, and he kept to it because he wasn't going to stalk or pester her. Sam was terrified he'd screw up again.

Althea

The bus rumbled along for hours, and with each passing hour, Althea was happier and happier. No one from the congregation had called the drivers on their phones to look for her in the bus, and now that she was well out of the jurisdiction of the town's police force, if the bus drivers did discover their stowaway when they pulled into a rest stop, she could make a fuss and get help.

She changed out of the long pink prairie dress all the unmarried church women wore and put on the jeans and t-shirt, hoping that they would help her blend in. She stuck a couple of the twenties into the pocket of her jeans so she wouldn't have to dig into the backpack when it came time to buy something to eat. Ten grand took up some space, and Althea didn't want people to see the stacks of bills.

Althea couldn't remember ever wearing jeans, and they felt odd on her legs. It took her a minute to figure out the zipper thing and the button. These were thankfully loose as the boy she had stolen them from was pretty fat, but she had no idea if they fit her properly or not. For all she knew, her appearance could be very odd, but Althea was sure she wouldn't look any weirder than walking around in the sinful world in her prairie dress. Girls wore jeans; they talked about clothes in the accounting department, and some of the women wore jeans when they were at home.

Then the bus stopped. Althea had felt it slow down and turn, and she knew from the sounds they were turning into someplace with activity and not stopping on the side of the road. The bus rolled and swayed and then stopped, and she heard the two drivers leave, talking as they walked away.

There were people outside, but they were walking around. She heard men, which was alarming, but also women and children. A gas station? Should she stay on the bus or leave and see what fate had in store for her? She crawled forward and felt the door because she was sure there must be an interior latch, and after some searching, found it and popped it open. Maggot said there was another bus parked very close, but she could leave, so she carefully crawled out and shut the door behind her. Maggot guided her around the parking lot. He said that there were a couple of buses, but it was mostly semis, and they were at a truck stop with a restaurant where there were lots of people.

Althea asked if there were any of the congregation in there, and Maggot sniffed and looked and said no.

"Well, Maggot, we'll just go have a lil' poke around. Let's find a table, and we'll have a rest. Maybe I can buy some food. Ya'll tell me if'n you see anyone from the church."

So Maggot guided her into the restaurant and to an empty table, and Althea sat down and just absorbed the sounds and smells. It was overwhelming; she had never been in such a place before. She had heard about them, but no one had ever taken her to one. The girls brought in bags of food every now and then for lunch – McDonald's hamburgers and Taco Bell – but Althea had never eaten any of it; they didn't share.

"Hey!" The male voice was irritated. "You can't bring a dog in here!"

Althea turned her head to the voice, and she tried to smile. She was prepared for this.

"He's my guide dog. I'm blind."

"Oh, jeez – I'm sorry." And the voice meant it. Althea could always tell if someone was lying, and this guy was truly embarrassed. "Yeah, sure, you can have a guide dog. I'm used to seeing them in some sort of harness or a vest."

"He doesn't need anything like that." Maybe this man would help her. "He can do everything but read a menu. Can you help me with the menu? Can I order some food?"

Of course, he could, and she did. His name was Curtis, and he worked in McDonald's as the night manager. He brought her and Maggot some hamburgers and fries and a Coke and even, after talking with her a bit, ordered her an Uber to take her to the bus station where she could find a bus to take her onwards to Dallas. Curtis never asked how a blind woman ended up in his McDonald's and why she was travelling alone.

The Uber took her to the bus station, and the woman who drove it came in and helped Althea buy a ticket to Detroit, not Dallas. She was very nice and even gently suggested to Althea that she turn her t-shirt inside out as "Trump for President 2028" wasn't going to do her any favours in Detroit.

Back at the house, no one noticed Althea was missing until she didn't show up for breakfast. By that time, she had been travelling for ten hours and was passing through Louisville on her way to Detroit. Rev Jimmy was beside himself, but everyone assured him that blind Althea was too stupid to get far, and she must be somewhere in town. The entire congregation spent the next two days searching for her. They never found her, of course, but it wasn't for lack of trying, and Rev Jimmy told Sister Lily that the best they could hope for was that Althea had been raped and left for dead in the deep piney woods. They both prayed for that.

The Vietnamese Clan

When they finally landed in Vietnam, Conary's reunion with Hùng and Long was emotional and disappointing at the same time. Long's wife Lan was uneasy around the lords, finding them eerie and unsettling. She wasn't an orc; she was simply a person who had problems understanding and getting along with anyone who wasn't like herself. She didn't like black Africans or Norwegians, either, and she didn't know a single one. She didn't like Vrt from the moment she saw her, and because of that antipathy, Long was cool with Vrt, too.

Vrt didn't give a shit. On the one hand, she really tried to do her best with Conary's kids because she loved Conary so much, but on the other hand, to her people who didn't like her were temporary blips of unhappiness that left flyspeck stains on a 3,500 existence, and their lives were too short to make any impact on hers. She tried; it didn't do any good. So she sat by the compound's pool and listened to music and flipped through fashion magazines.

Conary took Mai aside and asked her what Lan's problem was, and Mai just shrugged and said that Vrt was probably too pretty or maybe too scary. Or both.

Long and Hùng didn't understand the profound changes their dad had gone through in his journey to be a lord until they saw him. The last time they saw their dad, he was a painfully skinny, bespectacled, shaven-headed, seventy-five-year-old white guy with no facial hair. Now he was a lithe, bespectacled, white haired, goateed, white guy who looked younger than either of them. And he had elf ears. Big ones.

They had only been in the compound for about an hour, and everyone was sitting by the pool having lunch and catching up when one of the little kids asked Conary to do some magic. They expected him to pull a coin out of the kid's ear like any goofy grandpa. But no, he did real magic and disappeared and then reappeared across the room.

A terrified Lan exploded and ran to her bedroom, slammed the door, and refused to come out. She told Long that he might be okay with being related to some sort of big-eared alien, but she was not, and she wanted her kids away from the freaks, too.

Hùng and Mai yelled at Long and Lan for being so disrespectful to the Old Man, and Mai was beside herself, alternating between apologising to the lords and screaming at Lan for being a fucking idiot. The Old Man might be weird, but he had always taken care of them, and right now he was their meal ticket.

Grace didn't know what to do and sat in shocked silence as far away from the argument as she could get. Conary was miserable and embarrassed that Grace and Vrt found themselves in the middle of a loud, raucous, mind-numbing, Vietnamese inter-clan feud. After a few amazed minutes of watching the two families scream at each other, Vrt simply raised an eyebrow and suggested that she and Grace go back to the plane and sleep there until the family settled down enough to see them with some politeness. Without elves to port them, she asked Conary to call the limo for them, which he did.

On the way out, Vrt kissed Conary on the cheek and said that it would all work out. If he wanted to stay the night here, it was fine with her, and she would see him tomorrow. He smiled weakly at her and glowered at his sons and said he hadn't made up his mind yet.

In the limo, Grace was the first to break the silence.

"Blimey! That woman's crazy!"

"She'll calm down. She knows how to pluck this chicken. I noticed no one was talking about moving back to the shacks they lived in and that she never once said that they should give up the dirty elf money." Vrt turned to Grace. "I know you were born of humans, and so was Conary, but you're turning into lords, and this is what I've seen over the years. While humans find us scary and odd, I find their obsession with coins just as bizarre and rather pitiful. I like nice things, but I like my independence more. Humans will sell their short time on this earth for coins. Elves and lords don't trade in coins with each other. We barter until there is balance. They do a lot for us – everything for our comfort.

But even in Before Times, before we were destroyed as a tribe, we kept them safe from orcs and bad humans, and we made the Scent that gave them babies."

She smiled. "Have you ever wondered why elves don't like us going a-roaming? It's because we don't mind being independent, and they're afraid we'll forget them, which means they won't get defended and they'll lose the Scent they need. I can go back and live in the taiga. Ratna lived in her mountain. Jack lived with his ravens. We don't need the pretty clothes and catered meals if we find the cost too high. You'd go and live in some shack and be happy weaving – and I could go on. The point is, both elves and lords have a balance, a trade-off that benefits each other. Humans trade with coins, and balance is seldom there. They try to take advantage of each other to make a profit at someone else's expense.

Back in Before Times, lords lived apart from each other, and lord women settled with an elf clan who took care of them and any lord children. Male lords followed the women, so an elf clan had two lords to protect them and make Scent. They had every incentive to make us stay with them to the point that they actively worked to make us dependent. Talk to Caddy one day about how frantic the Lowestoft elves got when she roamed. If we women roamed, it was a disaster for the elf clan, and they had to lure in another one. They used us, and we used them so we had a balance. The elves knew we could leave at any time, and they couldn't follow us because of terrior. No elf can physically prevent a lord who's determined to leave.

Lan and Long will wake up in the morning with a balance-sheet headache and decide they like elf and lord coins more than independent poverty, and they'll be sorry for being rude. Very sorry."

Grace could see that. Her mother had been like that in an extreme, unhealthy way. She would have sold her own daughter if the coins had been enough to make it worth her while, and then moaned when the coins ran out.

"Well, I still think she's crazy. It's all very self-destructive to me."

"Yes, it certainly is. Here we are, back at the plane. We'll have a quiet night in and see what tomorrow brings."

Althea

Althea stank; she knew she did. When she reached Detroit, she asked for help at the bus station and was directed to a Salvation Army visitor's information desk. It took her a long time to get up the nerve to go there; she didn't want anything to do with "salvation," not at all, but in the end, the old woman at the desk was very helpful. When Althea told her she had money and wanted a room by herself, the woman arranged a nearby hotel and made sure Maggot could stay, too. That's when Althea learnt guide dogs could go anywhere with blind people, not just into restaurants.

When Althea said she needed to buy personal items and clothes, the woman asked her if she was running away from an abusive relationship and needed to go to a women's shelter. That gave Althea pause, but in the end, she decided not to go to anyplace like that. She didn't want to find herself under anyone's control, not even a well-meaning social worker. She knew all about social workers. What they thought was helpful sometimes wasn't. A social worker might think that calling the Congregation was the kind thing to do. The ones she had known over the years were usually gullible, and the smart, street-wise ones often had their hands tied by the law and paperwork.

It was clothes and personal items, like soap, that Althea needed, and the Salvation Army lady told her about a small discount store on the way to the hotel. There, a clerk helped Althea buy dog food, shampoo, body wash, a toothbrush and toothpaste, a pack of underwear, a t-shirt, and a tracksuit. The bill came to $243.58. Althea knew she was being cheated, but she paid it without comment.

Between Maggot's help and asking around, she navigated the busy streets and shops and made it to the hotel, which was on the lookout for her. Occasionally, she smelled a bad person, but she always managed to smell them before they smelled her, and she was able to avoid trouble that way. The man at the hotel desk ordered her two pizzas and said he'd bring them up to her room, and she was very grateful. She was starving.

Grace

Grace had a date.

What is it about a healthy young man that makes them all so handsome? His name was Josh, and he was certainly healthy and he was definitely good-looking. He was one of the RumLot Security team soldier-bodyguards who guarded the lords on their trip to Vietnam, and when he was on duty, he was as professional as any senior RumLot manager could want. But Grace knew he was there, and he smiled at Grace a full second longer than was absolutely necessary. If he was standing next to her, he always said something funny. There was frisson.

After the diplomatic mission was over and everyone was back to their old routine, Grace ported to Lowestoft to see Caddy and Kyrylo, and she ran into Josh in the shop's back offices. He seemed genuinely pleased to see her, and they had a nice chat – and he asked her if she would like to go out to dinner some evening. Maybe go listen to a band he knew was playing in Norwich.

Just like that. A guy asked her out for a real date. Not paired up with a terrified, pre-arranged escort to a diplomatic function. Not a group thing where she was just tagging along with other couples. Not a nameless guy who cut in on the dance floor just to brag that he had danced with a lord. A real date with a *hot* guy who had been born in the same century as Grace.

When she told Caddy and Kyrylo that she had just been asked out on a date, the smallest of shadows went across Caddy's face, and then she was fine. Kyrylo just grunted and asked who it was, and when she said Josh's name, he said, "Oh, he's a good one. He's an Arsenal supporter, but I guess you can't have everything." And he shrugged.

Unbeknownst to Grace, that evening her sisters had a late-night conference call about the tryst. Even Vrt was on it, although her screen was black because she forgot to turn on the camera. Not that it mattered much; they were either blobs on the screen or animated AI cartoon figures.

Vrt and Ratna were worried. They were from Before Times, and, from their upbringing, stepping out with humans was simply not done. It kept a lord from bonding with another lord and making lord babies. The human couldn't move on to a proper human relationship either, and sadly, in a few years, the human inevitably died, leaving the lord bereft. All Ratna could see was loss and grief, and she had her own human/lord relationship history to draw on. And humans didn't bond properly. This guy could pair up with Grace, and then, when he got bored or realised attaching to a lord had its own set of problems, just leave her. Then what?

Alizah pointed out this was just a date. It was just a nice evening out, and the girls were jumping way ahead of themselves.

Besides, who else was Grace going to go out with? It seemed to her that Sam had cooled down on Grace just like he had cooled down after an initial rush on her and Ratna. He didn't bring Grace Cokes any more, she giggled.

Caddy agreed. She had her own history with human Ricky and others and understood the pain of loss as well as the pain of breaking up, and her clan couldn't protect Grace from either. Alizah was right. Until another male lord showed up, Grace's choices of partners were limited, and no one should expect her to take vows of chastity. If she and Sam faded into a brother and sister relationship, then Grace would have to find romance somewhere else, and she was only twenty-one now. She could have decades – maybe centuries – of being single.

They would say nothing unless Grace asked for advice. They'd watch to see how it went and be there to pick up the pieces when everything went pear-shaped. Which it would.

Josh

For his part, Josh was surprised and thrilled that the young lord had said yes. At twenty-eight, single, and with a sweet job at RumLot Security, he wasn't hurting for dates. He also owned a mirror. But while he had a pretty good opinion of himself, he wasn't a bad guy. He treated the women he was with well and didn't two-time them. He just hadn't found one to stick with yet.

But this Lord Grace, she was hot! He didn't know her that well, but from what he had seen she was genuinely a sweet girl and seemed to have a brain in her head. But most of all, she was a lord, and between the bodyguards that meant wealth and power with a huge dollop of lord randiness to sweeten the offer. Jesus, the lords liked to fuck!

At least the RumLot bodyguards didn't have to deal with an endless stream of bed-hopping groupies and hookers like other professionals did with normal celebrities, but horny lords were still a constant topic of amusement with the human bodyguards who kept them safe. The elves who guarded and took care of the lords just shrugged. As one said, lords do what lords do. The humans who worked for them had no idea about the elves' relationship with lords and Scent; all they knew was that elves were constantly changing the sheets of one couple or the other.

Josh saw it for himself. During the trip to Asia, his duty assignment was to sit in the back of officer country on the RumLot private jet, guarding the curtained entrance between the press dogs and the VIPs. He made sure that no one in the press had one too many beers and decided to sneak in and use the VIP head and maybe snag a private interview on the way.

The VIP area was a lounge with little tables and plush chairs to curl up in. Ahead were four small sleeping cabins, and ahead of that was one very large, very luxurious master cabin. Lords Vrt and Conary slept in the master cabin on this trip.

The gorgeous Lord Vrt was sitting at one of the tables, idly flipping through a magazine or staring out the window and watching the clouds, while across from her, Lord Conary looked over documents on his tablet, and Josh saw her kick him. Lord Conary looked up, and she gave him a sexy little smile and a single little head shake to the cabin. Josh couldn't see his face, but he could well imagine the lord's famous devilish grin, and the man quietly wandered back. Then Lord Vrt got up, and the expression on her face would be forever imprinted in Josh's brain and would be his go-to jerking off image for the rest of his life. Her eyes glowed hot, she smiled, and one hand stroked her ear. It wasn't a cheerful smile; it was a lusty smile, and she licked her lips. She licked her fucking lips! She walked to the back. Forty-five minutes later, Lord Conary resumed his seat, his hair still wet from the shower. A few minutes after he returned, Lord Vrt was back in her seat, looking like the cat who stole the cream. A satisfied woman. Lord

When Josh mentioned that the lords had indulged in a little cabin time twice on the long trip to Asia the other guards laughed, and every one had their own story of sitting out in a hall listening to giggles, bed squeaks, and other noises, or the time one guard took almost an hour wiping down handprints off Lords Cadence and Kyrylo's mirrored dressing room on that cruise ship. "Hand, foot, butt – you name it prints," she laughed. "Even on the ceiling!"

When Josh asked Lord Grace out to dinner, her eyes glowed. He was looking forward to it.

Althea

The next morning, Althea walked back to the bus station.

When she inquired at the ticket office about buying a ticket to Ottawa, the woman didn't even look up. "Yes, ma'am, that will be sixty dollars American, and you'll need proof of ID."

"ID?"

She sounded tired. "Yes, ma'am, a driver's licence will do."

Althea just stood there, confused, and then the ticket seller looked up to realise that this blind person would not have a driver's licence, not even a learner's permit.

She didn't apologise. "A passport? A NEXUS, SENTRI or FAST card?"

"I don't have any of those things."

"Then I can't sell you a ticket, dearie."

Then the man in the line behind Althea cleared his throat, and with that, Althea moved to the side, an emaciated, forlorn scrap of a woman standing in the middle of the busy bus station, people running around her in all directions as if she were no more a living being than the bollards. Men, women, children, they all had a place to go to, and no one seemed to have any problems getting there. She had fully expected to just be able to go across the border, and she didn't know what to do.

Maybe Uber could drive her across, and she could pick up a bus on the other side.

That was all she could think of, so she asked the next person who rushed by where the Visitor's Information Desk was and was pointed in the right direction. The man at the desk heard her story and thought for a minute.

"Look, lady, the Canadians won't let you in without an ID, but if you go up to passport control and ask for help as a blind person, they might bend the rules. It's a long shot. Play the blind thing up. The other thing is to ask for asylum. That's another long shot since you're coming from the US, but hey, that will get you legal help, and maybe a lawyer can grease the skids."

With that advice, he called Althea an Uber to take her to the passport control station on the US/Canadian border and wished her luck. She smiled and thanked him. She had luck on the entire escape so far; she had no reason to fear that her good fortune wouldn't hold.

The Uber dropped her off at the passport control station and looped back. Most people went through in their cars, but there were a few inside, mostly bike riders who couldn't ride through the busy vehicle checkpoints and those with problems who couldn't be waved through the barriers.

Pulling out her cane, just for the theatre of it, Althea walked into the passport control building and stopped, listening and getting her bearings.

In the middle of the reception area, Althea stood, a painfully thin, young, mixed-race woman with frizzy, white-streaked orange hair that foamed to her waist and hid her slightly pointed ears. Maggot stood at her knee, tense. Even though it was pretty cold outside, all she had on was a badly fitting, polyester tracksuit, a Detroit Lions t-shirt, and broken-down tennis shoes. She looked lost, and she was.

A uniformed woman at the entrance saw the opaque sunglasses, the scruffy, unleashed dog who looked like he was mostly border collie, and the white cane, and she introduced herself as one of the passport and customs greeters and asked if Althea needed help and where she wanted to go.

"Canada. If y'all could jus' point me in the right direction, that'd be great." The accent wasn't Detroit; it was pure American South.

She laughed and said that if Althea could come with her, off to one side, they'd check out her papers and send her on her way.

Althea told Maggot to follow the woman, and they took a few steps to a small table where the woman discovered that Althea had no ID at all. Not a passport, not a birth certificate, not any of the fast-track IDs. The greeter didn't ask if Althea had a driver's licence.

"I'm sorry, miss, but we can't –"

And that's when all hell broke loose.

There was a blood-curdling scream. "DEMON!" Althea jumped, but she didn't know what was going on.

The greeter spun and slammed a panic button.
Althea smelled the orcs. Males. Two of them. They pushed their way through the crowd towards her, and out of nowhere, two armed officers ran up and grabbed one. One orc jumped at the officers, and Althea heard someone hit the floor. More officers were running up; she could hear their feet. A dog was with them. Maggot put himself between Althea and the melee, and Althea heard him growl.

Two shots. Pain. The last thought she had before her interior world went as black as her exterior world was "Maggot! Who is going to tak e. Ca re of – "

The crazy man who stole the officer's gun during the fight was taken down by the two dogs, one of the border patrol's Belgian Malinois and the woman's guide dog. The other man was rolling on the floor, two officers struggling to cuff him. Police and agents poured into the building, guns drawn, and pushed the screaming, panicked border crossers outside.

The blind woman was sprawled on the floor, and for a moment, the officers were sure she was dead. But they did CPR and stopped the bleeding as best they could, and within minutes the EMTs were there. They blue-lighted her to the hospital in Windsor, Canada.

Althea had passed through the border after all and hadn't had to produce a passport.

In the ambulance, one of the EMTs pushed away the masses of hair as he worked to insert an airway down her throat. He looked up.

"Jesus! John! This is a lord! Look at the ears! She ain't human."

Grace

When date night came, Grace wore a sexy clubbing outfit that showed off her curves without making anyone think she was rentable by the hour. She was ported directly to the restaurant where Josh was waiting, and when he saw her he was properly impressed, giving her a quiet whistle and a kiss on the cheek before telling her she looked beautiful and guiding her to their table. He was the personification of the perfect date.

Grace was a bit shy and quiet at the start, but that was okay with Josh. He'd been out with shy girls before and just did a little more chatting and filling in the air time with questions than he normally would have. Soon she relaxed, and they talked and talked.

After dinner he took her to the club he had promised, and that's when Grace really came out of her shell. That girl loved to dance! The band was great, the place was packed, and the dance floor was a loud, hot, pulsating, laser-lit, glittering, heaving mass of humanity (and one lord) who were just out for a good time. He was able to get in a real kiss, and she didn't pull away or giggle. She kissed back, and her eyes glowed which was incredibly sexy. Josh hoped no one else saw, but with all the weird lights in the club her eyes were just two more spots of light.

During the break between sets Grace said she needed to go to the ladies, and Josh escorted her there. He wasn't going to let her walk anywhere by herself; he noticed some guys paying Grace a little too much attention, and his bodyguard instincts alerted. If she were alone, they'd move in on her.

Josh had his hand in the small of Grace's back as they snaked through the packed club, and suddenly she stiffened, gasped, and her nostrils flared. His RumLot training kicked in. Orcs. As a human, he couldn't smell them, but after training, he could identify the tribe, and it never ceased to amaze him who turned out to be one. Before being hired by RumLot, he'd had no idea what an orc was, but now he saw them everywhere. What he did know was that they were always trouble even when no lords were around. With a lord in the room, they were dangerous.

He looked to the left where the guys who were leering at Grace stood, and it wasn't them. To his right a man lunged at Grace, his purple eyes glittering and beer-covered hands out to get a little booby feel before he slapped the snooty bitch into next week. Josh stepped in between the guy and Grace, pushing the orc back so hard he fell. But being an orc he just bounced back.

And that's when the brawl started. Within seconds the place erupted into a flailing mess of screaming women, flying fists, thrown drinks, bouncers, and black eyes. Josh spun around to where Grace was, and there was nothing in the Grace space but the fading sparks of an elf port. That was the last he saw before someone punched him in the face and broke his nose.

A half hour later he was sitting alone in a cubicle at the Norfolk and Norwich A&E waiting for a doctor to come by and patch up his nose when Grace ported in. An elf soldier stood behind her.

She wasn't crying, but Josh could tell she was close to it. Her face was scrunched up with worry, and her wet eyes glowed bright green.

"Are you okay?"

"Oh, I'm okay. I just need a doctor to reset my nose, and I'll be going home. But what about you? I saw that you ported out, so that was good. I'm glad they were watching."

She nodded, and Josh saw her lip tremble.

"Oh, luv, don't cry. Next time we –"

"I can't have a next time, Josh. Gods, you were perfect, so it's not anything you did, but –" She wiped the corner of her eye. "I'm a lord. I can't do normal human things like go out and have a fun date with a great human guy."

"Now Grace –"

"Josh, I'll get ported out the minute I hiccup. But any human I'm with takes the hits – or the shots. It's a broken nose today; it could have been a stabbing. I can't let a human take that risk just because I want to have a bit of fun." She looked at him, her eyes welling up with tears, and shook her head. "I'm orc-bait, Josh. I am what I am, and there's no use pretending differently. I'm orc-bait forever."

Josh nodded sadly.

"I had a wonderful evening, Josh. Thanks for that. Really."

He grinned. "Well, Grace, it was certainly a date I'll remember the rest of my life!"

"Me, too, Josh. Me, too." And she kissed him on the cheek and ported back to Aelfeham House.

Kyrylo

Kyrylo had the report about Grace's date and the melee in his email almost as soon as it happened. The young lord was fine, the human RumLot guard she dated had a broken nose, and the elf guard who had shadowed her that evening reported what Grace said to Josh in the A&E cubicle almost verbatim.

Josh had acquitted himself well, Grace had learned a hard lesson, and Kyrylo had one more thing to worry about with Ivana. They needed to find more lords and fast. To a lord twenty years was just around the corner, and who would his little girl pair with when the time came? Sam?

Kyrylo read the report and sighed. He was incredibly lucky he had found Caddy, and to pile miracle on miracles, they were also compatible. They would have been compatible if they weren't lords and fate had thrown them together. She was the first lord Kyrylo had met, and he fell hard for her from the first, but he wasn't her first acquaintance with a lord. She knew Neptune, Jack, and House before she met Kyrylo, and she easily could have stayed with Neptune. What was poor Ivana going to do? Or Grace? Run off with Lester and Rurik?

He showed the report to Caddy but didn't say anything about his fears for Ivana, Grace, or Sam living lonely lives. That would simply be transferring a worry to his bond-wife, and she could do nothing about it.

They had other things to worry about now, anyway. The Canadian government called and said that another lost lord had shown up in Canada. The Elf Nation was informed it was a woman, and she was in bad shape in a hospital in Windsor, Canada, but they wouldn't have time to send a security team there.

The best they could do was for RumLot Security to hire an international medevac jet, and one landed in Windsor two hours later. Kyrylo tasked Jameson and Darnya with managing her evacuation to the UK.

Dr Mandy

The doctors in Windsor Regional Hospital Emergency stabilised the woman as best they could. By the time Althea was transferred to intensive care Dr Mandy was already on the phone and teleconferencing with the head of trauma surgery, a wonderful, no-nonsense woman by the name of Dr AnTwan'a Franklin. Dr Franklin wasn't hopeful, and after Dr Mandy saw the unknown lord's vitals her little elf face scrunched up. They were going to lose this one.

For Dr Franklin, the experience of consulting with an elf doctor in Ukraine about a fatally damaged lord was beyond surreal. The blobby shadow of the elf doctor was terse, asked the right questions, and seemed competent, but Dr Franklin could tell she was upset from her voice.

"Stabilise her, and if you need to, put her in a coma. Any kind of life support. I need twelve hours, Dr Franklin. Twelve hours. Pump her with as much nutrition and water as you can get in her. I mean massive amounts, way more than you would give a human. Lords have extremely high metabolisms. We'll medevac her back to the UK where elves can tend her, and we'll either cure her or build a pyre. I'll be back with you in an hour, and you can tell me her stats, and I'll let you know about the medevac."

"I'm sorry, Dr Mandy. We'll do our best."

"I know you will, Dr Franklin, and we won't forget that at the end. Pray to your one God, and I'll pray to all the rest, and we'll all do our best."

Alizah

Alizah heard rumours about Grace's date from the housekeeping elves when she ported in for breakfast at Aelfeham House. She and Jack didn't have elves in their penthouse, just a human cleaning crew, and usually ate breakfast at home. But if she went down to the first floor and called for an elf there was always someone on duty to pop her over to Lowestoft or Aelfeham House.

She wanted to hear all about the date from Grace, but the early reports weren't good, so when she sat down with the guys she didn't say anything. Vrt didn't gossip with the elves and probably didn't know. Sam certainly wouldn't, and Conary wouldn't say anything if he did know. Jack, when he wandered in, wouldn't have asked either. Men were just so strange sometimes. They'd want to know all about the fight, but would they ask Grace how she felt about it? Probably not. They'd just ask if she was okay, and when she said yes, they'd go get some more scrambled eggs.

Of course, Alizah was both right and wrong. Everyone but Sam knew about the date and its disastrous ending. Conary and Vrt had read the report. Without meaning to, they were both slipping into the role of second-in-command advisors, and now much of what was funnelled to Kyrylo was copied to Conary. It turned out Conary was pretty good with the diplomatic stuff, and after proving his worth with Grace's rescue and the public side of the Asian trip, Kyrylo consulted with his son-in-law more and more. If Conary thought Vrt would be interested he'd tell her, but when he asked if she wanted a personal email account she just gave him the dead-fish look, and that was the end of that.

Tuân heard through his Ranger contacts and told Ratna who talked to Vrt. As Kyrylo said many times, there were no secrets, just information with delayed or alternative distribution.

So when Grace came down for breakfast almost everyone knew what had happened the night before, and no one said a word.

Conary and Vrt

Conary and Vrt stood at the front door of Sen's lovely house in Oulton Broad. He squeezed her hand and gave his bond-wife a smile. She was nervous, and while no one outside would ever know, he knew.

After the disastrous meeting with Long and Hùng in Vietnam it wasn't any wonder that she wasn't looking forward to meeting this new wing of the Aeldor family. Sen was going to be fine. Conary knew she wouldn't be rude. Long and Hùng's children – that might be another kettle of ca kho to.

Conary was their grandfather, and back in Vietnam, when he was living in the back of Sen's house, his other set of grandkids came around on holidays and occasional visits. But after they grew up, as children have a habit of doing, they found their own lives becoming more important than visiting their weird old grandpa. So the boys' kids grew up not knowing him as well as Sen's children.

Now Conary was more than three-times-a-year weird grandpa. Now he was truly bizarre, off-the-scales-weird grandpa with a new, even weirder wife.

But he had to visit them and give them a chance, and this was the perfect opportunity. Hùng and Mai's son Tun and daughter-in-law Linh now had a newborn baby boy, Tang, making Conary a great-grandpa. As soon as the baby was born Tun and Linh flew back to Vietnam to show him off to the proud grandparents, and now they'd just returned to Sen's house where they stayed while they tried out their new life in the UK.

Conary and Vrt stood on the porch dressed in nice civilian clothes with a baby present in hand and the goal to reconnect with the family, have a nice BBQ in the back garden, and fuss over the new baby. It was a perfectly normal family get-together on a perfectly normal Saturday.

Conary took a deep breath and knocked on the door.

The door flew open, and an excited Sen beamed a wide smile (which, Vrt saw, was exactly like Conary's) which started warm, froze, and her eyes widened. She hadn't seen her father since he walked off with Tuân to go to London and find his mother. He was different now. Very different.

Then Conary grinned back, and his eyes twinkled behind the owlish glasses.

"Hey, Sen! How's my girl?"

And Sen knew that whatever changes appeared on the outside, her dad was still her Old Man on the inside, and she threw herself at her dad with a big hug and dragged him inside laughing and crying and calling everyone to the door to see the Old Man and his new wife.

The adults arrived cautiously, but prepared to welcome this new/old family member. Later, Conary would say to Vrt that it was good that they all had already met Tuân and had gotten used to his very modest changes first before being confronted with Conary's more extreme transformation. Sen's boy Tuân had left Vietnam looking like a skinny kid, and when she saw him later, after her move to Suffolk, he was a strong, broad-shouldered, lithe, confident man with a goatee, subtly pointed ears, and his own weird bond-wife. But to his mother he was still her Tuân. The Old Man was so different that they could pass him on the street and not know him.

The children bounced in on spring-loaded feet and had no reservations at all, demanding hugs from the Old Man, asking impertinent questions ("Why did you grow a beard? I didn't know you had hair! Can you make your ears wiggle?"), and wanting to hold Vrt's hand and show her their toys.

Vrt was polite and smiling and tried to put the adults at ease, but she quickly became distracted by the children. She loved children, and her love was obvious to anyone. If this exotic creature found their children charming, how could a parent not be happy with that?

They all went out to the garden and had *banh mi* sandwiches and *bun cha* pork on the grill and piles of other dishes. Having fed Tuân a couple of times, Sen made sure there was a lot of food, and Conary feasted and rolled his eyes and complimented every dish. The elves might search TikTok and find Vietnamese recipes, but nothing beats homemade food, and he missed his daughter's cooking.

Vrt gave Tun and Linh the baby present, a lovely elf-made baby blanket. Linh proudly brought the baby out from his nap to see his great-grandfather and handed sleepy little Tang to Vrt first. She picked him up and smiled down at the baby, and Conary saw her face freeze. She looked over to her bond-man, her eyes wide.

"Oh gods," he thought. "The baby is an orc."

She gently handed the sleepy, yawning Tang over to his great-grandfather, and Conary cradled him in his arms and jiggled him a bit. Tang opened his eyes, and Conary looked in them, and back to Vrt, his own eyes wide and startled.

"Oh gods," he said. "This baby is a lord."

Althea

The doctors in Windsor had never had a patient like this. Every half hour they pumped as much nutrition and water in the lord as her stomach and veins would take. And every time they did she would have something like a seizure, and her body would heat up to the point they couldn't touch her without gloves, and an eerie green light would snap and spark all over her skin. She melted all the tubes and sensors, and the nurses would gingerly replace them while the maintenance team disabled the ICU's fire alarm. The anti-bed-sore air mattress exploded, scaring the shit out of the entire ICU staff, and one nurse ran out and refused to come back.

But after each seizure the woman would settle and cool again, and her vital signs would be a tiny bit better. She still looked like she was a day before walking out of Dachau, but internally she was, to Dr Franklin's utter astonishment, stabilising. Maybe the Ukrainian elf would get her twelve hours after all.

Dr Mandy stayed on the teleconference line, and she was fine with the weird electrical spasms. In between moments of high drama there were lulls, and the two doctors had little chats. When Dr Franklin asked what the elves were going to do when the woman was in the UK, the blob on the screen that was Dr Mandy shrugged and said the only thing they could do was put her in the cauldron to be reborn and hope for the best. She thought the lord only had about a ten or fifteen per cent chance of making it, but that was better than no chance, and she explained what the cauldron was and its risks.

"The last person we put in there was a human, and he came out as an elf. It doesn't happen often, but now and then we get a chimaera like a satyr, minotaur, or a pan. It's rare, but each failure is a tragedy. They don't lead happy lives. Sometimes they're brain-damaged. Recently we've had a good run here with two coming out better than they went in, but like any operation, you can only give odds, not guarantees."

Stranger and stranger, thought Dr Franklin, and she went to oversee the next feeding.

Three hours later the medevac plane was ready to go, and the lord was transferred to the airport. Two of the Windsor ICU nurses volunteered to go along, saying they at least had a few hours of experience with this weird and wonderful magical creature, an offer that was gratefully accepted. With plenty of nutritional supplies, water, and hastily acquired oven mitts from the hospital kitchen, they were on their way to Heathrow. Oh, and they didn't forget the dog. Maggot was kennelled, and while he howled, once he was on board and smelled the lord he was okay.

Althea and Vrt

When Althea's medevac plane landed at Heathrow, the jet was still taxiing down the runway when six elves ported onto the plane, along with Jameson and Darnya. They scared the stuffing out of the ICU nurses. Jameson explained that they were going to port the gurney, and by the time he explained what was going to happen the elves had the gurney unlocked and were pushing the comatose Althea through a porthole. A minute later two elves popped in and unhooked the kennel and ported the dog out.

Stunned, the ICU nurses sat down, staring at each other, and then Darnya ported in and asked if any of them would like to follow and see what happened at the other end to the lord. How could they say no?

By the time the captain pulled up to his gate, there was no one left to disembark.

When Conary told Vrt that an unknown lord was being medevaced in and that she'd had her eyes gouged out years ago, his bond-woman dissolved into a puddle of tears. He didn't know what horrible memory that triggered, but when she fell on him, sobbing for the poor, mutilated lord, he was sorry he'd told her.

Then Conary explained that the new lord was in bad shape and going into the cauldron the minute she landed in the UK and that Dr Mandy wasn't optimistic because there was no one to anchor her to this world. Vrt shook herself out of her tears and stood back, wiping her eyes with the back of her hands, and grimly looked at Conary. "Then it will have to be us. She doesn't know us or love us, but by the gods we can love her and do what we can."

When the elves ported the gurney in the cauldron was ready, and Vrt and Conary waited off to the side, trying to stay out of the way. The ICU nurses ported in just in time to see a naked, emaciated lord unhooked from all the lines, everything manmade removed from her body, and gently slid into the simmering cauldron. A senior healer nurse scattered the herbs on top, and instantly the cauldron soup thickened.

Bowing, Vrt introduced herself to the cauldron, then sat down in a chair to settle in to begin her long vigil. Fascinated, the Windsor ICU nurses watched everything the elves and lords did.

Conary introduced himself, and in the middle of his greetings Vrt jerked up, her eyes glowing, and she turned to him. "There's a dog. Where's the dog? He must be here. He loves her."

With that, a distraught, howling Maggot was brought in, and Vrt spoke to him for a minute and told him that his master was very sick and he must tell her to stay in this world. He and Vrt must stand guard for ten days. He whimpered back and then immediately quieted down and lay with his nose on his paws, staring at the cauldron, guarding like the good-smelling lord told him to.

Vrt turned and told Conary, "The dog says his name is Maggot, and her name is Lord Althea. They come from a sad place called Alabama. He will guard and beg her to stay in this world."

Conary was pleased that he could understand the dog – a new thing learned! After Vrt and Maggot settled next to the cauldron, he invited the ICU nurses to lunch in the Breakfast Room. When they didn't move, he turned back to them, his blue eyes crinkling. "I'm afraid you'll have to walk."

They spent the night in Aelfeham House, and the next morning they ate breakfast with a bunch of lords and then were ported back to the medevac jet for the return journey home and left with stories to tell for the rest of their lives.

Grace

When the Russian PT instructor told Grace to stop being a victim and to start being a survivor, Grace took that good advice to heart. Nevertheless, there were bad days when the old victim Grace sank into a suffocating black fog, and she wondered if her crazy mother was right after all; she really was a worthless piece of shit. She was depressed, she knew she was depressed, and she couldn't figure out why. On paper she was living a charmed life. She had a new family who truly loved her, a new body she had worked hard for, and a place in society as a lord that others could only dream of. So why couldn't she sleep, and why did she sit at her loom and, with no warning, start crying?

The difference between the Grace who had been chloroformed and stolen out of her mother's council house and the Grace stolen out of the Sochi palace was that the first Grace would try to drown her demons with food. Now she tried to outrace them on the track.

She still rose early and did her half hour, and Sam was still there, running around in circles to keep her safe. He still kept his distance from her, though. As soon as she returned from Asia, he had stopped texting her. No explanation – just stopped. She looked in his workshop to find out why, but he seemed so irritated and wanted to shoo her out, so she didn't bother asking. And she didn't go back.

She went back to her loom and had a good cry over that. She couldn't sleep that night, and a little midnight run helped get her tired enough to fall into a fitful sleep. The next morning, Sam smiled at her when she came down to breakfast, so she guessed he was just having a bad day.

Sam didn't know about the hours she ran in the middle of the night when she couldn't sleep. No one did except for the guard elves who watched the grounds at night, and she told them not to mention it to anyone. Other lords, she said, would just worry about security, and the guards were around, so she was safe. So they didn't say a word.

She began to get very thin, and no one knew why. The housekeeper elves told Dr Mandy the lord was eating well, and indeed she was. Worried about anorexia or bulimia, Dr Mandy started asking the (elf only) staff around Aelfeham House about Lord Grace, and when the night guards told her about the midnight runs, she decided it was time to have a little chat. But she didn't want to talk via video call because it was too easy to hide emotions or turn off the camera; she wanted to see Grace in person, and that meant Grace had to come to Ukraine. Dr Mandy certainly wasn't going to let any of the local Lowestoft healers practise on her precious lords; no way, Jose!

Since Dr Mandy wouldn't compromise patient confidentiality, she couldn't very well go to Ms Caddy and tell her that the youngest lord needed counselling sessions. Could she please bring her in for an appointment? So she thought about it and hit on a plan.

Grace was told she needed to go to Ukraine for a regular check-up. She would have a pap smear, a breast exam, and all the usual blood tests. Dr Mandy said not to worry, it was all very routine, but she wasn't going to let the local healers do any work on the lords any more, so the lords would have to go to Ukraine. It was inconvenient, and she was sorry, but at least Grace would be able to visit with Caddy and Kyrylo, and it would be a change of scenery.

The fact that there was no known incidence of any lord ever getting cervical or breast cancer wasn't mentioned. Dr Mandy didn't lie exactly; she just didn't want to bother the young lord with too much detail. When Grace came in, Dr Mandy was sure she would just forget to give the unnecessary tests.

Two days later, Grace came down for breakfast dressed in street clothes, complete with a hat, because it was always good form to visit Ms Caddy wearing a hat. When Ratna saw the hat, she asked Grace where she was going.

"Oh, I have a doctor's appointment with Dr Mandy, and I have to go to Ukraine. I'll stay with House tonight, and I'll be back tomorrow." She grinned and wrapped up a couple of bagels at the buffet. "And I get to see Caddy and Kyrylo and play with Ivana! So – ta-ta for now! See everyone later!" And with a wave, she left.

After the door shut, a frowning Alizah turned to Jack. "I hope she's okay. She's looking a bit tired lately."

Jack shrugged, "I'm sure she's fine. She seemed cheerful enough." But Alizah wasn't buying it.

"No one sees Dr Mandy for sniffles. Caldron, broken bones, and Caddy's pregnancy, that's why they see Dr Mandy in person."

Alarmed by Alizah's comments, Sam turned to Conary. "Do you think she's okay?"

Conary looked surprised. "Well, I'm sure she's fine, Sam. I haven't heard anything bad about her health, not a peep one way or the other." Sam knew Conary was getting a lot of inside info from the primaries, but since he directly said he hadn't heard anything to worry about, Sam believed him.

It was on the way to his workshop that it hit him like a freight train. Grace was going to the doctor. The big doctor, not a local healer, and she sure wasn't going in the cauldron; she was perfect as she was. She didn't have a broken bone like Vrt's foot. Then either it was something else, or she was pregnant.

Unknown to everyone, Sam was well aware of Grace's date. He didn't know about all the details, but he certainly knew it when the hairdresser and dressmaker came by, and he knew nothing official was going on. The elves ported in and out directly opposite his bedroom door. It was like Grand Central Station that night, and the elves liked to port at his end of the hall, not hers.

He heard her port back into the hall at eleven, and he heard her blowing her nose and gulping air as she walked to her room. She was upset. Sam got up once to go see her and then immediately turned back around and went back to bed. She'd say he was stalking her. He was doing his best to give her space and not bother her, and barging in on her now would instantly ruin all that effort.

He knew she was upset that night, but what if it was far worse? What if she was raped? What if she got pregnant?

Because of Caddy and Kyrylo's accidental pregnancy, the lords now had explicit lessons in lord biology, and if Grace was pregnant by a human, given that her lord genes hadn't expressed themselves yet, she could carry a human baby to term. She was still more human than lord, even if her eyes glowed and her ears had little points to them; she wouldn't gain her abilities for another thirty years or so.

What if she married the little shit who got her knocked up?

Just the idea of Grace marrying a human stranger and having sex with someone made Sam physically ill. He couldn't process it. He knew he was leaping to conclusions, but he just couldn't force the ideas out of his mind. So he did the only thing he could do; he went to his workroom and got roaring drunk.

Dr Mandy

Dr Mandy loved her lords. Some elves thought they were a necessary evil, but Dr Mandy genuinely thought this new crop was wonderful. Unlike the spoiled and lazy ones she had known during Before Times, this tiny clan of lords genuinely appreciated elves and wanted to earn their service. It was such a foreign idea that some of the older elves had a hard time understanding that this group was different.

They were such a tiny clan of a tiny tribe, and so much rested on their shoulders – not just the existence of elves but balance for the entire world. So when one of them was unhappy and not doing well, Dr Mandy would move Heaven and Earth to find out why and solve the problem.

She was a student of biology, and she had noticed that whenever a population of animals was decimated, either by disease or other forces, those that made it through the stresses were stronger for it. Dr Mandy did a lot of reading when she woke up in this new world, and she completely agreed with the principles of evolution. Humans like Darwin were very clever people, in her estimation, to have figured it out by themselves.

The other thing she noticed was that stressed populations, when the stresses were removed, bounced back remarkably quickly. They got busy and bred, and when they had babies, they often had multiples. Mandy saw that in the elf population. As soon as Ms Caddy started producing Scent (who the gods must have delivered; she was such a miracle), the elf population experienced a baby boom. Ms Caddy herself had produced two lords! Mandy fully expected to have one of the other lord women drop an egg any time now. Her bet was on Alizah, and she had put five coins on her at her favourite pub in Safe Haven.

But stressing a population also means that some of the population will break. Each one of these lords had serious, serious issues they'd had to overcome to get to where they were now. It was a wonder they weren't all raving lunatics curled up in a foetal position in the corner of an asylum. But then, the lords who did that were all dead. These were the survivors.

Now she had the problem of Lord Grace. Was she suffering from PTSD? That would be the easiest and most logical diagnosis. She'd certainly had a horrible upbringing, and her kidnapping had been, from what Mandy was told, traumatic.

Then there was body dysmorphia. A person couldn't be changed more than Lord Grace had been changed unless they went in the cauldron or morphed. She had lost two-thirds of her body and changed from a grossly obese, depressed blob to a cute, healthy young woman. Could she still be thinking that she was ugly, obese, and worthless?

Grace was ported into Dr Mandy's newly redecorated office, and Dr Mandy cheerfully greeted her, gave her a cup of tea, and right away she had Grace doing weird things just to keep her busy and loosen her up while Mandy babbled a mile a minute the entire time.

She looked in Grace's ears and commented that they were developing nice points. She looked into her eyes, she felt for lumps and bumps – and as she worked, she asked Grace about how she was feeling. Happy? Sad? Any panic attacks?

Grace did what she was told, even if it seemed weird, and answered the questions. She was too busy standing on one leg like a stork with its wings out to think of evasive answers, so when Dr Mandy asked about her sex life, all Grace could do was laugh and say she didn't have one.

Mandy was a bit taken aback. All lords screwed, and this one didn't? Was it a lack of desire or opportunity?

"Do you have a boyfriend? I mean, there's only one unbonded lord, and that is Lord Sam, but there's always humans – I'll tell you as a doctor not to bond with them, but hey, there's nothing wrong with a lord having a one-night stand with the right guy, especially under our circumstances now."

Grace gave up standing like a stork and instead sat down and had a sip of her tea. Her face scrunched up, and Mandy had a little twinge of professional satisfaction. There it was – she had hit a nerve.

"No, I don't have a boyfriend. I don't have sex. I've never had sex. I don't think I'll ever have sex."

"Why not?"

"Because I can't. I went out with a super hot guy, and he kissed me, and he was so nice. He got in a fight with orcs over me, and he still liked me, and I had to tell him I couldn't see him again." She started to cry, "I told him I couldn't see him again because I was a lord, but that wasn't the whole truth."

Mandy handed Grace a box of elf-sized tissues, and Grace pulled the entire wad out of the tiny box, but it didn't help. It was like blowing your nose with a cotton bud.

"What was the whole truth, dear?"

"The whole truth is that when I was kissing him, I thought, this is okay, but it could be so much better if –" And she sobbed. "I couldn't get into him. I tried. It was like kissing my uncle."

"Do you think of girls, dear? It's okay if you do; it's just who you are. Sometimes society pressures us one way, and –"

"NO! I think of Sam!" And now she was sobbing. "And he doesn't like me at all. Not that way."

Then Mandy knew. Grace was love-sick. She probably didn't even realise it herself, but she was bonding to Lord Sam, and he wasn't responding, so Grace was going through withdrawal. Since she had never kissed the lord or made physical contact, the bond was incomplete. She wondered if Lord Sam knew. Probably not.

"So, do you see Lord Sam very often?"

"Every day. I see him for breakfast, and he runs with me in the morning. His bedroom is across the hall from mine, and his workshop is next door." Grace hiccuped. "But he's avoiding me! He thinks I'm a jerk! He thinks I'm too fat!" And she started to sob again.

Mandy sighed. This was not going to be easy. They had been smelling each other for months now, whether they'd meant to or not. They started getting along, and Lord Grace began to fall in love with Lord Sam. But it was an incomplete bond, and he wasn't reciprocating. If he doesn't want to, he doesn't want to, and there's no forcing a lord to bond to another lord.

A lord who's fully bonded to another lord who isn't responding – that's a tragedy.

Unbonded lords can't live in such close proximity over such a long period and not be affected. Mandy wondered if Lord Sam had a sinus infection like Tuân did. Was he bonded to someone else? Was he still clinging to his dead human wife the way Vrt had clung to her dead bond-man?

So Dr Mandy did what Dr Mandy always did, and that was to explain the entire issue to Grace. When Grace left the office, she understood that her misery was the result of an incomplete bond with Sam, and her choice was to either complete the bond (if Sam was agreeable to such a huge commitment) or move out and separate. Then she wouldn't see him every day and smell his scent, no matter how faint. If she moved to Ukraine and stayed with Lords Caddy and Kyrylo, maybe in a year she could move back to Aelfeham House. Every place else, like moving in with Alizah and Jack or getting a flat in Lowestoft, had its own issues of one sort or another, and she'd still see Sam more than she should. Even then, moving to Ukraine would only work if the bond was still in the weak, beginning phase and if she worked hard to forget him. There were no guarantees.

Just thinking about moving away from Aelfeham House – and Sam – made her miserable and teary. But it was her only option. He just wasn't into her.

Instead of spending the night at House, Grace sent her apologies and asked the elf to port her to Calais. She'd go home tonight and think this disaster over.

Sam

Sam didn't get roaring drunk. He got mad. Tomorrow he would find out who Grace's date was and – well, he didn't know what he was going to do. He'd have to figure that out when he found out who the asshole was. But it would be bad.

He froze. What if she was seeing Neptune? Neptune was an Elemental Realm Lord, and only the stars knew how old he was. He had never bonded, and it's anyone's guess how many he'd seduced and how many furious cuckolds he'd battled over the years. They were all gone, and Neptune was still here, screwing anything with a hole he could stick his dick into. Grace could easily be ported to the sea, and they could meet there.

Didn't matter; he'd fight Neptune for Grace.

Sam furiously chipped at the huge hunk of granite, and every mallet strike was a blow to the unknown man who had hurt his Grace. Sweat poured off of him as he attacked the granite, and every punch was a futile blow against his fury and frustration. He had no idea what he was carving; he just had to bring some order to something in his chaotic life. So he carved.

"Sam?"

Sam whipped around, and his heart stopped. There Grace was, standing in his doorway, a marble statue of utter misery. He couldn't bear to see her so sad, and without thinking he gathered her into his arms and held her tight. She was shaking. Oh dear god, what had that man done to her?

"Grace – Oh, Grace – don't cry. We'll get through this –"

Grace buried her face in his neck, and he could feel her breath, her mouth. She looked up, her eyes glowed, and those wonderful lips parted. Sam couldn't help himself; he kissed her.

Grace kissed back. Furiously, passionately, she ate him up.

Then she pushed him to the couch, and when he fell back onto it she stopped and stood in front of him. She slowly unbuttoned her blouse and gave him everything he wanted.

When he was done, she had everything she wanted.

He was standing in the workroom's toilet drying himself off with a hand towel when he noticed a streak of blood on his leg. He had either hurt her badly, or she was a virgin after all, which meant he was the first, and she couldn't be pregnant. Or raped. Or anything.

Sam stepped back into the studio, and there she was still, stark naked, lying on her back on the couch, lazily stroking her own belly, absolutely sated.

"Grace, are you okay?" She turned to him and gave him a dreamy, afterglow smile. She was more than fine.

Vrt and Althea

Maggot and the Alpha sat at Vrt's feet, and she talked to Althea as the woman stewed in the cauldron. Sometimes she talked to Althea about the Before Times when she was a young girl living with her parents, and sometimes about her time as a newly bonded woman living with Prana.

Sometimes she talked about living on the taiga and how she learned to fight orcs and watch the humans as they grew and changed over 3,500 years. She talked about finding Conary and bonding with him and how much she loved him. She never talked about her first horrible encounter with orcs or how they had cut her up and had stolen away parts of her body, at least not when Conary, or anyone else, was around.

Vrt told Althea that as soon as Althea was reborn, she and Conary were going to go to Ottawa for a quick inspection of the new embassy and to meet with various representatives of the Canadian government. She talked about that and read background and position papers to Althea until Conary joked that the poor girl was going to rise out of the cauldron and stuff that damn three-ring binder down Vrt's throat.

What no one talked about was that Althea was now front-page news across the world. An American lord fleeing to Canada was shot by an American at the border. The American lawyers for the shooters argued in Canadian court that since the lord wasn't human, it wasn't a murder attempt because only humans could be murdered. The two men should simply be tried for common assault of the police officers and affray at most. Maybe a cruelty to animals charge if the Canadians wanted to get picky.

This prompted most of the world to fast-track changes in their legal systems, giving elves and lords equal status under their laws. The US dithered as the tiny group in the House of Representatives held the entire body hostage through procedural machinations. To them, their Americans for Humanity bill giving only humans any civil and legal rights needed to be debated and enacted, whether the majority of Americans felt the same or not.

Vrt didn't talk about that. She didn't want Althea to reject this world because of a few assholes. She could learn about that later.

Other visitors came and talked to the cauldron, too. All the lords did at one time or the other; even Sam took a stab at it, even though he felt weird talking to a big pot. He talked to Althea about different types of marble and how to sculpt each one. He could mansplain all he wanted, and Althea didn't say a word.

Elves came and chatted, the Rangers came and put their hours in, and Maggot was there every minute. The only reason he left was to go pee and poo, and that only took a few minutes. Then he'd race back to lie with his nose on his paws, staring at the cauldron.

Two days later than expected, when even Dr Mandy was starting to look grim, Althea rose to the surface in her egg sac, and everyone knew something would be born; they would just have to wait and see what it was. Five days later, Althea was reborn.

She had eyes.

She had eyes, and what she saw scared her. Colours! Movement! Shapes! Light! People! It was overwhelming and exhausting. Something in her brain from when she was a tiny baby remembered what seeing was like, so she was still wired to the visual world, and this new brain worked fine. She just had to get used to seeing, when previously she was entirely dependent on smelling, feeling, and hearing. Sometimes she just had to close her eyes and rest from the chaos of the visual world.

Althea didn't recognise Vrt when she first saw her, but the minute Vrt spoke, she smiled, delighted to recognise the voice. She didn't know what Maggot looked like, but as soon as the dog snuffled by (under strict orders NOT to touch or lick), she knew who it was. For the first three days, she was utterly sure she and everything else she could see weren't real but a dream.

From what Dr Mandy could tell, there was no brain damage. Althea had come through the cauldron with flying colours.

Now it was just a matter of gaining strength and adapting to Aelfeham House and her new world with her new clan. As Dr Mandy said, easy peasy.

Kyrylo and Caddy

The elves, as clever as they were, struggled to get the baby's car seat in the back of the Jag. Kyrylo had tried for a good half hour before he gave up and called in elves, and now he stood off to the side holding Ivana like a football and occasionally tossing her up in the air just to hear the happy squeals when she fell back into his arms.

"THERE!" And the elf mechanic stood back, well satisfied. "An evil contraption if I ever saw one, Lord Kyrylo, but it didn't defeat us!"

Kyrylo peered into the back seat to see how they had managed to wiggle the car seat in, but he didn't see anything that he hadn't tried, so it was a mystery to him how they did it. In any case, it was secured, and he thanked them and silently prayed that the car seat wouldn't scuff the leather upholstery.

Ivana was now trying her best to play patty-cake with his nose, so it was time to go get Caddy and the picnic basket and have their little outing. She had decided they needed a break – that he needed a break – and just for a few hours on his day off, they would go out for a ride in his beloved car and have a picnic. Just the three of them. No elves, no tablets, no guitars, no anything distracting.

As he walked up the steps to the porch, she did it again. Ivana pulled off his eyepatch and threw it on the ground, breaking the elastic band that kept it on. Kyrylo grimaced; he was going through about three of them a week now and kept a couple of them in the hall butler by the front door, another stash in his office, and still another pile in the bedroom. He hated having his dead eye exposed. It didn't bother Caddy at all. Of course, Ivana just thought that's what all daddies looked like, but he was still very self-conscious about it. He had been told too many times that the dead eye was creepy.

"Ivana! Leave daddy's eye alone!" Caddy walked out, an elf behind her hauling the full picnic basket.

"It's like she keeps aiming for it!"

Caddy shrugged and turned to get a spare patch out of the hall butler. "She is aiming for it! The black patch is something to grab. With me, it's my glasses. At least she didn't grab your nose. That hurts!"

"I should just go in the cauldron and fix this thing! That would do us all some good."

His wife hesitated. It was the smallest of hesitations, the briefest of pauses, and if he hadn't been looking right at her, he would have missed it.

She turned and gave him a sunny smile. Too sunny. And the three of them walked to the car and drove off to their family picnic.

Soon all three of them were sprawled on the blanket and dozing in the shade, the ravaged picnic basket pushed to one side. Ivana was asleep, doing her little starfish thing and mumbling baby complaints in her dreams. Caddy was lying on her back, her eyes closed. Kyrylo's head was on her stomach, and she idly played with a curl of his hair.

He decided to ruin the moment.

"So why don't you want me to go in the cauldron? Are you afraid I'll come out as an elf?"

She tensed, and her hand stopped twirling the lock of his hair.

"I never said I don't want you to go into the cauldron! That's your choice! I can't tell you what to do one way or the other!"

"You don't have to tell me anything, Zaychik. I know you too well." He patted her hand and held it. "You haven't answered my question."

"I'm not afraid you'll come out as an elf, but you have to admit it's not foolproof. I love you just as you are."

Kyrylo kissed her hand. "No, it's not foolproof, but Dr Mandy seems to be pretty good at it.

"Jack got his eye back. Althea got both her eyes back." He paused and then dryly added, "Binocular vision would be nice."

She was tense. "Of course, it would be. That's why I won't say anything if you do. It's up to you."

"But you're worried."

"I love you exactly the way you are. To me, you're perfect, and I love every scar and wrinkle. Every single one. Telling you not to do it would be selfish. I'll miss the old Kyrylo, though."

"Miss my scars!" He turned to look at her and was astonished to see her in tears. "*Zaychik*, how can you miss my scars! I'll come out the way I was supposed to be! Better! I'd come out as a complete lord, like you did. I won't have to wait twenty or so years to completely rid my body of junk human DNA. If we had another baby, there'd be no doubt it would be parented by two complete lords! That's all good, I think!"

She nodded and wiped away the tears. "Yes, that's true. I saw your face when we met Althea. I knew what you were thinking. It's been on your mind a while now. But I'll miss your scars. In a way, they brought you to me. If you hadn't been hit by that IED, you'd still be married to Katya, and I'd be alone."

Kyrylo opened his mouth to tell her not to be so silly, then closed it again.

"I'm pretty sure my marriage to Katya was over before I encountered the IED. But my scars didn't bring you to me; my scars almost kept you away from me! I was pushing you away because of my kink, so they didn't do us any good!"

And that's when Caddy started to cry.

"I love your kink!" She gulped and almost couldn't get it out. "I think your kink feels great. You have no idea. It's what I'll miss if you go in the cauldron."

He sat up and gawped, utterly gobsmacked.

"I've been with a couple of men in my life, and none of them felt like you do when you're inside. No one. Your kink hits me in just the right places. Maybe it's my G-spot, maybe something else, but we have great sex because of your kink, and I'd really miss that."

Kyrylo pulled his wife onto his lap and wiped her tears. "Oh, Zaychik, I'm not going to do anything to mess that up! I'll wait – think about it a bit. But if I lose the other eye or something happens, I have to go in."

She nodded, blinking away the tears. "Of course, you would. And if you decide to go in now, you go do it. I won't say another word. Two eyes would be a great thing, I know."

A hug and a kiss, and they were ready to move on. Kyrylo would think about it, and in the meantime, when he got home, he'd look up G-spot on the internet. He had no idea what that was.

Conary and Vrt

The visit to Ottawa was fruitful for everyone, and Conary and Vrt met with dozens of members of the Canadian government from all branches and departments. There was a warm reception, lots of hands were shaken and (blurry) photos taken, and it was all the normal "grip and grin" that Conary was turning out to be so good at.

Vrt patiently stood at his side, smiled a lot, said little, and made mental notes about the officials they met to discuss with Conary later. People tended to be more unguarded around a pretty face and often assumed that beauty and brains couldn't co-exist in the same person. She let them think that. It was useful.

At the end of the day, the Prime Minister invited the press in for a few photos, and, of course, questions were thrown out, mostly variations of "When will elves come to Canada?" and "Is Lord Ratna coming back?" and questions about Lord Althea's health and recovery. Then one reporter asked Lord Conary his opinion of the lawsuit filed in an American court that day regarding Lord Althea.

Conary looked puzzled. What lawsuit? Did something happen he wasn't aware of?

"Sir, just a few hours ago a lawsuit was filed in an Alabama District Court claiming that the Elf Nation has unlawfully stolen a piece of property from the Sweet Cedar Hill Church of Infinite Resurrection – the Lord Althea. Since Lord Althea isn't human, they claim she is the property of the Church, and they want her back. They are asking the US government to intervene."

Conary sucked in his breath, his back stiffened, and everyone in the room saw his eyes glow bright blue; the press pool became very quiet. He was furious, and they could see it. Vrt slipped her hand into his and squeezed.

He let out his breath and then smiled at the reporter, but his eyes didn't dim, and they certainly weren't smiling.

"It is sad that a few in the US want to be a slave-owning country again. I'm pretty sure the 13th Amendment to the Constitution hasn't been repealed, but things change rapidly, and this is the first I've heard of this lawsuit. There was a time when black and brown people in America weren't considered real people, and I truly thought that sort of bigotry was washed away with the blood of their Civil War dead and a hundred years of hard-won civil rights laws. In the meantime, the official Elf Nation reaction to this lawsuit is that the slavers involved can go fuck themselves. You can quote me."

And with that, he turned on his heel and left.

The headlines in the media were "Lord Conary Tells Slave Owners to 'Go **** Yourself'."

Back in the limo, Vrt turned to Conary and kissed him on the cheek. "That 'go fuck yourself' was pretty direct."

Conary laughed, "Oh, it wasn't original; a Ukrainian soldier said something like that to a Russian warship on the first day of the Russian War. It took a while, but they won against evil idiots. We will, too."

Instead of the usual official reception, that evening the Prime Minister invited the lords to a barbecue that featured plenty of real food instead of canapés, which cheered Vrt up considerably.

It was a lovely night in the gardens of 24 Sussex, and Vrt was enjoying a perfect steak while chatting with a couple from Alberta who were lobbying hard for Lord Ratna to come for a visit when the Ambassador from the US Consulate and a political Foreign Service Officer accidentally-on-purpose wandered to Vrt's picnic table and sat down. They introduced themselves as Mr ("Call me Greg") Patrick and Mr Mateo Escareno. The Albertan couple realised that they were done, and with a warm see-you-later to Vrt excused themselves to go get another beer.

"Lord Vrt, it's so nice to finally meet you! Are you enjoying the barbecue?" Before Vrt could say yes, he continued, "Of course, it's great! Y'know, we have fantastic BBQ in South Carolina. Now Mat here, he's from Texas, and they have their own version –" And he rattled on a few minutes about the differences between the two. Mat just sat there and smiled at the lord and nodded. She was the most alien thing he had ever seen. He cleared all lustful thoughts from his mind, just in case she could read them.

The choice for Vrt was to either keep eating her steak and let the man natter on or help him get on to whatever point he was here to make. She sighed internally. It was a good t-bone, grilled just the way she liked it, blue. Externally, she smiled, nodded, and kept eating.

"Maybe one day I'll be able to come down and try them out for myself. Lord Cadence is very fond of Tex-Mex and loves a good brisket."

Greg beamed. "We'd love to have you! I personally –"

" – But now we have security concerns." She popped a bite in her mouth and raised an eyebrow. "I don't for a minute doubt your welcome, Greg, but I'm afraid not all of your compatriots are as welcoming. Some think we're animals – or worse."

Mateo looked uncomfortable. "Not all of us agree with the rhetoric you're hearing, Lord Vrt. If you look at the polls, most Americans are live-and-let-live people. Please don't let a small group of extremists keep you away."

Vrt smiled. "Do you know how old I am, Mat? I'm very old and have always lived at the edge of humanity, watching and learning, and you don't live as long as I have by taking unnecessary risks with humankind. Two times Yanks have attacked lords."

Greg smiled. "I'm pretty old, too, Lord Vrt – pushing 70. And hey, I know life's too short to take risks – I get what you're saying, but we can promise you a safe visit."

Vrt cut another slice of the excellent steak. "I appreciate the invitation, Greg, and we'll look at how things play out. No one in the Elf Nation dislikes Americans. I'm sure you know my bond-man, Conary, was born and raised in Texas, and his mother, Cadence, lived there for many years. But I'm 3,500 years old, and I've survived millennia by knowing when to fight and knowing when to sit back and watch. While you promise security, it appears that we have no legal status as people in the US. I learned in my first century not to force myself on those who didn't want me." She smiled at Greg. "As you say, life's too short."

"Lord Vrt, that stupid lawsuit is just a PR stunt by extremists, and that bill – it's crap and won't be enacted. It would be unfortunate if a pissant bunch of yahoos turned our two peoples against each other. Very few Americans agree with them."

"We're not against, Greg. We are for those who welcome us." She waved her knife at the Canadians. "Maybe one day, soon, I hope, the US government will be more proactive in accepting elves and lords for what we are, but right now we don't see any movement in that direction. Where is the opposition to the 'crap' laws? Have your courts thrown out the lawsuit? The public might be elf-mad, but that doesn't mean I can walk across the border and not feel like a target. And if something happened, there's no guarantee your government wouldn't just shrug and hide behind legal quibbles."

"We're a powerful country, and it would be good –"

Vrt put her knife and fork down on her empty plate, just the way she was taught to do in etiquette class, and then, with her ability, moved the plate out of the way. Greg and Mat saw the plate move by itself across the table, and the lord's eyes flashed ever so slightly.

"Yes, the US is a powerful country, and it would be good to be on friendly, equal terms. I agree with that. But there are many types of power in this universe, gentlemen."

She stood up and smiled. "That was really good! If I come to visit you're going to have to work to top that steak. I think I'll get another!" She shook their hands and left to go find Conary and see if the grillmaster had another steak for her. And of course he did.

Lester

He came to terms with his bond with Lena, but it took some time. First Lester tried avoiding her, but that lasted about two days. He just couldn't stay away from her, and by the third night he was back in her bed, sniffing her hair as if it were crack and he was a drug addict going through withdrawal, which in a way he was.

Lena never noticed that he was avoiding her. After Lester ran out of the room in a panic from realising she was a lord and he had bonded to her, she just thought he was having some sort of intestinal problem and was pretty grateful he left the room if he was going to have the shits. The old, pre-baby Lester probably wouldn't have bothered.

Then, to get her out of his head, he went to one of the Tsar's hunting lodges for an all-male boy's weekend complete with hookers and had a three-day drunk that was so violent and ill-tempered that even his courtiers wondered what was happening to him. He couldn't do anything with the hookers. Nothing.

Lester tried to remember what he knew about bonding from the old days and was bitter at the realisation that he didn't know diddly squat.

He hadn't known many bonded lords back in Before Times, and none of them had talked to him about it, and he had certainly never been in a circumstance where he had to worry about it. In the Before Times, Lester hadn't had any lord girlfriends, and no one ever thought he was a good catch and tried to get him to bond with them. His father never gave him "the talk".

If he'd had elves around now, they could tell him what to expect and what to do. But he had none because they hated his guts. Just because he'd had a little, tiny, incidental contribution to their genocide. Nasty little shits certainly held a grudge.

So he had to just put up with it, and the fact that Lena was not bonded to him was terrifying. She was a lord who didn't know she was a lord, and one day she'd have an ability, and then what? There was no guarantee she would be weaker than Lester;

probably just the opposite. What would happen if she bonded to another lord? In the West, her freak, one-eyed father was gathering lords around him like they were iron and he was magnetised. Lester's intel units reported at least ten, and they were pretty powerful. Lena could go back to her daddy at any time and find a mate in his stable.

If Lena bonded with someone else and left Lester with an incomplete union he'd die of lovesickness, just as if she died herself and left him a widower.

So his only option was to get her to bond with him. If she did – when she did – he would be able to control her newfound abilities and guarantee his own health.

Lester was going to have to woo Lena and make her fall in love with him. It was going to be hard because, let's face it, Lena was a bitch. A really selfish bitch.

But he had no choice.

Lester was going to have to be nice to Lena as if his life depended on it.

Orcs

Orcs were on the move.

For years, The Wall had been there to keep the Russian military and the orcs who served and fought in it out of the border countries. Oh, they jumped The Wall and made regular incursions just to keep the NATO boys and girls honest, but on the whole the forays were small and limited to a few drones lobbed over the wall to bomb another abandoned Ukrainian farmhouse or a platoon raiding the sheds of a Polish industrial farm looking to steal whatever they could. Occasionally, a pack of undisciplined Russian marauders crept over The Wall and struck gold by hijacking a passing passenger car to rape and pillage. But the retaliation was swift and severe, and they didn't do it often.

Now small groups of people were showing up at quiet places at The Wall and climbing over to get into Russia. Even more took the costlier southern route, flying to Iran to pick up chartered transport to Turkmenistan and then travelling northwards to cross the frontier to Russia. Some walked across the vast open borders from Mongolia and China where they were quickly found by specialist Russian teams and welcomed as lost brothers. Some were lured by the promise of free housing in a socialist workers' paradise, but mostly orcs just wanted to be with their own kind.

The Orc Power campaign of the American First Lady had hit a nerve, and suddenly what was considered by the snooty left-wing liberals to be the failings of the underclass was something to be proud of. Aggression wasn't mindless; it was rebranded as assertiveness, a take-no-prisoners macho asset. Orcs were just standing up for what was theirs when they stole. Rape was just a he said/she said thing anyway and a matter of opinion. One man's rape was another man's consensual quickie. Orcs' superior strength and healing abilities were discovered and celebrated, and if that celebration meant bashing a few lib heads that was fine. Superior genes will out.

So individuals, on their own initiative, moved to a country where their misanthropy was celebrated, their instability was rebranded as simply being flexible, and where physical strength was far superior to mental ability. Orcs wanted to live where they were celebrated as a superior race. They longed for *lebensraum*.

Once they landed in Russia all was as advertised. They were given free housing built with human prisoner and slave labour, a food allowance funded by the farms of political dissidents, and free electricity created from Russia's vast oil fields. They paid no taxes but were expected to contribute to the vast network of bribes and graft. No one complained when the immigrant orcs trashed the free apartments and created vast slums because if they did, the dissidents would be sent to work in the gulag of farms or mines that fed and heated the orc housing.

Russia became an orc paradise, and Lester was their Tsar.

Judy

When Judy Sikao first walked into the detention centre she was blindfolded as all the lords were when they were moved around, but she could still hear, and she could certainly smell. She smelled the stench of what she would later learn were orcs, and she smelled the faint acrid note of death left from the former prisoners, the Uyghurs.

She was thrown into her cell, and there she stayed, totally alone, for a week. The Chinese guards didn't talk to her, and the only contact she had at all was three times a day when they shoved a tray of food into her cell. They were afraid of her; she knew that. They were waiting for Dr Ai to come from Beijing, and he was going to interview her. Zang, the guard who brought her food, was worried his wife was cheating on him.

Judy knew all that because she could read their minds.

Judy was diagnosed autistic when she was a child. She'd sit in a corner and cry because life was too confusing, too loud. Everyone screamed at her, talking with their mouths and with their minds and all at the same time until all she could do was crawl under her bed and shriek back at them.

As she grew up she learned to calm the noises, and special ed teachers at school congratulated themselves that they were saving her from her autism with their innovative therapies when in fact she just learned to tune out the noises. By filtering some out, she could pay attention to other things, like learning to read.

She was seventeen when she found she could calm the noise around her enough to learn to read, and, oh my, that was a blessing. People didn't talk to her when she was reading. They left her alone simply because she was reading, and the act of reading a book had a sacredness to it that meant she was not to be disturbed.

Reading also gave her mind something else to do that drowned out the overwhelming roar of other people's thoughts. Reading taught her how to act in public, and she stopped spinning and flapping her hands. She learned how to eat at a dinner table. Because she had spent her childhood under her bed screaming away the noise she'd missed out on friends and learning how to deal with other people. But reading socialised her even if she still wasn't able to talk to people directly. It was so hard to hold a conversation with anyone when their mouths said one thing and their minds said something else, but a novel let her get into someone's head and not have to deal with their noisy mouths.

She read fairy stories and science fiction, and in those tales she learned about others who could read minds. The Dead Zone by King was interesting if a bit OTT. Judy loved Jane Austen. Now there was a woman who could get into people's heads! Judy read psychology, sociology, and marketing; she learned every theory, school, experiment, and study out there and made herself an expert on how humans thought and why. The knowledge helped explain the noise, and with understanding her power over her own thoughts increased, and the thunder of noise wasn't so bad. By the time she was thirty she was totally in control of it. She had mastered the art of filtering.

Judy's parents were both Chinese immigrants and not well-educated. When they moved to the US, they worked in restaurants and eventually opened one of their own, a bagel shop. They had four kids other than Judy, so they were very busy, but while the kids assimilated into American culture the parents still had some Old World ideas.

The old Chinese community saw autism as a disease that could be contracted. Her parents, who had very noisy, disordered minds, didn't want their other kids to catch autism. Since Judy seemed to do better by herself it suited her parents to keep her isolated even within the family. Everyone seemed happier when Judy was alone in her room, so she grew up in a family but not a part of one. When she was three she was sent to a special school for autistic kids, and every possible day, for every possible hour, her parents made sure she was in some sort of public school special ed classroom – not because they thought it would do her any good but because it kept her away from the rest of the family and they could get on with their lives.

When she was twenty-one and could no longer go to public school she was sent to a group home in Tampa, and that was the last time she saw her parents. There she shared a room with another patient, and boy-oh-boy was that an utter failure. But at least this time she could articulate why she was having meltdowns and how the noise in the house was unbearable. So they put her in a one-room cottage in the backyard, not much more than a shed with a bathroom, and it was quieter there. The noise from the main house was muted by the distance, and she learned to tune it out and gradually learned to focus and listen to one voice in her head at a time.

She lived in the cottage for fifteen years reading books borrowed from the Tampa Public Library. Three days a week she went to a sheltered workshop where she worked alone fulfilling orders for lightbulbs from small businesses. Every box said,

"Packed with loving hands by patients joyfully working with the Greater Tampa Autism Trust. Let your light shine on." which Judy thought was cheesy.

Then the Trust lost its government funding and closed.

Judy was thirty-five and could almost pass as normal. She didn't know she was a lord because no one knew what a lord was back then. No one ever saw her eyes glow because when she was having a meltdown as a child she squeezed her eyes shut. Later, as an adult, she lived alone. There was never a lover to gaze softly at her at night and see the glow of emotion; she never had any reason to go out with anyone.

There were no lovers, but there were a few men who tried to molest her. Men who looked at her from across the room saw a very pretty Chinese girl who earned their attention and lust, but when they came closer she was god-awful ugly. Nauseating. She smelled bad.

She didn't want them anyway. Too much information in their creepy, horny brains. Too many pictures of what they wanted to do with her and to her, but never for her.

After reading about sex and such, she was pretty sure she wasn't gay, and she liked the way men looked and smelled, but when they came close with the intent to hit on her, she couldn't handle their neediness. She'd never met a man who just wanted her to love him or who wanted to make her feel good. They just wanted. She'd never met her Mr Darcy.

When the shelter closed she was on Social Security disability, and the social workers who were tasked with finding places for the shelter's patients found her a studio apartment in a massive, ugly, anonymous apartment complex. They showed her how to manage a credit card, use the bus, and took her three times to the Publix grocery store so she could learn to shop.

The social workers tried to make her get a phone to manage her credit card, but Judy didn't want a TV or radio or internet in her new apartment. The last thing she wanted was to add a noise-producing box into her life, and if she needed to do anything online, she did it at the library.

Then they left her alone.

Judy was fine with that. The studio apartment was just like living in the shelter, and while she didn't have to work packing light bulbs she did have to cook for herself. A good trade-off in her opinion.

The apartment complex was almost ninety per cent retirees who had moved to Florida to enjoy the sun while they waited to die. At thirty-five, she was by far the youngest person there, and she liked the old people. They had quiet thoughts. Some were going into dementia, and that just meant their mental processes were even slower. When she walked down the hall or out to the street to catch the bus and passed one of the geriatrics, their minds didn't scream at her, not like younger people. So she smiled a bit more, and they smiled back at the shy Asian woman, and before you knew it, she had a couple of friends who nodded to her in the halls and talked about the weather when she took out her garbage.

One day she was invited to a barbecue by the pool put on by the residents' association. Judy went, ate a hamburger so she didn't have to cook, and a couple of old guys asked her if she'd play some penny-ante poker with them. They needed more people at their table to make up a good game.

They taught her poker, and she won. Then they played again, and she won again. They played all night, and she won every game. Then they got mad, accused her of cheating, and she went home.

She realised a few things that night. One was that she could read the minds of her opponents very easily because they were concentrating on their cards, and there was less mind clutter to scream at her. The other important thing she learned was not to win at every game. But the last thing she learned was most important. She learned that she could use her gift in a gainful way – and it was entertaining. Reading minds wasn't just a burden to be endured; it wasn't a disability, but a talent she could use. She enjoyed playing poker, and she flat-out enjoyed winning.

The next day she went to the library and borrowed every book on poker she could find and read them all. She memorised all the different variations and games. She studied odds. She learned about poker tournaments, tells, high-stakes games, and casinos. She saw how her knowledge of psychology and how people thought would work with the game.

Then she returned to the library, and for the first time in her life she studied women's fashion magazines. With a page torn from one she went to the mall and bought a dress and high heels that matched a photo of a woman in a casino.

Judy had a plan, and it was pretty simple. She wanted to play poker, and if she was going to find good players, she wouldn't find proper opponents sitting around the over-chlorinated apartment complex pool. She'd go to a casino and see if she could sit in on a game there.

And that's exactly what she did. Oh, she was terrified! She had to get a taxi; then she had to go into the cacophony and chaos of a busy casino and walk past the rows and rows of

342

shrieking slot machines with their blue-rinsed players holding plastic cups of chips and find out where the real gamblers played poker and then make her way back to the card rooms. She bought a hundred dollars worth of chips and was given a seat at a table with five strangers who were happy to have a new mark.

Four hours later she walked out with over five thousand dollars. The money didn't matter; it was the sense of accomplishment that did. She'd won! She wasn't a defective loser freak! The people at the table all had thought she was a pretty little sucker when she walked in; she knew that because their thoughts were on top of their brains, loud and clear. When she finally left they were mad, they were frustrated – and they respected her. Judy was an equal, a formidable one.

When you know people think you're crazy or stupid because you can hear them say it every single day of your life and suddenly they respect you for winning – that was pretty intoxicating.

She played every night for the next month until the casino banned her. The floor managers took her to a back room and asked her how she was cheating and even offered to pay her for the knowledge so they could know for the next cheater. Was she wearing a wire? Did she get signals from an accomplice? But then, she always came alone. They couldn't figure it out.

When Judy told them she wasn't cheating and that all she had to do was look at the other player's faces and read their minds they didn't believe her, so she was banned.

But that was okay. She now had the money to travel and a healthy stake that allowed her entry to the best casinos.

When she was stolen by the Chinese government and locked into the prison Judy had been a professional gambler for almost thirty years. She was sixty-three but looked about forty, neither young nor old. She'd travelled all over the world playing poker, always making sure she didn't win too often, but often enough to fund a very nice lifestyle that allowed her to play in the top places. And she always had the money to earn invitations to play in the best games. She made sure she never ranked internationally higher than fifteen. Judy let the other players get the top spots, the endorsements, and the PR. She hid back in the pack where it was quieter.

She was playing in a high roller tournament in Macau when she walked into the elevator to go to her hotel room. The elevator doors shut, she smelled something funny, and that was the last thing she remembered.

She didn't know she was a lord. But someone in the Chinese government did.

Cho

Cho was pissed. Judy Sikao hadn't shown up for a high-stakes game with his best clients, and he had promised them she'd be there. Judy was there yesterday, playing in the Gold Room as a teaser, and, just as she always did, had won just enough to be a challenge. She was pretty enough to keep the old boys interested and the young ones sure they could bed her.

Of course, it was all a show, and Cho knew it. None of them would get anywhere close to her knickers, and the occasional losses in the Gold Room were just there to give the suckers a hope of a chance.

That was why she was his favourite pro. She wasn't greedy, and she knew how to play the game, and he didn't mean poker. Cho had known Judy for years. Years! His entire career.

She was a fixture on the circuit, and all the top-level casinos had a Judy story or two to tell. But in the end, she was always classy, always a draw, and never won so much that it made the clients surly. She had fun, and the clients had fun, and she and the casinos raked in the money.

Cho figured out that she was one of those elf lords about two years ago, and then everything – everything – made sense. They never could get a good picture of her on the security cameras, and for a long time they thought she was wearing some sort of camera-reflecting makeup. Cho even had his housekeepers tear her comp rooms apart to look for it, but other than red lipstick and eyeliner, she was a minimalist in that department.

She was a minimalist in everything. A cypher.

No sex, no men or women, no boozy nights with friends after the games, no TV on in the room, no internet to tap and trace. A bank account in Tampa, Florida, hooked into one credit card and a studio apartment there. US passport. No family, no clubs, no church, no university, no work history. No history at all outside of her casino tours. In that aspect of her life, she travelled pretty much constantly, and the casino security departments all knew her and she was well-documented.

And she won every single time she needed to. Cho never saw her lose money on a trip. Maybe on a day she'd lose, but she never walked out of a week in Macau with a net loss. And all the other casinos said the same thing. She never played against the house, just the clients, but she always made a good profit. You don't do that month after month for years without having some sort of angle, some sort of cheat. The gods of gambling just wouldn't stack the odds in her favour so consistently.

When he realised she was using magic of some sort, he told the Boss, who told him to keep Judy's lord thing quiet. Top secret. The Boss said it would be good to keep the EN on their side, and he wanted Judy to keep coming to his casinos. It could prove handy one day.

So when she didn't show up, he had the security people look for her. They came back and showed him a tape of her blob getting into an elevator, collapsing, and a couple of goons making the elevator go down to the parking garage, where they bundled her up and stuffed her in a van.

Judy was kidnapped right out of his hotel, and security was pretty sure it was the Chinese government from the looks of the van and how her abductors acted.

Cho called the Boss.

The Boss was pissed. So discourteous of the Chinese government people to come to one of his casinos without so much as a word and kidnap a guest. It was bad for business.

He thought about it for an hour or two and then called Mr Won, the lawyer. Mr Won had a lot of contacts with all sorts of people in the East Asian mafia families, but it was rumoured he also had contact with the Elf Nation. He knew, some claimed, Lord Conary, one of the big EN guys who was in all the news reports. Long ago, Conary Aeldor had done odd jobs for a lot of people the Boss worked with, before anyone knew he was a lord. They were almost all dead now, but there were still some around with long memories. His name was known.

The Boss figured that helping out a lord might pay him back big time later on, and the Boss was the boss because he played the long game. He knew the odds. Screw the government; they were rude. Disrespectful. He would bet on the EN.

Conary

Mr Won called Conary and told him what he knew about Judy Sikao. Conary listened, thanked Mr. Won, asked him to send any security tapes and evidence, and to keep him informed. Then he sent Mr Won's son a nice Rolex, compliments of the EN.

Rashid was given the information, and the RumLot intel guys started their investigations. It took a long time, almost a week. While China was very, very wired in, and the elf techs still had access to their computer system despite the government's obsessive secrecy and the fight to control internet access, it still took time. The problem was that they'd found a very top-secret program that gave every indication of being a biological research program for age extension that had a lot of internal discussion about lords, but the program itself was totally off the grid. You can't penetrate a computer system that exists completely isolated from the rest of the world.

But no man is an island, and neither is a super secret program that had a detention camp, bio labs, and scientists working for it. Someone, somewhere, would leak. A mistake would be made. It was a matter of finding a tiny leak in the flood of trillions of messages that inundated the Chinese ether.

What they found out was that Judy wasn't the only lord the Chinese had in a detention camp; she wasn't even the first.

The break they needed was an email of a routine report from the blood samples of thirteen patients being held in quarantine, who "had very high metabolisms," and the person who wrote the patient info put the age of one as 140. You don't send blood samples to a very high-level lab just to find out electrolyte levels. And a human patient who's 140 is either lying or dead.

The report had the name and address of the doctor who requested the information. After that it was easy.

Dr Ai

It was a good two weeks before Judy met Dr Ai. He had been watching her from the beginning, of course, but he wanted to break her down a bit before he hazarded a visit. If she had the ability to vaporise him the minute she looked at him, of course, he wasn't going to risk it, but she didn't kill the guards; she didn't do anything to them. She didn't seem to be very powerful at all.

The others didn't have any special powers either other than to make their eyes glow when they were upset. Most were kids, and for all of their glow-eyed weirdness they had not a speck of magic that anyone could see. Then they had one old guy who was almost dead. The only way they found him was that his family turned him in because he was so damned old, and they were tired of taking care of him. He didn't do anything other than mumble and pee.

Judy was a bit different. She was pretty well-preserved for sixty-three, but not out of the realm of possibility. She didn't look like a teenager. Her hair was black, but that was hair dye. She styled her hair with a permed Marilyn Monroe bouffant to mask the points of her ears, but underneath the hair dye and the perm her hair was about ninety-five percent white, and her ears were certainly pointed although not nearly as tall as the European lords' ears. Dr Ai knew better than to make an inference from a sample size of one, so he didn't know if that was just Judy or if the Chinese lords had a different set of genes. It would be bad if the Chinese lords were a weaker race than the European lords. If they didn't have the immortality gene that would be a disaster for his program.

When Dr Ai was ready to start talking with Judy via a link he had a screen installed in her room. The techs came in to do the work, and she was docile, sitting on her bed with the mandatory hood on with her hands on her lap and her ankles demurely crossed. He couldn't see her clearly, of course, but he could watch her blob on the screen, and the guards told him what she was doing.

He didn't know that she was listening to their terrified thoughts as they worked. She was worried about the guard who had his finger on a live trigger and was scared out of his mind. They all thought she was going to make them explode or something. In their frantic minds she saw images from newscasts and fleeting thoughts about other lords and their power. Lords who killed when they were attacked.

Now Judy really wished she had been an internet user. There seemed to be something going on in the world that she'd missed in her bubble life of casinos, hotels, and frequent-flyer airport lounges. She fleetingly remembered some of the images she'd seen in the guards' minds, but in the clutter of movie posters and video game adverts a newspaper with a drawing of a real lord or elf just blended in the background; if she walked by a TV screen with an elf on view it was just fantasy nonsense. She had obsessively avoided noise, but it turned out that inside the cacophony, there was information she was missing. Every one of the men who guarded her or walked down the halls thought she was a thing called a lord, and they knew there were more of them. And they were scared of her.

That was very interesting. The odds were changing with every bit of information she gathered. Maybe the gods had dealt her a good hand after all, and she just needed to learn how to play it.

For the first time in her sixty-three years, she wondered if she could use her ability to get in someone's head to kill. She didn't know if she was only a receiver of mind noise. Could she project a thought?

Dr Ai knew that isolation was a good way to drive people a bit stir crazy, and two weeks without any human contact would make his prisoner a bit more amenable to his overtures. She'd want to talk to him, he was sure. He didn't know Judy. She thrived on silence.

A voice came out of the TV while she was eating lunch.

"Judy, this is Dr Ai. Could we talk, please?"

She ignored it and kept eating her lunch. He spoke in Mandarin. She understood him perfectly well, but when she did speak to anyone it was going to be in English and in person. She was going to dictate the opening bid.

He tried several times and was always polite, but she pretended she didn't hear anything at all. A few minutes later a tech and a guard came in to check the sound levels of the TV. Like before, she was docile and did as she was told by the guard. In Mandarin.

They didn't see her little smile under the hood as she listened to the tech do sound checks and make sure the monitor was working. She didn't see the guard when he hammered her arm with the butt of his rifle and knocked her over.

"YOU ANSWER THE DOCTOR!!"

She lay on her bed moaning and clutching her arm, playing it up. The furious tech growled at the guard. "Do you want to get us killed?"

But the guard just shrugged, and then Judy tried something. She projected a thought. She could hear them walking out the door. She gambled and went into his mind and made him turn and made his trigger finger twitch. It was so easy. Just a twitch. The gun fired, and the guard killed the tech with one lucky blast.

Screaming at the top of her lungs Judy scrambled to a corner, imitating her best autism meltdown, but keeping the hood on. Alarms rang, and she could hear heavy boots thumping down the hall and panicked voices yelling. The guards were in a frenzy, and she could hear the mental cacophony of their hysteria despite her own very theatrical screams. They pulled out the body, slammed the door, and she could hear them beating up the guard who didn't know what had happened and why he had killed the tech.

She gradually stopped screaming, but didn't leave the corner for a long time, gently rocking and eavesdropping on the high emotions from the crowds in the hall. Judy hadn't had that much fun in ages.

Dr Ai

An incandescent Dr Ai pulled in the head of the military guard unit and threatened to put him and his entire family – his entire fucking ancestral village – in front of a firing squad if anything like that happened again. It was unforgivable; didn't the incompetent officer know he had an unstable guard? What if the crazy bastard had killed the lord?

The man grovelled, there was a purge, and Judy noticed new guards bringing her food. They were even more terrified than the last bunch because now they were scared of her *and* Dr Ai.

What a disaster, thought Dr Ai. If I can't get her to talk to me through the monitor I'll have to go in personally.

He still wanted to interview her, to make friends, and woo her with soft words and find out what she could really do. If he thought she was useless and he killed her for dissection there would be no going back to find out later she did have some magic they could have used. It would also help identify the purpose of any unusual organs in her brain or body that could be magic-related. They had already dissected one lord, but it had been a child and physically indistinguishable from a normal human. Judy was older than she looked and had pointy ears. There must be something there.

The next day, Dr Ai tried again through the monitor, and again he had no luck. She didn't even glance at the TV. He wondered if she couldn't hear or see it, even though humans could. After all, she couldn't be photographed; maybe there was something about electronic transmission that didn't work for her. She didn't have a phone on her when she was grabbed, and *everyone* had a phone.

They made her sit on the bed with the hood on when Dr Ai came in. He said hello, Judy, in Mandarin, and she looked at the sound of his voice but didn't say anything.

He didn't know it, but she was listening to his thoughts as they raced through his mind. She saw vivid pictures. Dissections. Other lords. Glowing eyes in the night. Fear. Lots of fear. Want. Want. Want. He wanted to live forever. Jealousy.

He sat down on a chair in front of her, waiting, and while he was trying to establish his dominance by waiting for her to speak first, she read his soul.

She didn't like what she saw.

The man was a sociopath. Classic. He was going to kill her sooner or later. He had other lords here. Children. He had killed one, and that thought came several times because he had enjoyed it. He took comfort in the child's death. A lord, who could live forever, had died by his hand. He was stronger.

He wanted, and in knowing his want Judy knew she had a winning hand. Under the hood, she smiled. Just like a poker player who wanted too much and so didn't figure the odds with logic, but emotion, Dr Ai's wants could be used against him.

She planted a want in his head while he waited for her and while he was under the illusion he was winning this hand. She made him want her. To have sex with her. To want to see her face, her beauty. To dominate and humiliate her.

He shifted in his seat, suddenly aroused, and she quickly left his thoughts, afraid to overplay her hand. She had planted the thought, and now was the time to let him absorb it.

"You can take the hood off if you want, Judy." He said it in English. She had won.

As slowly as a strip tease she took the hood off. Dr Ai had only seen her in drawings, and the drawings didn't do her justice. In front of him, in person, she was gorgeous. Her eyes glowed, and the thought flew through his mind – she was afraid of him, and that was even more arousing.

He asked her a few more questions, about her background, her name and birthdate, and things like that. Just to establish that he could. The answers were clipped; she offered nothing more than the minimum which he found irritating.

"Are you comfortable, Judy?"

"No, I don't want to be here."

"I didn't mean that. You're not going anywhere. You're too precious to be out in public aren't you? I meant do you need any more food or anything like that? Is there something I can tell the guards to bring you?"

"More meat. More veg, more rice, not so much noodles – that would be nice."

He got up to leave. In the end, Ai was happy with the interview. She had talked to him and asked him for something. As he walked out, he said, "Goodbye, Judy. I'll be back." And at that exact moment, he had a vivid picture of her kneeling in front of him, begging, her mouth open –

And he turned and left.

Judy didn't smile; that would have been too obvious, but she was very pleased with the interview, too. She was in his mind now – a Judy-shaped brain-worm he wouldn't be able to quit until he either fed it or killed it. Or died himself.

Now that she had Ai on the hook she began to plot her escape. For the last two weeks, she had been noting the shift changes and rhythms of the guards. The purge didn't change that; it only changed the personalities. She started listening as hard as she could, casting a wide net around the detention centre. It wasn't that big, and if she concentrated, she could pinpoint all of the guards as they manned their stations and came and went for shift changes. None lived in the centre, but they did have an office and a dining hall, and she could hear them gather there. It was noisy, and it was hard to tease out individual voices in the white noise of their collective mind, but she could do it.

She wondered if she could create a mass panic. They were already on edge. What if she could put fear in their minds the way she had put lust in Dr Ai's sociopathic brain? If they all ran away at the same time –

As hard as she tried she couldn't hear the thoughts of the other lords. Were they drugged, or could she not hear her own kind? The guards thought about them a lot so she knew they were still in the same detention centre just on different floors and kept apart from each other. Could she get them out, too? They were children. She couldn't leave them, but she didn't know how she was going to find them if she couldn't hear them.

All of this took a lot of energy, and her body glowed, but she huddled under her blankets and with the extra food she managed to keep her energy levels up. But, god damn, she was hungry all the time now.

Dr Ai came back the next day, and she teased him again. He thought she was answering his anodyne questions and that she was getting more comfortable with him. But today he left with a full-on erection and visions of sneaking into her cell at night when the guards were having their midnight shift dinner.

She still didn't know how she was going to get the kids out, but she did see for sure that Dr Ai had a large key ring on him, and he wasn't using a key from the guardroom to get into her cell. Her cell's key was on that ring, and the guards didn't put all of their keys on one ring, so he must have his own set. If they were alone and she killed him she could take his keys and gamble that they would get her into the other lords' cells.

Her hand still had a deuce staring back at her, and that was the kids. She had to figure out the layout of the compound pretty soon, the exits, and where they were. Dr Ai could come to her cell any night now. His narcissism and his lust wouldn't wait much longer, and Judy didn't want to have sex with him more than once. She didn't want to have sex with him at all.

Judy was still a virgin. She simply couldn't be with a man and his thoughts long enough to get aroused for a one-night stand much less to fall in love. Every man she had ever met who seemed to like her, sooner or later, would have a sexual thought that would just turn her off. When she grew older, she realised they couldn't control the mind-pictures that flashed through their undisciplined brains, and they didn't know she could see the nastier images. But when you're kissing a guy goodnight and he suddenly thinks of rape, even when he has absolutely no intention of acting on that thought, it was a turn-off, and he didn't get a second kiss. Being able to read a mind was handy in the short term, but it was isolating, too. Long-term relationships die with too much unfiltered exposure and honesty.

On the flip side, she'd never been raped or molested, either. She knew what was in the cards well before any rapist dealt his hand. The Chinese agents, by accident, did the only thing that would work when they remotely gassed the elevator. If they had sent a team of humans to grab her she would have mentally heard their intent before they crossed the room, and she would have run off.

Breakfast came and with it a new guard. She heard him on the other side of the door fumbling with the tray, and while he was messing around trying to fit it through the slot. She peeked into his mind, was immediately revulsed, and she almost left it. His foul mind stank and had purple shards of glass poking in it. It was a horrible, stupid mess of meanness and random thoughts about little girls, smoking hash, his balls itched – and what he was going to do next which was take the next tray to the next prisoner. He concentrated hard on that because if he didn't his slow brain was going to forget, and he'd get a beating from the sergeant. I won't forget. I have a list.

Judy sat up.

Fuckin' tray is hot –

Judy gave him a solution.

– but this piece of paper will protect my fingers –

He pushed the tray through the slot, and a corner of the paper poked through. From her side of the door Judy pulled in the tray and the paper at the same time.

She inserted the thought that it was okay to lose the list, not a big deal.

– Shit. Well, I'll have to get another.

He walked away, pushing the food trolley to the next cell, wherever it was.

Carefully, so the camera couldn't see, she tucked the paper in her shirt and picked up the tray as she always did and sat down for breakfast. She ate every bite.

It wasn't a list; it was a map of the building with red dots on certain rooms. The guard was so stupid he needed a picture rather than a list with numbers.

Dr Ai came at lunchtime, like he had before. A creature of habit it seemed. Judy wondered if he had a family, maybe a pretty, loving wife, two kids – and she shook her head. She'd never had any indication in his thoughts that any family was waiting at home. He'd either never had one or never thought of the one he had. Same thing.

He was done with the softball questions; now he demanded more meat. Could she lift things with her mind? No. Could she lob out pulses of light or flames? No, and she laughed which he didn't like. Could she fly? No.

"Then what can you do? What is your power?"

Judy shrugged. "I don't know if I have any power that normal people don't have. I'm a pretty average person, I think, who's good at poker. That comes from years of studying the game, studying people, and knowing the odds of every hand I'm dealt.

"Is being an idiot savant a superpower? I'm pretty bad with people, but I seem to be able to understand them." She smiled at Dr Ai and shot him a thrill of lust at the same time, and she saw him shiver. "But you appear to be good with me, Dr Ai. Is that your superpower?"

He sat up straight. "This is not about me. It's important that lords are understood, and we can't study you without your cooperation."

"And you expect cooperation by kidnapping me? Why didn't you just ask me for an interview at the casino if you thought I was one of these lord people? We could have sat down for a game of cards, and I would have talked to you for hours. That's what I do."

"You wouldn't have told us anything, and we still wouldn't have you under our protection."

"What are you protecting me from?"

Dr Ai looked around, and suddenly he felt trapped. How did this become an interrogation of him? He was supposed to be asking the questions. Judy knew she had pushed too hard, and she leaned forward. "But if I'm going to need a protector I'm sure you can do it. You look like a very strong man." She looked around and waved her hand vaguely. "You asked me what I needed. It would make me more comfortable not to have the guards staring at me when I'm showering and peeing. I'm afraid they're going to come in and –"

Dr Ai suddenly thought of the lord naked and a guard walking in, and his jealousy and anger burned white hot. Judy was his, and he didn't share. He stood up. "You don't have anything to worry about. The guards will do what I say. I'll make sure the cameras are off when you need some privacy. We're not barbarians here."

Judy smiled; she couldn't have asked for anything more. "Goodbye, Dr Ai, and thank you. I know you're not a barbarian! Sleep well. I know I'll sleep better tonight. Alone."

And as he left she shot a last thought to his mind. "If the cameras are turned off I can visit her, and no one will know."

A few hours later the tiny green light at the corner of the camera blinked off. It didn't come back on. Judy looked at the camera and walked to the shower. It didn't swivel. Then she walked to the other end of the room. It didn't move. Was tonight going to be the night?

Judy went to bed early. At one in the morning, she heard the keys rattling in the door, and Dr Ai slipped through, right on time. She looked at the camera; it was still dead. He was nervous; his mind was a riot of images and emotions. Lust was there, and so was hate, but not a lot of fear. He wasn't afraid of her.

He crept to her bed and pulled back the blankets over the small form – and nothing was there – just some clothes, a rolled-up blanket, and a pillow.

"Are you looking for me, Dr Ai?"

He spun around and there she was, between him and the door; her eyes glowed bright green. Now he had fear.

A step towards her. "Judy, I want –"

Yes, he wanted. He wanted her very badly, and she gave herself to him. A blast of noise from her mind screamed into his, and the terror she instilled made his body flood with adrenaline until his blood pressure soared to unsustainable heights and something had to give. What gave was a blood vessel in his brain in the cerebellar tonsils, and the section of his brain that controlled his breathing stroked out.

Dr Ai looked at Judy, and his mouth opened, but nothing came out. He was still thinking; he was starting to comprehend as she pulled her mind out of his, and that made her noise all the more effective, but it was too late for him. All she had to do was let nature take its course. Three minutes with no air, and he would be dead.

"My talent, Dr Ai, is that I can get into your head."

He sank to the floor, staring at her with fixed, terrified eyes, finally comprehending what her power was.

"And I just scared you to death."

After he passed out, she took his keys and walked out, locking the door behind her and leaving him to die alone. It seemed appropriate somehow.

She could see quite well in the hall even with the lights subdued for late-night energy conservation. It was good to see the Chinese government concerned about climate change. There were no guards in the hall; she could hear them at the canteen having their middle-of-the-shift meal. They weren't worried about their prisoners; their charges were all asleep, and being kids, who was going to break out?

In the long, silent hours she'd sat alone in her cell Judy had gamed many scenarios regarding the guards, thinking about how they would react and the odds of each possible outcome. Should she induce a mass panic? Make them all nauseated and sick? She didn't think she had the ability to do with them what she did with Dr Ai, not en masse. Dr Ai had gotten a specific, focused blast of mind noise. For the guards she needed to do something that would cover a lot of minds at once.

In the end, she decided to create a few extremely nasty hallucinations to drive them violently crazy and build from there. Panic and chaos are contagious, and she would try to set the stage. It was a risky bet because if it didn't work, she could be making the situation worse for herself. There was no way she could defend against a group attack if they turned on her. But all she could do was play the hand she was dealt.

The map said she was in front of one of the cells, and she could see the fresh scrapes where the dinner trays were pushed through the slot. It took a few minutes to find the right key, but she did. Inside was a boy, about twelve, and his blue eyes glowed in terror. She sent him a calming, you-are-safe-with-me thought, but she couldn't read his mind and didn't know if it worked.

"Put on warm clothes and shoes. We're breaking out. Don't talk."

As he dressed, she stood by the door and listened to the guards in the dining hall. Jumping from mind to mind, she found a weak one and inserted the hallucination. The guard looked up from his dinner, screamed, drew his pistol, and shot at the demon running at him. Of course, there was no demon; he killed people at another table. Judy jumped to another mind and inserted another hallucination, and that was enough. The entire company erupted into chaos. Even a human could hear the melee from where she stood.

In Ukraine, an automatic AI program was monitoring telephone, computer, and radio traffic in the area of the detention centre. As soon as the first frantic guard dialled out, the program shut down all communications to and from the detention centre until the situation could be evaluated. Judy, of course, didn't know that.

The boy was ready. She took his hand, and they went three doors down where she unlocked the next door. There was a little girl who appeared to be about five. He went in to get her, and Judy stood in the hall and sent her thoughts to the dining hall, looking for some more minds and causing more chaos.

And that's what they did for the next half hour. Their little group expanded as they went from cell to cell. Now and then Judy would cast her thoughts to the guards and push one or two over the edge, and they would start brawling again. Gunfire was sporadic as the guards faced off against each other, and there were a lot fewer of them now. By the time Judy reached the last cell the guards were all dead, wounded, or gone. She didn't hear any of them moving around.

She looked at her little group. She had two teenagers and one very old man. The rest were little kids and a baby that could only have been a few weeks old. She had no idea how they could leave such a small baby in a room by itself at night, but she guessed it was pure fear on the part of the guards. One of the older kids had thought to pack a bag of bottles of milk and a couple of diapers, so that was good. She made a sling from a sheet and carried the baby.

"Well, now we have to leave this place. Stay together, hold hands, and no talking!"

She knew she was crazy to bet everything she had on walking out into god-knows-what at two in the morning with a bunch of little kids (How many? She didn't even count) and one confused old guy who looked like he was about to fall over. All of them were so terrified they were in shock. But she calmed them when she felt their fear pick up, and they silently followed her like ducklings trailing their mama duck to a pond.

In for a penny, in for a pound. They had to leave.

Judy cast her thoughts wide, and the place was silent. Every time she sensed guards stirring, she blasted them with terrifying thoughts, and they either passed out or died. Soon, someone from the outside would notice that the guards weren't answering the phone, or a new shift would start to come in, so time was running short. She had to take the kids and hide them somewhere during the day. She had locked all of the cells behind her, and she hoped that would slow the new security people down, but who could tell? Probably not. Soon they'd be crawling all over this place.

She looked for the front gate, and there it was. In a panic to escape the madness of the dining hall someone had left it wide open. Judy herded the kids to the gate, passing about a dozen bodies lying in the courtyard, and they emerged onto an access road. They were in some sort of industrial area, and the streets were totally deserted and pitch black. Across a large, empty field she could see the black square outlines of warehouses silhouetted against the cold night sky. Judy led them down the street, trying to get her bearings.

"Hello."

She spun around towards the voice. They all spun around. A man was standing in the dark shadow of a scrubby pine, almost invisible except for his bright blue glowing eyes that floated in darkness.

"My name is Lord Tuân. We were sent here to rescue you – but I see that I'm a bit late, and you have rescued yourself. Do you need a ride?"

Judy nodded, her voice shaky. "That would be very kind of you."

Winner takes all.

Tuân and Ratna

Tuân and Ratna, along with five ethnic Korean operatives gathered from RumLot Security and the Korean Army, had been sent to check out the detention centre and look for weak points in the security. They hadn't been in the area a day when Judy made her breakout. The two lords were blocks away, walking around the neighbourhood on a recon, when they got a message on their phones that something was going down at the detention centre. When they ran to the front gate they saw twelve kiddy lords and two adult lords walking down the deserted street in a little, glow-eyed parade, their eyes dancing in the dark like fire flies.

While Tuân was introducing himself to Judy, Ratna called the Korean team who were checking out a warehouse that they'd rented as a base, and they were there in minutes. They were driving a panel truck, and everyone piled in the back.

The detention centre was fifty miles from the Korean-Chinese border, and a little over an hour later, a Chinese border guard who knew in his mind that the truck just had a load of papayas in it waved them through without checking, and once on the Korean side they were fine. Dr Ai had walked into Judy's cell at one am, and by five am the entire lot of them were in Korea.

China

The top ranks of the Chinese government were livid, but more than angry, they were terrified. Someone had entered their sovereign territory, broken into a top-secret detention centre, and stolen fourteen detainees, as well as killing almost twenty-five of their security guards. They could say nothing publicly.

What could they say to the wider world and to their own people? That they had detained lord children and were doing experiments on them, and now they were miffed because they had been interrupted? That they had kidnapped an American citizen and planned to do experiments on her, and now they needed her back? That some members of the elite want to live forever and are willing to do anything to make that happen? That they had pissed off the Elf Nation?

Someone had entered the detention centre. Something had happened, but in the end they had no evidence at all of an outside force which was eerie and frightening. All of the dead bodies in the centre had been killed by their own people. The three witnesses who lived said they all went mad at the same time, and they told of demons. Some of the guards tried to call out, but none of the phones and computer systems worked – until they did. There were no alarms, but nothing was wrong with the alarm system. Dr Ai had a stroke that the autopsy deemed to be entirely natural and was locked in one prisoner's cell. All of the doors of the prisoners were locked, and there was no evidence of forced entry. They were just gone. How did these lord children escape, if not by magic?

Could the magic of the Elf Nation be used against the NPC committee members in their own homes? Could they be made insane or have a stroke by long distance? Was there any safe place from their magic?

Internally they had been searching for lords within their population ever since Lord Cadence went public. The lords they found were marked and watched, and all were quietly rounded up at the same time, about a week before Judy was kidnapped. From the huge population of over a billion they found the twelve children and one old man. They didn't find any adults like Judy.

This meant the adult lords had either left China (doubtful) or didn't exist (doubtful) or were hiding. If the government said anything publicly about rounding up lords they would have an unknown number of adult lords of unknown power going even deeper underground and probably working against the government.

So they said nothing and did nothing and prayed that the lords didn't know exactly who had authorised the program and wouldn't come after them. Officially the program never existed, and unofficially every trace, every guard not on shift, every scientist who worked with Dr Ai, every written record or computer file were wiped away. As far as the upper echelons of the Chinese government were concerned they never existed.

The Chinese Lords

Aelfeham House had a major elf-spansion – a new children's wing complete with a school and a huge cadre of hyperactive elves to take care of them. Lord Farah took the assignment of being the house mother to them all. It took a while for the kids to adjust and heal, but children in a loving environment are resilient, and lord children have all the time in the world to get better. While there were rocky moments for all of them, in the end they became a joyful part of the lord clan, and just having them around turned Aelfeham House from a university dorm into a real clan home. They were certainly noisy.

RumLot Security was able to find two sets of parents who wanted their children back. Once they were told of the dangers of staying in China and given the option of moving to the UK both families chose to leave and were smuggled out. The rest of the parents couldn't be found or were dead. No one could ever find any trace of the parents of the baby.

Sen adopted the baby and named her Mei-Xia, and that meant Conary had another grandchild to add to the ever-growing Yule presents list.

The old man's name was Gang, and his body had deteriorated to the point of no return. A few days after getting to the UK, despite the best work of the healers, he never spoke, and he died in his sleep. No one ever found out what his abilities were, but given his great age and deterioration he surely had something but didn't know how to use it. He was given a proper lord's pyre, and they wished him peace on his journey and a quick return from the Void.

Judy was overwhelmed not by the noise but by the silence. She couldn't listen in on any of the lords' or elves' thoughts, and for the first time in her life she met people and didn't know what they thought the minute they laid eyes on her. Oh there were humans around, but she could filter them out. All of the ones who worked in the adult lords' area were reassigned, so Judy had a quiet space. It was the lords she had to learn to talk to. What were they thinking? What did they want?

After a few days of sleeping and eating she was back to her normal, full health and given the option of staying as a member of the clan and learning what being a lord meant or returning to her old life in the casinos. At first she thought she'd go back to the casinos; the lure of her old, hard-won and familiar world was strong. After a week of sympathetic people though, her people, talking to her like a regular person, of making friends and connecting, her old life began to look very lonely and not a little sterile. Judy decided to stay for the lord lessons then see how she felt about the future.

When Chi heard Judy say that at breakfast, he laughed at her with his high-pitched cackle, "Ha! You won't leave! We never leave! Who are you going to talk to after living here? Who are you going to fuck? We don't –" And someone flicked him with their ability, dumping him from his chair, and he shut up. But his point was made, even if inelegantly.

Conary was intrigued by this new lord's strange talent, and he talked about Judy with Kyrylo and his mother. When Judy was done with lord training and everyone was comfortable with her and she was proven trustworthy he thought her ability would be a great addition to a diplomatic and negotiation team. Her deep knowledge of human psychology was an asset even without her ability. The humans were always worried that lords could read thoughts anyway; Judy would give them something to worry about. The Primaries kept *that* thought to themselves, and they watched Judy go through training with great interest.

Caddy

Caddy was nervous about Canada. Yes, the Canadians were polite, very welcoming, and for their own reasons, secretly desperate for the Elf Nation to establish an embassy in Ottawa.

From the Elf Nation's point of view and on all objective grounds, what was the big hurry? The EN had plenty to do in

Europe, Caddy was the only lord who could waken an elf clan, and there were plenty, gods knew, plenty of European locations for her to work on. They hadn't even finished with the UK yet; what about Scotland?

The President of the Elf Nation knew she wasn't simply stepping a friendly foot on Canadian soil; she was throwing down a gauntlet to the rest of the world. She was saying that elves and lords weren't going to limit themselves to Old Europe but would live anywhere they wanted, and they wanted the entire world.

Asia, Africa, South America – they were all fair game, and any democracy that wooed the EN had a chance to establish relations with the EN. If Canada could have an embassy why not Australia or Japan? It didn't matter if an embassy came first or the elves did; in the end, when one showed up in a country, the other was sure to follow. No one doubted that the minute Lord Cadence cut the ribbon on the Elf Nation Embassy in Ottawa that elves would start popping up in Canada. It was just a matter of time, and the only speculation was how long it would take for the first elf to be spotted.

The Canadians knew what they were doing when they began to press for official recognition and mutual support from the Elf Nation. They weren't nervous about elves and lords; they had much more pressing reasons to be nervous. They were nervous about the frenemy to the south, the US.

Canadians weren't stupid; they knew how they were perceived on the world stage. If a country was the overlooked middle child, it was Canada. They weren't an old country in the minds of the world, and their peers in Europe dominated the room with the weight of two thousand years of culture, science, art, and imperialism. They weren't huge, wealthy, and brash like the US which careened around the world like a charming but spoiled brat, demanding to be heard and seen, hogging every other country's brainspace and attention.

They were Canada – vast, busy, mind-your-own-business Canada. Canada didn't invade other countries; it barely inhabited some of its own land. When asked, they helped promote democracy, giving blood and treasure during the fight against the Nazis and peacekeeping in Korea, Ukraine, and every other thankless task they were asked to help out with. Canada was the good neighbour you visited when you needed to borrow their leaf blower, and they always cheerfully ran to the garage and dug it out. They'd even help you bag up the leaves if they had the time.

What did it mean to be Canadian? It meant that when you visited London and sat in a pub someone would note your accent and ask what part of the States you were from. When you said, "Not American, Canadian" they'd smile. Everyone likes Canada! And then they'd turn away and forget you. If you were a businessman and walked into an international bank ready to set up a major factory you had to work a little bit harder to prove you had the money, the experience, and the hard-nosed guts to do it. If you were a world-class harpist from Montreal looking to tour in Europe you had to audition when the world-class harpist from New York did not. The only things a Canadian didn't have to prove themselves at was playing hockey and making maple syrup. Everything else they did on the world stage was greeted with a smile and low expectations. Canadians were nice. They were well-meaning. They were *shrug* Canadian.

Then days into Trump's second term he started blathering on about annexing Canada. While Americans laughed, Canadians were appalled. Just flat gobsmacked. They were used to being forgotten, but the profound disrespect from their closest neighbour was more than shocking; it was threatening. A hostile takeover of Canada? They were sure Americans would never do such a thing.

Or would they?

Trump eventually passed on, as all humans did, but his ideas did not. The proto-fascist leanings of his second term never went away – Meechum hadn't been created out of nothing, and he didn't get elected out of nowhere. He was simply the next step in the evolution of America. When you've been the biggest and baddest for a century it goes to your head, and extremism, whether it was from the right or left, always, always, always ended up in tyranny.

Ottawa didn't see any downside to inviting the EN to open an embassy. They knew what elves were; they saw the result of elf clans emerging all over Europe, and they needed allies to counter their huge and increasingly aggressive neighbour to the south.

And besides, elves were cute! They sold jam at farmers' markets and planted flowers outside of their quaint little houses. Elves were good neighbours who always watered your flowers if you went on vacation, if you asked politely. They minded their own business and paid their taxes. And if you shit with them they chopped off your fucking head. Much like Canadians when you think about it.

No, Ottawa didn't see any downsides. Caddy, on the other hand, worried about over-extending and pushing too hard, too soon. The Canadians were fine; it was the signal she was sending to the despots in the rest of the world that made her hesitate.

The embassy was finished; everyone knew it existed, so that horse had fled the barn anyway. The Elf Nation was expanding to the New World. She and Kyrylo prepared to fly to Canada to cut a ribbon, eat the excellent food, drink Canadian wine, and have a selfie or two taken.

Meechum

If the Canadians were appalled at the United States' new aggressive attitude towards them, a good slice of the US was miffed at Canada.

President Meechum was quite vocal. How dare Canadians push against the hegemony of the US? Canada was the younger sister to the US's older brother, and did kid sisters go up and tell their big brothers what to do? Did they rebel? Did they date people the big brother didn't approve of? No, of course not! Yet here was Canada (and every time he said the nation's name it was like he had a bad taste in his mouth) doing just that. Who did they think they were?

Canada's job, and he was quite clear about this, was to buy American products, provide raw materials for American factories, and keep their polar bears from invading Cincinnati. That was it. They had no business thinking they were their own country with their own foreign policy and aligning with *things* that weren't even human.

Privately, Meechum was worried about the EN. They were very popular amongst the common people, and he was still in a position where the proles had to be catered to. If he were to achieve his goal of a Presidency-for-Life, a goal that eluded his hero, Trump, but was achieved by his other hero, Putin, he still had some work to do. The EN was against dictatorships, no matter how stable or benign, and that meant Meechum was against the EN.

But it wasn't just that. There was magic, and his intel people were frantically trying to figure out exactly what that meant. No one knew. As one background analyst wrote, if they knew the limits to the EN's power they could fight against it, but they didn't. They had no idea how many elves were really out there or how many lords existed and what their magical powers really were. Every time they turned around a new lord appeared, but was that all of them? Where were they hiding? What was the EN holding back? If Lord Cadence could look at man and boil him into steam what was her range? How many could she boil? Could she just think about the White House and evaporate it?

Meechum was scared of the Elf Nation's immeasurable and unchecked power. If anyone was going to have unchecked power it had better be him! So he thought about it and put in the first steps to regain the upper hand. He began to subtly but relentlessly portray the lords as demons from hell and the elves as imps of Satan. It didn't matter if they showed no evidence of Satanic evil; there were enough in his own faction who would believe, and that's all he needed. Belief.

The Elf Nation

The RumLot Jet was now rebranded as the Elf Nation Air Force One (and Only), and with the ridiculous amount of security provided by the Canadian military Caddy, Kyrylo, and the entire circus landed in Ottawa with all of the appropriate pomp and circumstance any head of state merited.

And from Caddy's point of view that was the entire point of the whole inconvenient and stressful exercise. Her elves and her people were a nation and deserved an equal place on the world stage, and if cementing that impression in the public mind meant she had to walk a red carpet in court shoes and shake hands with a lot of people she didn't know, so be it. Countries in Europe recognised her elves and lords as real people, and now a country on another continent did.

The entire visit was choreographed to the last minute. Unlike the New York visit, Caddy and Kyrylo did all the PR events needed to get the Canadian people on Team EN, and with every hockey game visit, every meeting with a First Nations representative, every bow at every arts event in Quebec, they were met with riotous enthusiasm.

Every single interview either began or ended with " – and when can we expect to see elves in Canada?" And its corollary, " – and will Lord Ratna come back and live here?" Whoever was asked, whether it was Caddy, Kyrylo, Conary, or Vrt, the answer was always the same. Elves would come back when the time was right, and Lord Ratna was an independent person; best to ask her.

On the fourth day of the five-day Canadian visit, just as Caddy and Kyrylo were walking into the new EN embassy to cut the ribbon, a truck ploughed into the front gates of the EN embassy in London and exploded killing three tourists who happened to be walking by, injuring two EN employees coming back from lunch, and killing a third. All the occupants of the truck died.

The bomb inside the truck was huge, and the timing was designed to replace the worldwide coverage of the embassy opening with other news, and it succeeded in disrupting the celebrations at the embassy. While other leaders might have continued after a statement to the press, Caddy did not. She cut the ribbon and immediately thanked their Canadian hosts, apologised for leaving early, and the entire EN contingent returned to London. We take care of our own, she said, and with three employees killed or injured by terrorists, she wasn't going to party in Ottawa.

The truck was thought to belong to a Weizhi Julebu cell, a Chinese-inspired religious movement headquartered in New Jersey. The ultra-conservative leadership had once claimed their founder was a lord, but that claim had lasted only a few months and then quietly disappeared; it was thought that in the meantime the founder died of natural old age. The US wouldn't allow British or EN (especially EN!) investigators to enter the US to investigate the tenuous links, and the Weizhi Julebu leadership vigorously denied all involvement. After a lot of work, the EN intelligence people weren't sure either, and some of the evidence pointed to governments using the Weizhi Julebu as an unwitting cover.

In the end, all the EN could do was keep their investigative files open and remind the world that they would keep looking – forever.

Caddy and Kyrylo had another reason to rush home; they had their own tribe to comfort and tend to. Any attempt to destroy the bricks and mortar of the symbol of elf nationhood was really an assassination attempt on lords and elves, and while her lords, hidden in Aelfeham House, gave a brave face, they were severely rattled. Could a terrorist pierce the defences of Aelfeham House? Ivana, hidden in Ukraine? The lords left behind were very weak, many not much more than humans, and now there were children to protect.

The intelligence units and governments of the world didn't know how many lords there were, and the elves and lords wanted to keep it that way, so there was no calling for help from the human governments. That meant they were limited to their own RumLot Security soldiers and a pitifully small number of *terrior*-limited Warrior Elves. The big guns had to fly back.

But the lord tribe was growing. Between the day a year ago when Sam had walked into Aelfeham House, their tiny tribe had more than tripled. It was still extinct for all practical purposes, but not so much. There were twenty-two of them now, every one of the adults a traumatised survivor. Most were healing in the safe, nurturing support of their new clan, but some never would completely heal. All of them would forever carry their human-made scars as they lived their eternal lives and only the tiniest children could hope to grow up as "normal" souls in a stable and loving clan. The rest would learn to adapt to their new reality as best they could.

The world was waking up to the existence of lords and how they were different from the reborn elves. And like the orcs, hidden lords were looking in the mirror and realising who they were, too.

The tribe had started with a solo traveller, a roamer who had gathered her small family and cobbled together a proper clan with children to nurture and bonded couples to protect them. Now lords were contacting the Embassies and asking to join their fellow survivors. Caddy didn't have to search and gather lords any more; they were finding her.

She and Kyrylo knew that there were more hidden lords out there. There had to be. They were afraid, ignorant, traumatised, and hunted, but somehow they would come.

Internal Release

For immediate distribution.

From the desk of the President of the Elf Nation, Lord Cadence Aeldor.

My fellow employees of the Elf Nation,

It is with great sorrow that I attended today's memorial service for the wonderful men and women who died and were injured during last month's terrorist attack at our London embassy. We mourn the innocents who lost their lives simply because they were in the wrong place at the wrong time when the forces of hate decided to unleash their unprovoked attack.

It might sound odd that I don't emphasise this as an attack on elves and lords or Elf Nation employees, because on the surface, that's what it looks like. But it's not. It was an attack on everything all right-minded people want in life – freedom, justice, and Balance. It was indeed an attack on everyone, lord – elf, human, and orc – who want to live together in peace.

We in the Elf Nation will work as one to ensure that these terrorists will not win. We'll not bow down to any country or group of people who believe that, because their tribe is large, they are exalted and other people are less valuable.

It will take work to change ingrained beliefs that lords and elves are not real people and should not be a part of this wide world. This work could take years, maybe centuries, but lords, elves, and humans who support us won't back down. We have time on our side.

Today we mourn. Tomorrow we'll start again. We have much to do and a long way to go.

I'll see all of you at work.

Lord Cadence Aeldor

End of Book Four

Book 5

So Sweet a Changeling

Continue the adventure!

This and all books in

The Return of the Tribes Series

are available for download on

Amazon Kindle
or
The Rum Lot Publishing

www.rumlot.com

E-Publishing, Hardback and Paperback versions of all books are
available on amazon.com

Please Donate
to the Excelsior Trust

If you enjoyed this book (and we hope you did!), please consider a small donation to The Excelsior Trust, a registered charity that is dedicated to preserving heritage fishing boats, in particular The Excelsior, LT 472, a wonderful fishing smack that is featured in Book Two.

As part of the trust's mission to preserve Britain's maritime heritage, they also subsidise unique training and sailing experiences for young people.

https://www.theexcelsiortrust.co.uk/

https://www.theexcelsiortrust.co.uk/donate
Registered Charity Number 285899